Jenny Bond was born in Sydney, Australia, and earned a Bachelor of Arts and a Diploma of Education at Macquarie University. Prior to her reinvention as a writer, Jenny held the position of Head of English at Eaton House The Manor in London's Clapham. She also taught English and Drama for eight years at a selective high school in Sydney. Jenny's first novel, *Perfect North*, was published by Hachette in 2013. *The President's Lunch* is her second book.

Jenny and her husband and their two sons live in Canberra, Australia.

jennybondbooks.com
facebook.com/jennybondbooks
@jennybondbooks

THE PRESIDENT'S LUNCH

JENNY BOND

hachette
AUSTRALIA

For Sam and Ben

This is a work of fiction. Names, characters, places and incidents either are the product of the author's imagination or are used fictitiously. While a number of real historical figures and events are referred to, there is no suggestion that the events described concerning the fictional characters ever occurred.

Language used is appropriate for the time in which *The President's Lunch* is set.

Published in Australia and New Zealand in 2014
by Hachette Australia
(an imprint of Hachette Australia Pty Limited)
Level 17, 207 Kent Street, Sydney NSW 2000
www.hachette.com.au

10 9 8 7 6 5 4 3 2 1

Copyright © Jenny Bond 2014

National Library of Australia
Cataloguing-in-Publication data:

Bond, Jenny, author.

The President's lunch/Jenny Bond.

978 0 7336 2982 2 (paperback)

Roosevelt, Franklin D. (Franklin Delano), 1882–1945 – Fiction.

Roosevelt, Eleanor, 1884–1962 – Fiction.

A823.4

Cover design by Christabella Designs
Cover images courtesy of Trevillion
Text design by Bookhouse, Sydney
Typeset in Perpetua by Bookhouse, Sydney
Printed and bound in Australia by Griffin Press, Adelaide, an Accredited ISO AS/NZS 14001:2009
Environmental Management System printer

The paper this book is printed on is certified against the Forest Stewardship Council® Standards. Griffin Press holds FSC chain of custody certification SGS-COC-005088. FSC promotes environmentally responsible, socially beneficial and economically viable management of the world's forests.

THE FIRST TERM
1933–1937

Happy Days

1

CHICAGO, ILLINOIS
March 1933

Iris listened patiently as the seventeen-year-old inched his way through the book, his progress punctuated by frequent stops as he looked up from the page, seeking assistance. The young woman, with her cheek cupped in her palm, gently offered hints for each troubling word or sound. Then she'd smile broadly, her blue eyes and freckled nose crinkling. It was a child's book, *Hansel and Gretel*, that Roy had found or traded and had brought to her with a request from his parents that she teach him to read. Roy was obviously slow-witted but Iris supposed that being a little backward in times like these might be a blessing. As he read the final page she brushed her dark hair from her forehead and tightened the band that held her errant locks in check. The boy looked up from the page, distracted by the movement.

'Keep going, Roy,' Iris encouraged him. 'You're doing so well. Let's try to get to the end today.'

Roy was tall and good-looking, with a mess of blond curls poking from a tattered Cubs cap. Like nearly everyone at the camp, he seemed to have only one outfit – a pair of corduroy trousers, a dark green argyle sweater and a plaid shirt. When Roy had come to her door with his book a month ago it was the colour of his plaid shirt that Iris noticed first. She had sold or bartered away most of her clothes and it had felt as though she was giving away a part of herself. When she sold her favourite dress for a quarter, one made of dark plaid – the same pattern as Roy's shirt – she had cried at the realisation that she had nothing else to give.

Iris had walked with the broad, ambling boy back to his home on the corner of Easy Street and Prosperity Row. She'd had to slow her usual brisk pace so she didn't get ahead; Roy was often sidetracked, bending to pat a dog or stooping to pocket a dirt-caked bottle top he'd spied on the ground. The blanket that served as the shack's front door was pulled back, allowing light to enter the makeshift dwelling. The home was larger than hers and looked to be made up of two rooms.

The brick, wood and steel structure seemed sturdier than the crudely cobbled together one-room shanty on Hard Times Avenue that Iris had taken over when the previous occupants had moved on. The boy's mother was seated on a stool, patching a pair of trousers.

'Hello, Mrs Cullen. I'm Iris McIntosh. Roy says you would like me to teach him to read.'

The woman looked up from her work. 'Yep. He's simple, ya see. He's not got much goin' for him. He should knows how to read and write.'

Iris decided helping a young man become literate might not be such a bad way to spend her many idle hours. Since her 'fall', a term she used to describe becoming unemployed and homeless almost a year before, she had not worked for more than a week at a time. She needed a diversion, a purpose; she was only twenty-three, too young to feel useless. Mrs Cullen's suggestion reminded Iris of what she loved most about teaching – the opportunity to help another person. The hours spent queuing at soup kitchens and knocking on doors looking for work had erased this from her memory. She could barely recall standing in front of a class of faces, a few eager and others indifferent, book in one hand and chalk in the other. When the headmaster of Lincoln Park High School had called her and five other teachers into his office one Friday afternoon in April last year, Iris knew what was coming. Sure enough, Mr Walters explained that he would have to let go the last six teachers he'd hired. As the dismissed and dejected filed out of the room and down the corridor, the headmaster called Iris back.

'I'm really sorry, Iris,' he began. 'You're an excellent teacher and the kids really take to you.'

'What'll happen to my classes?' Iris asked.

'Classes will be combined. Some subjects amalgamated. We'll get by. This depression can't last forever.' He shook her hand and wished her good luck.

Iris hadn't set foot in a classroom since.

'We's heard you were a teacher, that you went to college,' Mrs Cullen was saying now. 'Tom and me don't expect you to do it for nuttin', though.' Roy's father, Tom Cullen, was regarded as the de facto mayor of the shantytown where she had resided for the past three months. 'Tom said you can eat for nuttin'. No need to contribute anythin' to the pot. Three squares a day.'

Iris agreed and asked Roy to visit her, with his book, at nine o'clock the next morning.

Iris had been tutoring Roy each morning ever since. He was sweet, attentive and hard-working. He was also making headway, albeit slowly. What more could a teacher ask? Sometimes he'd bring her gifts, tokens found around the camp: an old Coke bottle that became a vase; a rusty tin can she used to hold three stubby pencils (also offerings from Roy); and a stained, emerald-coloured ribbon that Iris washed and wore in her hair at her student's insistence. She dreamed that one day Roy might bring her a book to read or a current edition of the *Chicago Tribune*; even a not-so-recent copy of *Modern Screen* or the *Saturday Evening Post* would be appreciated – anything to end her debilitating isolation. But when she thought about it, what she longed for most was a brand-new cake of white, scented Lux soap still wrapped in its paper.

'That's excellent work, Roy,' Iris said. 'So good.' She rose from the crate on which she had been sitting and stretched out her long legs. Roy eyed her devotedly as she straightened the waistband of her tweed trousers and tucked in her shirt where it had bloused.

'I wish I still had some of my books, Roy,' she told him regretfully, hands on hips. 'I had a few westerns and adventure stories that I think you'd really like – *Treasure Island* and *The Lone Star Ranger*. But I sold them all.' She grimaced comically and he laughed. 'We'll keep going tomorrow,' she said, patting him on the shoulder.

Roy placed his hand on her hip and looked up into her dark blue eyes. 'You're so pretty, Iris,' he said.

Iris started; Roy had never touched her like that before. She picked up his baseball cap from where he'd left it on the floor and put it back on his head. 'Thank you, Roy. But you should be going now. I'll see you tomorrow.' She attempted to pull away but the young man strengthened his grasp and stood. He was holding her tight around the waist.

'But you're so pretty, Iris.' He stood and moved in closer, knocking the crate he was sitting on backwards as he did so. He pressed hard against her and Iris could feel his erection against her stomach. She managed to move her hands up to his chest to push him away but was only able to budge him an inch.

Iris looked up into his smiling, eager face. Although her heart pounded in her chest and her throat was tight, she tried to keep her tone relaxed and even. 'Really, Roy, you must go. This isn't proper. I'm your teacher.'

'Just a little kiss, Iris. You're so pretty.'

He leaned in to kiss her, mouth open wide, his arms tightening around her until she could barely breathe. She opened her mouth to scream but the noise was stifled by his large hand. Her panic was overlaid by a sense of unreality. Surely this couldn't be happening.

'Don't make a fuss, Iris. I just want a little kiss.' Roy placed his hands around her throat and lifted her head to his. An image from her childhood, of her mother and father, flashed into her mind. She hurriedly smothered it. With her body free, Iris swung her arms and kicked out with her legs. It was hopeless. He was too big and too dim-witted to understand the consequences. She was a rag doll. She closed her eyes as he lowered his wide, wet mouth to hers. Her stomach pitched and swayed violently and in a last desperate attempt to free herself Iris wedged her hands between her chest and Roy's torso and was able to unbalance him.

He stumbled and released her, and she fell back against the floor. Roy was approaching her, his hand to his fly. He was still smiling.

Then she did scream. The sound was loud and shrill and surprising and stopped Roy in his tracks. An expression of bemusement came over his face. Within seconds a crowd had assembled in her tiny home.

2
WASHINGTON DC
March 1933

When the cab turned right into Desales Street she could see her friend waiting in the doorway. She would recognise that frame anywhere: tall, slim and slightly stooped. Her hands were pressed into the pockets of a tired green overcoat. Hick thought the faded garment ill-fitting and unattractive, but it was one of Eleanor's favourites. Her bucket church hat was also well-loved by Eleanor. It was green like the overcoat, with a satin bow to one side that had, over the years, lost its pertness. Next to Eleanor stood a broad man Hick identified, despite the early morning light, as Harry Dewey of the Secret Service – another of Eleanor's favourites.

Her friend had given her brief but detailed instructions on the telephone the day before. Hick was to meet Eleanor in a cab at the side entrance of The Mayflower at seven forty-five am precisely. She would not divulge to Hick where they were going or, in fact, whether Hick would even be accompanying her. It was unlike Eleanor to take such risks, especially on the morning before Franklin's inauguration. Reporters and photographers would soon be swarming the hotel.

Hick instructed the driver to make a U-turn and pull up in front of the waiting couple. As he did so, Hick leaned across the back seat and grabbed the door handle. When the vehicle came to a stop she pushed the door open and Eleanor slid into the car. Dewey closed the door and Eleanor placed the palm of her gloved hand to the window in a gesture of thanks.

The driver's eyes filled his rear-view mirror. 'Rock Creek Cemetery, please,' Eleanor said. Surprised, Hick looked at her friend, but she couldn't see Eleanor's eyes. The interior of the cab was gloomy and Eleanor had her hat pulled low over her brow in a gesture Hick now realised was both a defence against the cold and a rudimentary disguise. Ignoring her friend's questioning glance, Eleanor placed her hand over Hick's, which was spread flat on the seat between them. Hick turned her hand and squeezed Eleanor's fingers, savouring the feel of the soft calfskin of Eleanor's glove.

As they drove north along New Hampshire Avenue Eleanor remained silent with her head turned towards the window. When she was able to glimpse Eleanor's face Hick noticed a change from her usual disposition. She was unable to define the expression exactly, but she'd seen it once before. It was during the 1932 Democratic National Convention. While the Roosevelts and their entourage were gathered in the governor's mansion during the days of tense ballots and deal-making, Hick was holed up in the garage of the same residence with a handful of reporters assigned to cover the convention. She remembered emerging from the garage early one morning to find the governor's wife sitting by herself on the porch. On seeing that Hick was bleary-eyed and starving, she'd asked the exhausted reporter to breakfast.

They had shared a substantial meal together on the porch, alone except for Eleanor's dog Major, who lay under the table across his owner's feet. Very little in the way of conversation passed between the two women during their forty-five minutes together. But despite her graciousness, her warmth, her hospitality and the certainty that her husband would win the presidential nomination, Mrs Roosevelt was conspicuously sad.

When the cab stopped at the entrance to the cemetery Eleanor stepped quickly out onto the sidewalk. As she did so she asked the driver to wait.

Hick hastily searched her purse and found a five-dollar bill which she gave to the driver. 'We shouldn't be long.' She also handed the man the copy of the *Washington Post* she had folded in her handbag. 'It's the early edition.' The driver nodded and smiled, and Hick left the vehicle, closing the door behind her.

'So, what's this all about?' Hick asked.

'Follow me.'

3
CHICAGO, ILLINOIS
March 1933

Iris sat contemplating the events of the previous day. Had she encouraged Roy? Had she been too familiar? He possessed the natural cravings of a man with only the self-control of a child to keep them in check. As he was led out of her house by three of her neighbours he began to cry. Iris heard confusion in his tears as he attempted to explain.

'But I just wanted a little kiss. I didn't mean no harm.' The sound of his breathless sobs accompanied by a sense of her own wretched state induced her own tears and she cried steadily the entire morning.

At nine o'clock there was a knock on Iris's door. Hers was one of the only dwellings to possess a front door. When she had arrived in December the shack had a large piece of corrugated tin propped up against the entrance. She had found the door on North LaSalle Street and had balanced it carefully on her wooden barrow. A neighbour cut the door to fit and attached it. She gave his wife her last pair of woollen socks in return.

Surely it couldn't be Roy knocking, she thought. Perhaps, like a child who'd been naughty, he had long forgotten the previous day's mischief. But to her surprise when she opened the door she found Tom Cullen. Iris gestured for him to enter but he moved no further than a foot from the entrance. Iris noticed he had buttoned the shirt that he wore under his denim overalls to the neck, and when he removed his hat she saw his hair had been combed carefully. Iris couldn't remember seeing a straighter part.

'Mr Cullen,' Iris said.

Cullen cleared his throat and stared at the ground, his hat gripped tightly to his chest.

'I'm sorry about yesterday, miss. Me, my missus, we had no idea . . . We never thought Roy would . . . anything like that.'

'Of course. Please sit down, Mr Cullen.' Iris pointed to a fruit crate by her cobbled-together stove.

He shook his head. 'I just come to tell you that we appreciate all that you've done for our boy, but I reckon there's just no fixin' some.'

Iris considered this for a moment. 'I don't think that's true,' she said. 'It's not a matter of fixing. He's a good person at heart. I think we just need to remember that he's a man now. We have to treat him a little differently.'

'You're mighty understanding, miss. But I've discussed it with the other Founders and we've decided the boy can't stay.' The Founding Fathers were the five men who first squatted on the piece of land on Randolph Street in 1929. From those five and their families a community of nearly three thousand people had been born. No one could remember when the tongue-in-cheek moniker 'Founding Fathers' had been formally adopted by the tribe.

'I really don't think that's warranted . . .' Iris began.

'He can't stay, miss,' Cullen repeated firmly. 'As much as it pains me, Roy's gotta go.'

Iris couldn't believe what she was hearing. The man was going to evict his own son. 'You can't mean that, Mr Cullen. He just needs to be taught right from wrong, about men and women.'

'There's nothing more to be said about it.' Cullen still hadn't moved from his spot just inside the doorway. He still hadn't looked at Iris. 'The boy can't see the error of his ways.' The man paused for a moment and cleared his throat before saying more quietly, 'I fear for your safety, miss.'

She took the seat that Cullen had refused and placed her head in her hands. 'Has Roy done anything like this before?'

'Nope.'

Iris couldn't let it happen. Despite his size and strength, Roy would never survive on his own.

'Then perhaps it's me who's the problem,' Iris said finally, looking at the mayor.

He returned her gaze.

'Thank you for coming to see me, Mr Cullen,' Iris said, standing and holding out her hand. 'I'll be gone by the morning.'

4
WASHINGTON DC
March 1933

Hick followed her friend as she walked briskly along the cemetery's paths. It was difficult for the portly journalist to keep pace with her long-limbed friend and occasionally the forty-year-old was compelled to break into a clumsy trot. After a few minutes, Eleanor came to a halt and took a seat on the granite bench facing the Adams Memorial.

The reporter positioned herself next to her friend on the stone seat and looked at her watch. It was eighty-thirty, but she could still feel against her face a thin cloak of mist in the air. Hick raised her eyes to the sky. It was cloud-covered, but she recognised it as the kind of cloud that broke up without too much of a fight when the sun really got going, even in March. She looked at Eleanor. The other woman sat motionless, her hat still pulled low on her face, staring at the hooded, bronze statue in front of them. The urge to break the silence was overwhelming.

Hick examined her friend's profile. The corners of her eyelids drooped down, transforming her grey-blue eyes into teardrops. Strangers often equated this feature with tiredness or sternness, seeing only the shape of the eyes, and not their playful, inquisitive glint. Her nose was perfectly straight and so feminine, Hick thought. Her mouth was slightly open, her teeth protruding impatiently through full lips. She always looked as if she were about to speak, as if a flood of words were being dammed, desperately waiting for the perfect time of utterance.

Although she was too cynical to believe in love at first sight, Hick did believe her feelings for Eleanor were born on their first meeting in 1928. She was assigned to interview the governor's wife and Eleanor had invited Hick to tea in her East 65th Street home in New York. Hick had found the invitation strange. After all, no other interviewee had ever served her tea and biscuits. But she was immediately captivated by Eleanor Roosevelt. The way her long, slender hands so nimbly manoeuvred the teapot and cups was mesmerising. Hick was fascinated by her host's control of a pair of ridiculously small tongs as she deftly placed cubes of sugar into the brew without a trace of a splash.

Eleanor was gracious and warm during the interview, but also guarded. While this usually annoyed the reporter, in this instance she didn't care. Hick had ended her article with the sentence, 'The new mistress of the Executive Mansion in Albany is a very great lady.' Her editor hadn't liked her choice of words. He had called the sentence 'clunky' but the phrase summed up precisely how Hick felt. For seventy minutes she had been in the presence of greatness.

While Hick recalled the day, she sat gazing at the soft spot at the corner of the mouth that she so loved to kiss. Then Eleanor finally spoke.

'Do you know the story behind this memorial?'

'Bits and pieces, I suppose. Henry Adams commissioned it for his wife Clover. She killed herself, didn't she?'

'That's right. She was forty-two and drank potassium cyanide.' Eleanor paused. 'In the old days, when we lived in Washington, I was much younger and not so very wise. Sometimes I'd be very unhappy and sorry for myself. When I was feeling that way, I'd come here and sit and look at that woman. And I'd always leave feeling better. And stronger. I've been here many, many times.'

'Are you unhappy now?' Hick asked, placing her hand on Eleanor's knee.

'No, just a little hurt.' Eleanor paused again. 'I asked Franklin if I might help him after tomorrow, answering his mail or something. He looked at me so strangely and told me it would be an insult to Missy.'

Hick stared at her, astonished. 'You have better, more important things to do than acting as secretary to the president. You are so far above that. You shouldn't see his response as an affront; if anything it's a compliment. Even Franklin knows that answering his mail and getting his coffee is beneath you.'

'Missy does slightly more than that. She's his right hand, his companion,' Eleanor said.

'I know. Missy is invaluable and a great friend to you both. But really, Eleanor . . .' Hick groaned in frustration.

Eleanor nodded, but Hick could see she was still troubled. There was more to it, she thought.

After a few moments Eleanor continued, 'He's also invited Lucy Mercer Rutherford tomorrow. Arranged special seats for the ceremony and a car to pick her up. We'll be separated for most of the day. I'm sure he has arranged time to be alone with her.'

'It's probably just a rumour started by someone like Alice Longworth, who enjoys seeing you rattled.' Hick moved closer to her friend along the bench. Their thighs touched.

'It's no rumour and my cousin knows better than to provoke me. Louis told me – to warn me, he said. He wanted me to be prepared.'

'Didn't Franklin's mother forbid him from ever seeing her again and threaten to cut the purse strings?'

'Yes, at the time Sara did. But it has been fifteen years. Franklin's going to be president tomorrow. Those sorts of threats don't really count for much any more.'

Hick was unsure how to respond. On the one hand she was annoyed, and jealous, she admitted to herself, that Franklin's thoughtless gesture cut so deeply and had reduced her friend to such insecurity. On the other, she knew she should comfort Eleanor and offer support.

'If you can have me there then surely Franklin can have Lucy; it's only fair, Eleanor,' she said, attempting frivolity.

'Most people think Clover Adams committed suicide when she fell into a depression following her father's death, but that's only partly true.' Eleanor stood and walked to the statue. She placed her hand lightly on the figure's bronze head before continuing. 'Her husband was obsessed with another woman, Elizabeth Cameron. She was known as the most beautiful woman in Washington. She was also Clover's best friend.'

'How do you know all this?' Hick asked. 'You would have been a child, a baby, at the time.'

'Uncle Teddy and Aunt Bye were good friends of the Adamses. Aunt Bye told me the story when I was a teenager. Henry and Elizabeth's love affair was infamous in Washington. They didn't even try to hide it.'

Hick could see how the story would resonate with Eleanor. She walked over to her friend and placed her hands on her shoulders. 'Your husband has been selfish and insensitive, that's a fact. But you have nothing to worry about. Tomorrow you'll not only be First Lady of this nation but also, in my eyes, the most beautiful woman in Washington. This town is fuelled by gossip and power and there's nothing you can do to change that. All you can do is ignore it or play along. I dare *anyone* to laugh at you or pity you. No one will be able to touch you.'

Her words had no effect. Eleanor sighed deeply then looked at her friend directly. 'Back in the old days, here, I was a different person. You wouldn't have loved the person I was then. I was silly and anxious. I worry because I have come so far, learned so much . . .' She trailed off, unable to finish her thought.

'Keep going, Eleanor,' Hick urged.

'I worry that I'll be required to be a congenial First Lady and nothing more. Shake hands and pour tea and receive bouquets. I worry my work will be sidelined.' She paused. 'That must sound so selfish.'

'Don't allow Franklin's thoughtlessness to mar what tomorrow means for you and all the good you'll now be able to achieve. You might be married to the president-elect, but you have been your own person for a very long time, Eleanor.'

'Thank you, my dearest.' Eleanor bent uncomfortably and placed her head on Hick's shoulder. 'Mitsouko,' Eleanor remarked of her friend's fragrance. 'I've always adored the smell of peaches and cloves. It was what you were wearing when you first visited us at Hyde Park. Remember?' Hick smiled then eased Eleanor's head against her shoulder again as she recalled the day.

It was sometime before the National Convention and the reporter had come to tour Hyde Park, Franklin's home town in upstate New York. Hick spent the entire day with Eleanor and Franklin at their home, Springwood. As they sat by the fire after dinner, Franklin assumed responsibility for conversation. Ceaselessly smoking and smiling, he worked hard to charm the journalist. Eleanor sat knitting. Occasionally, the women caught each other in a curious glance.

It was during the campaign, when Hick was assigned to cover Eleanor's movements full-time, that their relationship had grown into something more than cautious glances. On a train from Topeka to Salt Lake City, as a storm pounded against the windows of the drawing room they shared, Eleanor had recounted to Hick her life story. From her 'odd sort of childhood', as she called it, to the freedom of her school days in Europe, her marriage to her fifth cousin to her present dread of being First Lady, Eleanor had opened her soul to her new friend.

When the train finally outran the rain in the early hours of the morning the pair were snuggled on the berth in their nightgowns. Hick stroked her friend's arm in silence, astonished by both the privilege and the pain in her tale.

Now, as a cold wind swept across the cemetery, Hick wrapped her arms around her friend's waist and nuzzled her face against Eleanor's coat. The faded garment smelled fresh and recently laundered. They stayed this way for a number of minutes. When Eleanor lifted her head Hick could see she had been crying. She wiped her friend's cheeks with the back of her hand.

'Your hand is cold,' Eleanor said quietly. 'You should wear gloves.'

'I'm always losing them.'

'I'll find a special pair for you, leather with fur lining. You wouldn't dare lose those.'

'True.' Hick smiled. 'Shall we get back? Are you feeling better?'

'Much. I'm sorry to be so silly. Thank you for being here.'

'You're not silly, my darling. What are friends for?' And they walked arm in arm back to the waiting cab.

5

CHICAGO, ILLINOIS
March 1933

Iris prepared to leave the camp nauseous with unknowing. She had few possessions to pack – a change of clothes and underwear, a bedroll, a hairbrush and her toothbrush, and a saucepan which she tied to the outside of her haversack. The Cullens thanked Iris and gave her some bread. This she added to her meagre baggage, along with the one book she'd kept: *The Portrait of a Lady*. Despite her poverty, Iris had been unable to part with Isabel Archer.

It was not even seven in the morning. The sun had barely risen and was failing to penetrate a dense blanket of cloud. The cold stung her face. Iris stood at the door of her dwelling for a minute and looked out to the street. Fires burned in metal drums, lighting up the shantytown. Men and women were already positioned around the fires. It was a community, she thought; not one she would have chosen, but a community nonetheless. She walked the mile through the camp to Randolph Street. As she exited the camp and her foot hit the sidewalk she realised she was alone again.

She had no idea that in only a few hours, more than seven hundred miles away, the new president would stand on the East Portico of the Capitol. He would speak to a crowd numbering one hundred and fifty thousand about fear – nameless, unreasoning, unjustified terror. Iris also had no idea in which direction she should head. She stopped for a moment. Hurried workers rushed by her on their way to work. Occasionally someone would inadvertently jostle her. Neither a 'sorry, miss' nor an 'excuse me' were uttered. In less than a year she had gone from respected and valued to invisible and hopeless. She had no money and no prospects.

When her mother died she had felt a similar sense of destitution. Discovering her mother lying in bed when she came home from school was unusual. Mrs McIntosh would typically wait for her first student to arrive, setting the sheet music on the stand, adjusting the strings of her violin. Iris would sit and begin on her homework or read while her mother tutored. It was Tuesday. Her mother had two students on Tuesday, Iris knew: Albert Murphy and Maree Pugh. Albert would be there any minute. Iris grabbed her mother's shoulders and shook her. She yelled, slapped her face even, but she couldn't rouse her. The thirteen-year-old put her cheek to her mother's mouth, willing herself to feel a hint of breath. She pulled down the covers and pressed her ear hard to her mother's chest, holding her own breath in desperate anticipation.

Nothing.

There was a knock at the door. She wiped her eyes with the back of her hand and went to the door.

'Mama's not feeling well,' Iris said to her mother's student.

The boy looked at her blankly. 'What am I supposed to do?' he asked.

'Go home, I guess,' Iris said as she closed the door on the boy's consternation. She hastily opened it and shouted, 'Tell Maree, okay?'

'Okay,' he replied on his way down the steps.

Iris went back and sat with her mother, wondering where she might find her father. She knew most of what her mother told her about his activities was a lie. She knew what he told both of them was fantasy. Sometimes he didn't come home for days. There was a time when Iris's mother used to explain that he was working out of town. These days she didn't correct the neighbours who asked if Torrie was on another bender. She merely nodded politely and made her way up the steps and into the building, her shoulders erect.

Although it had grown dark before Torrie McIntosh came home, Iris had not left her mother's side. When he found his wife and daughter he sobbed wildly. Lying down beside his wife, Torrie put his arm across her body and cried into her cold face. Iris wasn't certain what she should do but she knew her father wasn't capable of any action. She went and knocked on the door of her downstairs neighbours, Mr and Mrs Woods.

'Poor, poor Abigail,' they whispered to each other as they hastened up the stairs behind Iris.

'That poor child. What's to become of her?' Mrs Woods whispered to her husband as she made tea in Iris's kitchen.

Iris could hear their concern from the sitting room.

Alone again a decade later, Iris began walking towards the YWCA on North LaSalle Street.

6
HYDE PARK, NEW YORK
May 1962

I can tell you for a fact that my nerves were a wreck. As soon as I walked up to the gate and stood looking at that house my legs turned to jelly. I was scared to death. Well, I'd never seen the White House before, only in newspapers and magazines and the like, and I just had no idea how grand it was, how very much like a wedding cake.

Of course Dad, my late husband, had no inkling how I was feeling. In fact, it was his idea to take a stroll and visit what would become that afternoon our new home for the next four years. We didn't know it then, but it was actually to become our home for the next twelve years! He was just standing there, commenting on the garden. You know, wondering how many gardeners it would take to rake all the leaves and prune the hedges.

All I could see were the windows. What seemed like thousands of windows. Windows that I would have to clean. I thought it would calm my nerves if I tried to count them – perhaps there weren't as many as there seemed, you know. How wrong I was! I stopped counting when I reached ninety. I was close to tears, I remember. I was about to turn fifty-nine and this was to be my very first paid position. I didn't know what I was thinking saying yes to Mrs Roosevelt when she offered me the position of White House housekeeper. But when she took my hand that day at Hyde Park, knowing how blue Dad had been from being down on his luck for so long and all, and offered us both a job, well, I just couldn't say no to her. Her blue eyes were so full of sympathy. But how was I going to manage cleaning all those windows? By this stage Dad realised I was scared and tried, in his own way, to comfort me.

I remember he said, 'It will only be for four years.' Well, that didn't help at all. My fears just started snowballing. Is that the expression? My fears were definitely snowballing. Then I remembered that we didn't know a soul in Washington – apart from the Roosevelts, that is. Then I realised that by that afternoon they wouldn't even be the Roosevelts, our neighbours from Hyde Park, any more. They would be Mr President and the First Lady.

Dad led me over to a bench and we sat there for a while staring at Pennsylvania Avenue and watching the men set up barricades and the like. When I seemed more myself, I recall Dad saying, 'You know you're already famous, don't you?' Well, that made me laugh. Because although I hadn't even stepped through the doors of that stately mansion yet, the newspapers had already come up with a lot of fancy titles for me – names like 'First Housekeeper of the Nation' and 'The Little Lady Who Rules the President'. I knew what he was trying to do. He was trying to make me see the silliness of it all, show me it was just a job. It worked and I started to feel better straight away.

I learned to cook by my mother's side. She cooked following the Viennese tradition. That was where she was from, Vienna, in Austria. I'd follow her around the kitchen and she'd give me small pieces of dough and the like to play with. Then we'd bake what we both had made in the big wood-burning range in our kitchen. I recall baking a chocolate cake for my eleventh birthday. That was when I first flew solo, as they say, in the kitchen.

I truly believe that the kitchen is the heart – no, the soul – of the home. Every woman should learn how to cook. It's essential to a happy marriage and a happy home. Absolutely essential. I've heard modern women, career women, say that learning to cook would ruin their figures. What poppycock! It has never done mine any harm. Anyway, to me cooking and housewifery are as important as any other job a woman might do. I know there'll be women out there who'll sniff at that comment, but it's true. It was my cookery skills and talent as a homemaker that got me the job at the White House, and at a very comfortable salary, I might add.

Mark my words, there are not too many career women who have chatted with the Queen of England and who know that she actually prefers coffee to tea, or who have bumped into Miss Tallulah Bankhead as she was coming out of the ladies' powder room and passed the time of day, or who know that Mr Ernest Hemingway prefers his bed to remain untucked. He was a funny one. He hated hospital corners, the kind that Mrs Roosevelt insisted upon.

Anyway, I couldn't have said no to Mrs Roosevelt. By the winter of 1932 it seemed like everyone we knew was out of work and everything I had faith in was crumbling away. We read the newspapers and listened to the radio and everything just seemed so bleak. Of course, we didn't know we were living through 'The Great Depression'. We were just trying to keep our heads above water. I don't think folks started using that term until later.

My father's people came from Germany, you know. They arrived in Minnesota, but were fleeced straight away by Yankee con men who sold them a plot of bad land. Still, they worked that land day and night until they turned that patch of poor soil into fine, fertile farmland, and they built a safe home. That's where I grew up, on that very same patch of land.

Then I married Dad and we moved to Hyde Park and we built our own life together there. But in '31 the people who owned the house decided to move back in, after twenty-two years. The Gilbertsons were very sorry but the housing shortage was to blame, they said. Dad had only lost his job as bookkeeper at the feed store a week before. We moved in with Garven, my eldest, his wife Mary and their firstborn, Bobby. As kind-hearted as Mary was, there just wasn't room enough for all of us. But what could we do? I think for women especially the home is all-important. I could see all around me those homes being snatched away from women by the depression. Why, it happened to me! I had to do something and Mrs Roosevelt assured me that there would be work enough for Dad and me. After all, I'd kept house all my life. How different could keeping house at the White House be?

7
CHICAGO, ILLINOIS
March 1933

Iris stayed at the YWCA for a week. It was all the girls were allowed if they couldn't pay for lodging. During that time she scoured the city for a job, but there were thousands of unemployed in Chicago and barely any positions for women. The few vacancies would attract hundreds of applicants, with the job usually going to the first through the door. Iris attempted to find work at one of the big hotels as a maid or kitchen hand or laundry help, but advancing into the lobbies of these majestic establishments was both daunting and humiliating, with the bellboys shooing her out before she had even asked to speak to the manager. What I wouldn't give for a new dress, a little make-up and a haircut, she thought as she walked along Monroe Street from the Palmer House Hotel. I could easily get a job if I looked more the part.

On her way back to the hostel Iris walked past breadlines that snaked down streets and around corners. She pulled her coat tighter around her chest. Everything was bleak. What if the situation doesn't improve? she wondered as a light sprinkle of rain dusted her nose. It was the sight of the children clutching their mothers' hands that disturbed her the most. How would they remember these times in adulthood, and what sort of adults would they become?

On her final evening at the YWCA, Iris sat on her bunk and closed her eyes. It was five minutes till lights out. Women and girls hurried to and from the bathroom. Mothers tucked in their children, usually two to a bunk, and kissed them goodnight. Others lay on their beds, reading a faded magazine or newspaper they had found. Iris believed herself to be sensible and resourceful; she'd done an outstanding job of looking after herself since childhood. Yet now she was terrified by the thought of what the next day held. Her father had often told her to grab life by the throat. Iris felt she was floundering, struggling to grasp at something when nothing was there.

'Penny for your thoughts,' her neighbour, Ginny, said as she sat down next to her on the bed, her auburn hair bouncing carelessly on her shoulders. She stretched out her left leg and gracefully straightened her stocking, admiring her shapely limb in the process.

'Just wondering what I'll do tomorrow,' Iris replied thoughtfully, contemplating where Ginny had got those stockings.

Ginny was seventeen and, despite her circumstances, remarkably optimistic. She had no one either and, until a month ago, had been employed as a maid to a family in Streeterville.

'Stay,' Ginny answered gaily.

'I can't pay,' Iris said. 'I've been looking for a job and there's nothing. I've been to all the schools that are open, hotels, diners, hospitals, shops. There's just nobody hiring. Nobody hiring women, anyway.'

'I know how you can make some money,' Ginny said furtively.

Iris looked at her, eyebrows raised in query.

'Come out with me tonight,' the girl whispered. 'There's always men who are willing to pay for it.'

'Pay for what?'

'Honestly, Iris,' Ginny said. 'You know.' She lowered her head and looked towards her lap.

'Oh, you mean pay for *you*. Sell yourself, you mean.' Iris faltered for an instant and cleared her throat. She hadn't meant to sound prudish or judgmental.

'Just a part of yourself,' Ginny corrected her primly.

Iris considered how much that part was worth. She stared at Ginny for a moment, at her silky hair and flawless, creamy complexion. Her wide brown eyes displayed not a hint of cynicism.

'A dime,' Ginny continued when Iris failed to respond. 'You can charge a dime.'

It was less than Iris had imagined.

'Where do you go with the men?' Iris asked, simultaneously intrigued and concerned by Ginny's revelation.

Ginny, mistaking Iris's curiosity for enthusiasm, answered casually, 'Usually into an alley or back street somewhere. Sometimes in the fella's car, if he's got one.'

'It's not safe and it's illegal,' Iris said, unable to help herself. 'Anything could happen and the worst probably will.'

Just then the lights went out. It was eight o'clock. Ginny moved closer to her along the bed. Iris could feel the girl's warm breath on her face as she spoke. 'You're worrying about nothing,' she whispered. 'Most of the fellas are real nice and those that aren't, well, it's all over in a jiffy.'

Iris touched her hand softly. 'I can't, Ginny. I could never, no matter how terrible the situation.'

'From where I'm sitting, Miss Iris, the situation couldn't get much more terrible,' Ginny said scornfully. She grabbed her bag and left the room.

Iris placed her head on the pillow and stared into the darkness, contemplating Ginny's suggestion. She heard a mother in the next bunk quietly singing to her children. It wasn't a lullaby, though; the woman was singing 'How Deep Is the Ocean'. Ginny was right, her own situation couldn't get much worse. But to sleep with strangers for a dime? It was just survival, Iris reasoned; Ginny was doing what she had to do to survive. Yet it seemed to Iris that there had to be another way.

8
WASHINGTON DC
March 1933

The door of the Oval Study opened. Framed in the entrance was the president, cigarette in his mouth and sitting ramrod straight in his self-fashioned wheelchair. This had been the president's chief mode of transport for the last twelve years since suffering polio as a thirty-nine-year-old. It hadn't taken him long to grow frustrated with the wheelchairs that were available commercially. They were cumbersome and barely fit through doorways, making them entirely impractical for the novice politician, who preferred to think and move fast. If he couldn't use his legs, he told people, he was going to use something that was just about as reliable. Roosevelt added bicycle wheels to a simple wooden dining chair pilfered from the kitchen at Springwood, and voila, he had a wheelchair that was fast, efficient and that he could manoeuvre easily. He looked over his pince-nez at the assembled guests and grinned mischievously.

'I think this would be a good time for a beer.' Franklin wheeled himself into the room as the gathering applauded.

The radio was still on, the Dorsey Brothers performing 'Ooh! That Kiss'. Anna rushed to turn the volume down when her father entered. 'That was wonderful, Pa. You sounded wonderful.' The willowy twenty-seven-year-old went over to her father and kissed him on the cheek.

'One week,' Harry Hopkins said, shaking his head in bewilderment. The president's adviser had worked in government for more than twenty years and knew there was no precedent for the speed with which Roosevelt got things done. Red tape and bureaucracy meant nothing to this man. 'Just one week and you've already salvaged capitalism.'

'Eight days actually, Harry, but I'll accept your salutations regardless.' Roosevelt unbuttoned the coat of his grey double-breasted suit, a sign it was time to relax a little.

Following in Anna's wake came the president's wife, who bent to press her cheek against her husband's. Roosevelt's private secretary,

Missy LeHand, shook the president's hand. The rest of the party, which included most of the cabinet and White House staff, the Roosevelts' eldest son James and a few friends, followed suit, surrounding the president, shaking his hand and offering their congratulations on the success of the address.

All of a sudden the well-wishers were pushed aside in a theatrical arm-waving gesture. 'I said, I think this would be a good time for a beer,' he repeated more forcefully.

'You might have to do something about the Volstead Act first, boss,' called Louis Howe from his seat on the sofa in the corner of the room. 'Anyway, I would've thought you'd prefer something a little stronger.'

The president laughed and approached the crumpled reed of a man who also happened to be Secretary to the President and his closest friend. 'You're right, of course. You got me elected, Louis; your next order of business will be to tackle the drys on my behalf. Prohibition has had its day!'

'I'm afraid the only beverage on offer tonight is non-alcoholic punch and wine,' Eleanor commented flatly as she brushed her hands down the skirt of her sober burgundy dress. Anna had been with her mother when she had purchased the dress. She had called it unflattering and shapeless. Eleanor had bought it nonetheless.

Eleanor did not approve of her husband's need to entertain in this manner and neither did she understand it. It was narcissism at its most shameless. While ordinary people suffered, having lost their jobs and homes, in this room nobody would ever have guessed that the country was wedged deep in the pit of an economic depression. Despite the triumph of her husband's 'Fireside Chat', a term CBS had coined for the evening's informal radio address to the nation, she found the frivolity distasteful.

'Will you take a drink, Mrs Roosevelt, when prohibition is repealed?' Henry Wallace asked, his square jaw jutting obnoxiously.

Eleanor smiled serenely at the Secretary of Agriculture. Vile man, she thought as he brushed a thick shock of his grey hair from his forehead. She had steadfastly and openly lobbied against Wallace's appointment. He was an odd man who held strange ideas about many things, including agriculture and spiritualism. He tried too hard to compensate for his obvious lack of social skills; his small talk was amateurish, in Eleanor's opinion.

'Eleanor will continue her teetotal lifestyle, Henry,' the president interjected. 'I would expect nothing less. She has an iron will. Even on our honeymoon in France, Eleanor refused to take a sip of wine. I have always admired her temperance. For her it's not a matter of law; it's a matter of principle.' Although Franklin's words were spoken in good humour, there was no mistaking their sincerity.

'Of course, of course,' Wallace stammered. 'It's just that I can't remember . . .'

Eleanor cut him off sharply yet courteously. 'My father was an alcoholic, Mr Wallace.' The room fell silent. 'This has never been a secret. My brother also has a weakness in this area. I'm not a supporter of the Volstead Act. I think that under the present circumstances, if people can afford to have a drink in moderation, it might be beneficial. In fact, I despise the lawlessness and bootlegging that has been able to flourish with prohibition. What I cannot abide is overindulgence, Mr Wallace, to the point where it destroys families and also, on many occasions, the individual.'

She said nothing that most of the room did not already know. Was Wallace trying to impress his colleagues with a dig at the First Lady? she wondered. Eleanor was not ashamed of her family history and she was not going to cower in the face of Wallace's attempts to unnerve her.

'Now, Mr Wallace, your glass is empty. Can I get you a refill?'

'No, no,' he replied. 'I'm quite alright at the minute.'

Eleanor moved to the sofa and sat next to Howe, who squeezed her hand. The ash from his cigarette had fallen onto his lap. She quickly swept the ash into her hand to be deposited somewhere later. 'You're brilliant, my love, and Wallace is a weasel,' he said under his breath. His chameleon-like eyes looked at her intensely. 'You know he's teetotal himself, don't you? And a health nut. He's always on some fad diet or another.'

Eleanor shook her head. 'No, I wasn't aware he didn't drink.'

'He's just trying to impress the big boys now that he's in the cabinet.' Howe turned his gaze to Wallace. 'I just can't stand that big, oblong head of his.'

Eleanor laughed quietly. 'You have a charming turn of phrase, Louis, but' – she scanned her friend critically and attempted to change the subject – 'I should buy you another suit. You need to look after the clothes I buy you.'

Howe squeezed her hand again. 'I mean it. That twerp had it coming. You are brilliant.' He coughed and Eleanor rubbed his narrow back soothingly.

'You're like a dog with a bone,' she whispered in his ear.

Howe wiped his mouth and took a sip of water. In the last decade he had become her mentor, friend and adviser. It amazed her that such a brilliant political mind, such a virtuoso, could be packaged so misleadingly. Wizened from liquor, illness and cigarettes, and scarred from a bicycling accident when he was a youth, he appeared much older than his sixty-two years. Yet without the five-foot-four-inch strategist neither she nor her husband would be where they were this evening.

Eleanor briefly scanned the scene. She noticed that the Secretary for Agriculture wasn't the only casualty of her rebuttal. The gay atmosphere had darkened considerably. In an effort to lighten the mood she said loudly, 'Tonight my husband is the brilliant one. What did you say, Harry? He has managed to save capitalism in a week?'

Harry Hopkins raised his glass, his mouth curving into a quizzical grin.

'It's a first step,' Howe said to Eleanor. 'There's still a long way to go. But you know what he's like when he gets some momentum and a little encouragement.'

She nodded. Franklin thrived on this sort of adulation and she had seen him work tirelessly through the election campaign. Every speech at every whistlestop served as a thrust. Despite his exhaustion, his mind became sharper, his ideas more acute, his words more honed. Regardless of his privilege, he was relaxed and at ease with average Americans. The staid, lacklustre Hoover never stood a chance.

Eleanor stood and walked to a wastepaper basket near her husband and brushed her hands over it, ridding them of Louis Howe's ash. Without addressing anyone in particular she said, 'Solving the banking crisis is one thing, but this Economy Act that the president has in mind, surely that's a new deal for no one.'

'Mama, don't start,' James pleaded, placing his head in his hands.

Most of the people present had witnessed similar displays of political sparring between the Roosevelts before, whether here at the White House or at the governor's mansion at Albany. In spite of the occasional objections from the president's inner circle concerning his wife's private and public criticisms of the administration, Franklin thrived on these verbal bouts. More importantly, his policy decisions were the better for it. The Roosevelts rode on the same donkey but they had very definite and diverging ideas regarding the beast's direction.

'Cutting veterans' pensions and medical support, firing all federally employed women who happen to be married to federally employed men.' Eleanor shook her head disapprovingly.

'Now, now. It's about finding money to strengthen the economy, dear. The inflated benefits of veterans eat up one-quarter of the federal budget,' Franklin argued. 'And don't forget that government salaries, including my own, will be dramatically cut. Everyone is going to have to make sacrifices.'

Eleanor raised her eyebrows. Franklin's fortune was independent of his salary as president. 'It doesn't seem like too many are making sacrifices here. Taking money out of the pockets of veterans is criminal.'

'Not to mention ending the careers of many women employed by the government,' Hick added. 'What are they going to do? Go home and have babies? I've heard some couples are planning to divorce just so the wives can keep their jobs. It's ludicrous.'

Eleanor nodded firmly. 'I am a teacher and I know that the planned budget cuts are going to affect schools.'

Franklin laughed loudly. 'You're not a teacher any more, you're the First Lady, and I can't see the cuts affecting the young ladies at Todhunter.'

Eleanor was proud beyond all measure of what she had achieved at the ladies' college. She not only co-owned the New York institution, she had taught English there for almost a decade. Still bitter at being forced to quit her teaching duties and furious at her husband's mocking tone, Eleanor continued heatedly, 'Teachers will be fired and schools will close. Some already have. This nation's most precious resource will suffer and you'll have unemployed teachers adding to the queues at soup kitchens and on breadlines.'

'You may be overstating the case, Eleanor,' the president said. 'One cannot make an omelette without breaking a few eggs. Anyway, it's all temporary. If schools close, they'll not be closed forever. If teachers lose their jobs, they'll not be unemployed forever. These measures are a means to an end.' Franklin took a sip of his punch and went on in a more serious tone, 'I'll tell you what I told Congress.' The entire gathering hushed and turned towards him. 'For three years the government has been leading the country along the road to financial ruin. The mounting deficit has slowed the economy, multiplied the unemployed and brought on the collapse of the banking system. We need to throw everything we have at this problem. I won't be able to spend money if there's no money in the coffers. We have to build up our war chest.'

'Stealing money from the pockets of those in need . . . It just doesn't make sense,' Eleanor argued. 'It should go against all your instincts as a human being.'

'Well, that's politics. It's a game and I'm the quarterback calling the plays.'

Eleanor knew her husband savoured this metaphor. 'Well, I think your plays are penny-pinching and needlessly cruel,' she retorted.

'I am aware of that,' Franklin replied sombrely. 'But you have to take the long view, Eleanor.'

Dinner was announced and they all filed into State Dining Room. It was the first time the space had been used under the 32nd President, and it seemed extravagant to Eleanor. The official dining room of the president should only be used for visiting heads of state, she had argued; that was the tradition. But Franklin had laughed at her concern; they could make their own traditions, he said. Tradition wasn't going to crowd him and over twenty guests into one of the smaller dining areas.

James toasted his father with non-alcoholic wine that had been chosen by his mother, then dinner was served. As the plates were placed in front of each guest, Franklin looked first at the meal, then at Eleanor. Her expression was difficult to read.

'The missus believes it would be wise for the residents and guests of the White House to eat economically. Gone are the days of champagne, caviar and a rolling feast of eight courses. We, my good friends, are going to be leading by example and showing America how to eat well in a depression.'

Eleanor was pleased with Franklin's support of her economy drive. 'It's not just a project for the kitchen,' she added. 'We're cutting back in all areas. Repairing instead of replacing drapes and bedding, that sort of thing. Making do with what we have until we see better times.'

'An admirable policy, Mrs Roosevelt,' Henry Wallace said. 'A grand idea.'

'Well, I don't know, Mama.' Anna was looking at her plate, unconvinced. 'What do we have here?'

'Stuffed eggs, darling. Tonight we are having a menu created by the Home Economics Department at Cornell University. The entrée and dessert cost a mere seven cents per diner.'

'But where's the soup?' Franklin asked.

'There's no soup. Those rich cream soups that you like so well are expensive to produce and extremely unhealthy. I know you enjoy them but we all have to make sacrifices, dear.'

The president looked at her shrewdly for an instant then turned his plate counterclockwise in an attempt to make its contents appear more appetising. When this did not have the desired effect, he turned his plate back the other way.

'Would you like to say grace, dear?'

Franklin nodded and took the hands of those seated on either side. Louis Howe commented later that it was the longest grace he had ever heard the president utter, and he had been dining with the Roosevelts for twenty-two years. Delaying the inevitable or praying for a miracle was the most likely explanation of the prolonged blessing, he concluded. Howe did not touch his dinner that evening. He was not a big eater, preferring cigarettes to food, and the three beige egg halves nestled before him did not appeal. Even the mashed potatoes looked odd, he thought. Lumpy and dull. He laughed to himself at the sight of such poor fare on the grand presidential china. It was the setting's first outing, he guessed. The ordinariness of the eggs and potatoes sat oddly beneath the mighty eagle perched on the plate's rim.

The president finished his entrée dutifully, but as he looked around the table he noted that, besides his wife, he was the only diner with the necessary fortitude to do so. Missy, who was seated to his left, had cunningly cut the eggs up and moved them around her plate, hiding small portions under her partially eaten potatoes. Anna, seated to his right, had eaten the whites of the eggs but the stuffing remained on the plate. She had not touched her hearty mound of under-cooked potatoes.

'Do you think for eight cents per head the kitchen staff could add some flavour?' Franklin said to his wife. The table broke into laughter.

'Economical cooking is not about taste,' Eleanor remonstrated.

'But food should be tasty, Mama.'

'Anna, food should be affordable, nourishing and easy to prepare.'

'Our new housekeeper, Eleanor,' Franklin said seriously. 'Do you think she might have bitten off a little more than she can chew?' Once again, the table began to laugh.

'Henrietta Nesbitt is an excellent housekeeper and she runs the kitchen expertly. One would never guess she had no previous experience in the field.' Eleanor's demeanour prevented the party from finding her final comment amusing.

'Then what qualifies her for the position?' Anna enquired.

'She has run a home efficiently for forty years. She has raised children and grandchildren and cared for her husband. I say that qualifies her.'

'But at the White House she's responsible for a staff of forty,' Franklin pointed out in exasperation, even though he realised his wife's position on this issue would not be altered. He argued more for the sport than from any desire to emerge victorious from the debate.

'Besides, the Nesbitts have fallen on extremely hard times,' Eleanor explained to the table at large. 'The last three firms that her husband has worked for have failed. At his age he cannot find employment. That's why I have also hired Harry Nesbitt as steward. He's an accountant. I say that qualifies him.'

'So, Mama, are you going to save the country one American at a time?' James queried.

'Yes, if I have to.'

The plates were cleared and dessert was brought out. A limp scoop of pudding, barely brown, squatted apathetically at the bottom of the bowl, without ice-cream, cream or custard to mask its awfulness.

'For goodness' sake, Eleanor . . .' The disappointment in the president's voice was plain. 'Isn't Henrietta Nesbitt's speciality baking? I can remember apple pies and fruitcakes and that German coffee cake she used to make for the functions at Albany. What do you call this?'

'Prune pudding,' his wife responded tersely. 'This isn't one of Mrs Nesbitt's recipes. It's from Cornell. I know it doesn't look very appetising, but I can assure you this dish is very nutritious and inexpensive.'

Eleanor glanced around the table. None of the guests seemed convinced. A different approach was required to win them over.

'I'm sure once she finds her feet in the kitchen Mrs Nesbitt's talents will shine,' she finished optimistically.

'God help us all,' Howe muttered under his breath, pushing aside his bowl and lighting another cigarette.

9
CHICAGO, ILLINOIS
March 1933

As the president celebrated his triumph, Iris McIntosh left Illinois. Five years earlier, at eighteen years of age, she had arrived in Chicago with a grand sense of purpose. There had been nothing for her in Baltimore after she completed high school and she had been eager to begin a new chapter. The previous one had been difficult. While a couple of the girls from her year went to secretarial college, few had any ambition to continue their education. Miss Burke, her English teacher, told Iris about the two-year teaching course at Eastern Illinois University. She thought Iris would make a fine teacher, she told her student. What's more, Iris found the security that the brick walls of an educational institution offered extremely tempting. Her shining grades and positive references from her teachers in Baltimore secured her place. Iris departed Baltimore believing her entire future had been mapped. This was a comfort to the young woman.

Now, when she crossed the state line into Indiana in the passenger seat of a Buick owned by a Fort Wayne pastor, she realised she was returning to her birthplace. Her direction wasn't intentional. She had no plans, but she was happy to be leaving Chicago. The last weeks had been testing since departing the YWCA. Sleeping in abandoned factories at night, queuing at soup kitchens during the day and looking for work – she was drifting and she didn't know where. It seemed to her that she was rootless, without the customary anchors of family, home or career. While some, she considered, might find this liberating, she found it extremely disturbing.

The pastor, whose name was Milton, made pleasant small talk during their four-hour journey together. Iris had met him at a soup kitchen on Wabash Avenue. He was moving stiffly from table to table, chatting with the diners. He was visiting the Wabash soup kitchen to gain insight into how such an establishment might be operated, he told Iris. His church was planning to open something similar in Fort Wayne.

When she heard this she immediately procured the ride. The times had made her opportunistic. Bold, she sometimes thought, although she preferred to think of herself as resourceful. He was nice enough, she reasoned, despite his wet lips, sallow skin and oversized Adam's apple.

It was after midnight when they left Chicago. Iris leaned her head against the window of the car, pulled her grey woollen hat low over her forehead and closed her eyes. Her stomach was full, fuller than it should be, but she relished the sensation. She was exhausted.

As they drove, Iris passed in and out of sleep. She did not speak to Milton again until the car stopped, just before dawn, at Fort Wayne. 'You slept well, Miss McIntosh,' he said, and then added, 'Like the apple.' He laughed, a little too much. 'You didn't even stir when we stopped for gas twenty miles back.'

Iris smiled half-heartedly and stretched her legs as far as she could.

'This is my home,' Milton said, pointing to a modest wooden cottage sitting next to the First Presbyterian Church. 'Would you like to come in for breakfast? My wife's bacon and eggs are the best in Fort Wayne.'

Iris could barely remember the last time she had eaten bacon and eggs. It might have been at Lou's on Lincoln Avenue early in the previous year, about three months before she lost her job. Iris had met a colleague, Lois Page, there one Sunday morning. They had chatted about Clark Gable and Myrna Loy and Lois's new hair style, blithely unaware they would both be unemployed by April.

'Thank you very much, that would be lovely.'

Iris decided she would have a big breakfast, wash her face and then thumb a ride further east.

10
WASHINGTON DC
March 1933

When the journalists were ushered into the Oval Office that morning, the president was already seated behind his desk with Louis Howe standing to his left and his press secretary, Steve Early, to his right. Hoover had made a practice of meeting reporters in the East Room, standing behind a podium. His press conferences were formal occasions where all of the questions were submitted in writing beforehand. Roosevelt intended for this to be an off-the-cuff affair but the reporters were made suspicious by the change in routine.

The mood is too sombre, the president thought. Not what I had in mind at all. As he was wondering what he could do to lighten the atmosphere, a tall, slim young man who looked to be in his early twenties broke ranks and approached Roosevelt's desk. Despite his well-cut navy suit, the reporter's dark hair was uncombed and dishevelled. But his eyes were sharp, the president noticed. Keen. They had a glint – amusement or doubt, Roosevelt couldn't discern which.

'Good morning, Mr President. I'd like to thank you for inviting me here today.' He stretched his arm over the desk and offered his hand. 'Sam Jacobson from Associated Press.'

'Well, it's good to know you, Sam,' Roosevelt replied. 'I'm glad you could make it. I can tell by your accent that you're not from around here. Queens?'

'Yes, sir, Forest Hills.'

'Did you vote for me in '28?' the president asked, grinning.

'No comment. Voting in the United States is done by secret ballot, sir,' Jacobson said pleasantly with a crooked grin.

Roosevelt opened his mouth wide in a soundless laugh. 'Right you are, young man.'

Jacobson turned to resume his position and noticed that a queue had formed in his wake. Everyone wanted to shake the hand of this man, it seemed. After all, he was the country's last hope. Jacobson wondered whether Roosevelt realised the weight that rested on his shoulders. He hoped so.

By the time the door to the Oval Office was closed behind the assembled pack, Roosevelt guessed he had shaken the hand of more than one hundred reporters. (Early told him later it was exactly one hundred and twenty-four.) Now they stood, notepads at the ready, pencils poised. Five or so photographers perched on chairs at the back of the pack. The president smiled warmly and waved an arm to the photographers, indicating that they should cease firing. Then he welcomed, more officially, the members of the press.

'But before I take any questions I'd like to go over some ground rules,' he said.

A chorus of muted groans echoed through his audience.

'Now, now, fellas; they're nothing to worry about,' he assured them. 'We will be meeting here, in this room, every Wednesday and Friday. Now, I'm not going to answer any iffy questions or those which for various reasons I do not wish to discuss, or am not ready to discuss, or I do not know anything about.' His final comment garnered a laugh from his audience.

'I do not want to be quoted directly unless my press secretary here, Steve Early, okays the quote first. Attribute straight news simply to the White House. There'll be a lot of off-the-record discussion and if any of that makes it into the news the person responsible will be out. You got it?'

The reporters nodded their heads in agreement and scribbled in their notepads.

The president sat for some time, attempting to catch the gaze of each man in his office.

'Well, I guess I don't have any real news, but I would like to say this. The Banking Bill, the amendment of the Volstead Act and the Economy Act, well they're good in themselves and needed to be implemented – to stop the panic, raise a little revenue and balance the budget. But those three measures do nothing immediately constructive for the economy. They don't put people back to work or raise farm prices.'

Every reporter in the room raised his hand at that point. Roosevelt considered them carefully then gestured to the young man who first shook his hand, a small reward for breaking the deadlock earlier. 'Sam Jacobson from AP,' Roosevelt said.

'Does the administration have any measures or policies in mind that would achieve those goals?'

'Nothing is set in stone, and I don't want to be quoted on this, but I was thinking of a system where we would pay farmers not to produce crops beyond an amount set by the Secretary of Agriculture. This would reduce surplus and raise farm prices and therefore income.'

'One more question, Mr President,' Jacobson said quickly.

Roosevelt nodded once.

'What about German militarisation? What steps will this administration take to stop the threat of fascism?'

'We might just wait to see if fascism is a threat before we take any steps,' Roosevelt replied.

Early gestured to another journalist.

'Francis Jackson, the New York Times. Are you saying that agriculture would be controlled by the government?'

The president nodded.

'Doesn't that smack of communism?' Jackson cut in.

'Not at all. I'm not advocating collectivisation; I'm arguing the opposite. Production needs to decrease. Next question.'

'Richard Lee Strout from the Christian Science Monitor. That will take care of farm prices, Mr President, but what about unemployment?'

'One idea I had in mind was a civilian conservation corps recruited from the unemployed to build bridges, plant trees, dig reservoirs, cut firebreaks, that sort of thing. The details have not yet been finalised.'

'And these unemployed would be paid?' Strout continued.

'Indeed. Thirty dollars a month, with twenty-five of that going back home to their families. But as I said, the details still have to be hammered out.'

'John Stephenson, the Washington Post. Do you think there'll be opposition from the unions?'

'We'll cross that bridge when we come to it.'

For the next forty minutes the president and the press bantered and joked about his first ten days in the White House. Louis Howe later remarked it was one of Roosevelt's finest performances. Sam Jacobson called it 'virtuoso' that afternoon as he was typing up his notes. He wrote: 'Whatever his legacy turns out to be, Franklin Delano Roosevelt will go down in history as the most charming President of the United States.' He told his editor that evening over a beer that he'd never met anyone with a greater talent for sidestepping a direct question while giving the questioner the impression that the question had actually been answered.

■

Even though it was ten thirty in the morning when Monty Chapel entered the president's bedroom, he was not surprised to see his commander-in-chief still in bed. His first press conference had been yet another conquest and every paper ran an identical front-page photograph – Roosevelt seated among a crowd of one hundred and twenty-four journalists. FDR was now alone. A tray lay across his lap bearing a plate of half-finished scrambled eggs and a cup of coffee.

Monty's usual genial smile was absent from his handsome face as he threw a copy of the *Washington Post* onto Franklin's bed. 'Have you read it?' he enquired.

'Yup.'

'Well, what are you going to do?' Monty's baritone was an octave or so lower than usual.

'Nothing. The press conference was a great success. I'm looking forward to Friday's.'

'No, not that. The article on page four, at the bottom.' The forty-two-year-old economist indicated with his index finger then ran his hand through his thick, brown hair, trying to maintain his composure.

Roosevelt held out the tray to Monty, who promptly shifted it to a table in another part of the room while the president wiped his mouth with a napkin. When he was satisfied his face was sufficiently clean he crumpled the linen cloth into a ball with his right hand and, propping himself straighter in bed with his left, expertly threw the napkin towards the table and onto the tray that had recently been removed from his lap.

'Yep, I've seen that too.'

'Well?' Monty persisted.

'I'm not going to call in Douglas MacArthur, if that's what you're worried about.'

'I'm not.' Monty unbuttoned the coat of his navy pinstripe and smoothed his hand down his tie. 'But I think action should be taken immediately. We can't allow the situation to escalate. Nobody wants a repeat of last summer.'

'Help me into my chair,' Roosevelt ordered, pushing his legs off the side of his narrow, metal-framed bed.

Monty obliged, grasping the president under the armpits and transferring him from the bed to the wheelchair. Standing at six feet two inches, Roosevelt was only slightly taller than the economic adviser, but the weight of the nation's leader always came as a surprise to anyone asked to perform this task. Despite his withered legs, his upper body was broad and muscled.

Roosevelt lit a cigarette and wheeled himself over to his desk. He picked up the telephone. As he did so Missy, who had already been working for several hours, entered the room briskly, walked over to the desk and deposited a number of papers in front of him. She squeezed the president's shoulder and he placed his hand over hers briefly before she left the room through the door that led to the East Wing.

'Louis, are you decent?' Roosevelt said into the phone. 'Get over here. I've got a job for you.' He hung up and looked at Monty. 'I'll put Howe on it. He'll sort it out.'

'But are you going to give them what they want?' Monty planted both hands on the president's desk.

'I can't. There's no money, Monty. I can't give them their bonuses early when I've just cut their pensions. There are no funds in the kitty.'

Monty stifled any further argument when he heard Howe coughing outside the door. He moved to the window that overlooked the Jefferson Memorial. After listening to a minute or so of intense racking, Monty was forced to close his eyes and lean his forehead against the chilly pane. He imagined Howe's besieged lungs as two deflated footballs. Asthma and emphysema had taken their toll on the president's chief adviser.

At last there was a knock and Louis Howe entered. He closed the door behind him and approached the president's desk.

'Good morning, boss,' Howe said, then nodded in Monty's direction. 'Good morning, Mr Chapel.'

Monty moved across the room to greet him. He respected the man for his intellect and his loyalty and delighted in his acid tongue. Howe rarely spoke about his background but he had confided to Monty that he began his career as a journalist in Indiana. He had never mentioned school or college.

The president looked up and grinned at the sight of the two starkly different men standing before him. Louis Howe wore an old light-grey suit that Roosevelt figured was at least two sizes too large. He noticed a coffee stain on Howe's yellow tie and a cigarette hole in his lapel.

Monty Chapel, who stood at least seven inches taller than the shrivelled Howe, looked impeccable as usual, hands in pockets and foot tapping as he waited for an acceptable resolution. Franklin knew Monty's wardrobe came from Brooks Brothers in New York.

'What's up?' Howe asked.

'Monty is worried about the Bonus Army. He wants to give them money. I want to give them jobs.'

'I'd like to offer them both – they deserve it,' Monty interjected passionately. 'They fought for this country, in the not-so-distant past, and this depression has left them high and dry.'

'Bolshie,' Louis Howe mumbled, following the comment with a wry smile in Monty's direction. 'Are you going to get in line if there's a payout?'

The president smiled at Howe's audacity. The adviser enjoyed riling the group of men the press had dubbed 'FDR's Brains Trust'. Most of them Howe regarded as privileged professors from the east who lacked political savvy. He had never endeavoured to hide his resentment when Franklin turned to them for policy advice. However, the president knew that while Louis Howe was undoubtedly the most skilled political strategist in the country, when it came to policy he had little interest and even less idea.

'I don't think it's bolshie to want justice and compensation for the men who served this country,' Monty rebutted coolly. 'Many of those veterans were physically wounded and are still burdened with psychological scars. Last year, when they marched into town, the cavalry charged into their camp with tear gas, bayonets fixed, with no regard for the women and children who were there. MacArthur, Patton, Eisenhower . . .' He shook his head in disbelief. 'They burned them out of the camp. People died. Do you remember?'

'Look, Monty,' the president began, 'that's not going to happen. I'm not Hoover or MacArthur, thank heaven, and you know I would never act in such a fashion. They'll get their wartime bonuses in 1945, exactly when they were promised. I haven't taken their bonuses away. Furthermore, although we have cut their pension, jobs are forthcoming. We all lived through the Great War; you were on the frontline, granted, but I visited the battlefields. I was witness to the sacrifices those men made. I'm just asking for one more sacrifice for their country until the work relief programs get the go-ahead.'

The president frequently used this analogy. Monty believed he genuinely felt that the nation was locked in a war against economic circumstances. Although there was no human enemy, Roosevelt saw their current foe as even more formidable than the Germans had been fifteen years before. But for Monty, who at twenty-five had found himself knee deep in mud in Verdun, the analogy didn't seem quite right.

Roosevelt saw that Monty's stony face was softening. 'Louis, set up a camp for the veterans – maybe at the old army base at Fort Hunt. I don't want them squatting in vacant buildings on Pennsylvania Avenue again or setting up another shantytown. They'll want three meals a day, medics, sanitation, whatever you think. Set up a meeting with whoever is running the thing.' He turned back to Monty. 'Happy now?'

'No.' Monty added, 'I'm heading back to New York tomorrow. I'm needed at Columbia for the next few weeks. I'll be interested to see the progress when I return.'

'Have a little faith,' the president said. 'Within a few months most of them will have paid jobs with food and clothing provided. They'll gain a sense of purpose and be helping the country win this war.'

Monty nodded reluctantly and looked at Howe.

Howe smiled and shrugged his bony shoulders. 'Sounds like a plan. I'll get on it.'

11
FORT WAYNE, INDIANA
April 1933

Iris departed the pastor's house with a full stomach three days after arriving. It was longer than she had intended to stay but the pastor and his wife encouraged her to prolong her visit. She walked for what seemed like hours, unable to hitch a ride. Iris had come to realise that people were made uncomfortable by the female poor, far more than their male counterparts. It just seemed unnatural, she supposed, that a woman should be alone and without a husband or family. People assumed that the woman must be to blame for her predicament. To be a single woman without income or a home must be one of the most degraded positions in society, she thought. It was the equivalent of being Negro.

On the outskirts of Fort Wayne Iris came to a freight yard. It seemed deserted.

'Miss,' someone whispered from behind her. 'Get out of sight or they'll chase you off.'

Iris turned towards the source of the warning and saw a woman huddled behind a stack of large wooden crates, the kind that cotton or wool were transported in. Iris hurriedly crouched down and joined the woman in her hiding spot. There were two other occupants, she realised: a pair of twin boys about ten years old.

'The train down there' – the woman pointed to the far end of the yard – 'it's about to leave soon. Last stop Harrisburg, Pennsylvania.'

'Is that where you're heading?' Iris asked.

'Yep.' The woman smiled and stole a quick glance at the train. Three men in blue coveralls were now boarding the engine. 'You don't seem like you've done this before.'

Iris shook her head. 'I haven't. I've been thumbing rides.'

The woman held out her hand. 'I'm Molly and this is Benny and Carter.' The boys greeted Iris shyly.

Iris began to introduce herself as a loud hiss was released from the engine. She was quickly shushed by Molly. 'Get ready. Just follow me,' the woman instructed as the train began its first steady movement along the rails.

Wearing a faded skirt, thick wool stockings and boots not dissimilar to Iris's, Molly placed her bag on her back and tightened the strap across her chest. She took the hands of her sons, and after a swift glance in each direction, jogged with them toward the last wagons. Iris ran alongside the trio. As they ran, Iris noticed men, women and a few children emerge from behind shrubs and containers until at least fifty people were running for the train.

Two guards appeared from a cabin in the yard, half-heartedly waving truncheons and shouting threats. They were ignored as the stowaways were absorbed by the carriages.

Molly ran towards a wagon where the large wooden door had already been opened. She released her sons' hands and they climbed aboard expertly. Once they were safely on the train she climbed in after them.

'Come on, Iris!' she yelled. 'It's now or never.'

Iris grabbed the handrail, her legs moving faster than she'd thought possible. Her toes were barely skimming the surface of the ground. She threw in her bag then hauled herself up and into the carriage.

As she fell onto her back on the carriage's dusty floor, she began to laugh.

'Quite an experience, isn't it?' Molly said. 'I ran track in high school; I never imagined I was training for this.'   •

Iris, unable to speak and still sucking in air fiercely, nodded. When she caught her breath, she said, 'I ran track too, but I don't think I ever ran as fast as I did just then.' She sat up and focused on the other occupants of the wagon; as well as Molly and her boys, there were two men. All were setting up their makeshift accommodation in separate areas of the carriage, in between crates stamped with the General Electric logo.

'Come, sit by us,' Molly said, patting the floor next to her. She was handing out crackers to her sons.

'I've got a little bread and some cheese,' Iris said. She produced a paper package from her bag. The pastor's wife had handed it to her when she'd departed Fort Wayne that morning. Iris untied the string and became aware of the concentrated stares of Benny and Carter, both unconsciously edging towards the package. Iris laid the bread and cheese on the floor.

'My, that's a whole loaf of bread!' Molly said. 'Where in the world . . . ?'

'A good Samaritan,' Iris replied.

'Ask, and it will be given to you; seek, and you will find; knock, and it will be opened to you,' Molly recited. 'Matthew. It's the only thing I remember from Sunday school.'

'Probably very good advice,' Iris said, and the women laughed.

Benny and Carter looked to their mother for permission. Molly nodded and smiled. The boys took one slice of bread and one small piece of cheese each.

'They're very good boys,' Iris commented.

'They have to be,' Molly said. 'They're only seven. I wouldn't be able to do this if they weren't the angels they are.'

'They look older,' Iris said.

'They're tall for their age; they take after me,' Molly said, rubbing Carter's head.

'Where are you coming from?' Iris asked.

'Seattle,' Molly answered.

'You've come a long way.' Iris was amazed. 'Riding the rails?'

Molly nodded and stretched out her legs. 'We've been on the move since Christmas, more or less.' She yawned and pushed her greying hair from her face. 'There were a couple of stops where I picked up a little work – piecework, that sort of thing.'

'You're a seamstress?' Iris asked.

'No, a librarian who can sew,' Molly replied. 'What about you? May I?' she asked, reaching for the bread.

'Of course,' Iris said. 'I was a teacher in Chicago, but was laid off last April. I'm going to Baltimore.'

'Then you should get off at Columbus,' Molly suggested. 'The train stops there, someone told me.'

'Are you going to meet your husband in Harrisburg?' Iris asked.

Molly laughed. 'You're sweet, Iris, but no. He left us before Christmas. He was a foreman at Todd Shipyards. They laid him off and then he laid us off.'

'That's awful,' Iris said, shocked.

'I'm through trying to figure out why. It's too exhausting.' Molly shrugged. 'I guess without work he felt no good to anyone.'

'What's in Harrisburg, then?'

'My sister and mother. My sister's husband still has a job and he reckons he can keep us all until this is over. My mother's got some savings too. Luckily she's never trusted banks. Kept her money in a coffee tin. It'll be tight, but I've promised to pay them back every single cent. I'll try and pick up some work, if I can. But most important, Benny and Carter will be in school again.'

Iris offered a strained smile. There was an end in sight for Molly and her sons; once they reached Harrisburg their struggle would be over. But Iris had no inkling as to how or when her own struggle would end.

12
HYDE PARK, NEW YORK
May 1962

Mr Chapel was a funny one. He always asked me to call him Monty, but I couldn't. He was so grand and important, in a low-key kind of way. He'd often come to my office and request something extravagant for dinner – filet mignon or caviar or some such thing – tongue in cheek, I think. He knew we were on an economy drive. Some of his suggestions just made me laugh. He was always on at me about hiring a sommelier. Well, I didn't even know what that was. I remember asking Dad and he was just as befuddled. Finally, after he had harangued me for weeks, I mentioned Mr Chapel's suggestion to Mrs Roosevelt. She just shook her head, informed me that a sommelier was a fancy French name for a wine steward, and instructed me to tell Mr Chapel that such an employee was not needed in the White House. Domestic wine and champagne would do just fine.

There were people going back and forth all the time. Family, friends, colleagues and so on. Mrs Roosevelt kept an open house. Everyone was welcome. After working there for a short time I got to know most of the folks' likes and dislikes, especially the president's. For special occasions he always requested fried chicken with Maryland gravy or Chicken à la King. He rarely got them, of course. They may have been his preference but I was responsible for the president's health, and with his blood pressure both of those meals were out of the question.

Despite what he said, though, I knew he loved sweetbreads and brains, and the way I fixed liver and beans was one of his favourites. All those comments he made about not liking my menus and the way the food was cooked, why, he was just joking. He had a peculiar sense of humour at times.

I met Mrs Roosevelt through the League of Women Voters back in '28. It all really began with my dining chairs. They were mission oak and really handsome, solid chairs. One of the neighbours borrowed them for a wedding one time and then word got out and my chairs became quite sought after. Anyway, Mrs Saltford asked one day whether she could borrow them as she was hosting the first meeting of the League's Hyde Park branch and she also invited me to the get-together. Back in the early 1900s I'd supported suffrage but up until that afternoon I'd always voted Republican.

Well, Mrs Roosevelt was the guest of honour and she gave a very lovely speech. She was so eloquent and, well, I was just drawn to her kind face. After the speeches and what have you, somehow I was elected to the office of treasurer for the League. I had never held any sort of office before in my life and I was very nervous. Mrs Roosevelt must have noticed my uneasiness and she immediately walked up to me, introduced herself and began to reassure me. She told me she had only become interested in politics when her husband was stricken with paralysis in 1921. She had no experience in politics before that time and was also very apprehensive. Well, she took to politics like a duck to water, so what did I have to worry about?

We became friends and every time she was in the neighbourhood, just passing by, she would stop for a cup of coffee and a piece of pie, no matter how busy she was. We had a great deal in common, both being mothers and grandmothers. She was younger than me by about ten years and her two youngest were still away at school. She missed them terribly, but that's the way rich folk raise their children, I guess.

That's about the time I became a Democrat. I guess I had voted Republican in the past because that was Dad's leaning. But that evening when I went home after the meeting I broke the news to Dad that I would be voting for Franklin Delano Roosevelt for governor. Well, can you believe he had come to the same change of heart but for entirely different reasons? His decision was prompted by chicken breasts. Now that's a tale that always makes me laugh . . .

13

RIPLEY, WEST VIRGINIA
May 1933

The two youngest children rode up front with their parents, but the rest of the family, which consisted of three boys and a girl and two dogs, was huddled with Iris in the back of the Ford pickup under a tarpaulin that smelled of grease. As uncomfortable as it was, it beat standing by the side of the road in the rain.

They had picked her up just outside Columbus, Ohio. The rain was coming down so hard that she had not heard the name of the man driving, but he indicated the open back of his truck with his thumb and she had climbed in and found the children and animals taking shelter. The girl, who Iris reckoned was about seven years old, wordlessly lifted the corner of the sheeting and allowed her to crawl into their sodden den.

As Iris strove to contain her shivering, she wondered whether they had crossed the state line yet into West Virginia. The sound of the rain gradually eased from a downpour to a shower and within minutes she began to feel warmth penetrating their refuge. The eldest boy threw back the tarpaulin and they all squinted into the sunlight.

The boys remained mute, but the little girl introduced herself as Betsy, short for Elizabeth. Iris complimented her on her pretty name and then the truck stopped. The driver opened his door and got out.

'I'm sorry, miss. We don't have enough food for you. We've just brought enough for the family and we only have gas money,' he explained as he helped the children from the truck.

'I understand. I ate this morning. I'll be fine,' Iris lied.

The tray of the truck was empty apart from two suitcases and a couple of boxes that were covered by a second tarpaulin. Iris eased herself from the side of the vehicle onto the road where the family sat together. Her stomach groaned. She hadn't eaten since the pastor's bread and cheese the day before. 'My name is Iris McIntosh. I didn't hear yours before, when you stopped.'

The man introduced himself as Henry Wilkins. His wife was Ruth. He didn't bother to introduce his six children. He informed his passenger they had just passed through Ripley, West Virginia, and would be in Charleston in a few hours. Iris had never heard of Ripley, but she had visited Charleston once with her mother. They had taken the train from Baltimore to visit a second cousin of her mother's, but Iris could no longer remember the woman's name. Mary, she thought, or perhaps Marion.

She had served cake, Iris remembered, with beautiful white meringue frosting. Her mother allowed her a second slice because she had been such a good girl on the train. Marjorie was her name, Cousin Marjorie. Iris experienced a strange, fleeting sense of relief.

Henry sat on the ground with his family in the scant shade made by the truck while Iris hovered nearby. She took off her hat, squeezed it out and laid it across the side of the truck in the sun. Then she did the same with her coat. She wasn't sure whether this was the end of the road for her and the Wilkins family or whether she'd be welcome to travel a little further with them. She looked both ways along the stretch of highway. There were no other cars in sight but there were many people on foot hauling suitcases and children and household belongings, all hoping for rides. People roamed and roamed, eventually leaving one big city for another in the hope of better prospects somewhere else. The country was being endlessly crisscrossed by hopeless nomads. Iris wondered whether their tracks would be indelible.

Ruth unwrapped sandwiches from waxed paper and divided them among the group. As she did so Iris heard her mutter, 'Sorry, Miss' to the ground.

Finally Iris worked up the courage to ask: 'Would it be a trouble if I travelled with you for a time. Depending where you're heading, of course.'

'We're going as far as Culpeper, Virginia,' Henry answered. 'My brother has a farm there. He ain't doing great, but he said he'd put us up for a spell, times being what they are and all.'

'Where are you coming from?'

'Oskaloosa, Iowa. Had a farm there – corn mainly – that went belly-up. The bank took it all. We sold everything else that we could,' he said matter-of-factly.

'I'm sorry to hear that,' Iris said. 'I'd be grateful if I could ride along with you until Culpeper.'

Henry nodded and then instructed his brood to hop back into the truck. Iris was thankful that neither Henry nor his wife enquired into her situation. Ruth took a cloth sack from the front seat and handed each of her children and her husband an apple.

Then, fishing in the bottom of the sack, she withdrew another. 'There's one left,' she said, handing the remaining piece of fruit to Iris.

'Thank you. Are you sure you can spare it?' Iris looked from Ruth to Henry. The latter simply shrugged his shoulders and slid in behind the wheel of his truck.

'Yeah, they'll just fight over it. It's better if you eat it.' Ruth got back into the passenger seat of the pickup.

Iris sat down and crossed her legs. One of the dogs lay beside her and pressed his muzzle into her hip. She examined the apple for a moment before taking her first bite. It was bruised. The engine started and she bit through the red skin and into its flesh. It was floury and, under ordinary circumstances, she would have thrown it straight into the trash. But these were not ordinary circumstances.

14
WASHINGTON DC
May 1933

Eleanor paused in the letter she was writing to look at her friend, who was seated on the sofa. Hick seemed odd sitting there, reading in front of a hearth in which no fire crackled, the First Lady thought. Her gaze shifted to the mantle and the photographs that stood there – pictures of family and friends were ranged along its length – and then higher to the portrait of William Henry Harrison. The portrait was not one of her choosing and yet there it hung. Eleanor could have swapped it with the likeness of a greater known or more charismatic president but her heart went out to Harrison, who had occupied the White House for just thirty-two days. Hick's legs were folded beneath her rump. Major and little Meggie were asleep beside her on the sofa.

'What are you reading?' Eleanor asked.

'*The Pastures of Heaven* by a Californian author, John Steinbeck,' Hick replied without looking up from the book. 'He's very good.' She absently placed her hand on Meggie's head and began to stroke it softly.

This was what she loved most about Hick, Eleanor thought. Franklin never had enjoyed domesticity. It had been a very long time since she had been a figure in a similar domestic tableau with her husband. In the early years of her marriage, Eleanor had been an utterly different person. Always pregnant, unfailingly dutiful and painfully timid, she was kept separate from her husband's social and professional life. She preferred it that way. Even before the fracture, neither of them appreciated the interests of the other. 'East is East, and West is West, and never the twain shall meet,' she mused. She placed her pen on the incomplete correspondence and rose from her chair.

'What's the matter?' Hick asked.

'Will you come with me tomorrow?'

'Isn't Howe escorting you?'

Eleanor nodded. 'Yes, but I'd like you to come along as well. I'm not sure why Franklin wants me to go over there.'

'He wants you to appease them, show the veterans some compassion. Those men at Fort Hunt cannot see a lick of difference between your husband and Herbert Hoover. The Bonus Army wants action. Franklin's hands are tied at the moment but they won't believe it unless it comes from the top. And you know he can't go over there and get pushed around through the dirt and mud. He'd look foolish. The president has great trust in your powers of placation.'

Eleanor turned to the window and examined the Washington Monument for some time. The sky was clear and there was a full moon. The obelisk took on an ethereal glow. She wasn't sure she possessed any of these powers that were apparently so blindingly evident to Hick and her husband. It seemed that all she had any talent for was rankling people. Apart from Louis and Monty, most of the players in the current administration despised her views. Eleanor had seen how they winced each time she opened her mouth to speak. Admittedly, she had not tried to hide her views, but how could she? The policies the group were working on completely disregarded women. There were one hundred and forty thousand homeless women and girls, thumbing their way from city to city looking for work or, worse, selling themselves. Yet they were ignored by the administration.

Even the female-only press conference that Hick had arranged that morning had provoked the ire of most of the Cabinet and her husband's advisers, who all seemed to believe that her opinions would get the administration into hot water. Eleanor was pleased that the press conference was a success and she had already scheduled them weekly. She hadn't checked this with her husband. But surely positive publicity was worthwhile even if she was prone to expressing a dissident opinion?

'You haven't answered my question,' Eleanor pushed, turning to face Hick.

'You know that I'm heading back to New York tomorrow.' Hick looked up from her book. 'A neighbour has been feeding my cat since the end of February, when I came down here. Then there's my mail, and I have to get back to the office'

'Why don't you move in here permanently?' Eleanor suggested.

Hick hooted loudly. 'Because my career would be over.'

'Don't be ridiculous,' Eleanor laughed.

'My loyalties would be divided, Eleanor. They already are. How can I report objectively on this administration when I'm privy to the greatest scoops in American history and I can't write about any of it because of you?' She stood and lit a cigarette in an attempt to calm herself. Major and Meggie leaped from the sofa and positioned themselves near Eleanor.

Hick inhaled deeply then continued, 'Frank asked my advice about his inauguration address. I read what he'd written and it was gold. My editor would have given me his firstborn for that sort of material and I wasn't able to offer him a thing. I left the room and cried like a baby for the missed opportunity.'

Eleanor didn't say a word.

'If anything,' Hick went on, 'I've been thinking I should spend less time here, distance myself from the White House.'

Eleanor asked quietly, 'Distance yourself from the White House or distance yourself from me?'

'Don't be stupid. I love you, Eleanor. You've got your apartment in the Village. You used to spend three days a week in New York.'

'That was when I was teaching. I'm needed here now.'

'Look, this situation is becoming impossible. My work is suffering. My career will suffer. Everything I've worked to achieve since I was nineteen and began at the *Minneapolis Tribune* will fall to pieces.'

Hick's words failed to move the woman she loved. 'I could find you something here, in Washington, at the White House,' Eleanor said. 'Or you could write magazine articles or a book. You've mentioned a book, I'm positive.'

'Can you really see me writing articles for *Ladies' Home Journal* about growing roses and patchwork quilts?'

'No, of course not. But you could be informing women about politics and their position in this country and the world. Most women are uninformed or ill-informed.'

'You mean I could be furthering your causes,' Hick responded flatly.

Eleanor did not react.

'That's not my style, darling.' Hick stubbed out her cigarette in an ashtray and put her arms around Eleanor's waist. 'I'll settle for nothing less than a front-page by-line in a national daily.'

Eleanor twisted the buttons on Hick's flannel shirt. A glimmer of a smile crossed her lips. 'I understand, but I don't accept. I will get you here, some day, by my side.'

'And that's exactly what I love about you the most: your tenacity,' Hick said. 'I wouldn't expect anything less.'

15

FAIRFAX COUNTY, VIRGINIA
May 1933

It took Iris a little over a day to reach Fairfax County from Culpeper, where she had said goodbye to the Wilkins family. Walking part of the way and hitching the rest, Iris eventually came to a stop, exhausted, and took in the scene. Individuals, couples and families lined both sides of the road as far as she could see. Many had their entire households with them, it seemed. Chairs were piled in jigsaw configurations on top of tables. Pots and pans, bedrolls and other household items were nestled into cracks or hanging by wire from the sides of the neat stacks. Iris wondered how these people had got here and where they were heading, but it didn't really matter, she reasoned. They were all stationary at the present moment, looking for a ride.

She continued walking and eventually reached a gas station diner on the highway in the early hours of the morning. It was closed so she slept for a few hours in the undergrowth by the side of the road. It was a clear night and it was cool, but her coat and bedroll kept her warm. When she woke her stomach was growling with displeasure. She had not eaten since she'd devoured the partially rotten apple in the back of the Wilkins' truck. She stood and entered the diner, noting a sign for the rest rooms. She hadn't seen herself in a mirror since washing her face in Milton's bathroom in Fort Wayne; she probably looked like a bum. Iris hastily walked the breadth of the diner, weaving through tables and avoiding the wait staff, to the safety of the ladies' rest room.

There she leaned on the basin and regarded her tired face for a moment before taking off her hat and removing the rubber band that kept her hair back. Her curls, once a source of admiration and compliments, were limp, made greasy by the grime of travel. She couldn't remember when her hair had last been cut but it was definitely before she was retrenched.

Taking the soap from the basin she washed her face thoroughly with hot water, scrubbing her chin, neck and the sides of her nose. She rinsed off the soap and looked in the mirror once more, staring hard into her own eyes. Iris blue, that was their colour, her father had told her when she was a child. That was why he and her mother had named her Iris, he explained. She closed them momentarily before drying herself with paper towels. There was nothing she could do about her hair until she was able to bathe, so she tied it up again and placed the hat back on her head.

Checking herself a final time before she left the restroom, Iris realised she still looked like a bum. Then she remembered Molly's words: 'Ask, and it will be given to you; seek, and you will find; knock, and it will be opened to you.' Iris had grown braver and bolder in the last twelve months, but she had never until this morning been able to summon the nerve to ask for free food. Yet she had never been quite this hungry before – so hungry she was bilious.

'Excuse me, sir,' Iris said as she approached the counter, 'I was hoping you might be able to spare a little breakfast. I haven't eaten anything but an apple for a few days.'

'Sure. Can you pay?' the bald man said without looking up from his newspaper.

'No. I've been unemployed since last April. I was a teacher,' she added, thinking the fact might lend her an air of respectability. 'But I was hoping there might be something you could spare. I'd be glad to earn it, washing dishes, clearing tables . . .'

'I don't need any more hired hands,' the man said abruptly, eyes still on his newspaper.

'I'll take scraps, anything. Please. There must be something you could spare.' Iris was gaining the attention of the diners in the restaurant. They were mostly men in suits. Her confidence began to crumble.

'Look, miss,' the manager said, leaning low over the counter so as not to be heard. 'The closest soup kitchen is in DC. If I start giving food to bums, there'll be no stopping it.'

'I'm not a bum,' Iris responded firmly.

'If it walks like a duck and quacks like a duck . . .' He shrugged.

Iris could sense every eye in the diner upon her. Her chest heaved. 'I'm very sorry to bother you. Thank you for your time, but I must be on my way.'

She turned from the bald man towards the exit, which seemed a hundred miles away. A few patrons stared at her as she passed their tables, but most looked at their meals. With cheeks burning and tears threatening, Iris endeavoured to keep an expression of pleasant defiance on her face as she passed through the door, as if it was her choice that she was departing.

Once outside Iris rounded the corner of the restaurant and, out of sight, began to cry.

■

Louis Howe awoke in the front seat of Eleanor's PD Plymouth to the sound of cheering. He sat up and looked out the window. The First Lady was striding towards the car, surrounded by veterans. The hem of her navy skirt was dotted with mud and her ivory Oxfords were caked with clay. Everybody in the crowd, including Eleanor, was grinning.

Howe stepped from the car in readiness to open the driver's door.

When Eleanor reached the car she turned and faced the crowd. After a moment of consideration she began. 'I never want to see another war. I would like to see fair consideration for everyone, and I shall always be grateful to those who served their country. I hope we will never have to ask such service again.'

Her farewell was interrupted by further hurrahs.

'Thank you so much for your hospitality this morning. I hope you all have a wonderful day,' she finished.

Eleanor slipped into the car with a wave and started the engine as Howe trotted back to the passenger side. Veterans followed the departing car at a jog as they drove through the gates of the camp. There was further cheering as the car turned onto the highway.

'So it went well, then?'

Eleanor nodded, refusing to take her eyes from the road, a look of satisfaction on her face.

'What did you promise them? I have never seen such a happy bunch of disenfranchised veterans,' Howe said, lighting a cigarette.

'Absolutely nothing,' she replied. 'Do you have to? In the car?'

Howe took a deep drag then stubbed the cigarette out on the sole of his shoe. He slid it back into the box before saying, 'I have met with those same men at least four times and also promised them nothing and each time I only just managed to escape with my life.'

'I found the gentlemen most affable. I joined them for coffee, they gave me a tour of their barracks and hospital,' Eleanor explained and then paused. 'I even sang a few old war songs with them,' she added.

'Is that so?' Howe shook his head in disbelief. 'You're a regular George M. Cohan.'

Eleanor allowed the hint of a smile. 'I simply apologised for their current predicament and then we chatted about the war and my work for the Red Cross back then. They were all extremely pleasant men.'

'Did you mention the bonus?'

'I informed them I had no news on their bonus.'

Howe nodded his approval.

Eleanor was reluctant to share any more details of her visit to Fort Hunt and her discussions with the veterans. Neither Howe nor her husband were able to comprehend that all the men wanted was to speak with someone offering a sympathetic ear. They didn't even mention the bonus; Eleanor had introduced that topic herself, feeling it would be less awkward if she raised the issue first. She showed interest in their plight and they were keen to hear of her experiences during the war. Compassion and understanding was all they were seeking, from someone who was willing to listen. But politicians always wanted to be doing the talking.

'I'm going to stop at that gas station up there,' Eleanor said. 'I need to clean the mud off my shoes.' She checked the fuel gauge. 'I should fill up as well.'

'I'm going in to get a cup of coffee,' Howe said as the car rolled to a stop. 'I need a pick-me-up. Would you like anything?'

Eleanor shook her head and turned to the approaching attendant. 'Fill up the tank, please.'

The young man nodded. 'Certainly, ma'am. You havin' a nice morning?'

'Very pleasant, thank you.' Eleanor walked to a roll of paper towels hanging by the bowser, ripped off a handful and then removed her shoes. She crouched down by a bucket of water used to clean car windows and wiped the mud from her Oxfords. It was a messy task and she was glad she had worn a navy skirt and not the cream Tommy had suggested.

'Would you like me to do that, ma'am?' the attendant offered.

'No, thank you, I can manage. But you might have to change the water in this bucket. I'm very sorry.'

The young man told the polite lady that it was no trouble. From the corner of her eye Eleanor saw him hastily replace the pump and move to a position in front of her, blocking the path of someone. All she could see from her position on the ground were two frayed boots protruding from the tattered hemline of a coat.

'Now don't you go bothering this nice lady. On your way,' the attendant ordered.

Rising, Eleanor saw a thin young woman wearing a dirty wool hat and a man's coat. It looked to Eleanor like a greatcoat from the war. She seemed tired and, when Eleanor looked into her eyes, she could see the woman had been crying.

'It's alright, sir, I'd like to speak with this young woman,' Eleanor said as she slid her feet into her shoes. The attendant stepped aside reluctantly but didn't move away. 'You can go now,' Eleanor told him. 'My friend will pay you when he's had his coffee.'

The attendant nodded suspiciously and walked away, looking back once or twice.

'What can I do for you?' Eleanor asked after a moment.

'I'm terribly sorry. I had no idea . . . You were bending down and I couldn't see your face.' Embarrassed and ashamed, Iris began to retreat.

'It's okay. I'm Eleanor Roosevelt, and you are?'

'Iris McIntosh,' Iris said clearly.

'Were you about to ask me something?'

'No, ma'am. I should be on my way. Please excuse the intrusion.' Iris turned away. 'I'm extremely embarrassed.'

'There's absolutely no need to be,' Eleanor said. 'Where are you heading?'

'Baltimore,' Iris replied, facing the First Lady.

'Do you need some money?'

'No thank you, ma'am,' Iris said.

'Will you join me for breakfast?'

'No thank you, ma'am. I must be getting along.'

'Where have you come from? How far have you travelled? You look tired, dear.' Eleanor was growing intrigued by this young lady. She appeared destitute but her manners and speech were equal to that of any of the girls at Todhunter.

'Chicago.'

'What did you do in Chicago?'

'I was a teacher, high school English.'

'What a coincidence. So was I until last year. Where did you teach?'

'Lincoln Park High School on Orchard Street. Are you familiar with Chicago?'

'I am,' Eleanor replied, moving closer to Iris. 'That's a good school. It has a fine reputation. Why did you leave?'

'I was laid off in April last year. Retrenched is the proper term.' Iris smiled. 'Budget cuts. No other positions were available so I decided to go home to Baltimore.'

'What have you been doing since then?' The First Lady reached out and touched the young woman's arm.

'This and that. Work has been difficult to come by, but I've made do.' Iris could barely feel Mrs Roosevelt's hand through her oversized coat but it was consoling nonetheless.

'Do you have family in Baltimore?'

'No. My parents died ten years ago and I have no siblings or any family that I know well enough to . . . but Baltimore was where I grew up.'

'We have something else in common, then, dear. I'm an orphan too,' Eleanor confided. 'What are your plans when you get to Baltimore?'

'I'm hoping to find a job, teaching hopefully. But if I can't I'll try something new. I'm not fussy . . . at the moment.'

'Wait there, please, Miss McIntosh.' Eleanor retrieved her pocket book from the car. She handed Iris her card and a ten dollar bill.

'Thank you, but I can't accept this, ma'am,' Iris said quietly as she handed back the money.

'Of course you can,' Eleanor said, folding Iris's fingers over the note. The First Lady's fingers were cold, but strong. 'You also have my card there. You should reconsider your destination. If you call on me in Washington next week, I'm certain I'll be able to help you find work. Call the number on the card and speak to my assistant, Miss Thompson. She will be able to tell you a good time to visit. I'll tell her to expect your call.'

Iris looked at the card intently for some time. 'Thank you. Thank you very much.' Iris offered her hand and Eleanor clasped it readily. As she looked into Eleanor's face she saw only concern. Iris felt a lump rise in her throat. 'I'm sorry. I've had a very trying morning.'

'Of course. I understand, dear. These times can be extremely hard. But think over my offer. And take these.' Eleanor reached through the car window to the dashboard and handed Iris her leather gloves. 'Your hands are like ice.'

'So are yours.'

'I'm getting back into the car. You can return them when I see you next week.'

Iris nodded and said goodbye hastily before the First Lady of the nation witnessed her weeping. She shoved the gifts into the pocket of her coat.

Eleanor watched the girl's retreat towards the diner. She noticed Howe standing a short distance away. He stamped out his cigarette on the ground and approached.

'How much did you give her?'

'None of your business,' Eleanor retorted, and then relented. 'Ten dollars, a pair of gloves and the offer of a job.'

'And I bet you another ten dollars that you will never see her again. This is why you need the Secret Service to travel with you.'

'There was no attempt at assassination, Louis,' she mocked.

'Worse than that. You've just lost yourself twenty dollars.'

Eleanor shrugged. 'Perhaps, but I have a very good feeling about her. She was a teacher, you know, in Chicago.'

'You're a soft touch, my dear.'

As they drove from the gas station, Eleanor looked in the rear-view mirror. There was no sign of the girl.

Beside her, Howe slumped in his seat and pulled his hat over his eyes.

'For goodness' sake, Louis! Why on earth are you so tired?'

'It's that bedroom you put me in. I can feel his presence. It's giving me the heebie-jeebies,' he replied. 'Well, not so much the room, but that four-poster bed . . . just knowing that old Abe used to sleep in it . . .'

'I'll have another sent down from Val-Kill immediately. We can't have you getting into bed with the Republicans now, can we?'

Howe's laughter induced a coughing fit. He rolled down the window and breathed in the cold air. It was amazing, he thought. Eleanor was at her most entertaining when she wasn't trying. In the early days, when he had proofread her speeches and guided their direction, any attempt on her part to be humorous fell flat. She was the polar opposite of Frank, who could have a room in stitches within seconds. But over the years Louis had mentored her, Eleanor had developed her own style, one that was elegant and refined, and it suited her perfectly.

■

Iris stood at the back of the diner near the trash cans for a long time after Mrs Roosevelt drove away. She removed the First Lady's card and the money from her pocket and examined them closely. It took her at least ten minutes to compose herself and weigh her options. She slipped her hands into the calfskin gloves and admired the First Lady's taste. Just then, her stomach released a loud complaint. She lifted her head and placed the card and the money in her pocket then walked confidently to the entrance of the diner and through the door.

Iris ordered the twenty-five-cent breakfast special which, on that particular morning, consisted of bacon, fried eggs, sausages, toast and a cup of coffee.

16

HYDE PARK, NEW YORK
May 1962

It was ten o'clock on a Tuesday morning in the first week of June that Iris McIntosh first visited the White House. Tommy, that's Miss Thompson, called down to my office and asked for coffee and cookies for four in Mrs Roosevelt's study. I went into the kitchen but Ida was in a flap and said she couldn't be expected to get a tray ready with everything else she had to do, so I did it myself. All that I had were cornflake macaroons. I laid about twelve cookies on a plate and placed them on a tray along with a jug of hot coffee, a jug of hot milk and four cups. Mrs Roosevelt liked to serve her own coffee in the French style. I called for Fields but he was occupied, so I delivered the tray myself to the third floor.

I can honestly say that I pitied the poor thing. Ike told me she looked a sight – hair untidy, no hat and wearing an ill-fitting cotton frock and coat that were both much too big for her. Ike's exact words when he came into my office that morning were, 'I can't believe they're letting tramps into the White House.' He was the head usher and a lovely man. And although he had definite Republican leanings, he was right, she did look like a tramp.

Mrs Roosevelt introduced me to the young woman like she was the Queen of Sheba herself and asked me to get a bath ready for her in one of the spare rooms on the third floor. Miss McIntosh would be 'residing' for a few days, she said. Tommy stayed for the meeting, as did Mr Louis McHenry Howe.

I was surprised, to say the least. Especially with the Lindbergh baby kidnapping so recent and all. Anna's children Sistie and Buzzie lived in the house, as did Elliott's little one. And James's daughter Sara was less than a month old. I feared for them. I honestly did. Mrs Roosevelt didn't know this girl from Adam's house cat. But Mrs Roosevelt was a trusting soul and so kind-hearted. She only ever saw the good in people. She must have seen something in Iris McIntosh that I didn't. Mrs Roosevelt had a sixth sense about people.

I talked to Dad about it and he reckoned Mrs Roosevelt was trying to make up for the shortcomings in her own children. They must have been a constant worry. Anna had left her husband, Mr Curtis Dall, and had taken up with a reporter from Chicago who she met during the campaign. And Elliott, her third, was trouble. He abandoned his wife and baby at the White House only four days after the inauguration. He ran away to 'discover himself' on the Texas range. Can you imagine? But it would be difficult for any child being brought up in the privileged way that the Roosevelt children were. Thank God that my own offspring were raised poor and had been given a lot of loving attention.

I showed Miss McIntosh to her room and laid out some clothes for her on the bed. There was a dress that belonged to Anna, a lovely navy frock that Anna hardly wore. It had white detail, pearl buttons and a Peter Pan collar. Mrs Roosevelt asked me to retrieve from her dressing room a pair of Enna Jettick tan leather Oxfords that she hadn't worn and Tommy sent out to the Palais Royal for some underwear and stockings.

Once Miss McIntosh was in the bath I asked her what she wanted me to do with the clothes she had been wearing. She told me to give them to Goodwill or burn them, if I liked. She had bought the dress and coat only yesterday for four dollars in a thrift shop on G Street. Well, that's where Dad and I were living at the time. We rented a cosy apartment on exactly that street. In fact, I knew the thrift shop she was talking about. I returned the clothes that same day on my way home from work.

She seemed like a nice enough young woman. While I was pottering about the bedroom she told me how she came to meet Mrs Roosevelt and how grateful she was they had run into each other like that, at the gas station in Fairfax County. She was thrilled that Mrs Roosevelt had given her the position as Tommy's assistant. She was a funny little thing, all skin and bone, sitting in that bathtub. She needed fattening up, there was no doubt about that. I washed her hair for her and it looked a great deal better but it still needed attention. I didn't learn her full story until later, but I could tell she had seen hard times. She had an Irish complexion, I remember thinking. Very pretty. Pale skin, dark hair and blue eyes. Dad was Irish and his mother had that same appearance. I always called it an Irish complexion. I asked her if her origins were Irish. She said her father's people were Scottish.

It's funny to recall how concerned she was that she had no experience as a secretary to a personal secretary. I recall we both laughed at that and I told her she seemed like a bright young woman who would pick things up quickly. I took a seat on the side of the tub and began telling her how I came to be the White House housekeeper with no professional experience and that I was doing just fine. She called it a baptism by fire. I thought that was a very clever way to put it, considering I spent a great deal of time in the kitchen and all.

17
WASHINGTON DC
June 1933

The following day Iris began work, sitting opposite Tommy in an office adjoining Mrs Roosevelt's suite. It was a large room painted in a pale blue, more suited to a bedroom than an office. Portraits of former presidents and flint-faced men whom Iris didn't recognise hung on the walls. Iris's breath caught in her throat for an instant as she stood by the window and glimpsed the outlook – the Washington Monument.

'Some view,' Tommy remarked from her desk in the centre of the room.

'Yes, it is,' Iris replied slowly. 'I can't quite believe it.'

'You get used to it,' Tommy said, but the newest White House employee couldn't imagine this ever feeling ordinary.

A breakfast tray of toast and coffee had been brought up to her bedroom at about seven thirty by one of the maids. There was also a small note of apology from Mrs Roosevelt explaining she had to catch an early train to New York. They would meet up at dinner that evening. While Iris was eating her toast and reading the note another maid knocked at the door and brought in a change of clothes. Iris wasn't sure where the second outfit had come from, but she finished her coffee and put on the garment obligingly. It was a little too large, so she guessed it must have been another one of Anna's cast-offs. The dress was very pretty though, Iris thought. The fabric was the palest shade of moss green, and white buttons, about the size of quarters, ran the entire length of the skirt. Iris particularly liked the three-quarter sleeves and the way the skirt fell over her hips and thighs. She tightened the belt around her waist, making the top section blouse at her midriff. Looking in the mirror she decided it would do well enough until she received her first pay cheque or gained some weight. There was nothing she could do about her hair until she had it cut. She bundled it into a loose bun at the back of her head and secured it with pins. It wasn't fashionable but it would have to do. Iris was just eager to get to work.

At precisely eight thirty Tommy knocked at her door and walked with her to the office they would now be sharing.

'How are you feeling?' Tommy asked as they travelled through the expansive East Wing corridors.

'A little nervous,' Iris replied.

'Just a little?'

'A lot, then,' Iris added, and the women laughed together. 'When Mrs Roosevelt offered me a position I thought I'd be working in the kitchen or the laundry. I never dreamed . . . Even the corridors of this place are daunting!'

Tommy had introduced her to a number of people en route – housekeeping staff, clerks and even one of the President's advisors.

'Apart from the maid who was dusting picture frames, I already can't remember any of their names,' Iris said, uneasily.

'Don't let it overwhelm you. It's just your nerves getting the better of you,' Tommy advised sweetly and squeezed Iris's hand. 'We're all just normal people, earning a living like everyone else. The President's West Wing is less intimidating. Apart from his office, it's just like a rabbit warren over there. Much more cosy.'

She explained that they would take it slowly the first day and handed Iris a pile of papers that needed to be filed and a stack of invitations that required responses. There was a small note clipped to each invitation that read 'yes' or 'no'. After running through White House telephone protocol Iris got to work.

Very quickly Iris discovered she was thrilled to be working again. And once she got into the swing of the day, spoke with Tommy about Mrs Roosevelt's work and began talking with different organisations on the telephone that were seeking the First Lady's endorsement, her anxiety about the job disappeared. The ideals that Mrs Roosevelt was striving towards, the policies her husband was initiating, they were remarkable. Without planning for it, Iris was now a part of this vision. She had seen pictures of the president and Mrs Roosevelt at newsstands, of course, but she had not read a newspaper with any serious interest for a long time. She had not voted in the previous year's election – she could not even recall when it had been. But her father had been a Democrat, and a proud one. There had not been a Democrat in the White House since Woodrow Wilson twelve years ago. Iris believed her father would be thrilled about Roosevelt's election.

For over a year Iris had been alone, working towards nothing except survival. While she didn't underestimate the seriousness of this goal, it was a goal from which she received very little fulfilment. But in the space of – she checked the clock on her desk – three hours, her sense of purpose had been returned and it made her smile. Iris sat straighter in her chair and set her shoulders back. She was beginning to know herself again.

'Hello there.' A man had walked through the open door to the office. Iris felt herself blush. She thought this might be the most handsome man she'd ever seen: a thoroughly pleasing amalgam of Clark Gable, Errol Flynn and Douglas Fairbanks – minus the pencil-thin moustache.

'Back from New York, I see,' Tommy said, standing. 'Montgomery Chapel, this is my new assistant, Miss Iris McIntosh. Iris, this is Monty.'

Iris stood and shook the man's outstretched hand, then Monty took a seat on the corner of Iris's desk and offered both women a cigarette. Tommy accepted eagerly. Iris declined.

'I got back this morning. I'm pleased to see there has been a new addition in my absence.' He nodded at Iris. 'And where have you come from?' he asked, lighting his cigarette.

'Chicago. I was a teacher there, but I was retrenched. I've been lucky to find a position here. Mrs Roosevelt and Tommy have been very generous.' Iris knew she was speaking too rapidly and divulging too much information. She felt herself blush again, her heart pounding slightly.

The handsome man perched on her desk was smiling at her. She guessed he was in his forties, judging by the lines around his eyes and the grey in his dark brown hair. Iris pushed her chair out slightly and crossed her legs. As she did so she caught his scent. He smelled of citrus.

'What a coincidence,' he said. 'I'm a teacher too, sort of. I teach economics at Columbia University. But I'm positive your students would have been more attentive than mine are. While I'm trying to teach them supply and demand, the only thing they want to talk about is FDR and the New Deal.'

'Monty's a professor, Iris. Don't let him fool you. And he's one of the president's advisers,' Tommy said. 'He's a member of the Brains Trust,' she added mockingly. 'Although you wouldn't know it to speak to him.' She gave a throaty chuckle.

'I'm sure your students would hang on your every word,' Iris remarked. 'Considering your position in Washington, you're probably seen as a celebrity. They'd probably rather discuss your role in current policy decisions than read about hypotheticals in a textbook.'

'You're very kind to say so, Miss McIntosh,' he replied. 'Have you spent much time in DC?'

'No, not really. I grew up in Baltimore and visited once or twice, but never for a long stay. I'm looking forward to getting to know the city.'

'Well, you must let me show you around. My home town is New York, but I've spent enough time in the capital to act as a fairly good tour guide. But I'll let you be the judge of that.'

Was he interested, Iris wondered, or simply being polite? Apart from Roy, she hadn't had any attention from the opposite sex in quite some time. Struggling to remember the signs, Iris looked at Monty again. He smiled. It was an easy, comfortable smile – and then he raised an eyebrow.

'I'll look forward to it, Mr Chapel,' Iris declared.

'Call me Monty, please. Everyone does.'

'Don't you have somewhere to be, Monty?' Tommy interrupted. 'Shouldn't you be debating with a senator somewhere instead of swanning about the corridors of power annoying innocent females?'

'You're a cruel woman, Tommy,' Monty said with a laugh. 'Stop trying to poison Iris against me. I wanted to make a good impression. I've actually dropped by to ask you two to lunch. While the cat's away . . .' He raised his eyebrows comically a number of times in the style of Groucho Marx.

'And some of us have work to do, Romeo,' Tommy said drolly. Iris hoped her disappointment wasn't evident. 'We'll grab a sandwich from the kitchen later.' Then she rose from her desk and shooed Monty from the office.

She closed the door and returned to her desk. 'Be careful, Iris. Monty's known as a bit of a ladies' man in Washington. Don't get me wrong, he's a charming guy and very funny, but . . . just be careful.'

'Thank you, Tommy,' Iris said quietly.

'Does that mean, "Thank you, Tommy, I will beware," or, "Thank you, Tommy, but mind your own business"?'

Iris looked at her for a moment, considering. 'A little of both, I think.'

∎

Mrs Roosevelt returned late that afternoon and shared with Iris a light supper of pea soup and toast in her suite. They chatted about Iris's first day. Eleanor was impressed with the girl's queries about her occupations and interests. They then discussed Eleanor's day in New York. Eleanor informed her she'd spent half her time at Todhunter and the rest of her time at the annual meeting of the Travelers Aid Society, an organisation founded to help young homeless people. Iris was not aware that the organisation existed. On hearing that, Mrs Roosevelt sprang out of her chair and made a quick note on the writing pad on her desk. 'I'll discuss that with them. We'll have to work to raise their public profile, if that's the case.'

Eleanor told Iris she had addressed the audience about the amount of people that had lost their homes in the last three years. Many of those were below the age of twenty-one, yet no New Deal legislature even contemplated their plight, let alone attempted to tackle it. The work and relief programs established under the New Deal were directed at men. Women, she said, were another matter altogether. Iris could have listened to her speak all evening.

'You seem well-informed, Iris,' Mrs Roosevelt remarked.

'Not really, my knowledge is sketchy. Tommy filled me in a little today about the New Deal and your work,' Iris replied. The truth was that Iris had questioned Tommy endlessly throughout the day and had spent her lunch break and two hours after work scrutinising recent issues of *The Washington Post* and *The New York Times*. The newspapers were still littering her bedroom floor.

Finally Eleanor excused herself, explaining that she had a great deal of correspondence to see to. Then she gave the young woman a light-blue envelope on which her name was written in beautiful script.

'This is your first week's pay,' Eleanor informed her. 'Go out tomorrow morning and buy yourself a few clothes. Wisconsin Avenue is good, so I'm told. You can't keep wearing Anna's hand-me-downs. Just make sure you're back by twelve; I have a press conference and I would like you to take notes.'

Iris thanked her benefactor and made her way back to her bedroom feeling slightly ill at the thought of the task the First Lady had assigned her. She lay on her bed clutching the unopened envelope to her pounding chest. She sat up and picked up the receiver of the telephone on her bedside table. She should tell Mrs Roosevelt that she didn't know shorthand. How could she take notes? She replaced the receiver. Mrs

Roosevelt would think her strange for not raising the subject when they were face to face. She would scribble notes as fast as she could and then type them up immediately afterwards, she decided. Besides, she had a very good memory. And Mrs Roosevelt would not require an exact transcript, surely. Neither would she assume that Iris knew shorthand. She was a teacher, not a secretary, after all.

Iris managed to calm herself with thoughts of her good fortune and of Montgomery Chapel. Then, still lying on her back on the bed, she opened the light-blue envelope and found twenty-five dollars. She rolled over and looked in her bedside table. She still had four dollars remaining from the ten that Mrs Roosevelt had given her at the gas station. Iris closed her eyes, breathed deeply and listed, in her mind, exactly what her wardrobe required.

1 8

WASHINGTON DC
June 1933

Over the next two weeks Iris gradually got to know her way around the White House and to recognise the people who worked there. Monty generally popped in to the office a couple of times a day for a chat and a cup of coffee, and sometimes they took strolls together through the gardens. Typically, Iris used these walks to quiz Monty on the policies he was working on with the president. While he still flirted, Iris noticed that he flirted with everyone – women and men. And it wasn't so much flirting, Iris came to believe, as showing an interest in people. A genuine interest. Consequently, she ignored the thoughts of a romance with Monty that would occasionally commandeer her thoughts. She had taken to having lunch with Mrs Roosevelt and Tommy and sometimes Mr Howe. From about four she was occupied attending afternoon teas for different women's organisations and charities. These were hosted by Mrs Roosevelt at the White House. Mrs Roosevelt spoke at these events, usually delivering a short speech that she had written herself, by hand. Sometimes, Tommy told her, there were two afternoon teas running concurrently. 'That makes for one hell of a logistical nightmare,' she'd added. 'A revolving door of scones and finger sandwiches.'

The intern (a title Mrs Roosevelt had unexpectedly bestowed upon Iris) had yet to meet the president. This seemed strange to Iris. She had lived in the same house as the President of the United States for two weeks and she had not yet laid eyes on him. Although she had come to know most of the staffers, Iris was uncertain as to the exact pecking order. Daily organisation was casual and familiar. Schedules changed hourly but no one seemed to care. When she enquired cautiously as to when she might meet the president, if ever, Mr Howe assured her that it would be very soon. The president was in the habit of knowing everyone who worked for him, but the strenuous demands on his time since taking office had prevented him from being as sociable as usual.

Iris thought she'd heard him the night before. As she lay in bed reading, close to drifting off, she heard a thunderous laugh from the corridor outside her room accompanied by a click of wheels, not unlike the sound of a bicycle. Her heart started beating heavily in her chest and she was reminded of Rochester's crazy wife from *Jane Eyre*, wandering the corridors at night when she escaped her attic prison. Iris's first urge was to leap from the bed, open the door and catch a glimpse of the phantom president. She decided against it when she realised she was wearing only her new lavender negligee. Instead she turned off her lamp and pulled the covers up to her chin.

On the Saturday morning of her second week she awoke with a feeling of immense promise. Was it really only a month ago she had been sleeping by the road? Those days seems like another life now. She got out of bed and opened the curtains, and the sun flooded across the burgundy rug. Iris caught a glimpse of herself in the mirror that made her pause. The sunlight from the window cast a silvery glow around her body. Then, standing there, admiring her own reflection, she suddenly recognised herself. She was a symbol for the new administration, a representation of what every American trapped in the gloom could expect to become. One by one people would be lifted from the doldrums, just as she had been. It sounded corny, she knew, but in that brief moment her path became clear, luminescent even.

She and Tommy had Sunday free and she was expecting an invitation from Monty to show her around DC. Mrs Roosevelt had also asked her to attend a meeting of the National Consumers League, where the First Lady would be delivering an address on the group's white label campaign. 'After many years of work,' Mrs Roosevelt explained, 'it's finally becoming government policy. Now consumers will know exactly who the ethical retailers and manufacturers are and they will be able to spend their money accordingly.' Mrs Roosevelt said the event would be over by two o'clock. Iris planned to get her hair cut that afternoon.

Iris bathed then dressed in one of her recent purchases. The dress was olive-green and dotted with thumbnail-sized pink roses, and it had a scalloped neckline. She was pleased her face and bust had filled out slightly in the previous two weeks and guessed she had gained five or six pounds.

Following breakfast she met Mrs Roosevelt downstairs.

'We'll take my car,' Eleanor said, leading the way. 'I'm a very competent driver and I feel better if I'm at the wheel, although the Secret Service hate it. They'll follow behind.'

'I've brought my notepad. Would you like me to take any notes during the meeting?' It had become the practice for Iris to document press conferences and meetings and Mrs Roosevelt had praised Iris's note-taking efforts, calling them 'detailed' and 'precise'.

'No, it's more a celebration than a meeting,' Eleanor replied. 'The League and I have been working towards this since the mid-twenties. It's quite a coup for us. Our hope is that it will put an end to child labour and dangerous working conditions in factories. Put an end to the unfair treatment of all workers.'

They drove for some minutes in silence, the First Lady taking corners and changing gears confidently, her eyes never leaving the road.

'By the way, Iris,' Eleanor said, 'would you like to join us for dinner this evening? There'll be a few of us there – John's come down from Harvard and Frank Junior will be down from Groton, Hick is coming in from New York this afternoon, Louis, Monty, Anna and James . . . oh, and my cousin Alice,' she added as an afterthought.

Iris turned her face quickly in Eleanor's direction. Eleanor smiled. 'Yes, Alice Roosevelt – or Alice Roosevelt Longworth as she is now.'

Iris's mother had kept a newspaper cutting of Alice Roosevelt on her wedding day tacked to the wall in the kitchen. Draped in white silk with a Cavalier King Charles Spaniel on her lap, she was nicknamed 'Princess Alice' by the press. Her wedding in 1906 was the social event of the year and as a child Iris had often sat and admired the fading newsprint above the table. Her mother had told her that while it was acceptable to admire Alice's beauty, she should never strive to emulate her behaviour. She was a scandalous, outspoken young lady who, as President Teddy Roosevelt's daughter, should have known better. She was wild and reckless, her mother had said, with far too many suitors. Recalling the clipping, Iris could see a strong family resemblance between Alice and Eleanor. It was the eyes – wide and intelligent. They dominated both of their faces.

'She can be intimidating,' Eleanor warned. 'Why, I was scared stiff of her for years. But she's our cousin and I strive to remember that she lost her mother when she was only two days old. It's not easy to be brought up without parents.'

'But her father . . .'

'He was the president. He didn't have a great deal of time for Alice. He spoiled her and appreciated her beauty but . . .' Mrs Roosevelt paused for a moment. 'He was never very present in her life. Anyway, she'll probably say something hurtful or outrageous about someone at the table. Never mind, it's just her way.'

■

That evening as she dressed, a wave of apprehension crashed over Iris then settled in her stomach. Mrs Roosevelt's comments about her cousin, combined with the likely presence of the president at dinner, made her feel queasy. When a knock came at her bedroom door, she fleetingly hoped it would be a maid with a note informing her that dinner had been cancelled. It was Monty. He took her in briefly before he spoke.

'You look lovely,' he said. 'You've had your hair cut. It is extremely fetching. It's so sophisticated – the final brushstroke on a masterpiece.' Iris wanted to say thank you but it didn't seem an adequate response for such a compliment. Monty entered her room and examined Iris in her entirety. 'All of you is extremely fetching. You look the part.'

The stylist at Elizabeth Arden's Red Door salon had cut four inches from Iris's hair and given her a deep side part – 'Like Fay Wray'. It had cost twelve dollars (Iris couldn't believe her extravagance), but the result was worth it.

Monty took her hand and spun her around slowly.

'I feel a little underdressed for dinner at the White House,' Iris confided. Her dress was made of sheer black rayon printed with tiny white hearts and fell to just below her knee. 'But Tommy said that even formal dinners here were pretty casual.'

'You look perfect,' Monty said. 'Absolutely perfect. A million bucks.'

'Thank you. I'm a little nervous. I feel as though everyone there is going to be judging me, because I'm the new girl.'

'The only trial we'll be experiencing this evening will be of the gastronomic variety,' he assured her. 'Everyone is very friendly. Just be yourself – no airs or graces – and you'll be fine.'

'Will the president be there?'

'Of course. But he'll adore you. He's always sympathetic to a pretty face. Shall we go down?'

He held out his arm and Iris took it.

■

When Iris and Monty entered the Yellow Oval Room the president's back was to the door. He was sitting in front of a butler's table where glasses, bottles of wine and beer were standing.

'I've never seen so much liquor out on show before,' Iris said in amazement.

'Don't worry,' Monty grinned. 'It's all above board. Beer and low alcohol wine are completely legal. The Volstead Act is fast collapsing. The entire country will be wet by new year.'

When she spotted Iris in the doorway, Mrs Roosevelt moved to her side. 'Good evening, you two,' she said. 'Iris, you look very pretty.'

Iris smiled and thanked her.

'Let me introduce you to my husband,' she went on, taking Iris's arm and leading her across the room.

'Franklin, I would like to introduce Miss Iris McIntosh, my new intern. Iris, I'd like you to meet the president.'

Roosevelt turned his chair to face Iris. Even though he was sitting, the phrase 'larger than life' immediately came to Iris's mind. His head, his hands and the expanse of his chest were far larger than that of other men, it seemed to her. And his lower jaw protruded mightily. It was a noble jaw, she thought. He placed his ivory cigarette-holder in the ashtray that was connected to his wheelchair and shook her hand. His grip was firm. He eyed her shrewdly over his pince-nez.

'Good evening, Mr President. I'm very glad to meet you. It is an honour to be working here,' Iris said. She had rehearsed the lines in the mirror a number of times while dressing.

'The pleasure is all mine. My wife has sung your praises. It's good to have you on board,' he said. 'But you have to call me "boss" – everyone around here does. You're from Chicago, I hear?'

'Yes, but Baltimore originally.'

'Wine, beer?' the president offered.

'A beer, please, Mr President,' Iris replied. Roosevelt smiled.

Conversation continued while Roosevelt poured her drink. He handed the glass to Iris then took a long drag on his cigarette.

'We're having wild duck tonight, from Maryland,' Roosevelt said. 'Well-wishers are always sending me gifts; most of them are completely useless, but yesterday I received a parcel containing six plump teals. Do you like wild duck, McIntosh?'

'Yes, very much, sir.' Iris was surprised at how excited he was over the duck. It seemed like such a trivial cause for enthusiasm, especially given what he had managed to achieve since March. The press had already nicknamed the period his 'One Hundred Days'. Since his inauguration exactly one hundred and one days ago, FDR had sent fifteen proposals to the Hill. In return, Congress responded with fifteen pieces of legislation designed to turn the nation's fortunes around. Although Mrs Roosevelt hadn't said so, Iris assumed this dinner was a celebration.

'It's delicious,' the president was saying now. 'But the cook has to remember that all it needs is a brisk chase over the flames. Overcook duck and it tastes like shoe leather, but you don't want it bloody either.'

'I'm sure Mrs Nesbitt is up to the challenge,' Eleanor interrupted. 'Now, Iris, come out to the balcony and I'll introduce you to some people.'

Iris was led out onto a small balcony overlooking the South Lawn and over to a man and woman talking by the railing. The woman was short and stout and, despite her considerable heels, the man towered over her. Iris didn't think they were a couple. If they were, they were an odd one. As they approached, the young man's eyes fixed on Iris rather than Mrs Roosevelt.

'Iris, this is my very good friend Lorena Hickok. She's a journalist at Associated Press.'

'It's good to meet you, Iris. Call me Hick. I don't think I'd answer to Miss Hickok or Lorena,' Hick said and then gave a loud laugh that made Iris start. 'This is my colleague from AP, Sam Jacobson. I don't think you've met him either, Eleanor. He's made quite an impression on the president, it seems.'

'So I hear,' Eleanor replied. 'You're a pot-stirrer, Mr Jacobson. A man after my own heart.'

'I don't mean to be, ma'am.' His eyes went briefly to Eleanor then returned to Iris. They were the darkest brown, with an agreeable sparkle. He put out his large hand, which totally encompassed Iris's, then took the First Lady's hand.

'I've read your articles about the Jewish crisis in Germany and this government's silence on the matter,' Mrs Roosevelt commented seriously. 'My husband sold his soul to the devil last year when he made that deal with Hearst.'

Jacobson nodded.

'While this country becomes increasingly isolationist the world is heading towards war,' she declared.

'Meanwhile,' Jacobson added, 'Hitler has abolished the constitutional government, declared himself supreme ruler of Germany and Jewish men, women and children are being brutalised at random on the streets of Berlin.' His voice was not cultivated by any means – Iris would even describe it as nasal – but the authority with which he spoke lent him a certain polish.

'Every American should be forced to read Lion Feuchtwanger's essay,' the First Lady went on. 'But in the meantime all we can do is keep agitating for disarmament and for this country to join the League of Nations and ratify the World Court. As long as we remain aloof, the League of Nations has no real power.'

'Will you two lighten up?' Hick exclaimed. 'I need another drink after that.'

Eleanor and Hick moved off, the former to see to dinner and the latter to the bar. Iris looked up into Sam's eyes. He was wearing round, wire-rimmed spectacles. He was obviously intelligent and friendly, but he made Iris nervous and she wasn't sure why.

She searched her mind for something to say as she sipped her drink. While she was aware that Mrs Roosevelt's internationalist leanings were in conflict with the government's policy of isolationism, she was not confident or sufficiently educated on the subject of German militarism to wade into a discussion on the topic.

'What do you do around here?' the reporter asked. Was his hair black, Iris wondered, or was it just the dwindling light?

'I'm Tommy's assistant,' Iris replied. 'Secretarial work. And you're a political reporter?'

'Yes.'

'Based in DC?'

Jacobson nodded and took a sip of his beer. Iris was aware he was studying her face.

'Is DC your home town?'

He shook his head. 'New York. Queens.' He smiled. 'Where are you from?'

'Chicago. But Baltimore originally.'

'I lived in Baltimore for a while. I did my cadetship at the *Sun*.'

'Really?' Iris wished she had something more intelligent to say. She breathed in deeply and took another sip of her drink. Why was she so anxious to impress this reporter she had met only minutes before?

Jacobson looked up at the sky and then cleared his throat. 'You look very nice tonight.' His tone had lost its authority. 'Your hair is . . . lovely. It reminds me of —'

'Fay Wray?' Iris interrupted eagerly.

'I was going to say Anita Page,' he responded. 'But I can see Fay Wray too.'

The laughter that ensued was spurred by both amusement and relief.

'Have you seen it?' he asked.

'Seen what?'

'*King Kong*,' Sam replied.

She shook her head; she had only seen the posters.

'It's good,' he went on. 'It's still playing over at the Tivoli.' Iris nodded in encouragement. 'I mean, if you wanted to . . . perhaps . . . I know it's hard getting settled in a new town but when you are, then . . .'

'Hey, Iris,' Hick called, before Sam could finish. Iris sighed at the lost opportunity. 'Eleanor wants you inside.'

Sam's eyes followed Iris from the balcony.

'Don't set your sights on her, lover boy,' Hick advised teasingly. 'From what I hear, she's already taken.'

'By who?' Sam asked, surprised.

'Chapel,' Hick answered, raising her eyebrows.

'Chapel? You're kidding,' Sam said indignantly.

Hick laughed loudly. 'So you find it unlikely that a young woman would be attracted to the best-looking, most intelligent guy on the East Coast?'

'No,' he replied. 'But she seems so sweet, naïve even.'

'Well, that's sure to change now that she's working here and dating Montgomery Chapel,' Hick commented as she turned towards the waiter serving canapés.

Sam stayed quiet as Hick chewed and swallowed a small round of toast topped with cheese spread.

'Of course,' Hick said as she wiped her mouth, 'I might be wrong. I'll see you inside.'

Sam nodded distractedly and remained alone on the balcony until dinner was called.

19
WASHINGTON DC
The same evening

When Iris went indoors she found Monty, drink in hand, sitting on the arm of a chair talking to Anna Roosevelt.

'I can see Jillian looked after you,' Anna said. 'Your hair looks divine.'

Iris thanked Anna for making the appointment for her at the hair salon as the tall blonde rose from her chair.

'Please excuse me. Mama seems to be a little upset over something.' She made her way towards her mother. Louis Howe was already by Eleanor's side.

'She's very beautiful, isn't she?' Iris said.

'Yes, I suppose so,' Monty replied, considering Anna Roosevelt as she spoke at length to her mother. 'I guess she was born with the best attributes of both her parents, Eleanor's eyes and stature and Frank's smile and charm – but I don't like blondes.' He turned back to Iris and winked.

Iris smiled and tucked a lock of hair behind her ear. Monty had become not only her best friend in the past weeks but had also assumed the role of mentor, guiding her through the dizzying maze of White House policy, procedure and etiquette. Moreover, he was attentive and noticed small changes in her appearance such as a new dress or shoes. His observations were always heartening.

'What's going on?' Iris asked, noticing Mrs Roosevelt's agitation.

'Mrs Roosevelt and Mrs Nesbitt want to get started on dinner, but the boss wants to wait for Cousin Alice to arrive,' Monty explained. 'She's already thirty-five minutes late. It wouldn't be the first time she's been a no-show. Apparently, the kitchen can't start on the duck until the first course is nearly completed. Timing is everything with this duck, according to the president. Meanwhile, the soup is ready to be brought up, getting cold in the bowls, according to La Nesbitt.'

'Quite a stand-off, then,' Iris said in mock seriousness.

'Indeed.'

'For goodness' sake, Eleanor, just tell her to pour it back into the pot,' they heard the president say. 'Why must everything be done to the housekeeper's timetable?'

'Fine,' Eleanor said and moved to the telephone. 'All we are attempting to do is cook this duck of yours according to your instructions. I don't know how long we are supposed to wait for Alice.'

'We'll wait as long as we need to,' Roosevelt said firmly. 'Nobody is dying of starvation.'

'It will all be fine, Mama,' Anna interrupted. 'Everyone is happy and we can wait for Alice a little while longer, surely.'

Eleanor looked at her daughter, her face grim.

'What say we give it another forty-five minutes, an hour tops,' Howe suggested. 'If Alice hasn't arrived by then we'll go in and have dinner.'

The president agreed and went back to his beer and conversation. Eleanor also acquiesced, but it was obvious to Iris from her tight lips and creased brow that she was not happy.

Forty minutes later, when hunger got the better of him, the president agreed to begin dinner. This seemed to upset Eleanor more than the delay. She picked up the telephone and gave the kitchen the green light before ushering her guests into the dining room.

Gus, Roosevelt's bodyguard, pushed the president to his position at the head of the table and Sam watched Monty seat Iris before taking his own place next to her. As a bowl of French onion soup was placed in front of each guest, Monty whispered in Iris's ear, 'This is appalling. Look at the colour. It should be a rich, deep colour, like treacle. This looks like a murky pond. The onions should have been cooked for much longer.'

Before Iris could respond, he continued in ever more distress. 'And look at the cheese.' He peered into the depths of his bowl. 'My god, she's used parmesan!'

'Shhh, someone will hear you. I'm sure it's not such a calamity.'

'But it should be gruyere!'

'I'm sure it's very tasty,' Iris said reassuringly. But even to Iris, who had stooped to some terrifying culinary depths in her recent history, the liquid in the bowl appeared unenticing.

She took her first sip. It was flavourless and watery. She scanned the table. No one in the room was eating with any gusto despite the late hour at which dinner had begun. Mr Howe had not touched his soup at all. As her eyes lit on Sam Jacobson, she noticed he was looking in her direction. A tentative smile appeared on his lips. She looked away hastily.

'Would you like wine, miss?' Fields asked.

'Yes, please,' she answered.

Fields poured her a glass of white wine and she brought it to her lips. It was sour.

'Sauterne from Texas, I think, McIntosh,' the president said quietly, and winked.

Iris did not understand the joke so she smiled weakly, reluctant to offend either the president or his wife during her first meal with them.

'So, McIntosh, tell me about yourself,' Roosevelt said, pushing his bowl away. It was only half empty.

The room quieted as it always did when the president spoke. The blood rose in her cheeks. She felt Monty nudge her knee with his encouragingly under the table.

'As I said, I've come from Chicago. I was a teacher there.'

'Iris lost her job, Franklin,' Eleanor added rather sternly. 'Over a year ago. Budget cuts.'

'I'm sorry to hear that. What have you been doing in the interim?' he asked, unconcerned by his wife's interruption.

Iris was hesitant to divulge her history in front of an audience, especially this audience. She doubted whether, apart from Mrs Roosevelt, the guests seated at the table tonight would sympathise with her; they might even see her as reckless or stupid. In fact, she was ashamed of what she had allowed herself to become – targeting a well-heeled woman in a gas station for money; she shuddered at the thought of it.

'Well . . .' She paused for a moment. 'This and that,' she said vaguely.

'But you haven't been teaching?' Louis Howe called from the far end of the table.

Iris flushed. Despite his ailing appearance there was certainly nothing wrong with his hearing, she thought.

'No.' She looked up from the tablecloth. All eyes and ears were on her. 'I wasn't able to find work anywhere.'

Iris didn't want to talk about her tribulations. While aware that her fall was caused by circumstances beyond her control, she was nonetheless humiliated. Then there was Monty. What would he make of her story?

As the bowls were being cleared and Iris was still contemplating her dilemma, the door to the dining room opened and a woman entered. Iris recognised her as Alice Roosevelt Longworth. Her hair was now grey and she wore a great deal of make-up, but Iris could still recognise the young bride from the newspaper clipping.

Despite the balmy evening she still had a fur wrapped around her shoulders. Except on screen at the cinema, Iris could not recall ever seeing anybody flounce before. However, Alice definitely flounced to the head of the table and kissed the president on the cheek; then flounced to the opposite end of the table and did the same to Mrs Roosevelt. She then allowed Fields to remove her fur.

'Good evening one and all,' she said gaily. 'I'm so sorry to be late.'

Iris thought it odd she made no excuse, but she figured that there was no need for someone in her position. This had been her home once, when her father was at the helm. Eleanor rose from the table, a warm smile stamped onto her face.

'That's quite alright, dear. Please sit down. You've missed the first course, but the entrée will be along shortly.'

'I could really do with a drink before I eat anything. Would you mind, Franklin? Would you mind indulging me? I've had an extremely exhausting day.' Iris wondered what an exhausting day for Princess Alice would entail, but she was thankful for the interruption caused by the whirlwind arrival of DC royalty.

'The duck is on its way up. We really can't put it off,' Eleanor said.

'What a funny thing you are, Eleanor, darling.' Alice laughed carelessly and addressed those seated. 'There's an image in my mind now of a flock of ducks waddling along the hallways of the White House, hopping in the elevator . . . it's really very silly.'

Her cousin's dismissiveness failed to erase Eleanor's smile. 'I believe it's a brace, dear.'

'Excuse me?'

'The collective noun for a group of ducks on the ground is brace, dear, or badling. Although the latter isn't in common usage. Flock is used for a group of ducks in flight.'

Alice looked at her cousin, stunned.

Franklin pushed himself away from the table. 'Of course you may have a drink, dear,' he said, all concerns about the duck seemingly forgotten. 'Fields, would you mind asking Mrs Nesbitt to hold the duck?'

Fields nodded and Eleanor resumed her seat at the table. Alice sat down too, next to the president.

'I believe you know most people here, Alice.' Roosevelt scanned the table. 'Except Miss Iris McIntosh and Mr Sam Jacobson.'

Alice politely offered her greetings to the newcomers then launched into a breathless account of her exhausting day. She was to have tea with Lady Astor at three o'clock and her car got a flat tyre. It took her driver over an hour to change it. She wasn't certain as to the problem, but it was extremely inconvenient.

Iris's thoughts returned to the duck. She found herself becoming quite incensed at the wait and she wondered what was happening in the kitchen.

'Alice,' Eleanor broke in, interrupting her cousin's monologue, 'Iris was just about to recount her experiences over the past year. You know, she has experienced this depression first hand.'

Iris's heart dropped. As she carefully straightened her silverware and refolded the napkin on her lap, she was aware of the scrutiny of the entire gathering.

'Go on, Iris,' Mrs Roosevelt prompted.

With little other choice, Iris had to tell the truth. She outlined her experiences of the past fourteen months. How, despite her best efforts to find a job, she was evicted from her boarding house. She was able to lodge for a few weeks with various friends in Chicago but eventually, along with many others, she found herself at a camp, a 'Hooverville'. She would get her meals either at soup kitchens or at the camp, where residents would each donate something found or scrounged to the pot for that day. If one contributed, one could eat. She was forced out of the camp by a young man's unwanted attentions and she spent nearly a month travelling from Chicago to Virginia, where she met Mrs Roosevelt in Fairfax Country.

When she finished the room was silent and an unfamiliar sense of empowerment took hold of Iris. She looked around the table. Some people's faces showed concern and sympathy while others, such as Monty and the president, seemed to be meditating on the seriousness of the times. It was one thing to read about Hoovervilles and soup kitchens in the newspaper; it was entirely another to have a bum at your dinner table. The most grave expression was that on Sam Jacobson's angular face. Iris couldn't quite discern its meaning.

'So these Hoovervilles, what are they like? Describe them to me,' the president said eagerly.

'I can't speak for them all, but the camp where I stayed was very well organised, with a mayor and city hall and street names, a mess hall . . .'

'Did you consider it a dangerous place?' the president wanted to know.

'No, not at all. It had a police department of sorts. A group of reasonable men who handled law and order.'

'But the young man . . .' Roosevelt said delicately.

'He was the son of the mayor; I was teaching him to read. He was a child in an adult's body . . . He made advances . . . Anyway, he was asked to leave the camp, that was the rule. But I thought it was an unfair decision. He wouldn't have been able to survive without his parents, so I left instead.'

The president nodded slowly.

'So you see, Franklin, this is an intelligent, educated young woman who was forced into a shantytown through the absence of choice. Yet none of the New Deal policies confront the question of unemployed, homeless women.' Eleanor was speaking loudly, emotionally. Her crisp, reassuring voice now echoed across the dining room with an edge. Iris shifted in her seat.

The wild duck that was served a moment later, more than a moment too late, did nothing to lighten the atmosphere.

Iris was grateful to Mrs Roosevelt and respected her greatly, but her heart went out to the president at that instant. His hopes for the duck had been incinerated. The man had achieved something extraordinary since March, regardless of his failure to address the plight of females, but the bird was a disaster. It tasted *worse* than shoe leather, Iris thought. While homeless, she had heard of people making 'hobo soup', a broth made from boiled shoe leather. Iris could not afford to be without her boots so she never attempted the dish, yet she was certain she would have preferred it to tonight's offering. Edible duck was a small thing to ask in return for the president's accomplishments, for his courage, for the sixteen-hour days and sleepless nights.

Dinner was completed quickly and the plates were taken away. By the time coffee was served it was midnight. Iris looked at the president as he drained his coffee cup. She caught his eye and offered him her sweetest, most compassionate smile.

He reached across the table and placed his hand over her own. 'It's good to have you on board, McIntosh. And I'm sorry for everything you've been through. I'm looking forward to getting to know you better, but now I must bid you goodnight. I'm done in.'

With those words, with that gesture, her fear of being seen as a bum evaporated. If her disgrace could be forgiven by a president, then what did she have to worry about? She had an overwhelming desire to hug him. Instead she said, 'Goodnight, Mr President.'

Roosevelt squeezed her hand tight.

He wheeled himself from the dining room. Gradually his guests began to leave the table. Monty excused himself from her side to chat with Louis Howe.

'You're extremely brave, Iris,' Hick said as she sat down opposite her. 'I'm not so sure I could go through what you have and come out the other side.'

'It's not difficult when you don't have a choice.'

'What about your parents? Eleanor told me they were dead.'

'They died when I was thirteen. My mother died first and then my father. Everyone said he died of a broken heart. But I don't believe that's a medical condition.'

'What did your father do for a living?' Hick asked.

'He called himself a poet. My mother called him a drunk.'

'Ah, the same profession as my old man,' Hick said. 'He was a heartless bastard. I got away the first chance I could.'

'My father was loving, just exasperating for my mother, I think.' Iris paused and looked at Hick. 'He just had that one fatal flaw.'

'Who brought you up, then?' Hick asked.

Iris looked down at her hands clenched under the table. 'My grandparents,' she answered.

'You're lucky you had them,' Hick said. Then, banging both hands on the table, she said, 'I'm beat. Goodnight, Iris McIntosh. It was lovely meeting you.'

When Hick left the table, Iris stifled a yawn and stood, smoothing down her skirt. When she looked up, Sam Jacobson was standing next to her.

'It was a pleasure to meet you,' he said. 'That was some story . . .'

Although she heard only kindness in his tone, Iris bristled at his use of the word 'story'. It implied a fantasy and nothing about her year on the streets had been anything like a fantasy. Moreover, she was tired. The telling of her tale and the questions that followed had been exhausting. 'It was all true, Mr Jacobson.'

'Of course. Forgive my poor choice of words. I just think that you've opened some eyes tonight. Politicians and bleeding hearts say they're fighting the depression. And they are, I guess. But they've never lived it or even seen it first hand.'

'I take your point, Mr Jacobson. But the president and Mrs Roosevelt are doing everything they can to turn around the fortunes of this country.'

'I'm afraid I'm not expressing myself very clearly, and will you please call me Sam?' Jacobson said. 'I'm not talking specifically about President Roosevelt and his wife. I mean politicians in general.'

'I should think an inability to express yourself clearly would be quite a handicap for a journalist. Goodnight, Mr Jacobson.' Iris turned away. She was immediately ashamed of her harsh words but couldn't muster the energy to apologise. She joined Monty and Howe at the far end of the table.

It was after one when Monty escorted Iris back to her room. When they reached her door Iris turned to face him. 'I'm embarrassed about tonight. I shouldn't have said anything. I'm worried that everyone will look at me differently.'

Monty took her hands. 'Don't be silly, kiddo. You were wonderful, refreshing. It would be the first time in years that anyone has been that candid in the White House. More important, it was the first time I've ever seen Alice Roosevelt silenced.'

He kissed the palms of both her hands. Something stirred in Iris and her spirits immediately rose at the prospect of Monty Chapel becoming more than her friend and teacher.

'Where's your family?' he asked.

'I don't have any,' she replied quietly. 'I'm an orphan, I suppose.'

He looked hard at her for a moment. Then she noticed a half-smile form on his lips. 'You're lucky,' he said. 'My parents are nuts. They're going happily insane up on Long Island. Fortunately, I'm an only child.'

Iris laughed.

'That young reporter from AP, Sam Jacobson, certainly took a liking to you.'

'I don't know,' Iris said, shaking her head in disgust at her own behaviour. 'We seemed to clash.'

Monty touched her cheek softly with the back of his hand and gently pushed the hair from her brow. Iris felt the tingle of goosebumps.

'Would you allow me to show you around DC tomorrow?' he asked. 'The usual sights, followed by dinner at Montmartre. You'll experience what French onion soup *should* taste like.'

'That would be lovely. I'll look forward to it.'

Monty moved in closer to Iris, pressing her back against the door. He bent and gave her a soft but lingering kiss on the cheek.

'You're not alone, kiddo,' he whispered.

She tilted her face upwards, but he backed away.

'Until tomorrow. I'll pick you up at eleven.'

He made his way down the corridor, whistling quietly as he went.

Before Iris turned off her light that evening she made a note on the pad next to her bed reminding herself to learn more about German militarism.

■

Hick entered Eleanor's sitting room. She found her friend sitting at her desk writing. Hick was wearing cotton pyjamas. Her feet were bare and she had washed her face clean of make-up. It was so clean, Eleanor thought, it glistened.

Eleanor was still in the same clothes she had worn at dinner.

'When are you going to bed,' Hick asked. 'It's two o'clock.'

'I just have one letter to finish,' Eleanor said without looking up from her correspondence. 'But you should go in.'

Instead Hick sat down on the sofa awaiting their customary debriefing. When Eleanor put down her pen and slipped the letter into an envelope, Hick said, 'So you've picked up another stray, I see.'

'Do you mean Iris?'

Hick nodded.

Eleanor described the circumstances of their meeting, an element of her story Iris had omitted at dinner.

'Boy, so she really is a stray. Quite a tale. Newspapers love a good rags-to-riches piece,' Hick said.

'I wouldn't call twenty-five dollars a week "riches".'

'Still, from tramp to presidential intern . . .'

'There's no story.'

'She told me her father was an alcoholic. Her mother died young then shortly afterwards her father died of a broken heart. Poetic. Tragic, really. Is that why you took her on? You saw her as a kindred spirit?'

'I didn't know that about Iris until now,' Eleanor responded evenly. 'All I saw in her was an intelligent, refined, modest young woman whose potential was going to waste. Can you stop being a newshawk for one night?'

'But it would make a terrific human-interest story,' Hick persisted.

'Iris is reticent to talk about her history,' Eleanor said. 'Anyway, after the courage she showed this evening I'm thinking of giving her more responsibility. That *Women's Home Companion* article each week is proving a chore. Tommy said I'm getting more than seventy-five thousand letters a week. She hasn't got time to read them all and I certainly haven't. I think Iris would be well attuned to other people's problems, making her an excellent person to sift the wheat from the chaff, so to speak. Her writing is solid too,' she added and placed her pen to her lips. She nibbled the tip for an instant. 'Perhaps she could ghostwrite some of the articles. Would that be ethical, from a journalistic point of view?' Before Hick could respond, Eleanor went on, 'I'll speak to her about it in the morning. Now, that's one person's future I've managed to organise this evening. Let's talk about your own.'

Hick arched her eyebrows. 'I thought that was settled.'

'But AP have cut your pay. You should try something else.'

'AP didn't have a choice. I've no malice towards them. My loyalty to you is a boundary, Eleanor. I can see that as plain as day.'

'Why don't I set up a meeting with my agent, just to see what's out there in terms of book and magazine opportunities?'

'It's late. We should get to bed,' Hick said flatly as she stood. 'Sorry about the duck fiasco. I think you need to find a more pliable housekeeper or a less stubborn husband.'

'It's still early days. Mrs Nesbitt will hit her stride in the kitchen and Franklin will just have to learn to lower his expectations.'

20
WASHINGTON DC
June 1933

'How are your feet?' Monty asked as they left the restaurant.

'Holding up,' Iris replied with a grin, thinking of the miles she had walked in her recent past.

Monty took her hand. 'Shall we go back to my hotel for a nightcap?'

Iris knew Monty stayed at the Mayflower when he was in town. She didn't answer immediately. Instead she stood on the sidewalk and breathed in the cool night air. The skirt of her pink print dress gathered around her legs in the breeze.

'I could take you back to the big house,' he went on as he rolled down his sleeves and put on his jacket. It was the first time Iris had seen him without a tie. 'But there are always so many people there, coming and going.' He straightened his hat.

He was right. Mr Howe and Gus Gennerich, the president's body-guard, were permanent residents and Hick was staying for a week as well. There were always Secret Service men walking the corridors. Mrs Roosevelt was in the habit of inviting people to dinner and to stay overnight or for as long as they wished. In addition, there were James and Anna and their families. It was only nine o'clock, and Iris knew that if they went back now they wouldn't find any privacy. She would begin looking for her own apartment in the morning, she resolved. She knew Tommy lived close by in a small apartment, as did the Nesbitts. It shouldn't be too hard to find something convenient and affordable.

'Yes, let's go to your hotel.' Iris looked at him and raised an eyebrow.

Monty hailed a taxi.

They travelled the short distance mostly in silence. Iris rested her head against the window and closed her eyes. She wasn't tired – just the opposite. She was invigorated. In the quiet of the taxi, Iris meditated on her day with Monty. They had wandered from memorial to memorial, to the Capitol and then to the Library of Congress. Time had run short, so they left the Smithsonian for another day.

Monty was an unusual man, she decided; an intriguing one. The night before he had made an unbridled fuss over dinner, yet today she watched him consume a hot dog bought from a vendor outside the Lincoln Memorial with unrestrained pleasure. At times he would joke and talk flippantly about serious issues, yet at the historic sites they had visited he was reflective, even solemn. Despite seeing him every day for a fortnight and spending many hours with him today, Iris knew very little about the man. Yet she knew she was attracted to him. Who wouldn't be? Iris had yet to find a flaw.

During the day, Iris had noticed other women looking at her and Monty together. She had wondered what they were thinking. Were they jealous or could they see through her polished veneer? Even though diligent and keen, there had been times over the past two weeks in the White House when Iris had felt out of her league – a bum in smart clothing.

She opened her eyes and faced him in the taxi. 'Why did it take you so long to ask me out?'

'It's only been two weeks!' he replied. 'I was being a gentleman. Plus, I'm older. I didn't want you turning me down. Anyway, what's the hurry?'

'How old are you?' she asked.

'Forty-two. Forty-three in December,' he answered plainly.

She smiled and closed her eyes once more.

'To be honest,' he continued, 'it was Jacobson. I saw him casting furtive glances in your direction at dinner last night. I knew I'd better make my move.'

Iris grinned. 'Competition.' At the mention of Sam her confidence grew slightly.

'Something like that,' Monty said softly.

'Mrs Roosevelt said you were a war hero,' Iris said with her eyes closed. Her head was swimming.

'War veteran would be a more accurate description.'

Mrs Roosevelt had mentioned his war service and Tommy always referred to him as a bachelor, so she assumed he had never been married. But then again, perhaps he had. From his tastes, manner and education she also assumed he was from a wealthy family. Long Island was where his parents lived, but he called New York his home town. But if Iris was honest with herself, she really didn't care about his history. He was caring and generous and extremely amusing. Why should she worry about his background? At that moment an image of Sam Jacobson sprang into her mind. She closed her eyes tighter for a second. When she opened them she asked, 'Who's Lion Feuchtwanger?'

'A German playwright and intellectual,' Monty answered.

'Mrs Roosevelt said something last night at dinner about every American reading his essay. What did she mean?'

'An article of his was published recently called, "Hitler's War on Culture". Internationalists like Mrs R. consider it a must-read. I'll get you a copy.'

'She also said the president had sold his soul to William Randolph Hearst.'

He looked at her and extended his arm, a request for her to come closer. He wrapped his arm around her as she leaned against his chest. To Iris it felt like the most wonderful place in the world.

'To secure the Presidential nomination last year, FDR assured Hearst that he would never support the League of Nations or the World Court,' he explained quietly. 'It rankled the missus no end,' he added in a fair imitation of the president.

'Where do you stand, Monty? Internationalist or isolationist?' she asked.

'I like to consider myself a man of the world, kiddo.'

'But really. . .' she began seriously.

'Shhhh,' he whispered, placing a finger to her lips. 'We'll talk about policy tomorrow. We have all the time in the world.'

■

Monty opened the door to his room. It was large. Iris thought one might even call it a suite. There was a sitting room with a writing desk and a sofa upholstered in gold brocade. A radio sat on a sideboard with various bottles of liquor and glasses. Aware that Monty occupied the same room whenever he was in the capital, Iris was expecting that she might find photographs or a few of the trappings of home, but the only personal item she discovered in the room was his attaché case leaning against the wall. She sat on the sofa and Monty poured her a glass of cognac.

'Have you had cognac before?'

'Only for medicinal purposes.'

He smiled. 'This is L'Esprit de Courvoisier. Smell it before tasting.'

Iris copied Monty and stuck her nose well into the large glass. 'This is going to sound silly,' she said, 'but it smells like fruitcake.'

'Yes, it does smell like fruitcake,' he agreed. 'Now take a sip.'

Going by the appearance and smell of the amber liquid she expected something cloying and sweet.

'What can you taste?'

'Coffee,' she said in surprise. 'It also reminds me of the cigars my father used to smoke. It doesn't taste sweet at all.'

'That's right. You have an excellent nose and palate.'

Iris had never before been paid such a compliment and she was pleased that neither her nose nor her palate had disappointed.

'How are you liking it at the White House, anyway?' he asked. 'We're always talking about the New Deal but never about what you do.'

'As a matter of fact,' Iris replied hesitantly, 'I've been given a promotion.'

'Already! Why didn't you tell me?'

'I was a little embarrassed, I suppose. Mrs Roosevelt only told me this morning.'

'Congratulations!' Monty cried, raising his glass. 'Don't be embarrassed. That's wonderful news! There's no room for the shy and retiring in DC, kiddo. If you're not going to blow your own trumpet then no one's going to do it for you.' He lowered his glass and said more earnestly, 'I'm so proud of you. I knew you wouldn't be Tommy's assistant for very long. What is it you'll be doing?'

She told him about the *Women's Home Companion* and they talked about it for a few minutes then, when there was a pause in the conversation, Monty said without hesitation or sheepishness, 'I'd like it if you spent the night with me.'

Iris had known that this would probably be the outcome of their evening together but the directness with which his proposition was delivered was startling. The heat rose in her cheeks and her heart began to hammer in her chest.

She placed her glass on the end table. 'I think I'd like that as well.'

'Excellent,' he responded softly.

'Just give me a minute.' Iris stood and made her way into the bathroom that adjoined the bedroom. It was the largest bathroom she had ever seen. As well as all the usual bathroom amenities there was a red velvet armchair in the corner. She sat on it for a moment and took a deep breath, wishing she was more experienced. After going to the toilet she walked to the basin and washed her hands. A tube of toothpaste lay beside the basin. She squirted a little onto her index finger and rubbed it along her teeth, then rinsed her mouth. It was futile to reapply her lipstick at this point, she decided. When she was satisfied she had done everything she could in preparation, she walked into the bedroom.

Monty stood naked by the bed, waiting. A lump rose in her throat. Iris had only had two previous sexual encounters with men and both had begun with them scurrying between the sheets in their underwear. She examined his body for a moment, becoming excited, aroused. His body was lean and muscular. His chest was hairless, but a light sprinkling of hair covered his tawny arms and legs. A pink scar ran from his right armpit under his chest to his stomach like an ominous fault line. He already had the beginnings of an erection, she guessed, although she had never seen one before. He approached and kissed her lightly on the lips.

'Allow me,' he said.

Over the next five minutes, Monty proceeded to lovingly and thoughtfully undress her. Unbuttoning her dress leisurely, he slipped it from her shoulders and draped it carefully over his arm.

'Raise your arms,' he requested.

She did so and he pulled her slip gently over her head and then lay the dress and the slip on a chair next to the bed.

'Let me admire you for a moment,' he said. 'You are very beautiful.'

Her eyes widened and her lips parted. He had used the word *beautiful*. Monty's voice was assured but soothing and she allowed herself to relax. Iris's mother had described her daughter's face as interesting. As Iris matured her face had gone from interesting to pretty. As for her body, Iris preferred to describe her lithe frame and long legs as athletic, although others had called her boyish. When the other thirteen-year-old girls' hips had broadened and breasts had swollen, Iris's had stubbornly refused to develop with the same zeal. Nobody – except her father, whose perception was often skewed – had ever in their descriptions of her appearance strayed into the territory of *beautiful*.

Monty sat on the edge of the bed and stared at her. Standing before him in only her underwear was a strange but liberating experience. She would have thought she'd be uncomfortable or embarrassed, but she enjoyed being the object of his desire.

With the same level of attention with which he'd removed her clothing, Monty made love to Iris that night. She realised she was no expert in sexual matters, but Monty forced her to redefine, in her own mind, the very nature of sexual intercourse. He caressed and delighted, explored and probed. When his tongue entered her she gasped in shock and he released a muffled laugh. Then came the excruciating pleasure.

'Oh my,' she said, panting.

Then he lay next to her and began to suckle her breasts. He seemed to gain an immense amount of satisfaction from this. A man had never done this to her before and as she lay there next to him it seemed completely natural. Her breath quickened as she began to sense the same inner stirrings she had earlier. She closed her eyes and tracked her hand down his scar until she reached his penis. Without thinking, she began to stroke it softly.

'Harder,' he instructed.

She complied.

After a few moments he said, 'Wait.' Rolling over to the bedside table he removed something from the drawer. Iris guessed he was putting on a sheath. When he returned to her, he pushed her legs open gently with his body and entered her.

When she eventually climaxed for the second time that evening, she allowed herself a moan. Monty followed suit then rolled onto the bed beside her. He lay his arm out invitingly. Iris immediately slid across the sheets into the shelter of the crook of his arm.

■

Iris awoke at seven and immediately wondered what the night before had meant. Would she be his girl? Would he propose marriage? Would they continue like this? She couldn't see herself marrying Monty. There was the age difference but also she just couldn't picture him as a husband. Still naked, she tiptoed to the bathroom. When she returned to bed, Monty was awake.

'Good morning, kiddo. You're very beautiful. Did you know that?' He propped himself up on one elbow.

Without answering, she slipped back under the covers and settled against his body. They began to kiss.

'I really should be going. I need to be at work at eight thirty,' Iris said.

'You can shower and breakfast here and then I'll get a taxi to take you back. That leaves us a good twenty minutes, as long as you don't take too long showering.'

Iris thought it a reasonable timetable and snuggled in tight against his warm body. Monty slid his hands between her thighs and whispered, 'Shall we try something a little different?'

Iris didn't know how different it could be, but she agreed with a tentative nod. Monty gripped the small of her back and flipped them both over expertly. Suddenly she found herself straddling him. He manoeuvred himself into her and then placed both hands on her hips in order to control their movement. When he was satisfied with the pace and approach, he laid back and gripped the railings of the bed, moaning softly. Their eyes were locked for the entire encounter.

Initially, Iris felt exposed. She had enjoyed their lovemaking last night, with Monty's body wedged tightly against her own in the dark, she unable to see his expression nor he hers. It was secure and safe and he was in control. But in this position, Iris feared she'd been handed too much responsibility. However, when the familiar quiver began deep inside her she pushed all concerns from her mind. No longer aware of herself or Monty, she allowed her instinct to direct her movement. Her sole passage of consciousness was honed in on that spot which seemed, at that moment, to be the very essence of her.

When it was over Iris found herself perspiring. Leaning her head against Monty's smooth chest, she exhaled loudly. A final release.

She remained against his chest, unsure of what to say, embarrassed by her loss of control.

As if sensing her feelings, Monty said gently, 'That's what love-making should be like. An outpouring. An uninhibited outpouring of passion. Don't feel self-conscious. It was perfect.'

'Thank you, Monty.' She kissed him on the lips and reluctantly threw back the covers.

21
HYDE PARK, NEW YORK
May 1962

The president was forever receiving gifts of one sort or another, and most of the gifts were food. This helped out with my household budget quite a bit. Mangoes and frogs' legs from Florida, persimmons from California, prize beef, ducks, quails, mountain sheep, caribou, venison, brook trout, oysters, clams, wild turkey, terrapin, salmon and ham. My goodness, the hams he was sent. Dad had to make a special ham cellar just to store them all.

Then there was the fruit, of course. Crates and crates of prize-winning fruit were sent to us from all over the country. Sometimes the fruit was accompanied by a queen. You know, a young lady who had been crowned the Cherry Queen or Peach Queen that year. I don't think any one of them ever met the president, but I was always on hand to welcome them and accept the gift. Usually, Mr Early would have a photographer there.

Mrs Roosevelt always bragged that the president had simple tastes and would be happy if he was served bacon and eggs every night. I don't think that was the case. I know he loved game birds and was especially excited when I notified him that a special delivery of ducks or quail or partridges had arrived. Sometimes he'd come down into the kitchen himself and inspect the birds. We used to hang the birds in the kitchen but soon there were so many that Dad had to turn an old airing cupboard into a storeroom just for the birds. The president was very specific on how they should be hung. He insisted they hang from their feet for up to ten days. Dad and I had been hanging birds for years and always hung them by their head for about five days. The president had his own way of doing things, but what he didn't know didn't hurt him.

That first year in the White House was extremely testing. You may laugh, but I had to consider diplomacy in the kitchen just as much as the president did in the Oval Office. One of our first state guests was

Emperor Haile Selassie of Ethiopia and Ras Desta Demtu, the Ethiopian ambassador. The pair were Coptic Christians and ate no meat, butter, cheese or anything made from animals. That threw up quite a challenge, I can tell you, considering I had to follow a budget and all. Well, I ended up serving them a menu of melon, clam cocktail with saltines, stuffed olives, blue fish with a cucumber and cress salad, pineapple ice and stuffed dates. I got a lot of criticism for my menus. If I stuck to economy cooking I was not meeting White House standards. If I splurged a little then I was blowing the budget. It was a tricky balancing act, made no easier by fussy guests.

I recall when the Japanese contingent came to lunch I had to hire a Chinese cook for the day, an older gentleman named Jing Oh. I wasn't sure what an Oriental menu should consist of and neither were Ida and Elizabeth, the cooks. So I thought bringing an Oriental in was a good idea. Anyway, when old Jing found out he was cooking for the Japanese, he stormed out of the kitchen in a fury, never to be seen again. I was left with the mess, of course, and threw together a pot of crabmeat soup and made up a batch of cornbread. Mrs Roosevelt explained to me later how the Japanese invasion of Manchuria had made the Chinese touchy, which may have explained Mr Oh's behaviour. I didn't pay him, of course.

Mrs Roosevelt was always right behind me, supporting my decisions one hundred per cent. And I did the same in return. It was in that first year, early on, that she fired all the white housekeeping staff, except me, and hired an all-Negro staff. She believed that staff in any one colour would work more harmoniously than a mixed staff. I had to agree. She got plenty of flack for that decision. But, she argued, unemployed white folk had an easer time finding another job than unemployed Negroes.

That was about the time of Ramsay MacDonald's visit to Washington. He was the British prime minister at the time. I think he was hoping to strike some sort of a deal with the president. The two of them didn't see eye to eye but I remember Mr MacDonald got on extremely well with Mrs Roosevelt. They shared the same views about world peace and disarmament. He was a lovely gentleman. Both he and Mrs Roosevelt were working hard to prevent another war. They could both see the writing on the wall as clear as day.

22
WASHINGTON DC
July 1933

'That's a dour little dress you're wearing, kiddo,' Monty said as he walked into Iris's office.

'Don't you like it?' Iris stood from her desk and looked down at the navy dress, flattening the starched white of the garment's dickey front. She supposed it was rather businesslike. 'I thought it was an ideal travelling outfit.'

'It's a little prim but perfect, I suppose, for two women travelling alone. You don't want to invite attention.'

'Well, I hope it's not that proper,' Iris said, feigning distress as she sat down.

Monty closed the office door and then kneeled down in front of her and placed his hands on her thighs.

'I've just come to tell you that I won't be going to Campobello with the rest of the crowd. Mrs R. has asked me to stay in Washington and thrash out this farming fiasco with Wallace and Hopkins.'

Iris could not help her disappointment showing on her face.

'What's the problem? Can't it wait?'

'Apparently not,' Monty replied as he slipped his hands inside Iris's dress and cupped the tops of her legs, just below her buttocks. Iris's eyes flashed quickly to the door. Monty had secured the latch. 'Wallace is destroying farm surpluses to create scarcity. Mrs R. is not happy.'

He began to massage Iris's thighs and she parted her knees slightly.

'What's to be done?' she asked.

'I'm supposed to come up with a solution. I'm going to propose to Hopkins that FERA buys the surplus and distributes it to relief agencies. It means a hell of a lot of negotiation between Wallace and Hopkins. Both of them are pig-headed. And I haven't even run it by the boss yet.'

Iris thought it a reasonable solution. Harry Hopkins was a sensible man whom Monty had worked closely with on many New Deal policies. They respected each other and, more importantly, as fast-moving head of the Federal Emergency Relief Administration, Hopkins would delegate surpluses quickly and to the most needy.

Wallace, on the other hand, was a more slippery fish, inexperienced as a politician and unpredictable as a man. Monty had concerns when he was brought on by FDR as Secretary of Agriculture, he had told Iris. He thought Wallace a strange choice and didn't understand the president's reasoning. Wallace was a disciple of a Russian mystic named Nicholas Roerich. While this didn't bother Monty, he wondered why it did not bother the president, who was, by and large, conventional in his views about faith.

Iris understood why Monty had to remain in Washington and, despite her disappointment, she agreed with him. At a time when people were starving, the burning of crops and slaughtering of livestock was an unpopular and short-sighted play.

Monty's thumbs moved towards her inner thighs. Her breath quickened.

'The president is unable to be contacted,' she said.

'I know. I thought I'd arrange it all then present it to him as a fait accompli.' He smiled. 'Anyway, this two weeks sailing up to Campobello is a holiday with his boys. I really don't want to bother him. He had no inkling when he departed that this Wallace thing would blow up like it has.'

When Iris was invited to the island by Mrs Roosevelt she'd had only a vague knowledge of Campobello and was unaware that the Roosevelts owned a summer home on the Canadian outpost. Monty told her that neither the president nor Mrs Roosevelt had gone up there for years, as far as he knew.

He paused for a moment. 'Where's Tommy?'

'Lunch,' Iris said. 'She'll be back soon.'

'Do you think we could nip to your old room for a few minutes?'

'The Brazilian ambassador is occupying it at the moment,' she informed him.

'I'm sure he wouldn't mind.'

'I have to be here when Tommy isn't . . . in case anyone calls.' Iris closed her eyes and placed her hands on Monty's shoulders. As she did so the telephone rang. Irritated, she opened her eyes and looked towards the annoyance.

'I have to get this. It's Mrs Roosevelt's line.' Monty released her reluctantly and she picked up the receiver. 'Yes, Mrs Roosevelt, he is.' She handed the telephone to Monty.

'I'm heading back there shortly,' Monty said into the receiver. 'Yes, they'll be ready before you leave this afternoon . . . Okay, I'll see you then.' He hung up and said to Iris, 'I have to get back, I'm afraid. When are you leaving?'

'At about four, I think. Mrs Roosevelt wants to reach Val-Kill by dinner. We're spending the night there. Then Mrs Roosevelt's friends Nancy Cook and Marion Dickerman will be travelling the rest of the way with us. Tommy's driving straight through tomorrow.'

'Nan and Marion will definitely approve of that dress. Be careful,' Monty warned playfully.

Iris looked at him, uncertain of his meaning.

'They're lesbians.'

'Who?' she asked, startled.

'Nan and Marion.' He laughed at Iris's shock. 'Don't worry, you'll be perfectly safe. They've been devoted to each other for many years.'

Iris was still contemplating this when Monty continued, 'You know about Hick, don't you? Mrs Roosevelt and Hick?'

'Mrs Roosevelt?' Iris gaped at him. 'Does the president know?'

Monty raised his eyebrows. 'Of course – that's where Missy LeHand fits in.'

'No!' she said loudly.

'Yes,' he responded. 'We all need love.'

'Have these sort of . . . arrangements been going on for very long?'

'The story goes that before the war the president began an affair with a young lady named Lucy Mercer. It went on for a few years before he was found out. I'm not sure of the details but divorce was spoken of. His mother threatened to cut him off. He had to sacrifice the love of his life for his political career and Eleanor never forgave him for the betrayal. From what I understand, after the affair with Lucy ended the Roosevelts became more partners, less husband and wife. In the subsequent years their friendship has been restored, but I doubt whether they have shared a bed since. Eleanor has softened over the years, but I don't think she has ever been able to forgive him. She allows him Missy's companionship as he allows her the friendship of Hick.'

Iris opened her mouth then closed it again, lost for words.

'Haven't you ever looked at a woman,' Monty asked seriously, 'and admired her beauty or her character and wondered what it might be like to kiss her or to touch her or to sleep with her?'

Iris thought on the question as Monty lit a cigarette. The idea of two women loving each other was not distasteful to her. There had been rumours about teaching colleagues and women at the camp. Others had always talked about these women in a scornful way, as if the only reason they were living with another woman was because they were unattractive and weren't able to land a man, but Iris was sure there was more to it than that. Thanks to Monty, she now had a better understanding of how women might go about pleasuring each other, but it was the day to day of their lives that intrigued her. Would they hold hands across the dinner table? Would they behave as a man and a woman in love might? Who would carve the turkey at Thanksgiving?

'No,' she answered finally. 'I never have. What about you? I'm sure the same feelings could apply to men.'

Monty smiled his most charming smile. His eyes crinkled and Iris stared into their depths, searching for an answer to her question. Brushing his hand over her head he said, 'Let's not talk about the Roosevelts and their eccentricities when this is the last time I'll see you for two weeks.'

'I'd just like to understand,' Iris persisted, standing. 'I don't think I'm a prig but maybe I am . . .'

'Don't worry,' he said soothingly. 'You're sweet – innocent and uncorrupted; it's what I love about you the most.' He held her shoulders and kissed her forehead lightly.

Iris's breath caught in her throat. Did that mean he loved all of her or merely a few of the traits that she possessed? she wondered. It was time to be assertive. Monty was more than a lover, he was her best friend. When he was in town they saw each other every day at work and spent each night together, either at the Mayflower or at her apartment – the snug, as he called it, on 6th Street. When he wasn't in town she missed him. He tutored her in policy matters and in the ways of DC society. Moreover their lovemaking, daring and exhilarating, was always on her mind.

'I love you, Monty,' she declared.

He didn't respond immediately and he didn't smile. He stubbed out his cigarette and met her solemn gaze. 'I love you too.'

Iris kissed him passionately on the mouth. 'I'll miss you,' she whispered when they parted.

'And I you, kiddo.' He hugged her warmly and kissed her quickly, once more, on the lips.

'Listen, I should go,' he said, and then as an afterthought added, 'I hear Sam Jacobson is going up on the press boat. He's quickly become one of the boss's favourites.'

'He's a nice guy,' she responded. 'Mrs Roosevelt has a high opinion of him as well.'

He nodded in agreement but Iris could tell he was troubled by the presence of Sam on the island. Iris kissed him once more as evidence of her lack of interest in the reporter. Monty's hand found Iris's breast through the stiffness of her bodice. He rubbed it gently until her nipple became evident and then he pinched it lightly.

'Be good. I'll see you at the end of the month,' he murmured as he pinched with more force.

Iris looked into her lover's eyes and pressed her body tightly against his. His thigh found her crotch and the couple stood like this, rocking deliberately, in front of Iris's desk for a few minutes, until Iris surrendered to a prolonged and breathy lament.

2 3
HYDE PARK, NEW YORK
July 1933

Iris enjoyed her evening with Nancy Cook and Marion Dickerman. Both women were unusual, unlike any other women she'd ever met. Nan was the more outgoing of the pair. Short and robust with close-cropped grey hair, her brown eyes were alert, and her warmth made Iris feel immediately comfortable. Marion was tall and slender and, although much more subdued and obviously younger than Nan, appeared to direct the events of the evening. It was Marion who prepared and served a late supper of spaghetti and meatballs. Despite Marion's apologies regarding the simplicity of the dish, Iris considered the meal exotic; she had never eaten spaghetti before.

Both of them smoked and drank bourbon (habits in which, Iris's mother had insisted, refined women did not indulge). Both drank red wine at dinner. Iris, who thought it more prudent to follow Mrs Roosevelt's example, sipped iced tea. After dinner the three older women showed Iris the factory where the Val-Kill furniture-manufacturing business was based. It was a venture the women had founded together in 1927.

'How many people do you employ here?' Iris asked.

'Anywhere between three and eight, sometimes more,' Nan replied. 'We originally started the factory as a means for local farmers to supplement their income. That was before the depression.'

'It's so lovely,' Iris said, running her hand along the surface of a drop-leaf table. 'You do fine work here.'

'Nan is the artisan,' Marion said. 'She honed her craft making wooden limbs for returned servicemen.'

'Marion is headmistress at Todhunter,' Mrs Roosevelt added. 'Another business we started together.'

Nan made Iris a gift of a large oak chest of drawers that she had recently completed, and arranged to have it trucked to DC. Iris loved the piece, though she had no idea how she would squeeze it into her 6th Street snug.

On their way back to the cottage Iris's mind drifted to Monty and she wondered what he would think of her discussing business with a trio of women who loved women.

'What are you grinning about?' Mrs Roosevelt wanted to know. 'You look like the cat who got the cream.'

'Nothing special,' Iris answered. 'You must be very proud of everything you've achieved.'

'I've been very fortunate,' the First Lady said serenely.

Over coffee they discussed politics. Iris learned that both Nan and Marion had been suffragettes and heavily involved in the Women's Division of the Democratic Party in New York during the 1920s. Although Iris couldn't follow much of the discussion – the conversation moved too quickly and the shared knowledge was too deep – she could tell that Mrs Roosevelt's friends were both intelligent and funny. She had not seen Mrs Roosevelt laugh with such abandon before. She seemed entirely relaxed and at home.

As they talked, Iris allowed her eyes to wander around the room and to the photographs on the wall. One struck her as extremely amusing. Mrs Roosevelt, Nan and Marion were standing on the porch of Stone Cottage wearing identical outfits – tweed plus-fours and jackets, long socks, tan brogues and neckties. Iris stood and walked over to study it more closely.

'That photograph was taken when the cottage was completed in '25,' Marion said.

'Eleanor had those outfits made,' Nan explained. 'We thought they were hysterical, but fitting. So did Franklin, as I recall. He took the photograph.'

Mrs Roosevelt was knitting. 'He was very proud of us, three women going into business together. He gave us the acreage and built the cottage and the swimming pool. I believe he was more excited about the project than we were at the time.'

'So you lived here too, Mrs Roosevelt?' Iris enquired.

'Periodically. When we came up from Albany. There was always such a crowd at the house. This was my sanctuary.'

'A sanctuary from Franklin's mother, Sara,' Nan added under her breath.

The three women exchanged meaningful looks.

'My mother-in-law can be rather . . .' The First Lady paused.

'Dictatorial?' Nan suggested.

'Tyrannical?' said Marion.

'Let's say "commanding",' Eleanor finished diplomatically. 'Stone Cottage became my sanctuary as Campobello had been, but it was Franklin's mother who purchased the cottage for us on Campobello Island in 1909 and, strangely, Sara gave me free rein to decorate and furnish the cottage as I pleased. It was really the first home of which I was entirely in charge.'

'How long has it been since you were last there?' Iris asked.

Eleanor replied, 'Twelve years.'

'Twelve years!' Iris exclaimed before she could check herself.

'Campobello was where my husband was stricken with polio in August 1921. It was the most trying time of our lives. After we left there in December of that same year I never wanted to go back again. Neither did he.'

■

The women departed Stone Cottage at Hyde Park shortly after breakfast and headed north, spending the night in Maine before travelling on to Campobello. As Mrs Roosevelt drove the Plymouth up to the two-storey home of red-cedar shingles and green shutters on Campobello Island after lunch on the following day, Iris wondered just how this residence could be called a cottage. There were a number of other cars parked out front on the road. Iris recognised one of them as belonging to Louis Howe. As the women stepped onto the gravel, James Roosevelt appeared from the house. He pushed his round spectacles along the bridge of his nose as he jogged to the car. He looked unmistakably like his father, Iris thought.

He kissed his mother on the cheek, offered Iris, Nan and Marion a cheerful greeting and then moved to the trunk and removed the bags.

'How was the trip?' he asked.

'Uneventful, but I had excellent company. How was yours?' his mother responded.

There was nothing in the world that the president enjoyed more than sailing, so as a reward for a gruelling four months in office, James had hired a forty-five-foot schooner called the *Amberjack II* for his sea-loving father to skipper up the coast to Campobello, with James, Franklin Jr and John acting as crew.

This modest scheme quickly become a substantial security nightmare for the Secret Service, who insisted that the *Amberjack* be escorted by two naval destroyers, one heavy cruiser and three coastguard cutters. FDR also wanted two additional boats in the convoy: one transporting friends to the island and the second carrying four of the president's favourite reporters.

'Pa was brilliant. You'd never know it'd been twelve years since he sailed those waters; he navigated by memory alone.'

'The Lubec Narrows can be quite treacherous,' Eleanor explained to Iris offhandedly. 'And Passamaquoddy Bay is always foggy.'

'When we sailed into Welshpool yesterday morning we were greeted with a twenty-one-gun salute, the entire fishing fleet and what must have been every sailboat and row boat in the vicinity,' James told them.

'Where is he now?' Eleanor asked.

'Playing bridge with the members of the press.'

'News from London?'

'I'm not sure. He received a few wires while we were out there. You'd better talk to Louis.' James hurried into the house with the suitcases.

■

Iris woke and examined the wallpaper of the bedroom in which she had been placed by Mrs Roosevelt. It was printed with violets, which were Mrs Roosevelt's favourite flowers, she had been informed by her hostess. It was a beautiful room, wide and airy, overlooking Friars Bay and the township of Eastport in Maine. It was the most glorious view Iris had ever seen, the water and sky an equal intensity of blue.

Looking at her watch she saw it was four o'clock. She had slept most of the afternoon away. She walked from the bed and opened the window wide. This was only the second time she had been on a seaside holiday. The first had been on a trip with her father. He had taken her to Atlantic City when she was ten years old. Iris didn't remember very much of their seaside excursion except the chill in the water and the saltwater taffy they ate. The five-day holiday was an impromptu one, precipitated by a nervous headache that had rendered her mother incapacitated for a number of weeks.

Standing at the open window in her slip, Iris brooded over how her father had managed to pay for that vacation. She closed her eyes and forced herself to recall where they had lodged. A guesthouse, she remembered. Meals were served there by an elderly man wearing a moth-eaten dinner suit. His hands had trembled as he delivered the food to the table. Had her father ever left her alone at any time? Did he wait for her to go to sleep and then spend the night gambling? Was that how he had financed the trip? Iris didn't think so. She couldn't remember being left to her own devices at all. But it was a challenge for her to evoke her father's drinking, his frequent disappearances or any of his bad habits. Instead she preferred to recollect his off-the-cuff poetry recitals, his love of dancing and his easy smile.

She decided to dress and walk down to the water. Mrs Roosevelt had said she wouldn't need Iris that afternoon. She dressed in a pair of light tweed trousers in the style of Amelia Earhart, a white blouse and wheat-coloured cardigan. On her feet she wore white sneakers. By the time she had got to the door of the house, the sun was masked by clouds and a cool wind had picked up. Louis Howe sat perched on the end of a deckchair on the porch. He was bent over, smoking, his elbows resting on his knees. Rather than looking towards the sea, his gaze was fixed on his shoes. He looked up as Iris passed by and gave her a cursory wave. Iris hesitated a moment, unsure whether she should stop and chat.

'Hi there. Is everything alright?' she ventured.

Howe raised his despondent gaze to her and shook his head briefly before looking down again.

Iris walked to the edge of the porch and looked towards the jetty about two hundred yards away. Mrs Roosevelt and Sam Jacobson stood there, talking. Iris could tell from Mrs Roosevelt's gestures that she was angry. Sam, dressed casually in fawn trousers and a white shirt open at the collar, gave an occasional nod. Sam appeared different from this distance. He was striking, it occurred to her, with his dark hair vivid against the billowing clouds.

Iris continued down the steps onto the lawn, uncertain whether to approach them or not. While she was still deciding, Mrs Roosevelt turned and strode the length of the jetty towards her. When she reached Iris she stopped and stared at her strangely. There were tears in her eyes, Iris could see, but they were not tears of sorrow. Her gait and the set of her jaw conveyed only one emotion: fury. Eleanor took Iris firmly by the upper arms and looked into her face. Iris's dark hair blew across her forehead and eyes but she couldn't push it back as Mrs Roosevelt's grasp was too tight. It seemed to Iris that Mrs Roosevelt wanted to speak but, as if thinking better of it, she released Iris without a word and continued her hurried passage to the cottage. Iris looked after her. When the First Lady reached the porch, she exchanged words with Howe, who stood, and the pair went into the cottage together.

Iris stood still for a few moments. Sam remained on the jetty, looking towards Eastport. After a minute he sat down and Iris, curious, decided to join him. Sam looked up, eyebrows raised in surprise, when she materialised beside him.

Iris lifted a foot. 'Sneakers,' she said.

Sam laughed and offered her a seat by his side.

'You must be cold,' she said. 'It's wild out here.'

'It was sunny not so long ago. The weather changes so quickly.' He looked at her and they smiled uneasily. Sam removed his spectacles and cleaned them with his handkerchief. He seemed quite calm, but Iris could read something in his expression. It wasn't the fury she had witnessed on Mrs Roosevelt's face. Sam looked more disappointed than angry.

'Are you okay?' she asked tentatively.

'Not really.'

'Is there anything I can do?'

'President Roosevelt has scuttled the London Economic Conference. He has completely torpedoed any chance there might be for peace in the future,' he said, and paused as he replaced his spectacles on his face. 'You know how he told us?' He shook his head in disbelief. 'While we were playing bridge.'

Iris wasn't sure how to respond. She understood that the aim of the conference had been to stabilise world currencies and that depended on the president hooking the dollar to gold.

'He's going to float the dollar, then?'

Sam nodded. 'He said it was in America's best interest to do so and he wasn't going to allow his country to be pushed around by foreign nations who still owed the States a massive debt from the war. He made it clear that he was speaking off the record, of course, but if we wanted to give the story a Campobello dateline, that would be a pretty good hedge,' Sam said sardonically.

'So London was a chance for economic equality, a way of keeping nationalism and rearmament under control?'

'You've done your homework,' he commented.

Iris shrugged. She *had* done her homework but they were Monty's words she had just uttered.

'He's a piece of work, that's for sure,' Sam continued. 'You know, Hitler is going to love this news. American leadership in world affairs is the only way to stop another war.'

Iris wanted to suggest that perhaps the president's primary objective at this point was to lift America out of depression. Save America and then America could save the world. But Sam Jacobson and Mrs Roosevelt were both passionate campaigners for world peace. She reasoned that neither of them wanted to hear an alternative perspective at the moment. Instead she said, 'Mrs Roosevelt seemed pretty angry. Is that what you were talking about?'

Sam nodded. 'Roosevelt didn't even tell her about his plans. I was forced to break the news to her when I bumped into her just now on the beach. Achieving world peace, disarmament, America's entry into the League of Nations, the World Court . . . that has been her goal since 1918. He didn't even discuss it with her.'

'That doesn't seem unusual. She's not a member of his cabinet, after all.'

'She's something more important than that, Iris. She's his conscience.'

Nothing more was said for a long while. It upset Iris to see Sam so distressed. She gripped her knees and glanced at his profile – his angular cheekbones, long, narrow nose and distinctive chin – and considered what it might be like to kiss him. His lips were thin but attractively shaped. He turned his head and faced her.

'Maybe the president's announcement wasn't planned,' Iris suggested. 'You said he brought it up over bridge. That doesn't seem orchestrated.'

Sam looked at her over the top of his glasses. 'The president's statement to us was about as unplanned as his inaugural address. He has known the outcome of London for weeks. Even though he hasn't been present at the conference, he held all the cards. He was just waiting until he was away from DC to break the news to the world.'

'I'm sorry,' she said at last. 'I can see this means a great deal to you.' It sounded lame. Iris paused for a moment and placed her hand on his arm and squeezed it gently in a gesture of commiseration or camaraderie, she wasn't certain which. All she knew was that her words needed support, a little shoring up.

He looked down at her hand on his arm. As she removed it she said in a lighter vein, 'I read Dr Feuchtwanger's essay. It was terrifying.' As soon as the words spilled thoughtlessly from her mouth, Iris realised it was an inappropriate topic to be conveyed in such a merry tone. Despite the crisp air she felt her cheeks burn.

'Realistic,' he uttered quietly without looking at her.

Reading the essay had made her understand more about Hitler's rise to power, fascism and the hatred of Jewish people that Hitler was fomenting. Monty also acted as tutor in this matter, filling in the blanks, answering her questions. But she wasn't confident to discuss the subject with a Jew. She worried her words would seem patronising. For some reason she couldn't identify, Iris was concerned about Sam Jacobson's opinion of her.

'You don't need to feel uncomfortable,' Sam said, as if reading her thoughts. 'Most gentiles have trouble discussing the topic of Hitler with Jews.' He smiled and then looked towards the sea. 'But we could talk about something else, if you'd like to sit here for a while longer. Do you follow baseball?'

She laughed and shook her head. They sat quietly for a while looking across the bay, then Sam spoke again.

'Did you ever dream, Iris, that one day you'd be on Campobello island, guest of the First Couple of the United States of America?'

'No,' she replied. 'My dreams were far more modest.'

'Really?' he said. 'I had great hopes when I was a kid of being a Major League ball player.' He grinned.

'Then how'd you become a journalist?' she asked.

'I wasn't anything special at baseball,' he stated matter-of-factly. They laughed.

He turned and examined her face closely. 'All your dreams can't have been modest,' he pressed.

Iris thought for a moment before responding. She lowered her head and gazed into the choppy waters.

'Well, there was a time, when I was younger, when I thought that I might like to try my hand at acting,' she said hesitantly. 'When I was seventeen I played Musician Number Two in my class's production of *Twelfth Night*. It was just a small part, but on opening night – the lights, the teamwork, the applause – it was like fire began to surge through my blood.'

'Why didn't you pursue it?' he prodded gently.

She shrugged. 'It was a silly dream.'

The truth was that when Iris had arrived home from the performance, breathless and giddy with excitement, she had informed her guardian Mrs Woods of her intention to become an actress. Mrs Woods had looked at Iris with a kind face and said, 'That will never do, dear. Actress is another name for harlot. Teaching is a much more sensible profession.' With her bubble burst, Iris considered the idea more clearly and realised that perhaps Mrs Woods was right. But that feeling of being on stage, under lights, surrounded by other performers in front of an audience and feeling like a princess, was one she had never forgotten.

'You'd be a great actress,' Sam responded sincerely.

Iris raised her head and a curious eyebrow.

'You're pretty enough,' he said by way of explanation. 'That's all I mean.'

She parted her lips to smile and felt herself blush. She looked back across the bay. 'But I don't think I'm talented enough.'

'I don't know,' he said wryly. 'As far as I can see there's not much difference between Hollywood and the White House.'

Iris turned to her companion ready to laugh but quickly realised by his clenched jaw and strained eyes that Sam wasn't joking.

■

That evening the president threw a cocktail party to which twenty-two guests were invited. It was a celebration of his triumphant return to Campobello. Iris attended, along with Sam Jacobson, who was in better spirits by seven o'clock. Mrs Roosevelt was absent.

Monty had told Iris that FDR's cocktail parties were not to be missed. Although he'd mentioned that, as a rule, Mrs Roosevelt rarely attended these gatherings – birthdays, anniversaries and other celebrations being the exception – he failed to inform Iris of Missy LeHand's role at these affairs.

That night, Missy played the hostess and performed all the tasks usually delegated to the mistress of the house. Her familiarity with the president – she held his hand, bent low to whisper in his ear and called him F.D. – was surprising to Iris. Her behaviour struck Iris as impertinent, even disrespectful. Someone who didn't know any better would assume Missy was Roosevelt's wife. Obviously, Missy was more than a secretary but to Iris it seemed as though she was flaunting her relationship with the president. But apart from her no one, not even the president's children, seemed to think his rapport with his secretary out of the ordinary.

However, while the gramophone played Bing Crosby, Kate Smith and Al Jolson, and those assembled drank and laughed and danced, it was with an air of forced gaiety. But it was not the president's peculiar relationship with Missy that was responsible for the underlying gloom, Iris knew. There was a palpable sense of foreboding, and the efforts made to mask the atmosphere only seemed to intensify the menace.

Louis Howe was the only person whose weathered face reflected the truth. He was sitting by the window, a scotch and cigarette his only company.

'You look concerned, Mr Howe,' Iris remarked. 'Can I help?'

'No one is capable of curbing the tragic inevitability of this evening,' he responded glumly without looking her way. 'Not even me.'

'Are you talking about Mrs Roosevelt? She seemed extremely distressed this afternoon.'

Howe nodded. 'In the many years I've known them I've seen him upset her before, but this is different. Frank has managed to cut right to the quick with this play. Disarmament, world peace, economic equality . . . they're her babies. And Franklin's gone and killed them all.'

Iris saw in Howe's face the seriousness of the situation.

'I told him, Iris. I told him to discuss it with her first. By all means, go ahead with the plan, but discuss it with her first. She hates being left in the dark and she hates being made to look a fool. But it's more than that. She genuinely believes Franklin has jeopardised any chance of staving off another war.'

'Perhaps she might have calmed down by now,' Iris suggested.

'No chance. That woman is part elephant, part lion. She will never forget and she *will* go in for the kill. Believe me. I've been up there all afternoon trying to calm her down. She won't be reasoned with.'

'What about Tommy?' Iris asked.

'Tommy's up there with her now, but I don't think even she'll be able to appease the First Lady this time.'

Iris sat down next to Howe and studied the room. Frequently guests looked at their watches or the grandfather clock in the corner of the room. Laughter would stop abruptly and heads would turn suddenly towards the door in anticipation of Mrs Roosevelt's arrival. When she did arrive, it was late, about nine o'clock.

The First Lady stood at the door and announced that dinner was ready. She wore a simple maroon dress belted at the waist. Her hair was coiled into a bun at the back of her head.

The guests followed her outside. They were having the catch of the day; it had been cooked in the front yard by local fishermen and their wives as a special welcome to the president. Trestle tables were laid out on the lawn and covered in red, white and blue tablecloths. Balloons and lanterns in the same colours hung from the surrounding trees and the gables of the cottage. A three-piece band that had appeared on the porch played 'Happy Days Are Here Again'. It was perfect, magical. What a pity, Iris thought.

Mrs Roosevelt did not take a plate. She sat at one of the tables away from the president and quietly sipped iced tea. Her face was unyielding and she looked at no one in particular. Iris took a plate and a modest amount of food and, unsure of whether she should sit with Mrs Roosevelt, was relieved when Sam gestured for her to sit next to him. Iris watched as people took their places. The gusts from the sea were wild at times and cold, but for Iris, who ate cautiously while keeping an eye on the proceedings, the temperature was rising as steadily as the mercury in a thermometer.

It was when James stood to toast his father that Mrs Roosevelt finally spoke. There was a sense of relief among the guests when she stood and gestured her son to sit. Everyone had known what was coming. No one attempted to stop her, calm her or cajole. Staring at the president, steely-eyed, she began.

Why hadn't she been consulted? Why had he broken the news while at Campobello? Did he fathom what this meant for the world? Why was he burying his head in the sand in regards to Hitler? For goodness' sake, she cried, the man outlined his aims clearly enough a decade ago in *Mein Kampf*.

The berating took little more than a minute and Roosevelt remained silent throughout, wearing an expression of dignified equanimity. Iris supposed after living with Eleanor for twenty-eight years he knew what the domestic consequences of his political gambit would be.

When Mrs Roosevelt was finished, she took a final sip of iced tea and returned indoors. Tommy followed. Iris looked up to the second storey of the house and saw the light come on in her bedroom a few moments later.

Despite the best efforts of James and his siblings, who had organised the elaborate two-week celebration, the party was ruined. Gradually the guests crawled out from beneath the carnage and made their way back to the safety of their rooms or cars. Sam said goodbye to Iris and with the three other reporters walked across the lawn to the jetty where the boat they were staying on was anchored. Howe, hands in pockets, walked over to the president and spoke into his ear. Roosevelt nodded as Gus pushed him across the grass and into the house. Missy trailed close behind.

As a light rain began to fall, Iris sat on the steps of the cottage and watched the fishermen and their wives pack the remains of the celebration into the backs of their trucks.

24
HYDE PARK, NEW YORK
May 1962

You could say that during the first year my war as housekeeper was fought across three fronts. The first front was dust. The problem was that the president and Mrs Roosevelt were keen collectors of knick-knacks and pictures. The president's print collection was one of the largest and most valuable in the country. Everyone admired the prints and photographs that hung on the walls, but all I saw when I walked down the corridors and through the rooms were dust collectors. The curios and framed photographs that Mrs Roosevelt had on display took days to clean. By the time you finished, you'd have to start right over again from where you began!

Well, the second battle was theft. Trays featuring the presidential crest that went up to guestrooms never came back down. Those teeny-weeny salt spoons that we'd set out for formal dinners just seemed to evaporate. Poor Fields blamed himself, said he should have kept a closer eye on things, but you can't go accusing Italo Balbo or Lord Beaverbrook of stealing a fish knife in the middle of dessert, now, can you?

Finally, keeping on top of the cleaning was a never-ending battle for me and my staff, especially with all the people who would come and go, day in and day out. It was next to impossible to give the house a good going-over all at once. When Mrs Roosevelt or the president went on a trip I sent the maids in to give their rooms a thorough clean – drapes washed and pressed, floors washed and polished – the works! Even if someone just went out for the afternoon we'd take the opportunity to get in and give the room a good clean. It was relentless. And my, after a function, especially if it was a buffet function . . . I don't even want to think. The floors were always sticky with mess from dropped food and spilt drinks.

Christmas was always at the White House and Thanksgiving at Warm Springs and occasionally Hyde Park. All the family and a few friends attended. There were usually between twenty-four and thirty guests. The Roosevelts always wanted their Christmas dinner on Christmas night. Mrs Roosevelt would usually rush in close to serving, after having been busy as a bird dog all day visiting orphanages, attending parties for disadvantaged children and serving food at soup kitchens. She'd always have a small gift for every child at these functions.

I can still remember the menu for the first Christmas dinner in 1933. We were still practising economy cooking, but Mrs Roosevelt let me splurge a little because the turkey, sausages and the chestnuts were gifts to the president.

Clam Cocktail and Saltines
Clear Soup with Beaten Biscuits
Curled Celery and Stuffed Olives
Filet of Fish with Sauce Maréchale
Sliced Cucumbers
Rolls
Roast Turkey with Chestnut Dressing and Deerfoot Sausages
Cranberry Jelly
Creamed Onions
Green Beans
Candied Sweet Potatoes
Grape and Rubyette Salad
Cheese Straws
Plum Pudding with Hard Sauce and Ice-Cream
Small Cakes
Cookies
Coffee
Candy

I insisted on chestnut dressing for the turkey just like Mother Kugler used to make, but it was the president who insisted on a string of sausages surrounding the bird. He said Christmas wasn't Christmas without a string of Deerfoot Farm sausages.

Mrs Roosevelt liked to say that her 'official Christmas' began on Christmas Eve. She usually spent this day on official business, running around from charity to charity conveying the president's best wishes. She'd shake hands and pose for photographs on behalf of her husband. Then she'd go on to Lafayette Square with the president, who'd switch on the lights of the municipal Christmas tree. Then back to the White House for two Christmas parties. The first was in the Oval Office for the executive staff, the Secret Service detail and the White House police officers. The second was in the East Room for mansion staff and their families. You know, Mrs Roosevelt gave a present to every person there. She kept a small notebook listing what she gave each person each year so as not to double up. She was exacting in her choice of gift and always bought the White House staff something personal.

My official Christmas, on the other hand, began the day after Thanksgiving, when I began the baking of hundreds of fruitcakes that Mrs Roosevelt sent out as gifts. She'd bundle up parcels of fruitcakes, preserves, cookies and different candies that the kitchen had made and stockpiled throughout the year. Elizabeth and Ida made the preserves et cetera, but I insisted on having a hand in every fruitcake. It was the dark fruitcake that was my favourite. My recipe was laced with spices and filled the kitchen with festive smells. Although it was hard work, I enjoyed it. I can honestly attest to the fact that fruitcake-mixing can be heartily recommended as a cure-all for the blues. It puts you right in the Christmas spirit.

25
WASHINGTON DC
December 1933

Despite Monty's criticisms, notably of the addition of marshmallows to the grape and rubyette salad, Iris thought Christmas dinner was one of Mrs Nesbitt's better efforts. The turkey was dry, the beans overcooked and the sauce Maréchale lumpy, but Iris argued that it would be difficult to get the exact timing of every aspect of the meal correct when you were cooking for thirty people. Monty argued that this was the White House, and if the White House kitchen couldn't get something as simple as the cooking of a turkey right, what hope did the administration have of solving larger problems? Monty took food very seriously, Iris had learned.

'All I'm saying is that the quality of what you put in your mouth is important. Food is more than fuel. It's a mood enhancer, a tonic; it can alter the way you see the world or your personal circumstances,' Monty said to the gathering.

'I agree,' the president responded. 'But it's just as important to cook frugally in these straitened times. We can't be eating caviar when the rest of the country is sitting down to mutton or rabbit for their Christmas dinner.'

Monty nodded bleakly. Iris was relieved his comments had not triggered another argument between the president and Mrs Roosevelt. Since the incident at Campobello, the president seemed more attuned to his wife's feelings. Monty told Iris that this was most likely Howe's doing. Howe was more than Secretary to the President, political adviser and friend; he was also mediator and counsellor to the Roosevelts, and this was the toughest job in Washington.

Immediately after his return from the island the president had begun the process of establishing formal relations with the Soviet Union. Unrecognised by the United States since the Bolshevik Revolution sixteen years before, Russia was a major thorn in Mrs Roosevelt's paw. After a series of clandestine meetings with Maxim Litvinov, the Commissar of

Foreign Affairs, the president signed the document restoring diplomatic relations with Moscow at midnight on the morning of 17 November.

Mrs Roosevelt was thrilled and touted it to the press as the president's first constructive international act. Trapped between the demands of William Randolph Hearst and his wife, the president had pulled a very impressive rabbit out of his hat.

'However,' Roosevelt continued, 'I think we can say that the New Deal has been successful and a greater number of people have food on the table these holidays than last Christmas, even if it is mutton. The Civil Works Administration alone has put another three million people to work since November and Hopkins believes that figure will reach over four million by mid-January.'

'Four million *men* by mid-January,' Mrs Roosevelt qualified.

The president put down his spoon and looked wryly at his wife over his pince-nez.

'There's still no New Deal for women,' she pointed out.

'But, my dear, we assume that if men are put to work that will impact favourably on their wives and families.'

'Not all women are married.'

Iris was silently praying Mrs Roosevelt would not turn to her, requesting a first-hand opinion on the matter. She stared into her dessert, willing someone to change the topic.

'Now I think of it,' Mrs Roosevelt said, 'that will become a priority for me in 1934. You won't do anything about the problem but I think I can. I have a few ideas up my sleeve. Iris . . .' she began.

As if aware of Iris's anxiety, Hick cut off her friend's train of thought. 'What about you, Mr President, what have you got up your sleeve for 1934?'

'Are you asking as a reporter?' Roosevelt queried.

'I haven't had a by-line since July, Mr President. I'm playing on your team now, remember?'

'And a grand job you're doing.'

Iris bit her lip in concentration as she listened to the exchange. Since learning of Hick's relationship with Mrs Roosevelt, Iris had had to refrain from trying to read between the lines of the president and Hick's banter. She had to accept that some people just lived their lives a little unconventionally, Monty advised. There was nothing between the lines.

Hick smiled. 'I enjoy working for Hopkins. He moves fast and gets results. Since July I've been to thirteen cities investigating New

Deal America. I can honestly report that day-to-day life for average Americans has improved.'

This was true. Organisations such as FERA and the CWA had quickly turned around the lives of ordinary men by taking them off the dole and putting them to work.

'So, off the record, Mr President, what's next?'

'More of the same. Get more Americans back to work and, of course, rural electrification.'

'Killing two birds with one stone,' Monty emphasised.

'Indeed. Establishing rural cooperatives to build power lines and stations will create jobs. In turn, the countryside will have electricity. The Tennessee Valley Authority has made inroads into electrification, but more needs to be done to help the South. The Rural Electrification Administration's main focus will be supplying electricity to the countryside.'

'Impressive!' Hick said. 'It needs to be done.'

'It will be done,' the president affirmed forcefully. 'Nothing will help more to reduce poverty in the South than electricity.'

'Don't forget Germany. Berlin has quit the Geneva Disarmament Conference and the League of Nations. Hitler is determined. He is heading for war,' Eleanor put in.

As Iris listened she thought about her own agenda for 1934.

Her position at the White House was secure and she woke each day with a sense of purpose. But while she appreciated her good fortune to be assisting Mrs Roosevelt in her work for *Women's Home Companion*, she had been doing so for nearly a year now and was growing bored. Monty advised her to discuss the matter with Mrs Roosevelt.

'You've been here for nine months,' he told her. 'You're way beyond sorting her mail. You're too smart for that. Tell her you want a project you can sink your teeth into.'

'I do some writing too,' Iris added in defence of the First Lady.

'Even so, kiddo, you should be doing much more.'

It was good counsel, but Iris feared she would appear ungrateful.

As coffee was being served, guests began to change positions, move and mingle. Iris found herself, cup in hand, talking to Mrs Roosevelt.

'My idea, Iris, that came to me during dinner –' the First Lady led Iris to a seat on the sofa – 'was camps. Camps organised in the same vein as the Civilian Conservation Corps, but solely for needy women and girls. What do you think?'

'I think it's an excellent idea!' Iris exclaimed.

'I'd like you to head the project,' Mrs Roosevelt continued. 'We'll get Harry on board, but you'll be in charge. You're an intelligent young woman. You can't go on sorting my mail forever. It will mean travel and meetings and begging for funds, but I'm confident you're up to the task.'

Iris wasn't sure whether this was just another example of dumb luck or whether Mrs Roosevelt had noticed a change in her. Iris was overjoyed to be handed a greater challenge. A lump rose in her throat. She was thankful to Mrs Roosevelt but, more than that, she was proud of her own achievements.

'Now, on a different note,' Eleanor went on, 'what exactly is your relationship with Monty Chapel?'

Iris stared at her, dumbstruck and unsure how to respond. Their relationship was impossible to define. They were a couple, but weren't. They had never discussed marriage or children. They dated, but they were not really dating in the regular sense of the term. Their relationship seemed clandestine, but everyone at the White House was aware of it.

'I'm not sure.'

'It appears to be serious, so in the absence of a parent or close relation to advise you, I'd just like offer my guidance.'

Iris nodded her consent.

'Monty Chapel is amusing and fiercely intelligent; I often think of him as a charming rogue,' Mrs Roosevelt mused. 'He fought bravely in the war and was highly decorated.'

Monty rarely mentioned his background or his family. He had never mentioned his wartime experiences.

'But he's also a man of temptations,' the First Lady went on. 'He lacks impulse control. This is a subject I know something about.'

Iris didn't know whether she was referring to herself or her husband. She shifted uncomfortably in her seat.

'I assume your relationship with Monty is carnal. Have you taken care of birth control?' Her tone was forthright and unembarrassed.

Iris could only stare into Mrs Roosevelt's compassionate yet unwavering gaze. Discussing her sexual relationship with the First Lady on Christmas night was certainly a surreal twist to the evening.

'Monty takes care of that,' Iris said quietly.

'You need to take care of that, dear,' Mrs Roosevelt said firmly. 'Your career is on the rise. Don't hinder it with an unwanted pregnancy.'

Iris nodded obediently. Monty was cautious but there had been one time, maybe two, Iris recalled, when, in the heat of the moment, they had thrown caution to the wind.

'I gave birth to six children in ten years. I love my children more than anything but if I'd had a choice . . . I'll give you the name and number of a doctor, a very good doctor, who can fit you with a diaphragm.'

Iris cleared her throat. 'Okay. Thank you, Mrs Roosevelt.'

'Just be careful, that's all.'

The women wished each other a happy Christmas before Eleanor excused herself and retired. Iris remained seated on the sofa for some minutes, waiting for her astonishment to fade.

■

'Mrs Roosevelt was talking to me about temptations and impulse control,' Iris began when she and Monty returned to her apartment. 'She said it was a topic she knew something about. What did she mean?'

Monty loosened his tie. 'Is the heat on? It's freezing in here.' He edged around the Val-Kill drawers and sat down on the bed. 'You really need to get a bigger apartment. Alternatively, you could get rid of this horrible thing.' He gestured to the drawers stacked with piles of books, magazines and newspapers.

'I can't afford a bigger apartment,' she said.

'Let me help.'

'Then I'd be a kept woman.'

'Exactly.' Monty grinned.

'Anyway, Mrs Roosevelt has given me a promotion.'

'Really? Well done, kiddo. What kind of promotion?'

Iris didn't want to talk about her new role now; she was more concerned with their previous topic. As she walked the perimeter of the room checking the radiators, she pressed, 'Well? What did she mean about impulse control?'

'Her husband, her father, her brother, her children . . . the list is endless.'

Iris looked at him quizzically.

'Her father and brother – alcoholics. Her children do whatever they please, damn the consequences. Her husband destroyed her life when she discovered his affair with Lucy Mercer.'

'That's quite a list,' Iris said contemplatively as she removed her shoes and unfastened her stockings. 'I wonder if she's ever completely forgiven the president for Lucy.'

'I doubt it,' Monty replied, sitting next to her on the bed. 'How do you think Henrietta Nesbitt got the job?'

'What do you mean?'

'She's Eleanor's revenge. The president loves nothing better than good food and his wife hired the least-qualified person to run the kitchen. Finally, after fifteen years, she has been able to exact her revenge via his stomach.' Monty laughed.

'Mr Howe called Mrs Roosevelt an elephant crossed with a lion,' Iris remarked.

'An accurate description,' Monty agreed. 'Anyway, this is a pretty strange conversation to be having at Christmas.'

Iris shrugged. It all seemed so complicated. The concessions that had been made over the years were staggering. The bending and negotiating, the compromises. She wondered if the Roosevelts were truly happy. Perhaps they were. They inhabited the same world but trod very separate trails.

Monty sat down next to Iris on the bed and slipped his hand under her skirt.

'As tonight is Christmas, I thought we might try something a little different. A further gift to each other.'

'The bracelet was ample,' Iris said, smirking as she anticipated what was coming next. Monty had presented her with a silver charm bracelet that morning. It had hanging from its delicate loops only one charm – a tiny pair of boots such as a tramp might wear.

Ignoring Iris's sarcasm, Monty reached into his overnight bag and produced what looked like a butter pat. This was not at all what she'd been expecting.

Turning the pat over in his hands, he enlightened her. 'I thought I might remove those lovely silk stockings of yours and you could tie my hands to the bed rails. Then you can do whatever you like to me, with this.'

She shook her head slightly, not quite understanding his meaning.

'You may feel my behaviour warrants some form of . . . punishment.'

■

As Monty dozed during the early hours of 26 December, Iris brooded further over temptations. She turned her head and looked at his handsome face in the half-light. She was deeply in love with him, she realised. He was perfect and that was exactly the reason she could not envisage a future together.

When the paddle entered into their foreplay, Iris was stunned but she played along. He was thrilled, more aroused than she had ever seen him. In turn, she found the sexual experience thrilling as well. Their lovemaking reached a crescendo that night, but there was an element to it all that disgusted her. What did that say about her? she wondered. Perhaps she was a prude. Was this the compromise she was making to be with a man like Monty, who was driven by his sexual impulses? If not this, then what else? Terrified, unpractised boys who stared at a spot on the pillow next to her head until they climaxed? She delicately traced the scar on his abdomen with her index finger and wondered how he had come to receive such a striking memento.

Monty rolled over and put his hand on her breast.

'How did you get this?' Iris asked, pointing to the scar.

'Our position was shelled,' he murmured, lighting a cigarette.

That was all he said before noticing a book on her bedside table.

Reaching across her to retrieve it he said, 'The Works of Bertolt Brecht. Interesting.' He leafed through the pages.

'It was a gift from Mrs Roosevelt,' she lied.

Iris was thankful Sam had not written an inscription in the book as he had wanted. Since Campobello she'd seen Sam regularly at the White House. They'd even had lunch together on one occasion, at a delicatessen near Dupont Circle. She sensed he was keeping his distance due to Monty, even though they had never spoken of him. The gift was thoughtful. He explained that Brecht had once collaborated with Feuchtwanger.

Why the lie? She wasn't certain. Iris had come to admire Sam's passion, his intellect, his thoughtfulness and his humour. She had also come to think of him as handsome. Not in the same way as Monty, but he had a curious face, she decided. It was a canvas for his every thought and feeling.

Monty replaced the book and noticed another. He picked up her dog-eared copy of The Portrait of a Lady. 'Why do you keep this by your bedside all the time? I've never seen you read it.'

'I just like to have it close by,' she answered honestly. 'I read it . . . when I have the need.'

Monty flicked through the pages carelessly as he spoke. His cigarette remained in the corner of his mouth. 'I suppose you see similarities between Isabel Archer's life and your own.' He spoke authoritatively, even solemnly. 'Jacobson, of course, is Caspar Goodwood, while I'm the evil Gilbert Osmond.'

It struck Iris that he was extremely familiar with the novel. It had been by her bedside for months and he had never mentioned it. When had he drawn these parallels? she wondered.

They lay in silence as Monty read a page at random. She could hear the burn of his cigarette.

'Don't be ridiculous,' she scoffed, leaning over and taking the cigarette from his mouth and placing it in her own. 'You're far too wicked to be compared to Osmond.'

He threw the book on the table. By the time he turned back to her his gravity had transformed to mirth.

'Seriously, though,' Iris began hesitantly, 'a lot of people have warned me against getting involved with you. In fact, Mrs Roosevelt described you as a charming rogue.'

'I take that as a compliment.'

'I don't think she meant it as such,' Iris responded.

'You think it was a mistake getting involved?' Monty asked, staring at the ceiling.

'No, no, not at all. . .' she stumbled, surprised by the candour of the question. 'It's just that . . . it's just that you're so reticent to talk about yourself, your past.'

'For instance?'

'That scar, for instance.'

'I just told you.'

'Barely.'

'It was in Verdun,' he said. 'Our position was shelled by the enemy. Most of the battalion were killed or wounded. I was taken to a field hospital where they removed most of the shrapnel. As you can see' – he pushed the sheet down to his hips – 'they didn't do a very clean job closing me up.'

'Were you sent home?'

'I was, and the war ended while I was still recuperating. Anything else?'

'Yes, there is,' she answered. He raised an eyebrow. 'How would you define our relationship?'

Monty thought briefly. 'It is beyond definition.'

Iris pushed herself onto her elbow and gaped at him, incredulous. 'Excuse me?'

'If we refuse to define our relationship then we allow it to grow and evolve and change as we as individuals grow and evolve and change,' he explained. 'Don't you think that's a good thing?'

'I suppose,' she replied as she thought on his response.

'Is that all?'

'There is one more thing,' she whispered. Iris had never asked Monty about his sexual cravings. She could never find the right words to use and she didn't want to seem narrow-minded or judgmental. But this was a night of firsts so she decided to wade into uncharted waters. 'The spanking and being bound,' she whispered. 'Why do you find it so exciting?'

He placed his hands behind his head and considered the question for a few moments before answering. 'I think it's the absence of power. It's not genuine helplessness, it's a fantasy. But it's vulnerability nonetheless.'

She nodded slowly. Only a powerful man could utter those words, she thought.

'You could try it,' he began. 'I won't spank you, of course, that's an acquired taste. But being bound is . . .' he searched for the appropriate word, '. . . inflaming.'

Iris rolled onto her side and examined the scar. She knew intimately its every bulge, fold and crevice.

'Yes,' she replied in the spirit of firsts. Monty had shared a small part of himself with her that morning. She wanted to give him something of herself in return.

26
HYDE PARK, NEW YORK
May 1962

The campaign of 1936 was marred by Louis Howe's death. He was sick for a long, long time. He'd sit in his room all doubled up, wrapped in a cape that Mrs Roosevelt had bought him. He was frail for as long as I knew him, afflicted with asthma his entire life, but it was emphysema that got him in the end.

But he was a strange one. It seemed the sicker he got the more peevish he became. He'd call down to my office with the most ludicrous requests. One day he demanded rats' cheese; 'the stuff you put in traps,' he explained. I didn't know what he meant, so I just sent some sharp cheddar up to his room. Another day he rang down and yelled into the phone that I couldn't cook a steak to save my life and then went on for at least twenty minutes telling me just how it should be done. It was around this time he told the president to go to hell, and not in private either. The president turned the other cheek. He knew Mr Howe was not himself.

The meals he requested from the kitchen became odder by the day. I recall for supper one night he asked for cornmeal mush, clear soup, scalloped oysters, pork tenderloin, potato salad and cream puffs. I asked his doctor whether he could order such rich food and the doctor told me, 'He can order whatever he likes but all he can eat is orange juice and soup.' I had a mighty laugh at that.

In the end, he was so ill that he had to be moved to Bethesda Naval Hospital. He was in an oxygen tent for most of that time, I heard. When he was moved everyone thought it would only be a matter of days before he passed, but he hung on for almost a year there. When he was at his worst Mrs Roosevelt was at his bedside day and night.

On the night he passed, Mrs Roosevelt had to leave the hospital. She was committed to speak at a conference on better housing for Negroes. Since Mr Howe had become ill, she had let her obligations slide. Although she felt bad about leaving him, I reckon she just didn't want to renege on another promise. It said in the papers the next day that her speech was a triumph, that she had moved the Negroes to tears. She arrived home to the White House late that evening. The entire staff knew before her. I suppose that hurt as well. Mr Hopkins broke the news to her.

She handled all the funeral arrangements herself, every detail. The flags flew at half-mast that day. There were formal services in the East Room and then burial at the Episcopal cemetery in Fall River, Massachusetts. The president and Mrs Roosevelt caught the train up there, but they were only gone overnight.

I hate to speak ill of the dead, but I don't know what Mrs Roosevelt ever saw in Mr Howe. They were such odd companions; she so refined and he so rude. But, then again, she could find the good in Al Capone.

27
WASHINGTON DC
April 1936

Iris put down the telephone. It was four o'clock. Work was difficult today. She and Monty had returned to DC only last night from the burial. She stood from her desk and looked out her window over the Rose Garden. She no longer shared an office with Tommy and she often missed the lively banter, especially on days like today. The high, half-moon windows surrounding the president's pool were fogged. The president must be swimming, she thought. It was a daily ritual impeded not even by the death of his closest friend and confidante.

She and Monty had travelled the distance from Fall River to New York in silence. They stopped at Monty's apartment in Manhattan for the night. When she walked through the door she'd been astonished. Every room was crammed with furniture. The placement of some pieces made it impossible to enter a room without squeezing past an end table laden with tottering lamps and ornaments. Iris had never seen so many lamps. Floor-to-ceiling bookshelves lined the walls of the dining room and yet more books were piled on the floor, mostly volumes on politics, philosophy and economics, although Iris did find *Alice in Wonderland* wedged between copies of *Das Kapital* and Keynes's *Treatise on Money*. Drawers in the kitchen were full of corks or used matchbooks. Why didn't he throw these things away? she wondered. A cabinet in the bathroom was stuffed with old postcards. Iris would not have described the apartment as dirty or rundown, just cluttered. But it disturbed her that he would live in such a way. She didn't know him at all, she realised.

'I thought you owned a townhouse,' Iris said.

'I do. I've had it converted into apartments. I let the other four.'

Monty had taken Howe's death harder than she had anticipated. When she was ready for bed she entered the living room and found Monty sitting, drinking Scotch, staring at a medal in his hand.

'Is that yours?' she asked gently.

He nodded. 'It's the Victory Medal.'

'It's beautiful.' Iris took it from him and examined the striped ribbon and the Winged Victory hanging beneath. 'What did you get it for?'

'Serving.'

'Mrs Roosevelt told me you were highly decorated.'

'Everyone who served got this one.'

'Where are the others?'

He shrugged.

'Did you get them for Verdun?'

He nodded. She replaced the medal in his hand and moved to the window that overlooked Madison Avenue and 91st Street. There was not a soul to be seen.

'Is there anything you'd like to talk about?' she asked.

Monty shook his head. His face was rigid but not sullen. He was sad, genuinely sad, she observed as she went to bed alone. He was by her side when she woke at six in the morning. The trip from New York to Washington was less strained. Tiredness and despondency distorted his handsome face. For the first time since she had known him he looked his age.

'I hadn't realised you and Howe were so close; friends even,' Iris began when they reached the outskirts of Philadelphia.

'We weren't, really. But he was an old soldier, I guess.' Monty's eyes remained on the road.

'He was a fixture, wasn't he? At the White House, I mean,' Iris said haltingly. 'He'll be missed. There'll be a great void, I suppose.'

Monty said nothing.

When the pair entered the White House the next morning at eight-thirty they went their separate ways. Iris hadn't seen Monty since. Now, without any urge to return the telephone calls she had received while at Fall River, she left her office.

Iris began strolling the corridors. The usual buzz of hurried voices, the rapid clicks of a hundred hurried footsteps, even the untroubled tones of the White House grandchildren were absent. All the usual sounds that echoed daily down the halls had faded. Monty was not in his office as she passed by his door.

Within a few minutes she found herself sitting on a bench in the Rose Garden. It was April and the sun had no real bite yet, but Iris closed her eyes and lifted her face into the light. She wasn't aware of anyone behind her until a light tap on her shoulder made her jump.

'Sorry, Iris.' It was Gus. He bent his tall, muscular frame low and placed his hands on the back of the bench. He wore a robe over his swimsuit. 'The president would like you to join him in the pool house.'

Roosevelt was still swimming when she entered through the French doors. His powerful arms cut through the water, barely making a ripple. From shoulder to shoulder he must be three feet across, she thought. When he noticed the young woman standing by the side, the president stopped and gestured for Gus to remove him from the pool. The bodyguard, a former New York City police sergeant, waded down the ramp into the water. He expertly lifted Roosevelt out of the pool and into the wheelchair where his robe was waiting. The president immediately placed a cigarette in his ivory holder.

'Would you like one?'

'Thank you, sir.' Iris took a cigarette and leaned towards the president's outstretched hand as he lit it.

'When are you going to call me boss, McIntosh, like everyone else?'

'It's difficult. You *are* the president.'

He laughed. 'Yes, I suppose I am,' he remarked wistfully.

Roosevelt relaxed into his chair and took a series of long drags. Iris glanced at him quickly. He was staring down the length of the pool. The pair remained wordless until Iris finished her cigarette and stubbed the butt into the ashtray on the table between them.

'I'm sorry for your loss,' she said softly. 'I didn't get a chance to speak to you at the funeral or the burial. I know Mr Howe meant a lot to you.'

'We'd been together since 1911. Twenty-five years. He followed me everywhere. From the New York State Senate to Washington when I became Assistant Secretary of the Navy, then to Albany and then to the White House. He told me once that there was no trick to making a president. He said, "Give me a man who stays relatively sober, shaves and wears a clean shirt every day and I can make him president."' Roosevelt grinned. 'I think he was more dedicated to my career than I was.'

'He was one of a kind.'

'He and the missus saw me through polio. They took the reins when I was laid up. Worked together to make sure I wasn't forgotten. He was devoted beyond all reason, really. I wouldn't have won in '32 without him.'

Iris nodded. 'Everyone says he worked tirelessly on the campaign.'

Roosevelt sighed and fixed a second cigarette into his holder. A further contemplative silence followed.

'What am I going to do now?' the president said finally.

'What do you mean?' Iris wasn't sure if the president was talking about that afternoon or beyond that.

'The National Convention is in two months. The campaign kicks off in September. This will be the first time in my political life that I'll be flying solo. How will I do it without him?' He leaned across the table and placed his huge hand over Iris's.

Iris took some time answering. It was obvious he required a considered reply, not a platitude. She wasn't sure why he was seeking reassurance from her, but she was determined to provide it. His eyes beseeched it. It was her duty.

She began matter-of-factly. 'Howe's gone. It's a sore fact and the campaign will feel his loss. But it doesn't have to suffer because of it. There are plenty of others in the White House who are just as dedicated. Monty, Hopkins, Jim Farley, Stanley – you said yourself there's no better speechwriter than Stanley High. Tom Corcoran and Ben Cohen are the greatest advocates for the New Deal anyone will ever see. The list is endless. And don't forget Mrs Roosevelt. In my opinion, Mr President, she is this campaign's greatest asset.'

Roosevelt studied her curiously before speaking. 'You have a keen eye, McIntosh. A very keen eye.'

'Thank you, Mr President.'

'Do you swim, McIntosh?' he asked after a minute.

'No, I don't. I can't. I never learned.'

'Well, we'll have to change that. The health benefits of swimming are amazing and it's restorative. It never fails to give me a new perspective on a problem or wash away gloom, doubts, that sort of thing. I can teach you, if you want to learn.'

She nodded. 'But you usually swim with Mrs Roosevelt in the afternoons.'

'She's not coming down so much these days. She's taken on a lot of causes. She's in town less and less it seems.'

'She's very busy,' Iris said. 'But I'd love to learn.'

'Good. We'll meet here at four tomorrow. Then you can join us for Children's Hour, okay? And cocktails and dinner tonight?'

Iris hesitated. But she couldn't say no to the president. 'Of course,' she replied.

As she strolled back to her office, a distinct twinge of betrayal gripped her chest.

28
WASHINGTON DC
April 1936

Despite her three years at the White House, that evening was the first time Iris had ever attended FDR's Children's Hour, the sixty minutes each evening that the president devoted to frivolity and play of the grown-up variety. Monty, a regular when in Washington, had invited her on numerous occasions, but she'd always declined, fearful her acceptance would upset Mrs Roosevelt. As far as she knew, the First Lady had never been invited to Children's Hour. Missy played hostess. However, Iris's poolside chat with the president that afternoon made it impossible for her to refuse again. She had dressed carefully for the evening. Dinner was rarely formal at the president's table, but Iris wanted to look her best. She wore her most elegant day dress, making sure it was one that had never been seen at the White House. It was made of striking fuchsia crepe and the cross-banded bodice accentuated her waist.

As she dressed that evening Iris thought hard about the reasons Roosevelt had chosen to reveal his concerns to her. Was it her political insignificance or just a desire for a sympathetic ear? Perhaps she was just in the right place at the right time. Although Iris came to no solid conclusions, she was flattered he had let his guard down, exposed himself to her in that way. It put their relationship on a different footing. But Iris, without seeking the position, had inadvertently been invited into the president's camp and she worried how Mrs Roosevelt would react.

When she arrived at the sitting room of the Roosevelts' family quarters she cast her eyes around, seeking out Monty. He wasn't there.

'Welcome,' Sam Jacobson said.

Iris turned her head, startled.

'Why so glum?'

'I'm not. Just looking for a friendly face.'

'Well, you've found one.' He smiled warmly, then hesitated before saying, 'You look pretty tonight.'

'Thanks.' Iris was pleased her efforts had not been wasted and was quietly thrilled that Sam had noticed.

'Can I get you a drink?'

She nodded and Sam walked to the opposite side of the room where the president was at work at the bar, cocktail shaker in hand, cigarette-holder clenched between his lips. He insisted on mixing the drinks himself. Sam was frequently a guest at Children's Hour by invitation of the president, or at dinner by invitation of Mrs Roosevelt. Monty dubbed Sam and his ilk White House Regulars — people who had become favourites of the president or his wife. There were very few, however, who were considered favourites of both. Monty was one, and so was Sam. Louis Howe had been one. And now, it seemed, Iris had joined this elite club.

Sam approached Roosevelt and gestured to Iris. The president turned and offered his new confidante a cheerful salute. Iris was about to respond with a wave when someone grabbed her hand. Monty had arrived. He kissed her fingertips in mock gallantry.

'You're cheerful,' she said.

'Of course,' he replied. 'The Tweedsmuirs are coming to dinner.'

'And?' Iris had been told the Canadian governor-general and his wife were guests, but she couldn't understand why Monty was so excited.

'Don't you know?'

Iris shook her head, mystified.

'And you call yourself well read,' he scoffed. 'Lord Tweedsmuir is John Buchan!'

Iris shook her head again.

'Author of *The Thirty-Nine Steps*,' he explained.

Iris smiled. She was pleased to see Monty on such a high. The effect of Howe's death on him had worried her, but this evening he was restored.

'Ah, of course, darling.' Iris squeezed his arm tightly. She had not read the book, but she and Monty had seen the film together the year before.

'Excuse me for a second,' he said, spotting Harry Hopkins. 'I just have to mention something to Harry before I forget.' Monty gave Iris a peck on the cheek then departed.

As he did so, Sam appeared beside her, brandishing a martini.

'Thank you,' Iris said. 'Now you're the glum one.'

He raised his eyebrows humourlessly.

'You don't approve of Monty?'

'I approve of Monty. He's smart, funny, a first-rate adviser. The president couldn't have done better.' He paused before continuing more quietly, 'But I think you could.'

'You're jealous?' she asked, surprised.

Sam shoved his hands deep into the pockets of his trousers. 'A little, I guess. But I'd say that I'm more concerned.'

The surprise at his initial revelation was overwhelmed by irritation at his patronising tone. 'Concerned about what? We've been seeing each other for three years. It's not as if he's going to love me and leave me now.' She laughed a little too loudly. 'Are you concerned about the age gap or the difference in our backgrounds? Is it that he hasn't proposed? That his intentions aren't honourable?' She gave him a hard look. 'From where exactly does your concern stem?'

Sam was smart too, and she gave way to his opinion on most matters political, but she wasn't going to allow him to sway her on matters of the heart. For one, he plainly had an ulterior motive in colouring Monty suspect. And two, she had heard that he didn't date often, if at all. He had little, if any, experience with women. As a bachelor of better than average looks and a pleasing personality, he was a frequent target of the administration's secretaries and typists. Hick often teased him about this fact, saying that this phenomenon only highlighted the shortage of eligible bachelors in DC.

Sam shook his head. 'Forget I said anything. But don't you get the feeling that Chapel is just too good to be true?' With nothing more than a fleeting nod he left.

Martini in hand, Iris stood stranded in the middle of the room. She looked at Monty, who was now talking to Missy. His rich, clipped tones lifted her spirits. He turned to her and smiled, waving her over. Sam had no idea what he was talking about, she told herself.

■

Iris was seated next to Monty, who was seated next to Lord Tweedsmuir. Monty was thrilled and had been deep in conversation with the governor-general since they'd been introduced. Iris was thankful that the presence of the famous Scottish author distracted Monty from his customary condemnation of the meal. The president sat at the head of the table as usual and Mrs Roosevelt, who usually took the position opposite her husband, chose on this evening to sit opposite Iris and next to Sam.

She could feel their double-barrelled glare from across the table. It was impossible to dodge. Iris crossed her legs at the ankles and stared at her folded hands in her lap. It was better to accept her punishment, Iris thought. She had unwittingly injured them both.

'John,' the president began, with a wink at Iris. 'McIntosh here is from Scottish stock.'

'Clan McIntosh!' the author said enthusiastically. 'Your family originated in Inverness, you know.'

'No, I didn't know. I don't know much about my ancestors at all, only that when they settled in America they fought against the English in the Revolutionary War. Well, that's what my father told me,' she explained and then added uncomfortably, 'That was probably something I shouldn't have divulged to the King's representative in Canada.'

Her candour provoked laughter from Tweedsmuir and the president.

'Your clan motto is "Touch not the cat bot a glove".' The governor-general adopted a distinctive brogue.

'Pardon?' Iris enquired.

'Don't touch the cat without a glove,' he explained.

'Wise advice, I'd say,' Roosevelt remarked.

'Indeed.' Iris agreed. She glanced at Mrs Roosevelt, who was finishing her soup. No other diner had managed the feat.

'And what do you do here, Miss McIntosh?' Tweedsmuir asked as Fields removed his untouched bowl of chowder.

Before Iris could respond Mrs Roosevelt spoke for the first time since being seated. 'Iris coordinates our women's camps, Lord Tweedsmuir.'

'Tell me more,' he urged, directing the request to Iris. 'It seems like something my wife might be interested in.'

As the entrée arrived, Lady Tweedsmuir told the table of her work with relief agencies in Canada. 'Receiving a handout is one thing, but people need to have a purpose. They need to work,' she finished.

'Exactly,' Iris said. 'And that's what the camps are all about. They're the female equivalent of the CCC. The ladies get a wage of twenty-two dollars fifty a month . . .'

'Less than their male equivalents in the CCC,' Mrs Roosevelt added pleasantly.

'Yes, that's true. But we're working to get that raised,' Iris continued, striving to highlight the successes. 'The women perform a range of tasks from sewing and clerical work to toy-making . . .'

'Because physical labour of the kind the men in the CCC perform isn't deemed fitting for women,' Mrs Roosevelt added. 'The ladies could be doing much more, contributing much more.'

'What Mrs Roosevelt says is correct. Sadly their work is restricted by their gender . . .' Iris explained.

'Or, more accurately, the perceived stereotype of their gender,' Mrs Roosevelt corrected.

Iris nodded dutifully, masking her frustration. She had worked hard to establish the camps and Mrs Roosevelt was belittling her achievements. 'But at least they're kept busy learning new skills, earning a wage and they're contributing to the economy,'

'But in such a paltry way,' the First Lady said to the Tweedsmuirs. 'I had great hopes for these female camps . . .'

Iris heard no more of Mrs Roosevelt's objections, overwhelmed by anger, guilt and embarrassment. She stared blankly at the vase of yellow chrysanthemums in the centre of the table. Iris had never before experienced the First Lady's censure. It was worse than she had imagined.

'And how many women do the camps serve?' Lady Tweedsmuir asked, turning to Iris, who was still contemplating the floral arrangement.

Iris focused on the conversation once more. 'We have ninety camps serving more than five thousand women.'

'Impressive.'

'Not really,' Mrs Roosevelt interrupted civilly. 'Considering that more than three hundred and fifty thousand men are presently enrolled in the Civilian Conservation Corps.'

Iris felt Monty's hand squeeze her knee tightly under the table in a gesture of comfort. Monty knew better than to take on Mrs Roosevelt in one of her moods. Better to stay quiet and allow the tide to ebb.

With that in mind Iris withdrew from the conversation and reluctantly picked up her knife and fork. The veal was pallid. She stared at the dissected kidney that lay at its centre. The sight of the cross-sectioned organ did nothing to improve her humour. Nothing about this night was particularly appetising. Iris raised her eyes from the plate and reached for a dinner roll. Sam was looking directly at her. She could see only tenderness in his eyes.

'Well, you know, the camps have come under fire from Conservatives. They've been called Red Citadels, communist breeding grounds,' Sam explained to the gathering. 'That's probably put a lot of girls off joining the program.'

All eyes at the table turned in Sam's direction. He looked to Iris. 'For the life of me, I don't know how educating women can be called communist.'

'It's just narrow-mindedness, but it's true,' Iris said, renewed. 'We've gotten a lot of criticism from the conservative press. The CCC has as well, to a degree, but the idea of offering women work and education just seems downright un-American to some.'

Everyone laughed. A sign of solidarity. She smiled at Sam. A sign of gratitude. Mrs Roosevelt ate in silence.

'How's the campaign shaping up, Mr President?' Tweedsmuir asked.

'We have it in the bag, John,' Roosevelt replied. He pushed his plate to the side and leaned on the table. 'Fifty-three per cent of Americans believe the depression is over and my approval is up to sixty per cent. Unless something game-changing happens between now and November, we've got it sewn up.'

Iris looked to President Roosevelt, not believing what she'd heard. His reservations from the afternoon had vanished. His arrogance was astounding.

'But that's seven months away, Mr President,' Sam said. 'Anything could happen. The Republicans haven't even chosen a candidate yet.'

'The Women's Committee doesn't feel the same way, Sam,' Mrs Roosevelt said. 'We are taking the Republican threat very seriously.'

'Who've they got, Sam?' the president argued casually. 'Borah, Hiram Johnson, Pinchot. They'll go for Landon, without a doubt.'

'Alf Landon's solid,' Sam responded. 'He's brimming with integrity. He's the Midwest in a button-down suit. Americans like him.'

'But he's dull and his policies are weak,' the president stated.

'That's right,' Monty interjected. 'The boss has proven that Americans like a little charisma in their leader. Anyway, the Republicans could put up Gary Cooper and we'd still win.' He released Iris's knee and began to list the administration's accomplishments on his fingers. 'Since 1932 the national income is up by more than fifty per cent, six million new jobs have been created, unemployment has dropped by more than a third and industrial production has doubled.' He shrugged. 'The election this year is a one-horse race.'

Usually Iris loved to hear Monty arguing a point forcefully, but tonight it only irritated. She folded her arms on the table.

Noticing Sam's unease, Roosevelt spoke light-heartedly. 'Don't worry, Sam. I'll campaign. I'll do the whistlestops. I won't take America for granted.'

They were the right words, Iris thought, but they were spoken without conviction.

'It's nice to hear people talking about something other than the King and Wallis Simpson for a change,' Lady Tweedsmuir said lightly as half-eaten servings of veal and sweet potatoes were removed from the dining room.

'Or the Olympics,' her husband added.

'Where exactly does Canada stand on that issue?' Mrs Roosevelt spoke for the first time since slating Iris earlier.

'Jewish groups and leftist groups called for a boycott, as they did here,' Lord Tweedmuir told her.

'Rightly so,' Mrs Roosevelt said. 'Nazi Germany makes no secret of its racism, anti-Semitism and militarisation. We should have boycotted. The entire world should have boycotted.'

'But politics and sports are two very different things,' Roosevelt interrupted.

'Hitler doesn't agree with you. He said Jewish athletes were not welcome at the Games. Staging the Olympics in Berlin makes a mockery of the Olympic ideals,' Eleanor contended.

'There were thirty-five Jewish athletes in Germany who were excluded from the games because they were deemed non-citizens by the Nazis,' Sam said. 'The Olympics wasn't a sporting event. It was theatre, a way for Hitler to validate the Third Reich in the eyes of the world.'

'Shouldn't we address the colour line in our own backyard before we call for boycotts of an international sporting event?' Monty queried.

'What do you mean?' Sam asked, leaning forward.

'Let's face it, Sam,' Monty said, placing his elbows on the table, 'America hasn't exactly got a terrific track record when it comes to racism and segregation and deeming people non-citizens. The '32 Olympics proved that.'

'You can't compare Hitler's treatment of Jews with America's treatment of Negroes,' Sam responded heatedly.

'Why can't I?' Monty said in a biting tone. 'You can't tell me that Negro athletes are given the same opportunities as white athletes. The Jim Crow laws in the South make it impossible for black athletes to succeed. Jesse Owens, Ralph Metcalfe – in fact all the Negroes on the

Olympic team – come from northern universities that are there to serve white students. They wouldn't have been enrolled if they weren't outstanding athletes.'

'So you think sporting bodies should bow to Hitler's agenda and pull Jews from their teams?' Sam demanded.

'People in glass houses, that's all,' Monty said.

'Sam Stoller and Martin Glickman were pulled from the relay team an hour before the final, and replaced by Owens and Metcalfe.' Sam was red in the face now. 'The US Olympic Committee was heavied by Goebbels, who didn't want his Führer embarrassed by two Jews winning gold medals.'

'America still won the gold and that was the objective, wasn't it?' Monty narrowed his eyes.

'But at the expense of two Jewish athletes!' Sam exclaimed, striking the table with his palm.

Iris had never seen Sam so furious. After his spirited defence of her during Mrs Roosevelt's attack, she wanted to show him a sign of support. But anything she did or said, even a glance, would be a betrayal of Monty. Instead she raised her eyes from the tablecloth and turned to the president. He grinned at her shrewdly.

'Come on, fellas,' Roosevelt intervened. 'Both those lines of argument are only going to make me look bad.'

Sam and Monty laughed uneasily, their shoulders relaxing as they withdrew their elbows from the table, but Iris saw each of them fire a final, silent glance at the other.

'That's true,' Mrs Roosevelt said seriously. 'America's history of race relations is appalling and this administration's refusal to acknowledge the Fascist threat is equally so. When Haile Selassie addressed the League of Nations recently he warned that the West would perish if we don't act now to curb fascism.'

'Indeed,' Lord Tweedsmuir agreed, 'it's a terrible situation. I feel for the Emperor. Mussolini has a lot to answer for. The atrocities committed in Abyssinia by the Italians are beyond belief in this day and age.'

'They're using weapons, poison gas, on civilians. They're breaking all the Geneva agreements and no one is lifting a finger. Those poor people,' Mrs Roosevelt said, obviously distressed.

'Where's your beloved League now?' Roosevelt quipped to his wife.

Eleanor looked at her husband for a moment before speaking. She pushed her chair out slightly from the table and crossed her legs.

'Their hands are tied, wouldn't you agree, Franklin? England and France are too concerned about their own interests in Africa. They're happy to carve the continent up, give Mussolini a share rather than stop him. The League can't act without the backing of England and France. Meanwhile, America is still selling oil, among many other things, to Italy. The world is giving its support to a monster, fuelling his march. Where do you think this is going to lead?'

Unlike the time she'd berated her husband on Campobello Island three years earlier, Mrs Roosevelt's voice was ominously hushed.

The room remained silent until Fields began bringing in dessert.

Iris was pleased it was ice-cream. All she'd eaten during dinner had been a roll. She noticed Lord Tweedsmuir was served a plate of fruit. The president noticed also.

'I can't believe a reed of a man like you is on a diet, John. I don't think I've seen you eat anything all night. And you're forgoing ice-cream for fruit!'

'Not at all, Mr President,' Tweedsmuir replied. 'I've a number of allergies. My wife would call them aversions.'

'You should have let us know. The White House will cater to all requests, no matter how unusual.'

'I did. Well, my secretary did. But don't worry about it, the list was so long that I don't expect your kitchen to accommodate my tastes.'

'The White House kitchen should accommodate all tastes, John,' the president replied, turning to his wife. 'Eleanor, can you explain why last year we spent nearly twenty thousand dollars on a new kitchen, big enough to cater for one thousand people, and Fluffy Nesbitt can't meet the requirements of one person?'

'Fluffy?' Tweedsmuir asked, amused.

She turned to the governor-general. 'My husband's attempt at irony, Lord Tweedsmuir. I'm terribly sorry,' she apologised. 'I'm really quite embarrassed. First my dog bites your prime minister on the hand during breakfast and now this.'

Iris flashed her eyes at Monty. Meggie biting Mackenzie King had embarrassed the First Lady and amused the president, who had subsequently mentioned the incident flippantly at a press conference. The news wound up on the front page. Mrs Roosevelt had been incensed. It impressed Iris she could now speak of the matter with good humour.

'Canadians are going to think we are the most inhospitable nation on earth,' Mrs Roosevelt said. Tweedsmuir laughed heartily. 'There must have been a miscommunication. Can I ask the kitchen to fix you something else? I don't want you to go to bed hungry.'

Tweedsmuir graciously declined the offer.

'Mrs Nesbitt seems incapable of catering to anyone's tastes,' the president said in a grave undertone. He wasn't complaining, merely stating a fact. 'How many times have I asked her to stop serving sweet potato?' His voice rose slightly and he looked at his wife squarely. 'No matter how she tries to dress it up, it's still sweet potato. In the past two weeks I've had them boiled, fried, creamed, mashed, baked, with fruit and with marshmallows.' He paused. 'You don't think I notice, but I do.' The president's speech was delivered as powerfully as if he was speaking before Congress.

'I'll speak with Mrs Nesbitt, Franklin,' Eleanor said.

■

Coffee was served in the Red Room. Monty made a beeline for Lord Tweedsmuir, who was seated on a sofa. Finding herself alone, Iris took the opportunity to talk to Sam, who was standing near a portrait of Rutherford B. Hayes.

'Thank you,' Iris said. 'Thank you for your help tonight.'

He smiled wanly and sipped his coffee. 'Any time.'

'Is anything wrong?' she asked.

'It's the president,' he said. They turned towards Roosevelt, who was seated in his wheelchair on the other side of the room, next to Lady Tweedsmuir.

'During dinner he was extremely . . .' Iris couldn't find the right word.

'Cocky?' Sam suggested immediately.

She nodded.

'I suppose he's gotta be,' Sam reflected. 'He is the president, after all. If he's going to make us and the rest of America believe he will win, then he's got to believe it himself.'

'Then tonight was all an act?' she asked.

Sam nodded. '"We have nothing to fear but fear itself." It was just a speech, words on a piece of paper. He didn't know if he could save America when he was elected, but he had to make America believe he could. Becoming president is all about having bigger balls than the other guy.'

Amused at his turn of phrase, Iris laughed.

Sam smiled. 'You'd never believe I was a writer, would you?'

'You were pretty cocky yourself tonight,' Iris said after a moment.

He nodded, his grin fading.

'Proving you had bigger balls that Monty Chapel?'

'Childish?' he asked.

'Sweet.'

'Flattered?'

Iris nodded. They stared at each other for only a few seconds but the gaze was long enough to prompt Sam to clear his throat and brush his hand over his head.

'I'll tell you who's got the biggest balls in Washington,' he said, his composure recovered.

'Who?' Iris asked.

'Henrietta Nesbitt,' he answered. 'Armed with nothing more than a sweet potato that woman has managed to bring a president to his knees!'

■

'You were under attack tonight,' Monty said as he lay next to Iris.

'So were you,' she responded.

Monty rolled over and stubbed out his cigarette in an ashtray on the bedside table, then he rolled back and nestled his head on Iris's shoulder. He placed his palm on her stomach. She sighed.

'What's wrong?' he asked.

She shook her head. 'Nothing.'

He gently stroked the silk of Iris's slip with his thumb.

'Jacobson's finally got under your skin, hasn't he?' Monty asked.

Iris supposed that Sam did have something to do with her restless dissatisfied mood. It was difficult to hide anything from Monty. His perception and mind were razor-sharp. There was an attraction between her and Sam, and it was growing. But her feelings towards Monty had not lessened even a fraction. Their relationship had grown and evolved just as Monty had predicted. It was now so integral to her psyche and her heart that she could not imagine being without it.

'What are you talking about?' she asked, affecting carelessness.

'He's been all over you like a bad rash since you came to DC,' Monty observed. 'And you have feelings for him.'

'He's a friend, Monty, that's all,' she insisted. Then, changing the subject, she said, 'I made a fool of myself tonight. I should have been more prepared.'

Monty drew a slow, gentle line from her forehead to her chin with his finger. 'No one is ever prepared for an attack like that. Don't worry about it, kiddo. Apart from the Tweedsmuirs, everyone sitting at that table has come under attack at some time or other. Consider it an initiation.' He gently kissed her forehead and then her lips.

'The problem is that I've taken the camps just about as far as they can go,' she explained. 'They *are* seen as red and now, with the economy improving, they're not considered an option by many women. What's more, Mrs Roosevelt is out of town so much . . . she has so many other duties and obligations that she has to attend to.'

Monty kissed her eyelids and then each cheek.

'I was thinking . . .' she went on hesitantly. 'I was thinking about trying something different.'

'Like what?' Monty asked as he stroked the length of her arm with his fingertips.

'Policy,' she declared.

Monty was silent, considering.

'You're not laughing,' she said hopefully.

'Why would I?' he responded. 'It's entirely feasible. You're intelligent and tenacious enough, but . . .'

'But?'

'But policy isn't fly-by-the-seat-of-your-pants stuff. It's advising the president on matters that affect an entire nation. You'd need to go back to school. You need another degree. Economics or law or political science.'

She groaned. 'That'll take years.'

'It probably will,' he responded kindly. 'But you'll only be thirty, at the most, when you graduate.'

She sat up and pushed Monty onto his back, straddling him. 'I'm hungry, Monty,' she said. 'Really hungry.'

He traced the outline of her mouth with his fingertip. 'With that mouth you could devour all of Washington and most of the East Coast.'

'That's not what I mean,' she said, parting her lips.

'I know,' he replied as she drew his finger into her mouth.

29
WASHINGTON DC
July 1936

'Do you own a whisk?' Monty enquired from the doorway of her office.

Iris put down her pen and looked at him quizzically.

'A utensil with which to beat eggs?' he explained sardonically.

'I know what a whisk does, but I don't own one.'

'I'm coming over tonight. I'll show you how to make cheese soufflé.'

'What's the matter?'

'I'll explain tonight. I'll bring everything.'

That evening Iris sat on a stool in the corner of her kitchen, mesmerised as she watched Monty crack four eggs, using one hand, into a copper bowl. He was at his most graceful in the kitchen, she thought. He moved around the space executing an elegant ballet. He handed her the bowl and whisk. He spun towards the oven, opened the door and removed the pots and pans Iris stored in there and placed them on the stove top. He turned the oven on and then moved one step to the right and began grating a large wedge of gruyere.

'Firm peaks, kiddo,' he instructed when she stopped to sip her wine. 'Firm peaks.'

Iris continued to whisk the egg whites vigorously.

'It's a good thing you moved to a bigger apartment,' he commented seriously as he scraped the cheese from the chopping board into a saucepan on the stove. 'I could never have made soufflé in the kitchen at the snug.'

He stirred the contents of the saucepan energetically with a wooden spoon then folded the eggwhites in.

Finally he tipped the contents of the saucepan into a dish and ran his finger deftly along the inside of the rim.

'Why are you doing that?'

'It'll give the soufflé a top-hat appearance.'

Iris had no idea what he was talking about, but she always enjoyed Monty's imagery.

'It should be ready in about twenty minutes,' he said, once he'd put the dish in the oven. 'Now, where's my wine?'

Iris scanned the kitchen. Monty was a graceful cook, but he certainly wasn't a clean one. Cups, jugs, knives and bowls littered the bench and table. It would be her job to clean up after dinner.

When Monty had found his wine, Iris said, 'So what did you want to talk about?'

They moved into Iris's living room and sat on the sofa.

'Mrs R. She's got the entire team in an uproar.'

'But she's on Campobello,' Iris said as she shifted the newspapers, book and files on her coffee table to make room for their glasses.

'She's fired off a memo to the president, Stanley High, Steve Early, Charlie Michelson, Jim Farley, me, everyone . . . About our inaction in running the campaign.' He ran a hand through his hair. 'She sent a list of eight points outlining what should be done. She's the First Lady! Farley and Wallace are calling for her head.' Monty took the memo from his pocket and handed it to Iris.

She read it carefully. 'Well, she's got a point.' Iris had followed the campaign avidly and groaned in frustration whenever she read an article about Landon in the newspaper or heard him on the radio. His support was growing just by the mere fact that the president's camp remained silent. People would vote for the most visible man. For just how long could the Democrats rest on their laurels?

She shrugged. 'Not much has been going on and Landon's got a big lead in the polls,' she noted. 'He's got radio spots, hired publicists . . . Mrs Roosevelt's up on Campobello mobilising the Women's Committee and doing a hell of a job, but all her work will amount to nothing unless the president moves into top gear.'

'But sending a memo to Farley, the chairman of the Democratic National Committee and postmaster-general, telling him what to do?' Monty shook his head. 'I think she's finally gone too far.'

'She's a concerned voter,' Iris argued. 'The president has refused to take Landon seriously from the outset. He's swanning around on a yacht while Landon's camp is chasing down votes. Jim Farley tries to please the president too much. There's just no one around who the president will listen to any more.'

Monty leaned forward and rubbed his forehead. 'We need Howe.'

'Well, yeah,' she agreed. 'You told me he supplied all of the political strategy in '32.'

Monty nodded. Iris rubbed his knee and studied the memo for a minute or two before going on.

'You know,' she said slowly, 'she may be no Louis Howe, but isn't this memo a little like a political strategy?'

Monty grabbed the document from her hands and examined it again.

'When you look past all the barbs there's some really fresh ideas in there,' Iris pointed out. 'You boys just can't see them because you've been scolded.'

'I suppose it's a starting point,' Monty conceded, leaning over and offering her a kiss. 'You have some head on your shoulders. Have you given any more thought to going back to school?'

'Some,' she answered, absently straightening the magazines on her coffee table.

She had actually given it a great deal of thought and had sent letters to the Dean of Enrolments at the law schools of George Washington University, Georgetown University and Howard University. Sam had helped her pen the applications. Seeking the opinion of a writer, she had showed him a draft. Sam had read it slowly a number of times before saying, 'It's beautiful, Iris. It's beautiful writing but I don't think it's going to get you a spot at a fiercely competitive law school.'

'Why?' she demanded, eyes wide. 'Why would you say that? Do you think it's just a mad dream?'

He laughed. 'No, it's a wonderful dream but the letter is too heartfelt,' he explained. 'You need to consider your audience. You're not writing this letter to Mrs Roosevelt. You're writing a letter to lawyers, all of whom are male. You need to come across as more aggressive, more masculine, I suppose.'

She had nodded thoughtfully then asked him for assistance. They had spent a week's worth of lunchbreaks together at the deli by Dupont Circle drafting and then redrafting the letters until they were both happy. Iris was sad when the week was over and the letters were in the post.

But Iris couldn't tell Monty of the headway she'd made in her plans. He would be hurt that she hadn't sought his assistance. But if she had, he would have waved his magic wand and had her enrolled at Columbia the following day, tuition paid. Monty's was the kind of assistance she could not accept.

Monty lifted her chin and looked at her seriously. 'You should consider it some more,' he instructed as he stood and threw the memo on the table. He bent and kissed her on the lips. 'The soufflé will be ready,' he added as he left the room.

Within minutes he had reappeared with the dish and two forks. He placed them on the coffee table in front of Iris. Admiring the puffed, golden crown rising slightly above the dish's rim, Iris understood exactly what Monty had meant by a top-hat appearance.

3 0
HYDE PARK, NEW YORK
May 1962

Lord Tweedsmuir had the longest list of dislikes I can recall seeing. Of course, a lot of the guests at the White House had the odd thing their stomachs wouldn't tolerate, but Lord Tweedsmuir turned his nose up at soup, fish, smoked meats, pork, veal, turnips, sweet potatoes, sprouts, cabbage, tomatoes, onions, parsnips, carrots, celery, salad, creamy sweets, ice-cream and sauces. That was just downright fussy, I said. Anyway, his special diet didn't help him any. He died not long after that dinner, in 1940.

There were times, definitely, when I felt undermined by the press and the public. Both seemed to take special delight in ridiculing me. On one occasion the president's fussiness made headlines. It read: FDR DEMANDS NEW DEAL — REFUSES SPINACH — CRISIS STRIKES THE WHITE HOUSE. Those reporters thought they were very clever indeed. But they didn't know how that headline fuelled a raft of hate mail addressed to me by the American public. It was very distressing.

What people didn't know was that I had to deal with bigger issues than the president's likes and dislikes. It was my responsibility to make sure he stayed healthy. His blood pressure was a huge problem and it was up to me to make sure it stayed under control. That was difficult when the president refused most vegetables apart from potatoes. A lot of the time I felt my efforts went unappreciated by the president. Terse notes were sent from the Oval Office to the kitchen about the beans being overcooked or the spinach being watery. I stood my ground in the face of a lot of criticism. Mrs Roosevelt always supported me, of course.

I've come to realise now that the president was using food as an outlet for the incredible weight of responsibility he must have carried on those broad shoulders of his. Before any election campaign he became particularly pernickety and bad-tempered. He was bound to that wheelchair and unable to relieve the tension in any other way than to take it out on me. I took it all on the chin. I saw it as my job, my duty even, to accept the knocks. I was an invisible yet vital cog in the wheels of government.

The election in 1936 ended in a landslide win for the government. The president won more than sixty per cent of the popular vote. The only states he lost were Maine and Vermont. It was the biggest win in presidential history. Alfred M. Landon didn't stand a chance; America just adored the Roosevelts. The Roosevelts were at Hyde Park when the results came in. But when they drove back to Washington the next morning they were welcomed by three hundred thousand cheering people. I had another reason to be thrilled that the president was re-elected. Mrs Roosevelt had promised me that if she and her husband were to stay in the White House for another four years, I'd finally be able to buy new drapes for the East Room.

THE SECOND TERM
1937–1941

Hail to the Chief

31
WASHINGTON DC
February 1937

'Where are you going?' Iris muttered sleepily into her pillow. It was six thirty on Friday morning. Monty sat on the side of the bed tying his shoelaces.

'Go back to sleep, kiddo.' He leaned over and kissed her on the forehead. 'I've been called in.'

'Why?' Iris sat up blearily, curious to know what brand of catastrophe had occurred overnight.

'Not sure. Something to do with the Supreme Court. Missy didn't say too much over the phone.'

'Oh, okay.' She laid back down and closed her eyes.

'I'm sorry about today,' Monty whispered. 'We'll do it soon, I promise.'

They had planned to take a long weekend and drive to Baltimore. Even though the city had been her original destination when she left Chicago four years earlier, she had not returned since arriving in Washington. After starting work at the White House, it just seemed pointless to go back. Monty had pestered her, though. He wanted to get away from Washington for a weekend and Baltimore seemed the perfect destination. He had become increasingly entrenched in the capital and reluctantly took a twelve-month sabbatical from his position at Columbia, although they both knew it would be longer. The president had a knack of making everyone feel indispensible.

Iris couldn't remember very much about Baltimore, but Monty had informed her it was a city worth visiting and had spoken at length about the architecture and history of her home town. However, she was reluctant for Monty to see where she had come from, he who had inherited the family townhouse on Manhattan's Upper East Side.

She did recall one place her family had lived for a time, a two-room apartment on 34th Street in Hampton. Her father had rented it optimistically when he'd landed an occasional shift at the nearby mill.

It was dark and damp, she remembered, and the stench of mildew overwhelmed all other smells, even the yeasty odour seeping from her father's still. Her mother complained continually about the noise, the mould, the lack of light and space. Her father would smile and twirl her around, saying she was the most beautiful girl in America.

When her mother had discovered mould on her debutante gown, the scream that emanated from the bedroom terrified her twelve-year-old daughter.

Iris found her mother on the floor, slumped over the dress which lay on her lap. She cried for hours. She liked to tell Iris about her debutante ball. She'd take the white silk dress from the wardrobe and hold it high for Iris to admire. Sometimes she'd place around her daughter's neck her own mother's string of pearls that she'd worn that evening. Iris remembered the name of her escort, Harrison Dewey III.

When her father returned that evening he was tipsy. Iris was heartened that he was not drunk. He attempted to lift his wife from the floor and give her a twirl, but she stayed limp in his arms. When she went to the bedroom and closed the door he whispered, 'What upset her today?'

'She found mould on her debutante gown.'

He nodded as if he understood.

The next day her mother burnt the dress in a trash can in the alley below their apartment. Iris watched her from the window and couldn't remember anyone looking as sad as she did at that moment. Iris never saw the pearls again, either.

■

Iris could only describe the following week at the White House as tense. The president and the Brains Trust were holed up attempting to deal with the fallout of the Judicial Reorganization Bill the president had read on Capitol Hill the Friday before. The staffers scurried from office to office discussing the controversy in hushed tones. She had only seen Monty once since he left her in bed at the Mayflower. That afternoon Iris was roused from her work by a soft tap on her office door. Sam Jacobson stood in the doorway.

'Hi,' he said. 'Can I come in?'

Iris smiled and waved him in, gestering him to sit. She was pleased he'd dropped by. While she'd seen Sam around from time to time, she'd not spoken to him properly since their covert meetings at the Dupont

Circle deli many months before. Occasionally he'd drop by and ask her
if she'd had any replies to the applications they had worked on together.
They'd chat for a couple of minutes before Iris would excuse herself,
citing a meeting, telephone call or deadline. Since July she had reflected
often on her feelings towards the long-limbed reporter who now sat
across the desk from her. Iris had only come to one conclusion – it was
best to keep her distance.

'Any news?' he asked.

'Refusals from Georgetown and Howard,' she said glumly. 'But
I've been placed on a second-round list at George Washington, so not
all hope is lost.'

'That's great, really great,' he said. 'When will you know?'

Iris shrugged. 'Probably not for a while. It's really quite maddening.
I want to make something happen but I can't. It's out of my control.
I'm not sure what I'll do if I don't get a place . . . I must check my
mail fifty times a day.'

'You could see if Mrs Roosevelt has any pull over there. See if they
can't move you up the list,' Sam suggested.

'Do you think that would be ethical?' Iris said, leaning closer across
her desk. It was a course she had contemplated but she had dismissed
the idea, telling herself that it smacked of cronyism. Sam, however,
made it sound like this was the obvious step to take.

'I can't see any harm in it,' he said. 'There'd be stack of kids there
who only got through the door because of money and connections. Mrs
Roosevelt would just allow you to compete on a level playing field.'

Iris nodded and thought about how she could present the idea to
the First Lady. 'I'll think it over,' she said.

Sam smiled but didn't speak, neither did he make a move to leave.
Iris reordered the pens and papers on her desk and then noticed the
copy of the *Washington Post* that lay there.

'I read your article,' Iris began. 'I liked it.'

'I'd thought you might throw something at me when I came to
the door.'

Iris looked at him quizzically.

'You do realise you worship Roosevelt, don't you?'

She raised an eyebrow, and then unfolded the newspaper. She
scanned the front-page story rapidly then quoted aloud, "'The independence of the judiciary, this safeguard against oppression by government,
is the most precious possession of man. Because we have long had it,

we have come to take it for granted. No American is able to conceive a court as being anything different. He cannot conceive a court as being what courts are in Russia, Germany and Italy, mere agencies of the government. The Supreme Court is the custodian of the constitution until changed by the people." That's my favourite part. So eloquent, so . . . passionate.'

'I'm better in print than I am in person,' Sam said. He stared at his feet.

'I wouldn't say that.' Her honeyed tone prompted Sam to raise his head and look at her.

Iris wasn't sure why she was flirting. Monty's unavailability during the past week meant she had been living for the first time in many years like a single woman. Was it loneliness, she wondered, or was she enjoying the glimpse of freedom Monty's absence offered?

Sam looked at her seriously. 'How's Chapel faring through all this?' he asked.

'I'm not entirely sure,' she began, noting her own feelings of disappointment at the change of subject. 'I know he's been working day and night, furious with whoever it was that came up with the expression "court-packing".' She smiled at Sam's laughter then continued more solemnly, 'But he's upset, same as everyone.'

'The president has run some pretty risky plays in the past, but this one . . . this one takes the cake. It's just so . . . uncharacteristic, I suppose,' Sam said.

'After the election he thinks he's invincible,' Iris offered.

'Turns out he's not,' Sam replied curtly. 'Everyone – the press, Congress, cabinet – they've all come out against this, guns blazing. But he seems determined to see it through. The President of the United States can't afford a fatal flaw.'

'Pride?' she queried.

He nodded.

'There are worse flaws,' she said. The hurt in her voice was difficult to conceal.

'Has your devotion suffered a hit?' Sam enquired gently.

Iris really hadn't thought about it in terms of herself. What the president had done was underhanded. Attempting to stack the Supreme Court with judges sympathetic to New Deal legislaton was devious.

She shrugged. 'I don't think so. Ultimately what he's trying to achieve is commendable.'

'How do you figure that?' Sam said.

'Some of the New Deal legislation has been thrown out by the Supreme Court and they're still deliberating on other bills. The president just wants what's best for the country. There are a few New Deal policies that are under threat of collapsing.'

'Maybe he shouldn't have rushed the legislation in the first place. He's a lawyer,' Sam argued. 'He should have made sure the drafts were watertight before he took them to the floor.'

'My god, Sam!' she gasped. 'Can't you remember the winter of '32 and '33, when people were dying? Without homes, jobs . . . He rushed bills through to turn the economy around fast. He didn't have the luxury of shoring up drafts.'

'New Deal policies were sloppy – and do you know who's behind the current bill?' Sam fired back. Iris didn't respond. 'Cummings and Reed.'

Iris had heard Monty refer to the attorney-general and the solicitor-general as the Laurel and Hardy of the legal world. He butted heads with them constantly. Neither of them had any experience in constitutional law, she had learned, which was exactly what the Judicial Reorganization Bill set about to alter.

She stood and walked around the desk, trying to temper her reaction. Sam's eyes went to her red skirt. 'I agree,' she said. 'He shouldn't have acted in secret, but don't start tearing apart what he's done for people who were suffering. President Roosevelt adds up to more than this one blunder.' Her face was flushed with emotion.

Sam stood and took her hands in his. His expression was pained. 'I'm sorry,' he said hurriedly. 'I'm so sorry.'

'No, I'm sorry. I overreacted.' Iris sighed. 'The president was careless in his methods, I agree. But I sympathise with his motivation.'

Sam still held her fingertips. Iris looked down at their hands. Agitation coloured her words. 'Why do I want to kiss you right now?' she asked, tears gathering in her eyes.

'Sexual tension, I guess.' Sam released her fingers.

'I guess,' Iris echoed as Sam left the room.

■

Mrs Roosevelt always kept her door open. Tommy told her to keep it closed, that she'd get more work done that way, but Mrs Roosevelt refused. She said she liked to witness the daily hustle and bustle and she enjoyed it when people dropped in for a chat.

Iris knew Mrs Roosevelt was in town. Since her run-in with Sam more than a week before, Iris had wanted to speak with her. However, it seemed that she was constantly out, usually campaigning or championing a cause in some place other than Washington. Also, it was difficult for the president to travel so the First Lady took over many of his obligations as well.

She approached Mrs Roosevelt's suite but the door to her office was closed. Iris had telephoned Tommy to check she'd be in so it was strange that her door was shut. Iris had never seen it so. Even when the First Lady was out of town the door was open.

Iris knocked tentatively. No sound was forthcoming. She knocked once more.

'Come in,' she heard Mrs Roosevelt's muffled voice call from the other side of the door.

Iris entered. Mrs Roosevelt stood at the window looking out. She held Meggie in her arms, stroking the aging terrier's neck softly. When she turned, Iris could see the First Lady had been crying.

'What can I do for you, dear?' she said. 'It seems like weeks since we've talked.'

'Are you alright, Mrs Roosevelt? Is this a bad time?' Iris asked.

'Of course not. I'm just being silly, letting my emotions get the better of me.'

She gestured to the sofa and Iris sat. The First Lady joined her after placing Meggie on the floor. The Scottie curled up next to Major, who was stretched out on the rug.

'I'm going to miss those two,' Mrs Roosevelt said, indicating the animals lying in front of her.

'Are they going somewhere?'

'Little Meggie's been causing trouble again,' the First Lady explained. 'She bit a child in Rock Creek Cemetery when I was walking them last week.'

'I didn't hear,' Iris said, surprised.

'We think it's best if Meggie goes to a family that has the time to enjoy her.'

'And Major?' Iris gazed at the German shepherd.

'I can't separate them. They've been companions since Albany.' She paused and smiled at the memory. 'Mrs Nesbitt has helped me find a family in Hyde Park that is keen to take them on.'

Meggie and Major were Mrs Roosevelt's companions, Iris thought. It would be heartbreaking for the First Lady to say goodbye. But Meggie had grown increasingly hostile to strangers. Both dogs were fiercely devoted to their mistress. Major, a former police dog, had the training to control his behaviour. Meggie, sadly, did not.

'I'm sorry,' Iris said. 'But they'll probably be happier with a family in the country.'

'Never mind me,' the First Lady said briskly. 'What did you want to see me about?'

Iris began hesitantly. 'I'm not sure whether I should speak to you or the president about this.' Mrs Roosevelt nodded encouragingly. 'But I think . . . well, I've been thinking about going back to school.'

'How interesting,' Mrs Roosevelt said enthusiastically. 'To study . . . ?'

'Law.' Iris scrutinised her employer's face for any trace of scepticism. 'Constitutional law.'

'Very interesting,' Mrs Roosevelt repeated thoughtfully. 'You know it's not easy for a female lawyer, especially in Washington. The bar is a boy's club, one of the oldest and most impenetrable in the country. You'll have to work ten times harder to be taken seriously,' she warned. 'But I think it's a very good idea, Iris. You can make up for my husband's shortcomings. He was never a very good lawyer, you know. He never had a passion for it.'

Iris smiled, pleased to have Mrs Roosevelt's approval. She started to outline her efforts to achieve her goal, hoping the First Lady would offer assistance before she was forced to ask.

'I was wondering . . .' Iris started nervously.

'I'll do everything I can to help you,' Eleanor declared. 'I'll contact the Dean of George Washington University's law school this afternoon. All going well, we can cut back your hours here so you'll have more time to study. It will be hard work, but I know you can do it, Iris.'

'Thank you, Mrs Roosevelt,' Iris said. 'You don't know how much I appreciate your help.'

'I'll merely open a door,' the First Lady said with a dismissive wave. 'It will be your own academic merit and ambition that will see you through and out the other side.'

Iris nodded, close to bursting into tears of joy. Eleanor kissed her gently on the forehead.

'What about children, Iris? Can you see yourself as a mother?' Mrs Roosevelt's ability to change the course of a conversation still managed to amaze Iris.

Iris had briefly considered the subject after Mrs Roosevelt had advised her to obtain a diaphragm, but she really hadn't thought of children since.

'I'm not being condescending when I say this, dear, but most women will want a child at some point in their lives. Even if you don't think so now.'

Iris thought of Monty. It was difficult, impossible, for her to envisage him as a father. They had never discussed the topic of marriage or children.

'How old are you now? Twenty-seven?' Iris nodded. 'And you've been with Monty for four years?'

'Yes, that's right,' Iris replied.

Mrs Roosevelt nodded, sympathetically Iris thought, before continuing. 'It's a difficult balancing act – career versus motherhood – but it can be done. One doesn't need to win out over the other.'

'I'll give it some thought, Mrs Roosevelt,' Iris said before departing.

Iris had only made her way a few feet along the corridor when she stopped and leaned her back against the wall. Her chest surged and her hands went to her mouth, muffling a cry of happiness.

■

By the next morning Iris's place at George Washington University was secured. She telephoned Sam at his office. He wasn't at his desk. An hour later she tried again and there was still no answer. Iris called reception. Sam was in Philadelphia. He wouldn't be back until late. Iris left her desk and made her way to the West Wing to find Monty.

That evening Monty took her to Montmartre to celebrate. While waiting for their appetisers and sipping champagne, Monty began planning a further celebration, a weekend in New York. He'd been invited to the opening night of Rodgers and Hart's new musical *Babes in Arms*. Furthermore, he'd be killing two birds with one stone, he explained. Mrs Roosevelt had asked him to attend an exhibition called *An Art Commentary on Lynching*.

'Dreary, I know,' Monty groaned. 'But you know the situation with FDR and the South. It would be impolitic for her to attend, but she feels obligated to the NAACP.'

Iris did know the situation. During the lead-up to the election Mrs Roosevelt had been silenced. Her denunciation of lynching in the southern states, her support of the National Association for the Advancement of Coloured People and her advocacy of the Costigan-Wagner Bill, the anti-lynching bill, were to stop, the president and his advisers had ordered. Roosevelt needed the South to win. Although the muzzle had now been removed and the bill defeated, she thought it would be a flagrantly churlish move to attend the exhibition.

Iris nodded distractedly as she sipped her drink, wondering when she would have the opportunity to tell Sam her news.

She was slightly drunk by the time they departed the restaurant. As they walked home arm in arm, thoughts of Sam had drifted from Iris's mind. They discussed the weekend in Manhattan and contemplated a future in which Iris was a lawyer.

'I still can't believe it, Monty. Can you? Can you believe I'm going to be a lawyer?' she asked in her state of mild inebriation.

'Of course I can, kiddo,' he replied, smiling and placing an arm around her waist. 'I can believe anything of you.'

Iris began laughing at the implausibility of it all as they rounded the corner onto 30th Street. Her thoughts and mood hastily shifted gear when she saw Sam Jacobson sitting on the front stoop.

'Sam!' Iris exclaimed, trying to conceal a rush of excitement.

'Jacobson.' Monty nodded. 'What brings you here?'

'I was hoping to speak to Iris about something.' He stood and removed his hat. 'About a story idea I had.'

Iris could tell he was lying.

'Well, it's a little late, pal,' Monty said.

Iris had never heard Monty call anyone 'pal' before.

'Yeah, I'm sorry about that. This idea just struck me and I came over . . .'

Iris remained silent, her heart pounding, her mind still turning over.

'You've been out somewhere?' Sam asked pleasantly.

'Yes, we were celebrating,' Monty replied. 'Iris got in to law school.'

Iris looked at the reporter guiltily. The smile disappeared from Sam's face. He clutched the brim of his hat tight between his fingers. She had wanted to tell Sam the news herself, had wanted him to know how she appreciated his help and encouragement and how she missed their shared lunchbreaks at the deli. She wished she could tell him that she had tried to telephone him, that she had wanted him to be the first to know.

'Really?' he said slowly. 'That's some news. Congratulations.' He returned his hat to his head and made his way to the bottom of the stoop. 'I should be going. It's late.'

Before she was able to utter a word, Sam had reached the bottom step and was walking hurriedly down the hill towards M Street.

'I wonder what he really wanted,' Monty said suspiciously as they entered her apartment.

'What do you mean? I'm sure it's just as he said: he had an idea that he wanted to run by me.' Iris was certain that was not the case, though, and she was thrilled by his unexpected appearance. But if she loved Monty, which she did, why did she want Sam? Obviously the two men possessed very different qualities. Was it a case of her wanting too much, perhaps?

'Does he do that often? Run story ideas past you?'

'Occasionally,' Iris lied.

'He asks some pretty inane questions for a journalist,' Monty scoffed. '"You've been out somewhere?"' he mimicked.

'He's better in print than he is in person,' Iris replied mildly.

She had no idea where her attraction to Sam Jacobson had sprung from. It made no sense to her at all. Monty was more handsome, more charming, more agreeable, more erudite, more confident, more worldly, more everything. Yet she quivered at the thought of Sam's fingertips touching her own.

Monty settled down on the sofa and loosened his tie. Iris removed her shoes and joined him, burrowing into his side with a sigh.

'Thank you for tonight,' she said. 'It was fantastic.' She kissed him on the lips but he didn't react. 'What's wrong?'

'You know you can tell me if there's something going on between you and Jacobson,' he said reasonably. 'It's clear that he has feelings for you. You know me well enough to know I'm not going to erupt into a jealous rage. This could be how our relationship is evolving.'

His observation was sobering and she sat up straight and turned to face him. 'There's nothing going on,' she responded. 'I love *you*, Monty.'

Iris wasn't ready to evolve away from her relationship with Montgomery Chapel just yet.

3 2
HYDE PARK, NEW YORK
May 1962

I knew right from the start that Iris McIntosh was a smart young thing and so pleasant too. She always had time for a chat and a cup of coffee. Mrs Roosevelt helped her get into law school, I think. They were very close. Mrs Roosevelt saw her as a kind of proxy daughter, I guess. She was critical in making Iris into the woman she was to become.

But it was funny how Mrs Roosevelt helped Iris McIntosh more than she helped any of her own children. You know, when James was summoned to DC by his father when Mr Howe died, Mrs Roosevelt was dead against it. Even though it was a big boost to his career – James was only working in the insurance business in Boston – she argued that he was far too inexperienced to take on Mr Howe's role. Well, she was proved right in the end. James ended up in the Mayo Clinic with a perforated ulcer! He resigned after that and moved to California. The president just wanted to have his eldest son close by, I guess. Losing Mr Howe and Gus in the same year must have been hard.

It was the same with the other children. The president arranged jobs for them all over the country. Elliott went west and ended up working for William Randolph Hearst. Anna and her second husband, John Boettiger the reporter, moved to Seattle where they both worked for Hearst too. You can imagine how Mrs Roosevelt felt about that arrangement. The youngest sons, Franklin Jr and John, never really were touched by presidential influence. Both were still in school when their father became president. Perhaps being away from the White House was a good thing for them.

But despite the helping hand those children got from their father they received no special favours during World War II. All four of the boys served and were decorated.

Iris didn't ask for any favours and she was devoted to the president and Mrs Roosevelt. During those months when the president was so preoccupied with his ideas for the Supreme Court, when his appetite was at its most pernickety, she never said a harsh word about his decisions. I only ever heard her praise both of them.

33
NEW YORK CITY, NEW YORK
April 1937

Iris walked the perimeter of the gallery alongside Monty taking in the photographs, paintings and sketches. They were shocking, many of them macabre. The tenor of the evening was a stark contrast to the previous one: the opening of a Broadway musical followed by supper at the Russian Tea Room. Monty had bought her a Coco Chanel dress that he presented to her on their arrival at his apartment. She had never seen anything so lovely – black silk embroidered with glass beads and a matching cape. The evening was perfect. Now she was examining pictures of Negroes beaten, hanging limply from trees or lying mangled on the ground as white men, women and children stood proudly over their lifeless bodies. Monty whispered into her ear, 'From the sublime to the ridiculous.'

Iris nodded. 'It's awful.'

'Monty, Iris!'

They turned.

Hick was coming towards them – a much stouter version of her former self, though Iris noticed she still wore her customary red lipstick and high-heeled shoes. Iris's heart began to pound when she saw Sam Jacobson following in her wake.

'I didn't know you two were going to be here,' Hick said.

'Mrs Roosevelt asked us to come on her behalf,' Monty explained.

'I haven't spoken to Eleanor in a few weeks,' Hick said. 'I haven't been in DC for a while.' She gestured to her companion. 'Sam here's in town on a farewell tour. He's going to Spain in a couple of days to cover the war.'

'Really?' Iris said, an eyebrow raised. She hadn't seen Sam for weeks. He had taken an assignment in California soon after that night on her stoop. Iris had been disappointed when she was told the news by another journalist; he hadn't even bothered to tell her himself. The same distress washed over her now. 'How long has this been on the agenda?'

'Not long. Hick gave me the idea and I thought it might be good to get away for a while.' The look he gave Iris was evasive, aloof even.

'I wanted to go myself,' Hick declared. 'But Eleanor talked me out of it. She said I'd get myself blown to smithereens.'

'And you're covering the exhibition too?' Monty asked, diverting attention away from Hick's admission.

'I thought I might as well while I was in town.'

'Why don't we go and get a drink?' Hick suggested. 'There's a bar around the corner where all the reporters go. You've got all you need here, Sam?'

Sam nodded and placed his notebook and pencil in his coat pocket.

Within half an hour of arriving at the bar, Hick was well on her way to being drunk. She consumed her whiskey sours at three times the speed of the others. 'You know Frank stopped her going to that . . .' She waved her arm above her head, in search of a word. Her friends understood that she meant the exhibition. 'And the Costigan-Wagner Bill was her baby.'

'That's politics I'm afraid, Hick. You know the thinking is narrower in the South. The boss didn't have a choice if he wanted their votes,' Monty said.

'She was silenced, gagged, during the campaign. Every speech she gave had to get the State Department's seal of approval, and not just on domestic issues either.' Her voice was becoming louder. She drained her glass and turned, seeking out the waitress.

'She was corresponding with a German woman in London, a Jewish refugee,' Hick went on after ordering another drink. 'The woman was trying to get the president to notice what's going on in Germany. She appealed to Eleanor. Then the State Department started censoring her mail. They told her that diplomatic affairs should be left to the experts.'

Iris, Monty and Sam knew that Hick was divulging more than she should. 'Roosevelt was counting on the German and Catholic vote as well,' Monty said calmly. 'It's screwed up, but that's what elections are about – courting favour, wooing voters.'

Hick turned to Sam. 'What've you got to say?' she demanded aggressively. 'You're a Jew.'

'What can I say?' he responded evenly. 'I despise Hitler and every-thing he's doing. But until the world takes notice he's going to go right on doing it. President Roosevelt's silence sends Hitler the message that he has no real opponent. The president needs to act.'

Iris looked at Monty to see whether he was going to defend the administration. But Sam's measured analysis was accurate. Monty had no rebuttal.

'Did you read McLaughlin's article?' Hick enquired. In her piece in the *New York Times Magazine*, Kathleen McLaughlin had called the First Lady both an asset and a liability in the election.

'Writing that Eleanor had a private post office at FDR's bedside, a basket that she filled with notes intended to influence him – what bullshit!' Hick declared. 'Anyway, I don't even know why I'm talking about this. I'm seeing someone else now, in San Francisco.'

Hick's three companions looked at each other uncomfortably.

'It's all over between us,' she went on. 'She's always too busy.'

'Is that why you're going to Spain, to raise a voice against fascism?' Iris asked Sam.

'Ella,' Hick was saying. 'We used to live together and then she eloped. That was the *first* time my heart was broken.'

'It's partly why,' Sam said in answer to Iris's question. 'I need some air.' He stood and left the bar.

Iris watched Sam's retreat from the table. He was broader, she noticed. He had gained some weight but it was appealing. And his olive complexion had become attractively bronzed during his time on the West Coast.

Monty was watching Hick, who was swaying in her chair now, her eyes half closed, a cigarette burned down to a butt between her fingers.

'I think she needs air, too,' Monty said. 'I'll take her out the back. I don't want her seen by any old colleagues. Will you be all right here?'

'Of course, go and see to Hick.'

Monty attempted to discreetly lead Hick from the table to the back door of the bar. Iris could see him straining under her weight as he tried to guide her between the closely packed tables. When they were out of sight, Iris went out to the sidewalk. Sam was leaning against the wall at the corner of building, hands in pockets. Iris went and leaned next to him.

'When are you leaving?' she asked quietly.

'Day after tomorrow.' His reply was curt.

'Where in Spain will you be?'

'I'll be based in Bilbao.' He turned to face her.

'Were you going to tell me?' Iris asked forlornly.

'I was going to tell you that night I was waiting at your apartment.' He stepped towards her slightly.

She stood on her toes and whispered in his ear, 'Why didn't you?'

'You know why,' he replied, then paused. 'I was planning to write you a letter.'

Iris took a step back. 'What? A letter!' she said, outraged.

He shook his head in disbelief. 'What's going on here, Iris?' he said. 'You're gallivanting all over Manhattan in a Chanel evening gown with your society boyfriend being photographed on red carpets and I'm expected to pay court to you. Do you know all of the clubs he's a member of wouldn't even let me through the door? And you're the one who's insulted? You didn't even bother telling me about law school.'

Her shoulders slumped. She could not deny his charges. Monty wasn't bigoted but it was true that he belonged to clubs where Jews were not permitted. And she should never have allowed Monty to be the one to break the news of her acceptance into law school on her front stoop that night. Even the words, *Chanel evening gown* were a startling rebuke discharged from Sam's mouth.

'I tried to call but you were in Philly; I wanted you to be the first to know,' she explained feebly. She didn't attempt to defend Monty.

Sam turned and stared across the street for a minute. Then he faced her. 'Don't you ever wonder about Chapel, Iris?'

'Wonder about what?' she said, puzzled.

'For Christ's sake,' he urged. 'Open your eyes. You grew up in West Baltimore. Where are your street smarts?'

'What are you talking about?' she pleaded. 'If there's something about Monty I should know, then tell me!'

He looked at her for a few seconds then sighed. 'It's nothing. Just sour grapes, I guess.'

They stood silently for a while as Iris mused over Sam's outburst. What could she not see about Monty? Was he on the take? Was he shaping presidential opinion and drafting policy with the interests of a union or manufacturer in mind? But he had money. Loads of it. Perhaps Sam was speculating about his fidelity, she thought. Monty was handsome and charming but Iris never questioned his loyalty. Surely she would notice the signs of betrayal – a forgotten note, lipstick on a collar or the lingering aroma of a perfume that was not her own. She bit her lip. Maybe it *was* just sour grapes.

Iris glanced briefly at the door of the bar before speaking. 'You're going to a war. I just thought . . . This is a big thing you're doing. A big, dangerous thing. I just thought we were friends. I'll worry about you.' She took Sam's hand. 'I mean, I will *really* worry about you.'

Sam looked down at their interlaced fingers in silence.

Iris moved her arms up to rest her hands on his shoulders. He lowered his head to hers and they kissed. It was a lingering kiss that was both a thrill and a relief. He led her around the corner and into a side street. There they kissed again, more passionately.

'Don't go,' Iris whispered. 'Stay in DC.'

'What about Chapel?'

But she loved Monty and he was so firmly embedded in her life that the idea of breaking with him was unthinkable. Sam took her hesitation as answer enough. He began walking back towards the bar.

'Where are you going?' Iris asked, taken aback at his sudden exit.

'Spain,' he answered flatly, without turning his head.

■

'Are you looking forward to beginning school?' Mrs Roosevelt asked.

'September can't come fast enough,' Iris answered.

Iris enjoyed her weekly meetings with Mrs Roosevelt when they occurred. Due to the First Lady's schedule they were frequently cancelled. The meetings always took place over breakfast. Usually they'd talk about work and the women's camps and anything else Mrs Roosevelt thought Iris could manage. Positions at the White House were flexible. Often Iris would spend a day or two helping Harry or Monty or someone else with a project. She never minded that it took her away from her own work. Whether East Wing or West Wing, the White House staff were a family, her family.

'Come September, we'll cut your hours back. Perhaps take you off the camps and put you on something with Franklin's legal team or in policy. It will complement your studies nicely. What do you think? I'll talk to the president.'

'It sounds wonderful.'

'Tom Corcoran could teach you a great deal,' the First Lady added. 'How would you feel about working with Tom?'

'I'd be honoured,' Iris answered, pleased at the prospect. 'He's brilliant. No one knows the Constitution better.'

Eleanor opened the *Washington Post*. Iris leaned back in her chair. The sun shining through the lunette window was making her sleepy. She hugged her mug to her chest and closed her eyes. Most people mocked the First Lady's quavering tone, but Iris found it soothing as she read aloud from the newspaper.

'Look here,' Mrs Roosevelt said urgently, leaning forward across the table. 'The Spanish town of Guernica has been bombed. On the twenty-sixth – three days ago. The Germans raided the town by air.' She scanned the text. 'A quiet market town, it occurred at four thirty on market day, took the populace completely unawares, civilian men, women and children innocently slaughtered. The article estimates that more than fifteen hundred lives were lost. Ghastly. Just ghastly!'

Mrs Roosevelt closed the newspaper and stood. 'America fuelled that attack, Iris. We might as well have dropped the bombs. Those poor people. And where's Franklin? Sailing around the Gulf of Mexico on a fishing trip! He should be here to make a statement!'

Mrs Roosevelt walked to the window and looked out across the lawn. 'This embargo on Spain, it's criminal. It makes no distinction between aggressor and victim nations. America should be aiding the Republicans, not standing on the sidelines selling copper and steel to the Germans, who are turning it into bombs and bullets for the Nationalists.'

Iris put her cup on the table and rose from her seat. Her mouth was dry and she could feel sweat beading on her upper lip. 'Where's Guernica?'

Mrs Roosevelt turned. 'What's wrong, dear? You're deathly pale.'

'Where in Spain is Guernica?' she repeated.

Mrs Roosevelt picked up the newspaper again and ran her eyes over the article. 'Fifteen miles from Bilbao. Why?'

Nausea flooded her stomach and the cold was overwhelming. Iris fainted.

She awoke moments later to find Mrs Roosevelt kneeling beside her, holding a napkin to her mouth. 'You split your lip, dear. You hit the table on your way down. Can you sit up?'

Iris nodded and Mrs Roosevelt helped her to her feet and across the room to the sofa. 'Lie down, Iris. Here, put your head on my lap. Rest for a few minutes and then I'll get a cold cloth for your face.' She raised the napkin from Iris's lip and scrutinised the injury. 'It doesn't look too bad. Nothing permanent, I shouldn't think.'

'Sam's in Bilbao, covering the war,' Iris said, panicked.

Mrs Roosevelt regarded her thoughtfully for a moment. 'How long have you been in love with him?'

'I didn't know I was until just then.'

Mrs Roosevelt laughed mildly. 'I'll get on to the State Department. They'll check if he's been evacuated. I'm sure he'll be safe.'

'Thank you.'

Eleanor stroked Iris's forehead gently as her colour returned.

'Why do men feel the need to act?' Iris asked seriously after a few minutes.

'Everyone has the same urge, I believe, but only a very brave few take action,' Mrs Roosevelt explained. 'The president desperately wanted to serve in the war but when America entered the fray he was Assistant Secretary of the Navy. He made do with serving in a different way.'

Iris closed her eyes, enjoying the sensation of the First Lady's touch. 'My father tried to enlist,' Iris confided softly. 'They wouldn't take him. He was an asthmatic. He was distraught, I remember, and took it out on my mother.'

'Violently?' Mrs Roosevelt asked.

'He tried to choke her,' Iris said directly. 'My father only had two gears – fury and euphoria. It has taken me a long time to realise it. When I was young I thought he was perfect.'

'That's not unusual,' Mrs Roosevelt said. She examined Iris's lip closely. 'Does Sam know how you feel?'

'I'm not certain. We didn't exactly part on the best of terms.'

'And Monty?'

Iris shook her head. 'I can't see a future with Monty, but I can't see one without him either.'

'You need to do some thinking, my girl. You need to get away from DC and Monty for a spell. Come up to Val-Kill with me next week. I'm putting the finishing touches on the new cottage before the lecture tour begins. You can have Tommy's quarters. Nan and Marion will be in the city. I always do my best thinking up there.'

'All right,' Iris agreed, thankful for Mrs Roosevelt's decisiveness. 'Will you call the State Department now?'

'Of course, I'll call straight away.'

■

By the time her afternoon swim with the president rolled around Iris was still feeling anxious. Mrs Roosevelt had telephoned the State Department but there was no news of any Americans being wounded or killed. She was mildly relieved but longed for something more definite. When Iris dived into the water that afternoon she swam with intensity, hoping the water would wash away her uncertainty.

'You're a natural, McIntosh,' the president remarked when they had completed their laps. 'You're swimming like a champion.'

'Thank you, Mr President,' Iris said, panting. She floated on her back for a minute as she caught her breath.

When she emerged from the pool the president was already in his wheelchair. A cigarette was burning in its holder. Iris joined him.

'I've got something for you, McIntosh,' Roosevelt said as he stubbed out his cigarette. Reaching into the pocket of his robe, he produced a small blue box. 'I wanted to say thank you for the work you've done for this administration and wish you well with your future profession.'

Iris untied the ribbon and opened the box. A tiny silver gavel lay against the black velvet of the interior. Iris smiled widely and looked at the president.

'I noticed you wear a charm bracelet but it was Missy who organised the purchase. Do you like it?'

'I do, Mr President. I love it. Although I'm doubtful whether I'll reach the heights of judge.'

'You never know,' Roosevelt replied. 'You're smart, McIntosh. I sense we're going to need people like you in the near future.'

'Do you mean Spain?' Iris asked.

'Spain, China, Germany, Japan,' he replied. 'It's all going to come to a head sooner than we would like.'

Iris admired the charm as she considered the president's position. The heart of America beat isolationist, but if a world war was to begin it would be impossible for the United States to remain so. The president would have to convince Congress and the nation to march to a different drum.

'My wife told me about Sam's situation,' the president remarked. Iris closed the box and placed it on the table. 'I'll make some calls myself and see what I can find out.'

'Thank you, sir,' Iris said.

The president smiled. 'When will you start calling me boss?'

'I'm not sure, Mr President,' Iris answered. 'Perhaps when I've finished law school.'

'Is that a deal?' Roosevelt asked.

'It's a deal,' Iris affirmed.

■

Iris said goodbye to Monty in the first week of May and drove to Hyde Park early one morning with Mrs Roosevelt. The First Lady had grown increasingly incensed during the week following the attack on Guernica. Franco was claiming the Basques had raided their own town and Germany denied any knowledge of the bombing. Meanwhile, the Roosevelt administration made no comment. Mrs Roosevelt declared it a conspiracy of silence.

The First Lady called for relief measures and went public with her cry for help on behalf of the Basque people. A radio broadcast, magazine articles and a speech at Georgetown University condemned the Fascist regimes of Franco and Hitler and criticised America's isolationist policies. But Iris's distress was of a purely personal nature. She still hadn't received any information about Sam's situation. The names of the injured and dead were coming through to the State Department every day. So far his name had not been on a list. She contacted his boss at Associated Press, who had not heard from him since a few days before the twenty-sixth – but that didn't surprise him, he said. Sometimes it was difficult to communicate in a war zone. He'd had similar experiences with correspondents before.

Iris spotted a gas station. 'Can we stop here, Mrs Roosevelt? I'd like to use the rest room.' They pulled off the highway and rolled to a stop.

'I'll fill up, Iris. Is there anything you'd like?'

'Just the newspaper, please.'

Iris sat in the cubicle and placed her head in her hands. A coldness had penetrated to her very core. She felt sad and lonely and wanted Monty. He was the only person who was able to lift her spirits when she was so glum. What would a few days at Val-Kill achieve? she wondered. She'd go back to Washington just as confused, straight back to Monty. After all, he was the one she really loved, wasn't he? Yet the idea of Sam being blown to pieces in Spain was agonising. Iris sat in the cubicle and attempted to assess her feelings rationally. Monty was her teacher where Sam was her equal. Monty was her lover where Sam was her friend. Monty was compelling where Sam was engaging. The total sum of Monty remained just out of her grasp where Sam was entirely reachable. She had been with Monty for four years and couldn't break with him. Yet it was impossible to deny her feelings for Sam.

Back in the car and on the road again she opened the copy of the *New York Times* Mrs Roosevelt had bought. She searched the front page for news from Bilbao, but it was all Hindenburg. It was true, she thought; everything Mrs Roosevelt said was true – Americans weren't interested in international concerns. The Hindenburg bursting into flames in New Jersey was a much bigger headline than thousands of innocents being slaughtered in Spain.

She turned the pages ruefully as Mrs Roosevelt drove in silence. A story on page three covered the president's extension of the Neutrality Act of 1935. Iris didn't mention it to Mrs Roosevelt. She knew it would spark a diatribe and she was finding the quiet comforting. Then she saw it on page six, column one – Sam's by-line. 'He's alive!' Iris cried. 'Here's his by-line!'

Mrs Roosevelt took her hand and clutched it. 'What does he say?'

Iris read aloud: '"Tuesday was market day. There was little fear of attack. After all, Guernica was not a military centre. It was of no strategic value, had no defences, no munitions depots.

'"As the populace went about their business of buying and selling, the airplanes of General Franco, German and Italian planes piloted by Germans and Italians, unleashed one of the most brutal and malicious attacks in the history of warfare. First, small parties of airplanes threw heavy bombs and hand grenades in orderly fashion all over the town. Next came the fighting machines which swooped to machine-gun those who had run in panic from the dugouts. Many of these people were killed as they ran. Finally, as many as twelve bombers appeared at a time, dropping heavy and incendiary bombs upon the remains."

Iris stopped reading and leaned her head back against the seat. 'It goes on, but that's the main thrust.'

'Brutes,' Mrs Roosevelt said. 'A measured attack on a civilian population. Why do people go on trying to destroy civilisation!'

In that moment Iris didn't care about civilisation. She closed her eyes and breathed deeply. She was conscious of her body again, her heartbeat, the sound of Mrs Roosevelt's voice and the tyres on the bitumen highway. She opened her eyes and looked at the trees that bordered the road and smiled at how the sunlight filtering through their leaves and onto her legs gave her black trousers a brindled appearance. Iris knew in that instant what she needed to do.

■

It was just the two of them for the five days at Val-Kill. Iris and Mrs Roosevelt rose early, took long walks and ate large meals. Mrs Roosevelt always made breakfast, typically scrambled eggs with bacon or ham. Iris handled dinner. Lunch was usually forgotten. The rest of the time the First Lady spent preparing for her lecture tour or heaving furniture around the cottage. In the evening she taught Iris to knit. Iris spent her idle hours writing to Sam.

Draft after draft she threw in the trash. She knew precisely what she wanted to say, but when she read the words she'd written they seemed all wrong. It turns out, Iris thought, I'm not very good in person *or* on paper. She spent hours sitting by the pond, hoping the scene would inspire something brilliant, but by the fourth day all Iris had managed to generate was two letters to Monty. Iris decided to make one last attempt to write to Sam that evening after dinner. If she couldn't express herself this time, then it was just not meant to be, she decided.

'This is lovely, Iris,' Mrs Roosevelt said as they lingered at the table. 'I didn't know you could cook so well. The salmon is poached beautifully and is the sauce a beurre blanc?'

'Yes, that's right. There's nothing to it. Monty showed me,' Iris replied. 'He's a great cook, and you know Monty: he's not one to do things by halves.'

'No, he's not,' Mrs Roosevelt agreed. 'Iris, have you come to any conclusions in regards to your predicament?'

Iris placed her knife and fork on her plate and sighed. 'Yes and no,' she said honestly. 'I think I love Sam, and I want to write to him and tell him so, but I can't. Something is stopping me. It must be Monty.'

'Monty's not stopping you,' Mrs Roosevelt said reasonably. 'Is the fact that he's Jewish a problem?'

'I don't think it's a problem,' Iris said pensively. 'It used to make me a little nervous. His faith made him seem alien to me. But now I think of him as just a man, a journalist.'

'A lot of people will see it as a problem,' Mrs Roosevelt told her. 'I can remember refusing to attend certain functions if *my kind* were going to be outnumbered. It was just the way it was in those days. Although Franklin never had a problem with Jews, I was once very narrow in my views.'

As Iris contemplated whether Sam's faith could be the cause of her hesitation, Mrs Roosevelt continued, 'I remember when Franklin first brought Felix Frankfurter home for dinner many years ago. During the war, I think.'

Frankfurter was a Harvard law professor and a member of the Brains Trust. Iris's opinion of Frankfurter came from Monty, who respected his mind and his insight. The lawyer never came to Children's Hour and remained outside the inner circle. Iris wasn't certain whether this was by choice or circumstance.

'I informed Franklin when Felix had left the house that he was an interesting little man, but "very Jew",' Mrs Roosevelt admitted. 'What a terrible thing to say. If you love Sam you need to give the relationship a chance.' She looked at Iris. 'Sometimes we have to make painful decisions. But life's short.'

Iris looked to her enquiringly.

'Take Gus Gennerich, for example,' the First Lady said. 'Losing Gus to a heart attack last year hit the president hard. Gus had spent the last decade working for my husband. Seeing to his every need, carrying him, dressing him, bathing him, putting him to bed . . . the whole time waiting to live his dream. He'd bought a farm up here, did you know? He was living for that farm, but he couldn't break from Franklin. He was only fifty, Iris.'

'I didn't know that about Gus,' Iris said.

'Distancing myself from Nan and Marion has been the hardest decision in my life. But their dislike of Hick made the situation impossible. I've been forced to break from my two oldest and dearest friends, but I happily did it for Hick.'

'But Sam and I . . . it just doesn't make sense. He always says the wrong thing. I always say the wrong thing. He criticises my views . . . With Monty it's so easy.'

'Iris, I know this is a cliché, but the heart wants what the heart wants, even if it seems illogical. Anyway, love, relationships, they're not meant to be easy. They're hard work but so rewarding when you get them right.'

Iris nodded and the women began to clear the table.

Later that evening, Iris finished a letter to Sam. She didn't think it was extremely stirring but she guessed it expressed what she wanted it to. She addressed and sealed the envelope and propped it up on the dressing table. She went to sleep staring at the letter, contemplating the power of such a seemingly insignificant thing to change the course of a life.

34
WASHINGTON DC
July 1937

When Iris and Monty arrived at her apartment it was past midnight. She sat down, took off her shoes and put her feet on the coffee table. Monty poured them both a glass of brandy and then joined her.

'What about you?' he asked, astounded. 'Butter wouldn't have melted in your mouth tonight – "Thank you, Mr Hemingway. I'd be honoured to read your new work",' he said, mimicking Iris's polite response to the writer's offer of a book at dinner.

She grinned. 'What was I going to say? "No thank you, I'm not a fan".'

'You could have explained how you prefer the narrative style of James to his more masculine prose,' Monty replied sardonically.

'Ha ha,' she retorted drolly. 'He probably would have punched me.'

That evening Iris and Monty had attended a screening of *The Spanish Earth* at the White House. The documentary had been produced by Ernest Hemingway and Martha Gellhorn. The film was followed by dinner with the war correspondents as well as the film's director, Joris Ivens. Hick and Harry had also been in attendance, along with the president and First Lady.

'What did you think of the film?' Iris asked.

'It was informative but too sanctimonious,' Monty replied.

Iris nodded 'It certainly wasn't Frank Capra.'

He laughed. 'And those squab. Did you see Roosevelt's face when they were served?'

'As hard as rocks,' Iris agreed.

'I'm planning to tee off with one at the first hole at East Potomac tomorrow,' Monty chuckled. 'But you've got to hand it to Nesbitt, she always manages to bombard an evening from the safety of the kitchen.'

'I pity the man,' Iris said more seriously. 'He was getting it from all sides tonight.'

Hemingway and Gellhorn had spent the entire evening haranguing the president, demanding an assurance that America would join the war in Spain. Mrs Roosevelt had been on the attack as well. Despite Monty and Harry's best efforts to appease the couple, it had taken an unambiguous statement in regards to America's isolationist stance from Roosevelt to quiet the pair. That had been the final word on the issue.

'You'd think the least he could ask for is a well-cooked meal,' Iris observed.

'He's the president. He can handle it.'

'But can his stomach?'

Monty laughed. 'You're in better spirits tonight.'

Iris swung her legs onto Monty's lap and he began to rub her feet. She had been distracted and blue of late. Iris had written Sam a steady stream of letters since May. Not one of them had been answered. For the last few months Iris had felt as though she had been sucked into a void, a relationship limbo, as she waited for a response.

'Is it Jacobson? Are you worried?'

'A little, I guess,' she lied. 'But I'm more worried about starting school. September is creeping up fast. I get more nervous every day. I'm not sure I'm that smart.'

He patted her legs, reassured but not convinced, Iris thought. Unsettled by his silence, Iris said lightly, 'Hemingway and Gellhorn?'

'Definitely,' Monty answered. 'He's married but you can just see it. They're made for each other.'

'I liked her; she was fiery,' Iris mused. 'Although I couldn't do what she does. Living in a war zone, filing stories as the bombs drop around you.'

'You don't give yourself enough credit, kiddo,' Monty replied.

'What do you think Mrs Roosevelt and Hick see in each other?' she asked after a minute. 'Their split didn't seem to take. They have a lot of ups and downs, don't they?'

'I suppose, but I guess it's just comfortable, like an old dressing gown. You know you should throw it out . . .' Monty said. 'Besides, Mrs R. likes a project.' He squeezed her thigh affectionately and winked.

Iris nodded thoughtfully.

'What do *you* see in *me*?' Iris asked. Sam's veiled hints outside the bar still troubled her occasionally. Although she had seen no evidence of Monty leading a double life, there must have been more to Sam's pointed remarks than sour grapes.

'Are you serious?' he asked, putting his glass on the coffee table and turning to face her. He pushed her legs onto the ground. 'You're intelligent, funny, determined, ambitious, courageous, compassionate and not bad-looking either,' he said, before adding, 'You're the whole package, kiddo. I'm crazy about you.'

'Really?' she asked

'Really,' he stated sincerely.

Iris took his hand in hers and kissed his palm softly. 'I'm crazy about you too,' she murmured. 'I don't tell you that enough.'

'You're doing fine.'

'Let's go to bed,' she said. 'I'm beat.'

Iris and Monty didn't make love that night, but they went to sleep in the comfort of each other's arms.

35

HYDE PARK, NEW YORK
November 1937

It was the first time Iris had visited Springwood. She'd lost count of the number of times she'd been to Val-Kill, but she had never visited the president's childhood home, even though it was a mere two miles away. The scale of the house became clearer as Monty drove slowly towards it along the gravel drive.

He turned off the engine when they reached the front of the house. Iris marvelled at the grandeur through the windscreen. The warmth of her breath clouded the glass and she rubbed it with her coat sleeve. It was a home she could only describe as presidential – vastly different from the house on Campobello Island or Stone Cottage at Val-Kill. The flags, columns and crescent-shaped balcony encircling the first storey gave the residence the appearance of a lesser White House.

'Wow,' she said. 'I'm kind of glad I'm not staying here.' Mrs Roosevelt had invited Iris to stay at Val-Kill with her, Hick and Tommy over the Thanksgiving holiday.

'Awe-inspiring, isn't it?' Monty said. 'I'll miss you when you're at your ladies' retreat in the woods.'

'Don't be ridiculous,' she admonished. 'You'll see me every day and Val-Kill isn't far away.'

'Perhaps we can arrange a midnight rendezvous in the forest.'

She laughed, then leaned over and kissed him on the lips. 'A little cold, but I'm sure we can work something out.'

The couple left the car and entered the house. As they stood in the foyer and removed the trappings of winter, Iris took in her surroundings. The walls were crowded with an array of paintings and sketches, mostly featuring historic sea battles. A large portrait of Napoleon hung above the front door. The president's interest in ships and naval history was evident everywhere. A maid appeared and took their coats. She and Monty were well acquainted. He clasped her hand and kissed her cheek.

'The president is in the living room with Mr Hopkins and Mr James Roosevelt,' she informed them. 'And the door is closed.'

'Thanks, Mary,' Monty said. 'What about Mrs Roosevelt? Has she arrived yet?'

'Not yet.'

'We'll be fine until the president's finished.'

Mary departed, telling the couple she'd bring some coffee to the dining room.

'Will you be okay for a minute while I wash up a little?' Monty asked.

'Of course,' Iris replied.

She moved around the perimeter of the room, examining the pictures more closely before coming to a life-size sculpture in bronze of the president as a young man. The figure was seated, but his legs were cut off mid-thigh. She wondered if the work was commissioned before or after his polio and looked around its base for a clue. She found the year – 1911, before the disease – on a silver plate on the statue's pedestal. How prophetic, she thought. Behind the monument on the wall sat a collection of about forty stuffed birds, including swallows, owls, warblers, sparrows and many Iris didn't recognise. As she was gazing at the macabre flock she heard the heavy tread of a man's footsteps descending the stairs behind her.

She turned, smiling, expecting Monty. On the verge of saying something clever about the avian array, she was struck dumb at the sight of Sam Jacobson standing at the foot of the staircase. While his very appearance at Springwood stunned her, it was his transformed physical appearance that jolted her composure the most. His skin was ruddy from the sun and his v-shaped face had filled out into a pleasing, sturdy oval. His dark, disorderly hair was now close cropped and he sported a short beard. Although it was an impossibility, Iris would have sworn he was taller. It was his presence, she quickly realised. He now made a greater impact.

'Hello, Iris,' he said, moving closer. 'It's good to see you.'

Her throat was dry and she could feel tears forming behind her eyes.

'You look well,' he continued. 'I thought you might be here for the weekend. I thought so when Mrs Roosevelt invited me up for Thanksgiving.'

Seven months and she'd not heard a word. Iris had written him copious letters, one each week. He'd never replied.

'The president collected stuffed birds as a boy, apparently,' he informed her, indicating the collection.

His manner had altered somewhat as well. He was more assured. It seemed war zones agreed with him, she thought.

He edged closer. 'Your hair's a little longer, isn't it?' he asked, touching her cheek softly. 'It looks lovely.'

Iris could stand it no longer. She rushed past him and fled up the staircase, hoping to find Monty.

■

Although invited, Iris didn't attend Children's Hour at Springwood that evening. She stayed with Mrs Roosevelt, Tommy and Hick at Stone Cottage. They would drive up to Springwood for dinner at about eight. Although she was in no mood for it, Iris dressed for dinner in grey houndstooth slacks and a crimson blouse with long, breezy sleeves. She adjusted the wide collar in the mirror as she left the room. When she reached the living room she found Mrs Roosevelt sitting by the fire, knitting. It was still an hour before the women planned to leave. Hick was sitting at Mrs Roosevelt's desk, typing, and Tommy sat in another corner of the room in an armchair, her legs curled up under her, proofreading a number of Mrs Roosevelt's columns. The three women glanced her way when she entered.

'That's a pretty outfit, Iris,' Mrs Roosevelt commented. 'You look very attractive. I never think to wear trousers. I'm a product of my generation, I suppose.'

Iris smiled and took a seat on the edge of the sofa. She stared into the fire, her hands clutching her knees. She felt as though a boulder had come to rest on her chest.

'You look as if you're on your way to the gallows, Iris,' Mrs Roosevelt said quietly. Iris heard the click of the typewriter stop behind her.

'Would you like to join me in a drink?' Hick suggested, leaving the desk. 'I'm having scotch. What's your poison?'

Iris, unconcerned for once with Mrs Roosevelt's opinion, answered, 'I'll have a scotch too, neat.'

'Tommy?'

'Scotch is fine,' she answered.

'Okey-dokey,' Hick sang as she made her way to the kitchen.

The women were silent. Iris concentrated on the sound of Mrs Roosevelt's knitting needles and the fire's noncommittal hiss. Occasionally the First Lady took her eyes off the sweater she was making and glanced at her guest. When Hick handed Iris the drink she could barely lift the glass to her lips.

'I don't think I can go tonight, Mrs Roosevelt,' Iris said weakly. 'I'm sick to my stomach.' She hastily consumed the scotch Hick had served her.

'I didn't know Sam was back until the day before yesterday,' Mrs Roosevelt said. 'You'd already left with Monty. I thought it might be good for you two to see each other again. That's why I invited him.'

'But I wrote him so many letters and I never heard a thing from him. I feel like a fool. And this afternoon at the house . . . I just stood there. And Monty's here.' Iris placed her head in her hands and sat like that for some moments. 'It's all such a mess.'

Eleanor and Hick exchanged glances.

'You know, Iris, I can think of worse predicaments to be in,' Hick began. 'You've got two of the greatest guys in DC chasing after you.'

'To my mind,' Tommy interjected, 'it's gotta be Sam. If it was me, I'd choose Sam. He's more my speed.'

Iris bit her thumbnail and considered this advice.

'But I've got to hand it to you, kid,' Tommy continued. 'You've certainly managed to tame Monty Chapel. That's got to stand for something.'

Mrs Roosevelt shot her secretary a warning glance.

'Tame him?' Iris queried.

'Um, well, he did have . . . quite a reputation,' Tommy explained, suddenly busy with the papers on her lap.

'As what?' Iris persisted.

'He was known as a bit of a playboy, Iris,' Hick said plainly. 'He liked to have a good time. But that's all changed. Anybody can see that.'

Iris frowned. Why was she surprised? she wondered. Numerous people had warned her off Monty – Tommy, Mrs Roosevelt, Sam.

'Don't let the past worry you, dear,' Mrs Roosevelt said. 'You have a decision to make. It's a good thing it has come to a head.'

'The problem is,' Iris began wanly, 'I don't know if Sam wants me or not. Seven months and not a word.'

'Maybe he didn't get the letters or –'

Hick was interrupted by Mrs Roosevelt. 'Or maybe he was waiting for news that you had broken with Monty,' she suggested, looking pointedly at Iris. 'There could be a million reasons why he didn't write.'

'It's not just that,' Iris explained. 'I can't sit there at dinner tonight and at Thanksgiving lunch tomorrow with Monty and Sam, together.'

Mrs Roosevelt put down her knitting, rose and walked to the sofa. She sat down next to Iris.

'Listen, let's get through tonight and we'll worry about tomorrow afterwards. I've seated you between Hick and me. Tommy will be sitting opposite. Everything will be fine,' she assured Iris, placing her arm around her shoulders. 'We'll take care of you tonight, but you have to take care of business tomorrow, Iris. You must make a decision.'

■

Dinner was lovely – the Maryland chicken was fried just right – but Iris barely ate a bite. The support of Mrs Roosevelt, Hick and Tommy could not shield her from Monty and Sam. She rarely looked their way, but she could feel the force of their gaze on her all evening.

'Sam,' the president began. 'when did you get back?'

'Last week, sir,' Sam replied, placing his knife and fork on his plate. 'And the entire country seems to have shifted into reverse since I've been gone.'

'What are you talking about, son?' Roosevelt enquired.

Her husband's feigned ingenuousness infuriated Eleanor.

'The labor unrest, the budget cuts, the stock market,' she said. 'It must seem like quite a different country.'

'Did you know, ladies and gentlemen, that my wife is the first First Lady to join a union?'

'I joined the Newspaper Guild when I became a columnist,' Eleanor explained. 'I wouldn't stand in a picket line or strike, of course – at least, not in the immediate future.'

The gathering laughed.

'The Wagner Labor Relations Act was a necessary evil,' Harry Hopkins stated. 'The right for workers to unionise we see as fundamental to democracy. Unfortunately, it has resulted in a wave of sit-down strikes –'

'That have slowed industrial output to a trickle,' Mrs Roosevelt interrupted.

'I'm not going to use force on strikers,' the president stated.

'But you could force someone's hand,' Monty put in. 'This stalemate has been going on since June. Production at General Motors has virtually stopped.'

'We'll wait it out,' the president said casually. 'We've got to give the economy a chance to stand on its own two legs. Just let things stabilise. We need to stay the course. We can't keep pumping money into New Deal schemes forever.'

'But, boss, such massive, sudden cuts. The economy can't sustain it. Last month, the stock market had its worst day since '29,' Monty said.

'The press are calling it a depression within a depression,' Mrs Roosevelt added. 'The Roosevelt Recession.'

'The press like drama, Eleanor,' Roosevelt told her, eyeing Sam and Hick in turn. 'It's not as bad as that.'

'But it is, boss.' Monty insisted. 'It is as bad as that. What is called for is an immediate resumption in government spending.'

'Here, here!' Hopkins cheered from across the table, holding up his glass.

'Anyway,' the president said, in an obvious change of subject, 'how's the book coming along, Hick?'

'Great. Better than I'd expected, in fact.'

'And the new job?'

'The World's Fair job is surprising. I never thought I'd be running a publicity department, but I'm lovin' it,' Hick said enthusiastically.

'You're writing a book?' Sam asked.

Hick nodded. 'About the depression – based on the FERA reports I did for Hopkins.'

'That's interesting,' he said. 'I'm writing one too – about the war in Spain.'

Iris's head involuntarily turned towards him. 'Really?' It was the first time she had spoken all evening. 'Does that mean you'll be going back there?'

'That depends.'

She looked at him seriously for a moment, trying to interpret his meaning.

'The situation is getting out of hand in Spain. Atrocities are committed every day. Fascism is running riot all over Europe. America can't keep on this isolationist path for much longer. The world is about to explode.'

Sam had silenced the table.

'And it's not just Europe; there's the Japanese invasion of China,' Mrs Roosevelt added, shaking her head.

'Winston Churchill is calling for rearmament in England,' Hick added. 'He's fervent in his views about the Nazis.'

'America wants peace,' the president declared boldly. 'Last month I gave a speech in Chicago, testing the waters.'

'The "quarantine" speech?' Sam asked. 'I read about it. Reaction was mixed. The *New York Times* and the *Washington Post* were both very supportive. It was only the Hearst papers that were scathing.'

'It's the Hearst papers that make public opinion,' Roosevelt declared. 'America remains staunchly isolationist, like it or not.'

■

As coffee was served, guests left the table and moved into the library and living room. Iris was putting on her coat when Monty approached.

'I need some fresh air,' she explained as she hurriedly wrapped her scarf around her neck.

'Are you all right?' he said. 'You were so quiet during dinner.'

'I'm just a little tired. The cold air will work wonders.'

'Do you want me to come?'

She shook her head. 'You go in and have your brandy and cigar with the president. I won't be long.'

'We could go for a drive,' he suggested.

'I'm fine.' She smiled. 'I'll be back in a few minutes. Promise.'

Iris walked outside onto the porch. She breathed in deeply and the air stung her nostrils and then her lungs. The sky was clear and the moon illuminated the surrounding trees. Within minutes she had rounded the house and was standing on the edge of the bluff about a hundred yards from the Hudson. She looked back at the house. The first floor windows were aglow, while the bedroom windows on the upper storeys remained darkened. She sat on a bench and attempted to block out the voices coming from the library. The night carried sound so clearly, she mused. Iris listened only to the river. After a few minutes she heard the sound of a door closing, followed by the squelch of footsteps on the dewy lawn.

'How's law school going?' Sam asked as he sat beside her.

'Okay,' Iris replied, unsurprised Sam had followed her. 'It's hard work . . . challenging. I'm working with the president now on policy which helps with school . . . Although I know everyone we study in my class and my teachers look at me a little differently because of it . . . But that's for another time,' she finished, aware she was beginning to ramble.

'I got your letters. Thank you. Thank you for writing them.'

'Why didn't you reply?'

'I can't be the third party in a relationship, Iris. You gave no indication it was over with Chapel.' He paused for a long time. 'I love you, but it's got to be just you and me.'

'I love you too,' she murmured in response. 'I know I've treated you shabbily. I'm sorry.'

The mutual admission prompted them to look fleetingly at each other.

'I'd like to tell you that I understand but I don't . . . entirely.'

'Neither do I,' she replied. She turned toward the bluff. 'Are you going back to Spain?'

'What difference does that make?'

She thought carefully before answering. 'I don't want to invest in you if you're leaving.'

'That's a cold way of looking at it.'

'Practical, I'd say.'

He took her hand. 'Are you giving me an ultimatum?'

'I suppose I am,' she said quietly.

'I have to go back. There's the book I want to finish but also I really think I can make a difference. You heard what the president said about newspapers forming public opinion.'

They sat without speaking for a few minutes, holding hands.

'You could come to Spain with me,' he suggested

'And do what? My life is in Washington,' she reminded him. 'Besides, I'm no Martha Gellhorn. I need a hot shower each morning and a cold cocktail at five.' She looked out into the darkness. 'I love you, Sam. But I'm not giving up all I've achieved to follow you to Spain.'

She rested her head on his chest. He placed his arm around her and hugged her to him. The idea of leaving with him was tempting, almost irresistible.

After a few minutes Iris bolstered herself with a deep intake of the frigid air.

'I'm going to leave early tomorrow morning,' she told him all of a sudden as she sat up straight.

'And not stay for Thanksgiving?'

'It's too hard. I'll make an excuse to leave.'

'With Chapel?'

'Probably.'

'I don't understand . . . at all.'

'I need him.'

'No you don't,' he responded firmly.

They fell quiet.

'How long are you planning to be home for?' she asked finally.

'Just a week or so.'

Then she looked into his face and they kissed achingly.

'Please, come with me,' he whispered.

'You can't ask me that when you're not willing to stay. You must understand,' Iris pleaded.

'Then call it quits with Chapel.' He looked at her directly and wiped a tear from her cheek.

'Are you giving me an ultimatum?' she asked with a fragile grin.

He sighed and moved away. 'I suppose I am,' he responded.

Reluctantly, Iris ended the wretched scene.

'Goodbye, Sam. I guess the timing just isn't right. We've both got some things to finish.'

She stood and walked back to the house, fighting the urge to cry.

■

Monty didn't require any explanation when she asked him to take her to New York for Thanksgiving. She said she was exhausted and didn't feel up to socialising with the thirty or so guests that were expected at Springwood the next day. He merely nodded and was waiting outside Stone Cottage in his Citroën Torpedo at six the following morning. Iris asked Mrs Roosevelt to give her apologies to the president.

When they arrived at Monty's apartment a few hours later he turned on the heat and they took off their coats. Iris was tired. Her sleep the night before had been restless. She sat down heavily on the sofa. As she did so, the sofa knocked an end table which toppled one of Monty's lamps. As Iris watched the lamp rock precariously from side to side on its delicate base, terror at what was to follow forced an inadvertent cry from her throat. When the crystal lamp eventually smashed and sprayed shards across the parquet floor, she began to weep. Monty was by her side in seconds.

'I'm sorry, I'm so sorry,' she cried.

'Hey, it's just a lamp. I have hundreds of them,' he said flippantly, gesturing around the room.

Tears poured down her cheeks.

He placed his arm around her and hugged her tightly as she sobbed. 'It's more than the lamp, isn't it?' he asked after a couple of minutes.

Iris nodded.

'Jacobson.'

She nodded again.

'What's going on, Iris? I know he was outside with you last night. You were out there for over an hour.'

Iris hadn't realised it was that long.

'Is something going on between the two of you?' he said calmly.

She finally caught her breath and said, 'Nothing's going on.'

'But you love him?'

She offered an ambivalent shrug. 'He's going back to Spain.'

'Then he's an idiot,' Monty stated.

Iris looked into his face and smiled. 'Nothing happened. A kiss. Two kisses. It's all over. Well, it never really began.'

Monty touched her cheek.

'It's not just Sam. It's school. I'm making a mess of everything,' she blurted.

'What are you talking about?' he asked gently.

'I got my first paper back last week,' she began.

'The one about the Fourteenth Amendment?'

She nodded. 'It got a C–. I worked so hard on it, Monty! Professor Barnes said my theories were pedestrian and my arguments wooden. When I went to his office to pick it up, do you know what he said?'

Monty raised his eyebrows.

'He said, "Oh, how the mighty have fallen".' Iris winced; the memory of Barnes's condescending tone still stung.

'Listen, kiddo,' Monty said, taking her hands. 'People are going to try to cut you down to size. Barnes is just the first of many. Not only are you a woman but you're working with the president. You need to use their criticism to fire you up, not get you down.'

'But I didn't go to Harvard or Dartmouth or Brown. I know the other students think I'm only there because I work with the president. They must hate me! It's nepotism at its worst.'

'That's not nepotism,' Monty responded. 'Nepotism is the boss giving his twenty-nine-year-old son Louis Howe's job.'

'I like James and he's smart.'

'There's no denying he's a likeable guy and he's smart, but you're far superior in every way to James Roosevelt. I could see your potential the first time I met you in Tommy's office,' he said. 'You may not have had the opportunities that James, the president or Mrs Roosevelt did, but you're bright and you're determined. You'll outshine all your classmates. Just look how far you've come. It wasn't five years ago that you were living in a shantytown. Listen, if the president made it through law school, anyone can.'

She laughed at this and huddled against his side, reassured.

'So, you still my girl?'

'Always,' she replied. 'What about the kisses?'

'You're here with me now, aren't you?'

Iris supposed that she was. The decision had been made.

'What do you want to do today?' he asked, kissing her forehead. 'I don't have anything in the kitchen, but we could go to a hotel. The Waldorf does a very good Thanksgiving dinner.'

'Let's just go to bed,' Iris answered.

'Your wish is my command.'

36
HYDE PARK, NEW YORK
May 1962

My Thanksgivings were usually wild-goose chases, and I mean that literally. I remember one year, I think it was 1938, when the president got sent twelve wild geese, four wild turkeys and one domestic twenty-seven-pound turkey.

Well, I planned to save the big turkey for Thanksgiving lunch for the help. The wild turkeys were going up to Hyde Park and the wild geese were being sent out by Mrs Roosevelt as gifts. This particular year there was a special family Mrs Roosevelt wanted to help – a mother, father and two children who were all blind. They lived in Lancaster, Pennsylvania. She asked me to send them one of the wild geese.

Anyway, to cut a long story short, I asked one of the girls to send the birds off. I mean, I gave her a list of addresses. But the silly girl got it all wrong. She was just one of the kitchen help, you see. I didn't find out about the mistake until the day before Thanksgiving when the White House got a telephone call from the blind lady who said she couldn't fit the turkey in her oven! I knew straight away that she'd received the twenty-seven-pound bird instead of one of the wild geese. Wild geese weigh only about twelve pounds, at their largest. That meant, of course, that the help wouldn't have anything for their Thanksgiving lunch and there was still one wild goose unaccounted for.

Gosh, oh golly. I got on the telephone immediately and howled to my assistant, 'Get the big turkey back and find a goose for the blind family!' You may laugh now, but at the time it was no laughing matter. When I first took the job as housekeeper, the help were just so pleased to have a job. They never questioned their schedule or wages or quibbled about the tasks I asked them to do. But as the economy became stronger the quibbles became more frequent. I used to sweat over their schedules, making sure everyone was accommodated. It was about this time that the help also started asking for higher wages. I knew that if a turkey wasn't produced at one o'clock in the afternoon on Thanksgiving then

I'd be hearing from their union by two. Why, I thought my bird was well and truly cooked!

My assistant eventually tracked down a wild goose at the Willard Hotel. It was the hotel kitchens who were always my saviour in a crisis. Meanwhile, I rang Wells Fargo, who organised to collect the bird from Lancaster and dispatch it to DC as soon as humanly possible. At the DC end, the Willard's goose was sent to Lancaster. It all worked out eventually. But that night, the night before Thanksgiving, I stayed at the White House late, until about midnight, when the turkey finally arrived. To this day I never did find out what happened to that missing goose.

37
WASHINGTON DC
January 1938

Eleanor and Hick sat opposite each other on matching sofas in the First Lady's suite. Eleanor knitted and Hick pretended to read, but her eyes skipped randomly over the page, unable to focus. She sighed, folded the newspaper and stood. Moving to the window, she crossed her arms under her bosom and stared out. A rap on the door and the entrance of Tommy startled both women.

'Sorry to interrupt,' Tommy began. 'But I've just been on the telephone with your cronies at the Women's Peace League. They want you in for a meeting tonight to discuss Chamberlain's rejection of the Washington Conference.'

Hick turned immediately to Eleanor, her eyes both pleading and accusatory.

'Your schedule's free,' Tommy added.

'Of course. Arrange it, Tommy,' the First Lady answered after a second's thought.

'It'll have to be the one o'clock train.'

The First Lady nodded.

'Okay. Anything else?' Tommy asked.

'You came in here,' Hick snapped. 'Why would there be anything else?'

'Just asking,' Tommy muttered as she left the room.

After a moment, Eleanor placed her knitting in the faded tapestry bag at her feet and folded her hands in her lap. 'That was unnecessary, darling. What's the matter?'

'What isn't the matter?' Hick barked. 'I've come here to spend the weekend with you and instead of clearing your schedule, as you said you'd do, you're rushing off to meet with a bunch of save-the-world do-gooders.'

This outburst was entirely unexpected. Hick had been so calm, seemingly so happy lately. Stable. Eleanor began to speak, but Hick wasn't done. Thrusting her hands deep into the pockets of her slacks, she went on, 'What's more, we're never alone. People treat this place like a hotel and you're the most hospitable landlord in town. Hopkins is now ensconced in my room and I'm staying on a day bed in his daughter's room. You invited me here because we haven't been alone together since last August and I'm left feeling like I'm getting in the way.'

'You're not in the way,' Eleanor explained. 'But Harry's just lost his wife and he's not himself at the moment. It's better if he and little Diana stay here for a while.'

Hick sat down forcefully on the sofa beside Eleanor. 'Why do you have to help everybody? He's a grown man in charge of government policy. Don't you think he is capable of helping himself?'

'It's just in the short term and everyone needs help from time to time, no matter who they are.' Eleanor's eyes crinkled with concern. 'As for my meeting tonight, the Peace League is something I've been committed to for years. The world is at a critical point, Hick. I can't ignore what's going on in Europe. Franklin's Washington Conference would be a great step towards preventing war. Chamberlain's refusal to attend, well . . . it's catastrophic. The conference won't go ahead now. The League has to take stock. I'll get the late train back. I'll be in bed by midnight.'

'Why do you care so much? Why do you care so much about everyone else?' Hick's tone softened as she lay her head in Eleanor's lap.

Eleanor shrugged. 'Someone has to. The entire world is falling apart. I have a little bit of power that just might make a difference. Just like I can help Harry.'

'Everyone knew Chamberlain wasn't going to show up. He hates the president, ever since the stunt Frank pulled on the London Economic Conference in '33.' Hick said grumpily. But Eleanor could read the humour in her words.

'More fool him, then. Cutting off his nose to spite his face.'

'Pretty big nose too, I hear.' Both women laughed. Eleanor stroked Hick's forehead gently. Hick's eyes were closed and her face had lost its brittle edge.

'Is there anything else?' the First Lady asked.

Hick shook her head, but Eleanor noticed her lips tighten.

'What is it?' she urged.

'I just read the review of *This Troubled World*. It's fantastic. A rave, even. Better than reviews of your last book.' Hick spoke quietly, without opening her eyes, as though if she looked at her friend's face she would lose all courage to go on.

'It seems that while my life and career are going down in flames you've just published two bestsellers. Your column – your syndicated column – has about a trillion readers. You're crisscrossing the country on yet another lecture tour every time we speak. Meanwhile, I'm going backwards, working in a job that I hate.'

'I didn't know that, darling. I didn't know you hated it.'

Hick's features darkened as she sat up. 'If you know me at all, Eleanor, you should have known that. Kissing the asses of reporters, sucking up to the kids I trained . . . I despise it. I should be in Berlin or London or Madrid reporting, doing what I was born to do. Instead, I'm stuck here nurturing a bitterness so sharp that it's fast festering into one hell of a grudge.'

'What about your book? Why don't we meet with my agent again and talk about publishers?'

'Stop trying to help me!' Hick yelled. 'I know you got me the job with the World's Fair.'

Eleanor was aghast. 'I had nothing to do with it. That position was won entirely by your own efforts.'

Hick looked at her cynically and stood. 'I can see them all looking at me. They don't respect me because I didn't earn it.'

'I promise you, darling,' Eleanor insisted, 'I had no hand in it.'

'Even if you didn't directly, my very position as the First Lady's best friend gives me a lot of pull that I'm not comfortable with. Since I was a kid, since I left home, I've always done things myself. I'm an underdog, for Christ's sake!'

'I understand that our position is tricky to say the least. But I am the First Lady and you are my dearest friend. These are facts which I can't change.'

Silence settled over them, neither knowing how to move forward. Eleanor was the first to speak.

'If you're not enjoying working for the World's Fair, I know there's a spot at the Women's Democratic Committee. Molly Dewson is leaving soon and there'll be some reshuffling . . .'

'You just don't get it, do you?' Hick was exasperated.

She rose from her position next to Eleanor and walked to the fireplace. She examined the walnut-coloured mantel closely. It was only about fifty inches long by twelve inches wide, she guessed, yet Eleanor had more than forty framed photographs of her dearest friends.

'I'm going back to New York today,' Hick said. 'I need time to myself.'

'As you like,' Eleanor said. 'We could get the train back together.'

'If I hurry I can make the eleven o'clock.'

Eleanor didn't press. 'Will you be back on the thirtieth for Franklin's birthday?'

'Let's wait and see.' Hick gave Eleanor a quick peck on the cheek and left the room.

The First Lady looked at the clock. There was still enough time to organise her papers for the meeting and have a light lunch before heading to the station.

38
WASHINGTON DC
March 1938

'Pack your bags, kiddo,' Monty said brightly as he entered the office Iris now shared with Tom Corcoran. 'We're going to Warm Springs.'

'I know, Tom told me,' she replied. 'But I really can't spare the time. I've got a paper due on the congressional prerogative.'

'Get Corcoran to write it for you,' he suggested playfully.

Iris shook her head.

'Oh, come on. The boss really wants to show you Warm Springs and I'll help you with your paper when we get back next week.'

Just then they heard the familiar shuffle of Tom Corcoran heading towards the office and Monty said, 'The break will do you good. Cooped up in the office all day with Tommy the Cork can't be good for anyone.'

'Shut up, Chapel,' Tom mumbled as he entered. 'Stop pestering the female staff and get back to work.'

'I'm trying to convince Iris to come to Warm Springs,' Monty explained. 'Will you give her the lowdown on the congressional prerogative when we get back?'

'Sure, there's nothing I'd like better,' he said distractedly as he searched his desk. Files, folders and documents were shuffled and restacked in his efforts.

Iris smiled. She enjoyed working with Tom. Apart from Monty, he was the most intelligent man she knew. He was generous, amusing, smoked incessantly, drank heartily and, at only thirty-nine, was one of the most influential men in politics. He was often called 'FDR's hatchet man' by the press, but Iris saw him as an Irish Catholic dynamo who did whatever it took to get New Deal legislation through Congress.

'Done,' Monty stated emphatically. 'You're coming to Warm Springs.'

'Anyway,' Tom said, cigarette hanging from the corner of his mouth, 'we need her if our mission has any chance of succeeding.'

'What do you mean?' Iris asked. 'What are you two hatching?'

Monty sat on the corner of Iris's desk. 'A surprise attack.'

'We've got to get the boss to jettison the balanced budget,' Tom explained. 'Monty's put together a proposal for a spending program to put the economy back on the rails.'

'But we've got to get the boss away from the likes of Wallace and Farley and all the other naysayers before we can present it,' Monty added. 'There's nowhere he's happier than at Warm Springs. Liquor, good food, we'll all take a girl . . .'

'A perfect time to attack,' Tom finished.

'Is Harry going?'

The men nodded.

'Who's he taking?'

'Dorothy Hale,' Monty said cautiously.

'The actress?' Iris asked, surprised.

'The bad actress,' Tom answered.

'She's very beautiful,' Iris said. 'But Barbara's only been dead six months.'

'My guess is that Dorothy's trying to land herself a rich husband; she's in her thirties, a high society widow left with a lot of debts and a career that's stalled,' Monty speculated.

'It never left the ground,' Tom pointed out.

'Is Harry that well off?' Iris questioned.

Monty shrugged. 'He's comfortable, I suppose,' he replied casually. 'He's no Nelson Rockefeller, if that's what you're asking.'

Tom departed when the missing document was found, but Monty lingered a little longer, as was his custom. As he removed his cigarette case from his breast pocket Iris said irritably, 'Don't you have somewhere you oughta be?'

'I suppose so,' he responded, bewildered at her change of tone.

'You're always hanging around here as if I don't have anything more important to do than entertain you.'

'What's got into you?' he said, standing and replacing his cigarette case.

'I'm busy, that's all.' Iris picked up the telephone receiver and began to dial. She stared pointedly at the door. When Monty had gone she replaced the receiver.

Iris had never seen Dorothy Hale on stage or on the screen. She knew her by reputation only and by all accounts she was an extraordinarily bad actress. Nevertheless, Monty and Tom's jibes annoyed her. She was a woman just trying to get by, Iris thought. And how did they know her feelings for Harry weren't genuine? Moreover, Iris wasn't at all pleased to be going to Georgia. She didn't want to collude with Monty and Tom in their scheme.

Iris sighed in resignation and went back to work, willing the trip to be over before it had even begun.

■

The president fetched Iris and Monty from the station on Thursday afternoon. They spotted him behind the wheel of an open-top Plymouth PA when they alighted. Three men – farmers, Iris gathered from their clothing – leaned on the automobile and talked with the president. Iris could hear Roosevelt's laughter over the hiss of the train. Four men from the Secret Service stood on either side of the president's vehicle.

'Sit up front with me, McIntosh,' Roosevelt called after Monty had placed the luggage in the trunk.

The president reversed out of his spot by the side of the station, forcing Iris's head violently forwards. Her hands instinctively grasped the dashboard. The Secret Service raced to their cars and sped off behind the president. Brake, clutch and throttle had been moved from the floor to around the steering column. Roosevelt handled the controls of the modified vehicle confidently, honking the horn and waving to locals as he drove by, shouting greetings to people by name. Iris clutched the door with one hand and the dashboard with the other as the president took corners at breakneck speed. He must be doing at least forty miles an hour, she thought. She squinted against the sunlight and the dust the tyres whipped into the air. All the time the president was talking and grinning, pointing out places of interest, corn farms and cotton plantations he'd visited and the best place in town for a sundae.

'What do you think?' he asked eagerly when the car came to a sudden halt in front of a small wooden cottage at the end of a long gravel drive.

'It's lovely, Mr President,' Iris said, admiring the four-columned portico and the French doors leading into the home. She noticed the driveway, porch and entrance were level. 'It *is* a little White House, isn't it?' she replied in admiration, referring to the nickname of the president's Warm Springs residence.

'It is indeed,' he cried, slapping the wheel.

Iris's misgivings regarding the trip were allayed. She had never seen the president so happy.

When they entered the house, Roosevelt instructed Iris that the first order of business was a tour of the neighbouring rehabilitation centre the president had built in the twenties, and then a swim, just the two of them, in one of the pools.

At the hospital the president introduced himself to patients and asked each one about their experience with infantile paralysis and the treatment they were receiving. Iris felt like an interloper, an upright imposter mocking them with her healthy body. This was one club of which she could never be a member. But Roosevelt spoke with his usual easy charm. The president was never seen in his wheelchair in public. State of the Union, addresses to Congress, accepting the Democratic nomination, inaugural speeches – on each occasion he walked to the podium supported by a son on one side and a cane on the other. Fourteen-pound callipers on each leg prevented them from giving way beneath him. But at Warm Springs he was surrounded by equals. The patients would never question his capacity to lead based on his infirmity. They left the hospital with the president promising to have a swim with the children the next morning.

By the time they reached the pool the sun was setting. Iris took off her robe and walked into the water, which was hot, as hot as a bath. She lifted her feet from the bottom of the pool and was immediately floating. It was a sensation she had never experienced.

'Wow,' she called to the president. 'I don't even need to move to stay afloat.'

'It's the magnesium in the water,' the president explained. 'That's why it's a perfect therapy for polio victims.'

'It doesn't look like a hospital,' Iris remarked.

'It's not supposed to. I designed the grounds and the buildings to resemble a university campus,' he said. 'In fact, work is beginning on a school at the end of the year. Some of the kids spend months away from home and miss quite a bit of their education. Healing is about keeping the mind strong as well as the body.'

Iris lay on her back and looked up at the orange sky, moving her arms and legs gently in the water. The gentle splashing of Roosevelt swimming reached her. In a minute he was by her side. She lifted her head and noticed his legs were floating near to the surface. She smiled.

'I can see why you love it here so much,' she said.

'It's the only place I can be myself, completely,' he said. 'When I set up this place in '26 I put most of what I had into it, in terms of money. Eleanor was aghast.' He laughed at the memory.

'I was down here every chance I got,' he continued. 'Mama wanted me to retire and live the life of a country squire at Springwood. But I was only thirty-nine. I came down here first in 1924 and as soon as I began swimming in the springs I felt an improvement. It wasn't long before I was walking again. There was a lot more that I had to achieve. I wasn't going to give up on life just yet.'

Then he added, 'Eleanor doesn't like coming down here so much. Never has. I understand. She has Val-Kill. But as they say, absence makes the heart grow fonder.' He smiled affectionately.

'That reminds me,' he went on. 'I was glad to see that Sam Jacobson's back in DC.'

Despite the heat of the water a shiver ran through Iris's body. 'Sam Jacobson?' she repeated.

'The one and only,' Roosevelt responded. 'Front and centre at Wednesday's press conference. Firing off questions about fascism, militarism . . .' He shook his head.

Iris couldn't believe that Sam had been in the White House only two days before. 'I didn't know he was back.'

'He's finished the book and now he's looking for a publisher,' he said.

Iris lay on her back and submerged her ears. She didn't want to hear any more. The orange sky gradually turned pink. Iris watched the transformation. Then she closed her eyes, aware only of her own breathing and the sweet scent from the surrounding crape myrtles and nothing more.

39
WARM SPRINGS, GEORGIA
March 1938

When Iris entered the living room the other guests were already drinking. A large punchbowl containing ruby-coloured liquor had been placed on a small table. Iris approached the crystal vessel and gazed into its depths. It was tempting, she thought. As she was pouring herself a small glass, Monty placed his arm around her waist and kissed her on the cheek.

'Watch out, this hooch is potent stuff,' he smirked and filled his glass again.

Unaffected by the merriment in the room, Iris didn't respond. She turned her back on Monty and glanced around the room.

'Good news,' he went on. 'Harry arrived this afternoon when you and the boss were swimming. We'll lay out the plan after dinner. Look at him.' Monty nodded towards the president. Missy was by his side, hand resting on his arm. Roosevelt was talking animatedly to Tom, drink in one hand, cigarette burning in the other. 'He'll agree to anything.'

Before he could continue Iris said, 'I'm just going to speak to Miss Hale.' She left Monty standing by the punch.

Iris had spotted the actress immediately when she entered the room. She was stunning, exotic. Her manner and appearance were in every way the opposite of her suitor, whose long neck, narrow head and bulging eyes always reminded Iris of an ostrich. In the few minutes Iris had been staring at her, Hale's posture hadn't shifted, neither did she speak. Harry had his back slightly turned away from her as he chatted with Tom's wife. Dorothy Hale was out of place at this gathering, a solitary bird of paradise. She surveyed the gathering with a bemused half-smile on her full red lips, the only guest without a glass in her hand. Instead she clutched a silver cigarette case, engraved with a design Iris could not make out from a distance. But Iris did recognise something familiar in her demeanour. A kindred spirit, perhaps? Iris made her way over.

'Hi. Miss Hale?' Iris held out her hand. 'My name's Iris McIntosh.

It's lovely to meet you.' As the actress passed the cigarette case into her left hand, Iris recognised the engraving as a fleur-de-lis.

'Please, call me Dorothy.' She offered Iris a cigarette. Iris could smell her perfume as she leaned in to light it and closed her eyes for an instant, attempting to identify the scent before it was drowned in smoke. Jasmine, she decided.

The woman stood. 'Shall we go outside? It's so stuffy in here.'

Iris nodded and followed Dorothy through the French doors. As they walked towards the fountain at the front of the house, Iris examined her gown. It was cream silk, the skirt trailing behind her created a small train of about six inches. Persimmon velvet bands criss-crossed her back. The skin of her tanned shoulders was flawless. They were the colour of honey.

They both sat on the cool stone of the fountain's edge. They didn't speak until they'd finished their cigarettes. Iris looked toward the stars, occasionally sneaking a sideways glance at her new friend's lovely, regal profile.

'What do you do at the White House, Iris?' Dorothy asked.

'I work in policy with Tom Corcoran,' she replied. 'I'm also studying.'

The actress nodded but didn't seem interested.

'Your gown is beautiful,' Iris said admiringly.

'I'm overdressed,' Dorothy replied, shrugging her perfect shoulders.

'Are you working at the moment?' Iris queried.

Dorothy turned to her, brow furrowed.

'On Broadway or in Hollywood?' Iris elaborated.

The actress shook her head.

'Where did you meet Harry?'

'In New York. At a party.' She didn't offer any more detail and Iris didn't press. Hale swirled her cigarette in the water in a figure of eight and then threw the butt on the ground. 'It seems we're both attracted to older men. You're here with Monty Chapel aren't you?'

'We're here together,' Iris clarified.

'Of course you are,' Dorothy said as she lit another cigarette.

Confused by her response, Iris asked, 'Do you know him?'

'I know *of* him.'

Monty was a high-profile member of the administration and of New York society. Dorothy Hale moved in similar circles. It would be unusual if she didn't know *of* Monty. Yet her tone and emphasis were troubling.

Her response resonated in Iris's mind for a number of minutes until the doors opened and she saw Monty walking towards them.

'It's a lovely evening,' he observed, 'but I'm afraid dinner is about to be served.'

Dorothy rose and took Iris's hand. 'It's been lovely talking to you, Iris. I'll see you both inside.'

Once she had departed, Monty sat down next to Iris and lit a cigarette.

'I thought you said dinner was about to be served,' Iris said.

He shook his head. 'I lied.'

'Have you met her before?' Iris asked.

'Nope,' he replied casually.

'She said she knew *of* you.' Iris hoped she'd got the stress correct.

'Well, she probably does. What's got into you tonight?' He shifted to face her.

'How does she survive?' Iris went on, ignoring his question and extinguishing her cigarette under her heel. 'She told me she's not working at the moment.'

'She lives off the largesse of wealthy men,' he answered. 'She's had a string of rich lovers since her husband died. Harry is but one in a long line of many.'

'Have you ever stood in that line?' Iris remembered all the words of caution – and, of course, there were Sam's vague hints just before he left for Spain the first time.

'What are you talking about?'

'Well?'

'You're being ridiculous,' he scoffed. 'Why are you trying to pick a fight with me, Iris?' He rarely called her Iris. 'Is it because Jacobson's back in town?'

'How did you know?'

'I saw him on Wednesday. I thought you would have known.'

'I only found out today,' she admitted. 'Anyway, I told you, there's nothing going on.'

'I get the feeling you'd like for something to be going on.'

Iris looked at the ground for a moment. She was being unfair, she realised, by allowing the opinions of others to colour her view of Monty.

'Now you're the one being ridiculous,' she said more affably. She took his hand. 'I'm sorry. Dorothy Hale rattled me. She had a tone . . . I can't explain it.'

She and Monty sat for some time by the fountain, neither speaking. The sound of the gramophone reached them from the house. Monty threw his cigarette on the ground and stubbed it out with his shoe. He stood and held out his hand. Iris accepted his offer and rose. He wrapped his arms tightly around her and they danced to Bing Crosby singing 'Let Me Whisper I Love You'. She pressed her face into Monty's neck. He hummed the tune softly into her ear.

The truth, she realised in the shelter of Monty's arms, was that it wasn't only Dorothy Hale's remark that had her rattled. She was peeved that Sam was back in Washington. She had made her decision at Thanksgiving. She had walked away and left him sitting at the bluff. His return had shaken her resolve. When the song finished she and Monty kissed.

'You'll be okay, kiddo,' he said, his mouth curving into a crooked smile. 'I'll make sure of it.'

She hugged him forcefully.

'Hey, listen, I've just had a thought,' he began. Even though the music was over, the couple was still swaying slightly. 'You know work has just finished on the chapel over at the hospital, don't you?'

She nodded, unsure where this was heading.

'Why don't we get married there tomorrow?'

Startled, Iris pulled back and stared into Monty's face. 'But we've never talked about marriage or children or anything,' she stalled.

'What's to talk about? We love each other. We can have kids when we're ready. Although it'll have to be pretty soon if I'm ever going to play ball with them.' He laughed.

Just say 'yes', she willed herself. One little word. Just say it. 'Where would we live?'

'We could get an apartment in DC or a house. I know you love Georgetown. I'll let my apartment in New York and give up my suite at the Mayflower.'

'This is all quite a shock,' Iris said, flustered. 'I wasn't expecting a proposal tonight. Ever, to be honest.'

'What do you say?' he asked. 'We're made for each other, kiddo.'

'Are we?' she responded doubtfully.

'I always thought so,' he countered.

She glanced at his face. His high spirits had waned. She turned away quickly towards the fountain, sick with self-reproach. She wished Mrs Roosevelt was here.

'I need to sleep on it,' she said, aware it was a coward's response. 'I've got school to consider.'

'Among other things.'

Iris couldn't turn to look at him. She felt his hands on her arms. He kissed her on the back of her head and walked towards the house.

'I'll see you inside, Iris,' he called over his shoulder.

■

Dinner was a feast. Vegetable soup with okra, roast oysters, fried chicken with cream gravy and mush, string beans with bacon, and peach trifle. Iris moved the colours around on her plate, the food rarely touching her lips, as she stole rapid glimpses of Monty. Each glance only served to dampen her appetite further.

After she'd come inside Monty had avoided her. He poured himself a large glass of bourbon and consumed it quickly. Throughout dinner he'd not uttered a word in her direction. Iris had lost track of how much he had drunk, but by the time dessert was served he was well and truly smashed. Once dinner was completed and the remnants of the evening were being cleared away, Harry suggested the men decamp to the president's study.

Judy Corcoran put another record on the gramophone and Missy sat in an armchair, her head against the back rest, eyes closed, her foot tapping to the music. Dorothy Hale stood by the window, smoking. Iris felt ill. She suddenly found the atmosphere of the living room stifling. Feigning a yawn, she told the women she was exhausted and left the room.

Standing outside on the portico she breathed deeply, but the cool of the evening did nothing to quell her nausea. She stepped off the portico and rounded the corner of the house. Hunched beneath a pine tree, clutching her stomach, Iris heard a low voice.

'You okay, honey?'

Iris straightened and turned. A Negro woman stood there. She held her hands in front of her, at the ready.

'I'm sick,' Iris moaned.

'I can see that, honey.' The woman placed a gentle hand on Iris's back. 'Do you reckon you're done?'

Iris nodded.

'Come with me into the kitchen.'

The woman took her arm and led Iris back to the house. They entered the kitchen through the side door. Dishes littered the table and bench. She cleared a space at the table and sat Iris down. The young man who had served the president's table sat eating the leftovers.

'This here's my boy,' the woman said as she got a clean dish towel and soaked it under the faucet. Iris smiled. 'I'm Daisy Bonner, the president's cook.' She folded the towel and placed it on Iris's forehead. 'Hold it there, honey,' she instructed.

Iris did as she was told.

'You must be Iris McIntosh,' the woman surmised. 'The president told me about you. Said you were as smart as a whip.'

Iris attempted to respond, but her throat was choked with tears.

'Hey, Lonnie,' Daisy said to her son. 'Go out back and finish that.'

The boy nodded and left the kitchen with his plate. The moment the screen door shut behind him Iris began to cry. Daisy calmly took the dish towel from Iris's hand and silently replaced it with a clean, pressed handkerchief. She took the seat Lonnie had occupied and watched Iris sob. After a couple of minutes she spoke.

'Okay, that's enough now, honey,' she said, patting Iris's hand. 'That's enough tears for one night. I'll fix you a little ginger tea.'

Iris looked at Daisy. Her face was stern behind her thick, black-rimmed spectacles. Iris sniffed and wiped her eyes. 'That would be nice. Thanks.'

Daisy walked to the sink and filled the kettle. 'Now, I know it weren't my cooking that made you sick. You ate like a bird tonight. Lonnie told me it was the lady wearing trousers that weren't eatin' nothin'.'

A smile forced its way to Iris's lips. 'It wasn't your cooking. Dinner was lovely.' She explained, 'I upset someone tonight, very much.'

Daisy nodded thoughtfully and continued with the tea. After a few minutes of silence she handed Iris a cup of steaming liquid. Iris held it under her nose for a few seconds. The pungency tickled the back of her throat.

'Mind if I join you?' Daisy asked, indicating a second cup.

Iris shook her head. 'Not at all.'

Iris stared into the cup she clutched in her hands and then asked, 'How long have you worked for the president, Mrs Bonner?'

'Since he first come here in '24. I was the cook at the Meriwether Inn. Then when he tore it down to build the hospital he kept me on as cook. And when he visits I always cook for him here. I'm proud to say that I cooked that man his first meal in Warm Springs.' She laughed easily. 'I like to think that's why he keeps coming back.'

Iris thought of Mrs Nesbitt. 'It probably is,' she said.

Daisy finished her tea. 'Those dishes ain't going to clean themselves, Miss Iris,' she said, standing. 'Excuse me.'

Iris followed her to the sink and picked up a dish towel. 'I'll dry.'

'Be careful with that, honey,' Daisy instructed a few minutes later as Iris lifted the punchbowl to dry. 'That was a wedding gift to the president and Mrs Roosevelt from the first President Roosevelt.'

'I wish you hadn't told me that,' Iris said as she clutched the object more tightly.

As the women worked Daisy asked, 'Who did you upset? Was it Mr Chapel? He's been coming to Warm Springs going on eight years now and I never seen him drink so much as he did tonight.'

'He proposed to me before dinner and I didn't say yes,' Iris confessed. She needed to tell someone.

'Did you say no?'

Iris shook her head. 'I didn't give him an answer. I said I needed to sleep on it.'

'Sometimes that's worse than saying no,' Daisy suggested.

Iris looked at her. 'I know.'

'Mr Chapel's a funny one, that's for sure. He's got quite a head on his shoulders as well. Money, I hear, and he's just about the best-looking man that's ever set foot in the state of Georgia.' Daisy looked at Iris assessingly. 'He's a mite older than you, ain't he?' Iris nodded. 'But that shouldn't matter none if you love him.'

Iris did love Monty, without a doubt. But it was a strange sort of love, she realised, now that she had something to compare it to. Love bordering on dependency. What she felt for Sam was love without necessity.

'Personally,' Daisy continued plainly as she scrubbed a heavy pot vigorously, 'I don't see you two marrying.' She looked at Iris and pushed her spectacles up the bridge of her nose with the back of her hand.

'Why is that?' Iris asked keenly. She longed for the answer to the question she'd been asking herself for years. Perhaps Daisy Bonner, the president's cook, had the answer that eluded Iris.

'You see, honey, to my thinking, all women want to get married and raise a family. Don't kid yourself. You can call yourself a career woman all you want, but all women want to raise a family. It's just the natural way. Why do you think that Miss Hale is so quiet and sad-looking all the time? It's not money she's after, it's a family.'

'And you don't think Mr Chapel wants a wife and family?' Iris said.

'Uh-uh.' She shook her head. 'If he'd wanted to get caught, a woman would have done so by now. He may think he wants you, but it's more than likely the thought of losing you that he's trying to duck. He's lonely too, you see. But that's no reason to marry someone.'

■

It was past midnight before Iris and Daisy Bonner had finished. Even so, Daisy made them each a cup of chamomile tea to beckon sleep. There was not a sound to be heard in the house. When Daisy and Lonnie left the kitchen via the back door two Secret Service men took positions at the table. One of them produced a deck of cards from his pocket. Iris crept through the darkened living room, the wooden floors creaking under her weight, towards the room she and Monty were sharing. She could see light shining from beneath the door. It was close to two o'clock. Iris had been hoping to delay another encounter with Monty until the morning. Placing her hand on the door handle, she braced herself against his resentment, but in the silence of the hour she was able to hear the low grumble of his snore.

Apart from his shirt, which he'd unbuttoned to the waist, he was still dressed in the clothes he'd worn at dinner. Iris took off her shoes and walked to the bed. There was half a glass of bourbon on the side table and a cigarette burned in an ashtray. Iris twisted the butt into the glass base of the ashtray then she pulled off Monty's shoes and placed them under the bed. Leaning over him, she carefully unknotted and removed his tie. Iris looked at his face in the glow of the lamp and brushed his hair tenderly from his forehead. Then she gingerly inched his shirt open and examined his scar. It was as bold and as shameless as ever. Couldn't his intentions be genuine? she pondered. Was it really only the threat of Sam Jacobson that had inspired the proposal? Loneliness was an emotion she had never associated with Monty. She sat on the bed and placed her hand on his cheek. Would it be so wrong of her to accept?

Contemplating her situation in the dim light, she jumped to her feet when Monty suddenly rolled onto his side from his back. As he did so something fell to the ground that he must have had clutched in his hand. Bending down to retrieve the scrap of paper, Iris saw it was a photograph. A photograph of a young man in military uniform. She examined it closely.

It definitely wasn't Monty. While the boy in the uniform was handsome, his features were more finely cut and the hair that protruded from his hat was lighter than Monty's. Iris catalogued the possibilities. It couldn't be a brother; Monty was an only child. It would be odd, she thought, for a man to fall asleep with a photograph of any male relation, other than a father, clutched to his chest. And it couldn't be his father, she surmised, as the picture was too recent. Monty's father must be in his seventies or even eighties. This young man served in the Great War.

A friend, Iris concluded. A close friend who was killed. She remembered his reaction to Louis Howe's death. An 'old soldier', Monty had called him. She placed the photograph on the side table and turned off the lamp, then slid into bed next to him.

■

Iris didn't wake until Monty pulled the curtains back.

'Good morning, sleepyhead,' he greeted her cheerfully. 'It's nearly lunchtime.'

She rolled onto her back and looked at Monty through half-closed eyes. He was showered, shaved and dressed in a light-grey three-piece suit. Given the events of the night before, his sprightliness was disconcerting. Clearing her throat she asked huskily, 'How are you feeling? You had quite a bit to drink last night.'

'Good as gold,' he replied. 'Where did you get to after dinner? Tie one on with Dorothy Hale? You slept in your clothes.'

'I went for a walk,' she answered, sitting up. She turned to the bedside table. The photograph was no longer where she had left it. 'I wanted to think over your proposal.' Telling Monty that she'd spent most of the evening in the kitchen with Daisy Bonner would have led to a string of questions she didn't feel like answering.

'Well, you've got a little more time up your sleeve,' he said. 'The boss wants me back in DC pronto. He agreed to the plan and I need to go over the numbers. He wants something ready to take to Congress on the fourteenth.'

'Oh, but I thought we could talk about things . . .'

'I'm catching the twelve thirty train.'

'I'll come back with you,' Iris said as she moved to the edge of the bed. 'We can talk on the train.'

'Don't be silly,' he said lightly, working his hat onto his head, positioning it at just the right angle. 'You come back next week as planned. Enjoy the break. I'll be tied up with work all weekend anyway.'

'But I don't want to be here without you,' she insisted. 'I'm sorry about last night.'

'What's to be sorry about, kiddo? You said you needed more time. I understand. We'll talk on Wednesday when you get back. I'll meet you at Union Station and take you to dinner.'

Iris hated for him to leave with so many things left unsaid. Important things. She wanted to know about the photograph. But it seemed their talk would have to wait until next week.

Monty picked up his bag. He'd already packed, she noted. 'I'll see you back in DC.' As he leaned over the bed, about to kiss her, she leaped to her feet and embraced him.

'I love you, Monty, I really do,' she whispered. It was the truth. She needed for him to believe it. His jovialness was an act, Iris was certain of it. Despite her feelings for Sam, she couldn't lose Monty.

'I know.' He looked into her eyes seriously for a moment before leaving the room.

'Goodbye,' she muttered to herself after he'd closed the door.

Slumping onto the bed, she lit a cigarette. Despite only consuming half a glass of punch, she did feel as though she'd tied one on. Her head was foggy and a suggestion of a headache was forming behind her eyes. It was useless to consider Sam in this mess, she decided. He hadn't made contact since arriving in Washington. It was over. She had to forget about him. After all, she had built a relationship with Monty over the last five years. What's more, he had proposed! So what if that proposal had been driven by jealousy or loneliness, as Daisy had suggested? Surely that didn't prevent them from being happy together. The foundations of a delightful life were all laid out; Iris couldn't understand why she was so intent on demolishing them.

Iris changed into her swimming costume and left the house in the direction of the pool, determined to make up for the hurt she'd inflicted on Monty once she returned to Washington.

40

WASHINGTON DC
March 1938

As the train pulled in to Union Station late on Wednesday afternoon, Iris rehearsed in her mind the scene on the platform. She would see Monty standing among the porters and passengers, spinning his hat in his hands, the shadow of a smile on his handsome face. Running towards him, Iris would throw herself into his arms, kiss him and then announce her intention to marry him.

'I'm sorry I've been such a fool,' she would say. 'You're the only man for me.'

They would kiss again and he'd say something along the lines of, 'I love you, kiddo. You've made me the happiest man in the world.'

Appreciating the theatrics of it all, he might then lift her from her feet and twirl her around. Maybe he'd lower her into a dip and follow with a Hollywood kiss right there on the platform.

After he collected her bags and tipped the porter they'd take a cab to dinner, perhaps Montmartre, the scene of their first dinner together all those years ago. And then back to the Mayflower or her apartment. Perhaps they'd skip dinner. She didn't care. Iris only wanted to set this production in motion. She was desperate for her life to move forward. Inaction always distressed her.

The train stopped. She looked through the window in an attempt to spot him. She couldn't. Iris collected her belongings. Standing behind a queue of people making their way to the exit she bent low, peering out windows as she passed slowly through the carriage. When she finally alighted and stepped onto the platform she turned her head from left to right. Still no Monty. Was he attempting to teach her a lesson? she wondered. No, that wasn't his style.

Hesitating, as she hurriedly rewrote the scene, Iris considered calling Monty's office at the White House then decided against it. Why waste more time? He must be busy and his promise to meet her at the station was forgotten. The president had returned to DC the previous day. He would have wanted to work through the proposal straight away. She would surprise Monty at work.

'Good to see ya back, Iris,' Bert on the gate called as he waved her through.

'It's good to be home,' she responded cheerily.

'How was Georgia?' he asked.

'Just fine,' she answered. 'Have you seen Mr Chapel around?'

'Nope, he left about lunchtime. Just let me check.' Bert scanned the pages of his register. 'Ten minutes past twelve.'

The information stopped Iris in her tracks. 'Really? You sure?'

Bert nodded and looked at the page a second time. 'Yep. Ten minutes past twelve o'clock it says. The ledger doesn't lie.'

Iris looked at her watch. It was approaching six.

'Of course. Thanks Bert.'

Walking, almost running, to the West Wing entrance, Iris fretted over the undoing of her plans for their reunion. She was nervous. Monty's behaviour – deserting her at the station, leaving work at twelve – was totally uncharacteristic. He was usually so mindful, especially when it came to her.

When she reached his office the door was closed but unlocked. No light was visible behind the frosted-glass panel. She entered the room. His desk had been cleared. A knot formed in her throat. Slamming the door behind her, she walked through the labyrinthine corridors of the West Wing until she reached the Oval Office.

Iris tapped on Missy's door before entering. The president's private secretary was seated behind her desk.

'Iris, when did you get in? Weren't you due to arrive at nine?' Missy said. Her face was tense as she flicked through the pages of her large leather-bound diary.

Iris shook her head. 'I was always on the early train.'

'Oh, there must have been an oversight.' Missy cleared her throat. Her pale face was flushed.

Iris knew something was wrong; Missy was usually unflappable.

'Where's Monty?' Iris asked. 'He didn't meet me at the station and I went to his office. All his things have gone.'

Missy cleared her throat again. 'There has been an upset,' she explained, looking at Iris sympathetically.

'What?'

'Perhaps it's better if Monty tells you.' She glanced at the clock on the wall. 'There's still plenty of time.'

'Until what?' Iris demanded, her voice breaking with anxiety.

The door to the Oval Office opened. 'Come in, McIntosh,' Roosevelt said.

Once Iris was seated on the sofa in the Oval Office the president asked, 'Would you like a drink?'

'No,' she said, perched on the edge of the seat. 'I just want to know what's going on. Has Monty been fired? Was his proposal no good?'

'His proposal was excellent. I'm taking it to the floor next week. Some of the best problem-solving he's ever done.'

'Then where is he?'

The president paused for an instant before looking Iris squarely in the eyes. 'Monty's decided to take a leave of absence.'

Iris stared at him in disbelief. 'But he never mentioned anything like that to me. A leave of absence?'

'It all happened very quickly, dear. It was really only finalised this morning.' Roosevelt spoke soothingly. He came a little closer and took Iris's hand. Could this be her fault?

'He proposed to me,' she began. 'Monty proposed and I didn't accept immediately. I was intending to tell him yes today. I knew he was hurt, but I . . .'

'This has nothing to do with you,' Roosevelt reassured her, then groaned slightly. 'Monty's got himself into some trouble.'

'What sort of trouble?'

'On the train coming back from Warm Springs . . .' The president stopped and looked at Iris intently, as if attempting to convey with his eyes what he didn't want to say.

'I'm sorry, but I don't know what you mean. Just tell me,' she pleaded.

Roosevelt stared at her for another few seconds before continuing, 'Monty propositioned a porter.'

She was silent. The lump in Iris's throat moved to her chest. She wasn't certain what she was feeling at that moment, sitting opposite the president in the Oval Office, and she didn't fully understand the nature of Monty's transgression. She didn't even know there were female porters on trains.

The president was still looking at her, waiting for her to speak.

'Obviously, I'm shocked, upset,' she began. 'But why would this lead to a leave of absence? Surely this is a personal matter between Monty and me.'

'He's threatening to go to the press,' Roosevelt said bluntly.

Iris stared at him, puzzled. 'Monty?'

'No, the porter. Mr Francis Slattery.'

Iris's breathing quickened. She gaped at the president.

'You've turned very pale, McIntosh. I'm getting you that drink.'

The president hurriedly poured a glass of bourbon and handed it to her. 'You didn't realise it was a man, did you?' he asked quietly.

She shook her head and stared into her glass. Then she drank the contents in one gulp. It was shame that she was feeling now, she recognised it instantly.

'This Mr Slattery wants money. I've instructed Monty not to pay him. If he does, well, he'd have an even bigger story.'

'What's going to happen?'

'We're sending Monty to Tokyo in an ambassadorial role. We'll shut this Mr Slattery down one way or the other, but Monty's got to disappear for a while. He's a very public face in this administration.'

Iris understood. There was no other way. He'd let the government down and threatened the administration with a scandal.

'When's he leaving?'

'He's flying tonight.'

■

'I was waiting to see whether you'd come,' Monty said when he opened the door.

'I nearly didn't,' she said, entering his suite. Four suitcases stood in the centre of the room. 'Turns out you were right.'

Monty threw her an inquisitive glance.

'I am a prude.'

He laughed softly and set about making her a drink. Iris sat on the sofa, a sofa she had sat on hundreds of times before. Rubbing the fabric, she was suddenly overwhelmed by a sense of loss.

'I had it all planned,' she said, striving to keep her voice from breaking. 'A passionate reunion at the station, my acceptance of your proposal followed by a night of debauchery.'

'But I started on the debauchery a little too early,' he said ruefully. Monty sipped his drink thoughtfully before adding, 'I'm so sorry, kiddo.'

Iris nodded.

'You were going to accept?'

'Yes,' she murmured. 'I was so excited.'

Monty stared into his scotch for a minute. 'You still can,' he urged, placing his drink and her own on the table and taking her hands. 'Come to Japan with me. The irony is that this sideways step in my career will look pretty good on my résumé and it won't be for long. When this blows over we'll come back. What d'you say?'

She shook her head. 'I can't. Everything has changed. This' – she searched for an appropriate word – 'entanglement makes me feel a little sick.'

Iris could see she had wounded him with her words, but it was the truth. She could never look at Monty in the same way again. The spell he had cast on her in Tommy's office all those years ago was finally broken.

'Have there been other men?' she asked, afraid of the answer but desperate to know.

'On occasion,' he answered.

'While we've been together?'

'On occasion,' he repeated.

She sighed deeply and clutched at her glass. She took a long sip, astounded at her own blindness, struggling to believe this was really happening.

'Was my hesitancy on Friday night the reason for the porter?' she asked, looking up. She couldn't bring herself to mention Francis Slattery by name.

'Yes,' Monty said, 'and no. I was miffed – jealous, I guess. I suppose your hesitancy did affect my mood. But I saw this young man in uniform on the train and . . .' He paused for a moment. 'He reminded me of somebody.'

'The boy in the photograph?' Iris asked, already knowing the answer.

Monty nodded. 'How . . .?'

'Your last night at Warm Springs. You fell asleep with it in your hands. I wondered who it was.' She looked at him earnestly. 'Did you love him?'

'Very much.'

'What happened?'

'He was blown to pieces in front of me,' Monty replied without emotion. 'I couldn't do a thing to save him.'

'Is that how you were injured?' she asked quietly.

He nodded. 'It happened on the same day, yes.'

'I'm sorry.' It wasn't a platitude. Iris wanted Monty to be content. 'I wish you didn't have to go through that.'

Her life had veered so dramatically in the last few hours. There was so much Iris wanted to know in her desperation to make sense of what was probably inexplicable. When they finished their drinks, they held hands on the sofa without saying anything more. Iris stared at Monty's bags and considered what life without him would be like. She was angry with him for his actions, furious that he had scuttled her plans and destroyed his career in DC, yet she knew she would miss him terribly. She could already sense a chasm opening up inside her.

'You're everything to me,' she said finally. 'I don't know what I'll do without you.'

'Thank you for the compliment, kiddo. But you've always taken care of yourself just fine. You doubt yourself, but you have. Coming to DC, showing up at the White House . . . You're an amazing woman, Iris McIntosh. You're the best thing that's ever happened to me.'

His words only made it worse. Iris had never been any person's 'best thing'.

'I'm miserable that I screwed it all up.' He went on looking down at their entwined fingers. 'But it's just in my nature.'

'You lack impulse control.' Iris remembered her conversation with Mrs Roosevelt at Christmas dinner a few years previously.

'Indeed I do.'

'I wish we had more time.'

'That would just make it more difficult to say goodbye.' He held out his arm and Iris slid along the sofa. She nestled against him and gave over to her sorrow.

Monty stroked her back tenderly. 'There, there,' he said softly. 'If there's anything that you need, ever, your wish is my command.'

'You'll be my guardian angel?'

'I'll be anything you want me to be,' he answered seriously.

They smiled and embraced once more.

'My girl?' Monty whispered apprehensively in her ear.

'Always.' It was the truth. But at the same time Iris realised that without Monty she would have to become a very different kind of girl.

41
WASHINGTON DC
April 1938

On 14 April 1938 the president asked Congress for a special appropriation of $3.4 billion to revive the flagging economy – an economy that he had shot in the foot, Monty had declared only two weeks earlier in Warm Springs.

'Getting Congress to open the coffers is just the first step in repairing the boss's reputation,' Monty had explained to Iris. 'Ever since the Supreme Court debacle it's been low tide for this administration.'

Congress agreed to his request. At Children's Hour that evening everyone was thrilled. Roosevelt was cheery, Harry Hopkins and Tom Corcoran jubilant. Monty's name was not spoken. The group chatted merrily about the president's youngest son's upcoming wedding in Nahant, Massachusetts. Iris was expected to attend. The very thought made her weary. She left after one drink, blaming a headache. But it was loneliness, pure and simple, that was responsible. The chasm within that had begun forming on the evening Monty flew to Tokyo had only grown larger.

Iris walked through the White House gates and headed towards Lafayette Square. There she sat on one of the metal seats, delaying her return to her empty apartment. The sun had set a few hours before but there was a constant stream of people cutting though the square. Iris lit a cigarette and mourned for Monty. He had been integral to the New Deal. Only two weeks after his departure he seemed to be forgotten. Iris needed time to grieve and she was angered that nobody else, not a single one of his closest colleagues, saw the same necessity. No one, apart from her, had grieved over her father either.

Iris had been informed of his death by her neighbour, Mrs Woods. She had struggled to believe it at first. Her father was so young, not yet forty.

'Where?' Iris asked.

Mrs Woods's kind face was sombre. 'He collapsed in the street. It was his asthma.'

'I mean, where is he now?' Iris asked.

'At St Agnes,' Mrs Woods said. 'Some men took him there. It was too late. He died on the way.'

Even though she was only thirteen, Iris knew from experience that liquor triggered her father's asthma, and Torrie had been drinking more and more since her mother passed six months before. His absences from home had increased. Iris grew accustomed to caring for herself, learning to make herself scarce when the landlord was due to call for the rent. Occasionally Torrie would reappear with a little money, sometimes a lot, and give Iris enough for food and rent. Iris wanted to see her father one last time to say goodbye, even though he was dead, but Mrs Woods wouldn't allow it.

'You're to come and live with us,' Mrs Woods told her. 'Just until we can get everything sorted.' She hugged the girl tightly to her ample bosom, then showed her to the guest room and suggested that she have a rest.

It was while Iris was lying on the metal-framed bed that was to become her own for the next five years that Mr Woods arrived home from his job repairing streetcars for the J.G. Brill Company.

Iris rolled onto her side and hugged her knees to her chest. Her stomach was empty and its edgeless ache was the worst pain she had ever felt. Mrs Woods tapped lightly on the door.

'Iris, dear. Would you like anything? Are you hungry?' she asked.

'No thank you,' Iris said politely. 'I'm not hungry.'

Mrs Woods retreated into the kitchen with her husband. Iris could hear their whispered conversation in the kitchen as Mrs Woods began supper.

'I'll telephone her grandparents tomorrow,' Iris heard her say softly. 'Abigail told me to contact them if anything should ever go awry.'

Iris hadn't known she had living grandparents. She knew her father's parents were dead; he spoke of them often and in the fondest terms. Her mother had said that her parents were deceased as well. But she had rarely spoken of her mother or father. Still, the idea of relatives, even ones she had never met, was a comfort to the grieving girl.

'She's well rid of him,' Mr Woods commented. 'Drunk and idle. The worst of all men rolled into one.'

'That may well be,' his wife agreed, 'but his daughter loved him very much. Children don't see the faults in their parents.'

Mrs Woods never mentioned the telephone call or its outcome to Iris, but the girl went on living with the childless couple until she was eighteen years old.

When Iris raised herself from the seat in Lafayette Square she was still sick with longing for Monty. Why had he done it? she asked herself. Why couldn't he have just controlled himself? Then Iris thought of the porter, Mr Francis Slattery. Nothing had been mentioned of the scandal in the newspapers and she wondered how the situation had finally resolved.

42
NAHANT, MASSACHUSETTS
June 1938

The wedding of John Aspinwall Roosevelt to Anne Lindsay Clark of Boston took place on 18 June. There must have been three hundred guests, Iris guessed, packed into the historic Nahant church. But Anne's folks could afford it, Tom Corcoran informed her during the ceremony. After dinner Iris stood on the balcony of the Nahant Tennis Club, smoking. She had worn an Elizabeth Hawes evening dress that Monty insisted on purchasing for her when she'd admired it a magazine. It was sensational, she remembered him remarking of the deep magenta bias-cut silk gown.

Iris's eyes wandered from the sparsely lit tennis courts on her left to the spectacle of the dance floor on her right. She leaned against the doorframe, her thoughts mainly drifting to Monty. They had agreed not to write while he was in Japan and she imagined how different the evening would be if he were present.

She had spoken to neither the president nor Mrs Roosevelt all afternoon. She had last glimpsed the First Couple when they arrived at the dock in Salem the previous afternoon. Iris had driven up with Tom and Judy. They reached Salem about an hour before the president's yacht was due to arrive. The town was abuzz with well-wishers and media, hoping to catch a glimpse of Roosevelt and his motorcade as he travelled to the resort town of Nahant about ten miles away.

'Son of a bitch,' Tom said in amazement as they drove into town and caught sight of the masses lining the streets three deep. 'Who said the presidency was in the doldrums?'

'And look at the press,' Iris added.

There were newspaper photographers every few yards, standing on ladders and crates or perched in the trees that bordered the sidewalk.

'How many people do you think there are?' Judy asked.

'If there are this many along the road all the way to Nahant, then I would have to guess at least fifty thousand,' Tom answered.

The six-piece wedding band stopped playing while the band leader called all the unmarried women to the dance floor. Iris moved out of the light and finished her cigarette. She opened her small purse in search of another. The music began once more.

'You make quite a sight,' the president said as he approached. 'Standing as you are, mysterious in the shadows. You look lovely, McIntosh. How're things?'

'Fine, sir,' she replied. 'It was a beautiful ceremony. John and Anne seem very happy.'

The president nodded and then said sincerely, 'I hope they remain that way, but situations change. We have to adapt with them.'

Iris contemplated his counsel. He spoke from experience, she realised, as she thought of Missy and Hick.

'I'd like to ask you to dance, McIntosh,' he went on. 'I've been watching you tonight. You haven't danced at all.'

She smiled apologetically as she pulled up a chair next to the president.

'You know,' he continued, 'I believe I fell in love with Eleanor on the dance floor. It was at a Christmas party at her Aunt Corinne's house and no one was dancing with her. She was only fourteen but she was very tall and an extremely serious young lady. All the young men were quite terrified of her.' He smiled nostalgically. 'But by God she was striking. I was the only fella with the nerve and the stature to approach. Turned out she was an angel.'

'That's a lovely memory,' Iris said. She had never imagined the Roosevelts in love. They led such separate lives.

'My heart still skips a beat just when she's poised to speak,' he said. 'You know the way her eyes crinkle and her mouth opens slightly.'

Iris smiled in response; she knew exactly the expression he meant. 'Where did you get married?'

'In New York at the townhouse of Eleanor's cousin Susie,' he recalled. 'It was a grand affair. Her Uncle Teddy gave her away and stole the show, as is typically the case when a president is invited to a wedding.'

'So I witnessed this afternoon,' Iris said with a grin. Just then the band began playing 'Don't Be That Way' and the balcony was quickly deserted.

The president laughed. 'Tell me about your folks. Where did your parents tie the knot?'

'They eloped, Mr President,' Iris informed him. 'I'm not certain where exactly they married.'

'You don't say.' Iris could see his curiosity had been piqued. He lit another cigarette. 'Why was that?'

Iris shook her head. 'I assume my mother's family didn't approve of my father.' She stubbed out her cigarette and then looked at the president. 'I don't know the full story. I was just a kid when they died.'

'You were raised by your grandparents, weren't you?'

Iris hesitated a moment before shaking her head. 'They didn't want me,' she confessed. 'Elderly neighbours became my guardians until I was eighteen. They passed when I was at college.'

The president examined her closely, as though viewing an artwork for the very first time. Then he took her hand and squeezed it tightly. The pair sat on the balcony for quite some time without speaking, gazing out onto the perfect green of the tennis courts.

When the music stopped, Missy appeared on the balcony and spoke softly into the president's ear. He nodded.

'Duty calls, McIntosh.' He raised her hand to his lips and kissed her fingertips softly.

■

When the toasts concluded and people began milling back out to the balcony, Iris took her leave and hurried down the steps that led to the tennis courts. On the ground, she could hear the chatter and laughter of those above on the balcony, but she was confident she hadn't been seen. Removing her shoes, she walked carefully along the six courts, following the baseline of each as accurately as she could with her bare feet. She enjoyed the sensation of the cold, yielding grass beneath her feet and found the predictability of the white line reassuring.

As she turned the corner, intending to make her way along the doubles sideline of the final court, she heard a familiar trill.

'Iris, dear, what are you doing out here by yourself?'

Iris stopped and looked in the direction from which the voice had come. In an instant she saw the First Lady striding towards her, the blue of her gown radiant in the moonlight. The press had labelled the colour 'Eleanor blue'. Eleanor herself referred to the particular shade as hyacinth. It was the same colour as the gown she wore to her husband's first inauguration.

'I just wanted to be alone for a while,' Iris answered.

'You've been alone all evening,' Mrs Roosevelt said severely. 'This has gone on long enough.'

Iris looked at her, shocked.

'You've moped around for the last two months,' the First Lady continued. 'Enough is enough. Stop pining for the man who humiliated you.'

It was impossible for Iris to argue. Being hit by the truth so violently and unexpectedly was devastating.

'Talk to me, Iris. What's got into you?' Mrs Roosevelt demanded.

'I miss him; I miss Monty terribly,' Iris confessed. 'Nothing is the same. As stupid as it sounds, it's as if my life has stopped.'

The older woman's demeanour immediately softened. Placing her arm around Iris's shoulders she led her wordlessly to the raked seats usually reserved for spectators. The women sat for a minute before Mrs Roosevelt broke the silence.

'I know it feels like that. But your life hasn't stopped, it has merely changed,' she said compassionately. 'Perhaps even for the better.'

'I just can't see how anything good could come out of this,' Iris responded. 'I feel so empty. Nothing matters any more.'

'Fill the emptiness with something meaningful, Iris. You can't see it now, but Monty was a crutch.'

Iris turned to her sharply.

'Try standing by yourself for a little while. It will do you the world of good. You don't need him any more.'

Iris knew she was trying to help, but Mrs Roosevelt's words only served to increase her sorrow.

'Has anyone told you about Lucy Mercer?' Mrs Roosevelt asked kindly after a minute.

Iris vacillated before answering. 'Monty told me snippets.'

'Lucy was my secretary. The children adored her. I adored her. When I discovered my husband was having an affair with her I was distraught. Crushed. I realised he was no longer my husband. I was alone. The emptiness was insidious.'

'What did you do?' Iris asked.

'I got angry and then I was sad and then I worked,' she said matter-of-factly. 'I devoted myself to causes and committees dedicated to improving the lot of women and the underprivileged. I discovered I was good at something other than being Mrs Franklin Delano Roosevelt. I thrived and we steadily rebuilt our marriage, but on more equal ground. Then, when Franklin caught polio and spent such a long time recuperating, it was Louis who pushed me off the deep end into political waters. That was when I discovered I could swim.'

'I don't think I'm as resilient as you,' Iris said.

'Don't be foolish. Of course you are,' Mrs Roosevelt replied bluntly. 'You survived the depression by yourself, without anybody's assistance. Now you're working for this administration, studying to become a lawyer. Don't tell me you're not resilient.'

Iris had never thought of herself in these terms. She supposed she *had* lost herself in Monty for a time. And then there was Sam. So much energy she had devoted to thoughts of his well-being. Iris realised she had been buried by these relationships.

'The world is at a turning point,' Mrs Roosevelt went on. 'If it turns the way I think it will, then we need all the good people fit for duty.'

'I understand,' Iris said. 'Thank you.'

Mrs Roosevelt stood to leave. 'I'll see you at work on Monday, dear.' She patted Iris's shoulder and walked towards the clubhouse.

Iris was left by herself on the wooden seat as Mrs Roosevelt's Eleanor blue faded into darkness. Contemplating what the president and Mrs Roosevelt had discussed with her, she realised that this night she herself had reached a turning point, a critical fork in the road.

■

Without hope or agenda Iris waited in the corridor outside the Oval Office. She had resolved to confront Sam. It had been two months since his return from Spain and they had not yet had any contact. It struck Iris that the situation was becoming absurd and they were avoiding a meeting. DC was too small a place for them not to have run into one another. But, it occurred to Iris, she couldn't come to work each day anxious she would bump into him. She needed a clear, focused mind to manage her studies and her job.

The president's weekly press conference would soon be over. Iris had checked with Missy, and she knew Sam Jacobson was inside. She leaned against the wall waiting for the door to open and the reporters to be shepherded out.

A few minutes later she saw the journalists filing along the corridor, placing their notepads in their pockets and bags. The men who knew her waved or offered a greeting. Iris stood on her toes and craned her neck above their heads, attempting to locate Sam. He was one of the last to exit the president's office. When he saw her he stood to one side allowing the last reporters to pass, his gaze never leaving her face.

'Hi there, stranger,' Iris said when they were alone. 'How are you?' She offered him her hand.

'Good. How about you?' he replied, taking her hand and holding it briefly. He was clean-shaven but his hair remained close-cropped.

Her heart began to race and she remembered why she had fallen in love with him. The deliberate movements, the uncertain words, the bashful glances, the sureness that when he looked at her his heart was racing too.

'Fine. I just thought I should say hello. It's been a few months. You're probably in a hurry. Can I walk with you?'

He nodded and they began to walk in the direction of the exit.

'I won't say I've been meaning to call,' he began. 'Because I haven't. I've been avoiding you, Iris.' He offered no further explanation.

'I gathered that.'

'But it's good to see you,' he added hastily.

'It's good to see you too. How's the book going?' she asked.

'Finished. I'm looking for a publisher. The Spanish Civil War isn't the most attractive of topics to Americans, but I think Scribner's might be interested.'

'Congratulations,' she said. 'They're a good publisher. They publish Ernest Hemingway, don't they?'

He nodded and smiled. 'Nothing has been set in stone, but I'm going to New York tomorrow to have another meeting with them.'

'That's a good sign,' Iris offered.

'I guess.' He glanced at her. 'I was interested to see that your name was on the list of people going with the president on the tour he's starting on next month.'

Iris stopped and looked up into his face. 'What?'

'The campaign trip he's planning. For the Democratic primaries. To promote New Deal candidates. You're going with him, according to this press release.' He handed it to her.

Iris read the release rapidly where she stood. She hadn't been informed, but that was nothing new. For better or worse, the president liked to improvise. Still, she dismissed the topic hastily. This wasn't what she wanted to be talking about.

By this time they had reached the exit. It seemed like there was more that should be said, but why dredge up the past? she thought.

Now Monty was out of the picture, she was determined to keep her life simple. Before she could say goodbye Sam said, 'I'm sorry about Chapel. It's a tough break for you, but a good posting for him, I imagine. Had it been in the works for very long?'

'No, it all happened rather suddenly, actually.'

'Right,' he said, nodding. 'Tough break, though.'

She wondered if he knew about the porter. Was this the sort of behaviour he had alluded to outside the bar in New York?

They stared at each other for a minute, neither sure of how their meeting should conclude. Iris wished he hadn't mentioned Monty.

'I think there's been too much water under the bridge for anything to come of this, of us,' Sam said at last. 'It's the timing.'

'I agree,' Iris said quickly. 'We missed our chance, Sam. But it's good to know you're still a friend.' She held out her hand.

'It's been good seeing you.' He held out his hand and Iris shook it.

'Goodbye,' she said.

■

Iris was pleased with how her meeting with Sam had gone. As she sat in her office that afternoon with Tom, she concluded it was the best possible outcome. They had gone down the road of lovers and run into a barricade. With that in mind, they could now go forward along the avenue of friendship.

Steve Early entered the office and placed the press release Sam had shown her on Iris's desk. She handed it back to him immediately.

'I've already read it,' she stated, raising an eyebrow. 'It's nice to be told I'll be travelling across America for a couple of months.'

'It was last-minute,' Early explained. 'You know what the boss is like.'

'Anyway, you've finished school until September,' Tom pointed out.

'But I wanted to get as much reading done for next semester as possible over the summer,' Iris protested. 'You know Barnes is constantly on my back.'

Although she managed, Iris found it a struggle to balance school and her work. Furthermore, since writing an indisputable A paper for Barnes last fall she wanted to maintain the quality of her work. She didn't want him to think it was an anomaly.

'Seeing Roosevelt at work, first-hand – making deals and lopping dead wood – is more valuable than reading twenty legal texts. You can't pass up this opportunity.'

'What do you mean?' she enquired.

'The turnout at John's wedding was proof to the president of his popularity. He wants to rid the party of conservatives, anti-New Dealers, every doubter who objected to the court-packing and the cutback in spending,' Tom explained. 'He's sick and tired of being hindered by a deadlocked Congress. What you are about to embark on, Iris, is a congressional purge.'

'He may be dressing this up like a campaign tour, but it's a purge, no doubt about it,' Early agreed. 'He's raring to go and, my dear, it's going to get messy.' He and Tom laughed conspiratorially.

Monty had once told Iris that he could tolerate critics labelling the president a second-rate lawyer and a ham-fisted economist, but he would not abide them calling him a bad politician. 'The art of politics,' Monty said, 'is what Roosevelt excels at.'

Perhaps a change of scenery would be good, she thought. Steve and Tom were amusing company and it would be an opportunity to mix with a different crowd. There'd be a media contingent joining them, Iris imagined. Perhaps it would do her friendship with Sam good to be away from Washington, to begin a new chapter without constant reminders of the past.

'Which reporters has the president invited to come along?' Iris asked.

'The usual.' Early produced a notepad from his back pocket, flipped it open, and read the list offhandedly. 'Tom Silsby, James Pendergast, Sam Jacobson, Austin Sinclair, Barbara Morton.'

'Have they been told yet?'

'Not yet; I'm phoning them this afternoon,' Early replied. 'I'd better get on to that now.'

Early exited and Iris sighed. She tapped her pencil on her desk and stared at the telephone.

'What's up, Iris?' Tom said.

'Do you know if there's been any news regarding Francis Slattery?'

'Who?' he asked.

'Monty's porter.'

Tom shook his head slowly. 'He's gone quiet. He's just a kid. Probably thought better of wrangling with the White House.'

'Probably,' Iris said.

43
BALTIMORE, MARYLAND
September 1938

The president exited the Palm Room of the Hotel Belvedere. Steve Early stepped forward from his place to the right of the lectern to begin the 'mopping up', as he liked to call it.

The final press conference of the tour was coloured by the same negativity that had marred the entire two-month trip. Of the eight candidates the president endorsed for election in their state primary, only one had been victorious. Roosevelt's intervention in the election process had been lambasted by the press, criticised by conservative Democrats and derided by the Republicans. Washington reporter Charles Dapper had summarised the result of FDR's attempt to influence the outcome of the primaries in the morning's *Washington Post* by writing, 'President Roosevelt could not run for a third term even if he so desired.' Sam Jacobson had referred to the court-packing, the budget cuts and the primaries fiasco as 'Roosevelt's narcissistic trifecta'.

As Steve Early took the final questions from the reporters, Iris thought about returning to DC. It was only an hour before their train departed. She had visited eight states in two months and she was tired. The knowledge that she would be returning to school after the Labor Day weekend raised her spirits. Although it had been a unique learning experience, it was not the one she had been expecting. The tour had drained her and she was eager to throw herself into her studies.

'Tired?' Tom asked.

Iris nodded. The president was drained too, Iris could see. She could read the disappointment and resentment in his face. He had taken a punt that fell far short of the end zone. Whether this play was motivated by arrogance, as the media implied, or the desire to shore up the administration, as Iris hoped, the upshot was that the tactic was a complete disaster. The president had crippled the administration.

Furthermore, the absence of Sam Jacobson from the press

contingent had left Iris numb. She had hoped the trip could revitalise their relationship, albeit on a different footing.

Steve Early took the last question and the journalists began filing out. Iris and Tom waited near the exit until the final stragglers had left. Iris nodded at Ed Boyce, Sam's boss at AP, who had taken Sam's place on the trip. Boyce was walking with a younger, shorter man whom Iris didn't recognise, but he smirked at Iris as though he recognised her. Probably a Baltimore reporter, she thought.

When they had passed, Iris heard the Baltimore reporter whisper to Ed, 'Is that Chapel's girl?'

Iris turned quickly towards the departing men. She saw Ed nod.

The pair stopped just outside the door and lit cigarettes. Tom left Iris's side and began talking to Steve. Iris moved a few inches around the corner into the room, out of sight of Boyce and the other reporter.

'She's pretty,' the other man said. 'I wouldn't be foolin' around on that. But then, if you're a nance . . .'

'Hey!' Boyce cut his colleague off severely. 'Chapel is a good guy.'

'Well, I never met him,' the other man commented. 'But good guy or not, I don't know how his shenanigans were kept out of the papers.'

'How did you find out about that?' Boyce asked.

'There was a rumour. So it's true then?' Boyce nodded.

'Did you have anything to do with hushing it up or was it all the White House's work?' the reporter queried.

'Neither,' Boyce remarked casually. 'We work differently in DC. A public figure's private life is considered private. We don't play dirty. You know Sam Jacobson?' The Baltimore reporter nodded. 'He shut the kid down.'

■

Iris paid the taxi driver and stood outside the building that housed the Associated Press office on E Street. Filled with an epic sense of promise, she had hastily left Union Station, leaving Tom in charge of her bags. It was four in the afternoon when she stepped into the elevator and asked the operator for the sixth floor.

'I'd like to see Sam Jacobson, please,' Iris informed the receptionist seated at the entry to the AP office. 'Tell him it's Iris McIntosh.'

The woman picked up the telephone. 'Iris McIntosh is here to see you, Sam,' she said into the receiver. 'Yes, Iris McIntosh.' She looked at

Iris to check if this was correct. Iris nodded. The receptionist placed the receiver back into the cradle.

'He won't be a minute,' she informed Iris. 'Take a seat.'

But Iris couldn't sit. Her breathing was fast. Each second seemed to take an hour. At last she heard footsteps and Sam's voice thanking the receptionist. Iris turned. Learning of how Sam had acted to save Monty's reputation had opened something in her. Standing in the Palm Room of the Belvedere Hotel, she had suddenly been so overwhelmed with love that all her thoughts of an entirely platonic relationship with Sam evaporated. All at once Iris couldn't imagine a life that wasn't with him.

Sam stood opposite her, hands in pockets. 'Hi there, stranger,' he said. His voice was unemotional but not unpleasant. 'How're you doing?'

'Pretty good,' she replied. 'Have you got any plans for tonight?'

Sam shook his head. 'Nope.'

'Can we have dinner?' she hazarded.

Sam regarded her for a few seconds as if considering her invitation. Iris hadn't thought about what she'd do if he were to refuse.

'That would be nice,' he replied eventually.

Iris exhaled.

'Do you remember where I live?' she enquired.

Sam nodded.

'Then I'll see you at seven. I'll cook.' She stood a moment longer looking into his serious brown eyes. She noticed the beginnings of a smile before he turned and returned to his office.

■

When Iris had prepared the duck she changed her clothes. She was still wearing the same skirt and blouse she had worn to the press conference hours before in Baltimore. She marvelled at how everything had changed since then. Standing in front of her closet, Iris contemplated her options, biting her lower lip. She eventually chose a pair of navy trousers and a straw-coloured, short-sleeved knit top. She lay them out on the bed and ran the shower. When she was dressed she looked at the clock. It was five minutes to seven. Eager for the evening to begin, she was pleased when she heard a knock. Taking a final look at herself in the mirror, she took a deep breath and went to open the door.

Although she was expecting Sam, it was still strange seeing him and not Monty. It took her a second to gather herself and ask him in. He carried a bunch of flowers, a box of chocolates and a bottle of wine.

'I think I've overdone it a little,' he said wryly. He had changed out of the suit he was wearing earlier, Iris noticed, and now wore a white, opened-necked shirt and dark green trousers.

'It's sweet,' she said, taking the items from his arms. 'You're sweet,' she added softly.

Holding up the bottle of wine she asked, 'Can Jews drink wine?'

'Kosher wine,' he answered, placing his hat on the back of a chair.

She peered at the label. 'Is this kosher?'

'No,' he said, smiling. 'I only keep kosher when I'm in my parents' house.'

Iris wished she had known that earlier. Her visit to the market that afternoon had been fraught with frustration. It was crowded with people preparing for the Labor Day holiday weekend and so many dishes she would have liked to cook were prohibited to Jews. That was why she had settled on duck.

'I'm sorry, by the way,' she went on nervously as she put the flowers in water. 'You probably had plans for the weekend and I rushed into your office . . .'

'I would have cancelled a dinner at Chequers to spend the evening with you,' he said sincerely.

She relaxed. 'So, I trump Winston Churchill, do I?'

'Every time,' he said.

Sam opened the wine and poured it into the glasses Iris had placed on the table.

'L'chaim,' Sam toasted.

Iris lifted the glass to her lips and then hastily put it down. 'I want to thank you, Sam. I want to thank you for what you did for Monty.'

He looked at her and cleared his throat. 'How did you find out?'

'It doesn't matter.' She touched his arm. 'If Monty's actions had leaked into the public domain his career would have been ruined. I know what you think of him. It must have been difficult.'

'I didn't do it for Chapel,' he informed her. 'I did it for you. You were a very public couple, Iris. You would have gone down in flames with him. It wasn't difficult for me at all.'

'How?' she asked. 'How did you bury the story?'

'When Francis Slattery came into the office he met with me, just by chance. He could have met with anyone,' Sam explained. 'I was just there at the right time. Anyway, he told me his tale. I stalled, dug around into his life and discovered something that outdid Chapel's hijinks.'

'What?' she enquired eagerly.

'Francis Slattery is a card-carrying member of the Communist Party,' he said offhandedly as he sat on the sofa. 'Not that I care, but it was something I could use.'

'Being red trumps being a pansy,' Iris mused as she sat next to him.

'I guess,' he agreed. 'Anyway, I informed him that if we were to run a story, his allegiance to the Communist Party would be exposed. The FBI would be called in to investigate. He's just a kid. It didn't take much to scare him.'

Now that Iris had all the pieces, she contemplated the mess in its entirety. Sam's resourcefulness and his dedication to protecting her reputation impressed her greatly. She was also mildly excited by the ruthlessness he had displayed in handling the porter. It was a trait she had not witnessed before.

'Thank you, anyway,' she said. 'After everything that's happened, you didn't have to help.'

'I know.'

'Did you know, Sam? I mean, did you know about Monty's . . . proclivity?'

'There was always talk,' he said. 'Especially in New York. Not so much here. But I wasn't going to ruin the guy's good name based on rumours, despite my feelings.'

Iris felt her heart swell. 'As you might have guessed,' she said shyly, 'it's over with Monty.'

He nodded.

Iris stared at his solemn face and reached out to touch his hand. Sam had grown more handsome in the five years she had known him. Age, maturity and his experiences in Spain were responsible, she guessed. But it was not this that appealed to her so deeply at that moment; it was what she could discern behind his features. Iris could see his feelings for her clearly in his face's every aspect. They were etched along his long nose and his chiselled jaw, composed on his well-defined chin and prominent brow. But mostly they were inscribed in the veiled recesses of his dark eyes. She kissed him lovingly and then said, 'I'd better go and see to the duck.'

■

They consumed the duck with gusto. Iris had only eaten a sandwich on the train. The knowledge of what lay ahead when she arrived in DC had triggered a peculiar sensation in her stomach, a muddle of elation and terror, but now she felt entirely at ease. She and Sam chatted about ordinary things. Spain was not mentioned; neither was politics. Iris gathered that they were getting to know each on a new level, unencumbered by Monty or the White House or world affairs. They were just two people having dinner – two people in love. They even spoke affectionately of their first meeting, another evening when duck had been on the menu.

'You don't strike me as a cook,' Sam said when they had finished.

Iris hesitated before responding. 'My father used to cook quite a bit. My mother had no talent in the kitchen. Sometimes, not very often, my father came home with a duck.'

'Was he a hunter?' Sam asked. 'Didn't you grow up in West Baltimore?'

Iris shook her head and grinned. 'No, I'd say he would have won them in a card game. On one occasion the bird was still alive, but he didn't have the heart to kill it.'

Sam laughed. 'What happened?' he asked.

'I had a pet for a while, until my mother left the window open and it flew away.'

'Your childhood sounds much more colourful than mine.'

'Colourful was one word for it.' She smiled and changed the subject. 'How did your meeting with Scribner's go, by the way?' She rose and began to clear the table.

'It went well,' he replied, brightening. 'They're going to publish my book. The contract has been signed.'

'That's wonderful, Sam, I'm so happy for you,' she responded enthusiastically, but it struck her that she wanted to say more.

Sam helped her clear the dishes and, once finished, they moved to the sofa.

'I still love you,' she confessed. 'I don't think I ever stopped.'

'I know I've always loved you,' he admitted with unexpected boldness. 'The minute I laid eyes on you, I knew you were the one. You walked towards me along the balcony with Mrs Roosevelt and I'd never seen anyone so striking. I was completely tongue-tied and you were trying to talk to me and I was so nervous and then you blasted me after dinner. From that point on it was hopeless for me.'

'I was nervous too. You seemed so clever and street smart. You unnerved me, I suppose . . . or something . . . Now I'm the one who's tongue-tied.'

'And then I tried to ask you out . . .' Sam placed his head in his hands theatrically at the memory of his stilted, clumsy advance.

Iris stood up from the sofa and took Sam's hand. He raised his head, surprised.

'Would you like to spend the night?' she asked.

His lips curved into a smile. 'Are you sure?'

'I think the timing is finally right.'

∎

Iris lay in the crook of Sam's arm as he dozed. She placed her hand between her face and his chest; the prickly hairs were a new sensation to her. As she squirmed in an effort to get comfortable, Sam woke and kissed her forehead.

'That was wonderful,' he said. 'I hope . . . did you? I want to make you happy, Iris, more than anything.'

She shook her head. 'I didn't – but that's okay. It doesn't happen every time. It's different for women.'

He grimaced. 'I rushed. This was something I've imagined for such a long time, and then you just came walking out of the bathroom naked . . .'

'We were intending to make love,' she pointed out. She kicked off the covers and rolled onto her back.

Sam propped himself up on his elbow and gazed at her nakedness. 'You're not inhibited at all, are you?' he asked.

She shook her head. 'Not any more,' she murmured and rolled onto her side.

'I'm sorry I rushed things,' he said, placing his hand on her hip. 'I want it to be wonderful for both of us every time.'

'It doesn't matter,' she replied kindly. 'Let's just say I like a bit more small talk before I get down to business.' She stroked his arm lightly with her fingernails. He grinned at her choice of words.

'I've never talked about sex before with a woman,' Sam confessed.

Iris kissed him on the lips. 'Have there been many women?' she asked. 'In Spain?'

'A few,' he answered as he gently circled her nipple with his fingertip.

Iris closed her eyes and exhaled. 'Spanish women?' Her breathing quickened and Sam fondled her breasts more firmly.

'No, Americans,' he whispered. She moved closer. Sam kissed her lips before continuing, 'But they weren't like you.'

'What do you mean?' she asked.

'Perfect.'

Iris looked at him. 'I'm not perfect, Sam.'

'In my eyes you are.'

'It's dangerous to see me like that,' she responded seriously, then tilted her head back as Sam peppered her neck with kisses.

'I don't care,' he said.

Iris wrapped her legs around his body and kissed his lips ardently.

When they came together for the second time that night it was wonderful.

Iris woke in the morning to the smell of eggs cooking, feeling more rested than she had in many months.

44
HYDE PARK, NEW YORK
May 1962

There's no denying it, those mid-term elections in 1938 were a disappointment for the president. He dropped by my office one morning in November and threw the morning's newspaper across the table at me. 'What's on the menu tonight, Mrs Nesbitt?' I remember him saying. 'Republicans in the House have doubled and there's also eight more in the Senate. I need some cheering up.' The president didn't let much get him down. I heard him say a dozen or so times, 'Once you've spent two years trying to wiggle one toe, everything is in proportion!' For the life of me, I can't remember what was on the menu that day, but it usually couldn't be altered. Menus were planned a month out. If one meal was to change, just on a whim, it would throw out my entire schedule.

The president's appetite was getting more and more picky in those days. I think he found it difficult managing the nation's expectations. When Hitler invaded Austria the president turned off food altogether. You see, the United States in those days was fiercely isolationist. Even if the president wanted to lend a hand in Europe he'd first have to undo years of this kind of thinking. 'Peace at any price,' he called it.

I have to admit, the whole situation made me sick to my stomach as well. You know, when the Nazis marched into Vienna they were welcomed! There was no resistance and Hitler's army were thrown flowers. When I heard that on the radio it made me ashamed to be of Austrian extraction. But the real losers on the day were those of Jewish faith. Then, before Hitler had any time at all to devour Austria, he turned on Czechoslovakia. That man's appetite couldn't be sated.

If I could have had the president's ear during those months I would have advised military intervention. That's certainly what Mrs Roosevelt was promoting and she was a stauch pacifist! Germany needed knocking down to size. Even if the polls didn't show it, public opinion was shifting. My boys, Buck and Garvan, were both of enlistment age, but I wanted to see Hitler put in his place once and for all.

Now, speaking of finicky appetites, you can't tell me that food peevishness isn't contagious. It was about this time that Mr Hopkins moved into the White House permanently. He had the Blue Suite. Mrs Roosevelt became his daughter's guardian. I think Mrs Roosevelt was expecting the worst, but little Diana and the First Lady just adored each other. It was just after that actress, Dorothy Hale, jumped out of her apartment window. Mr Hopkins was pretty shaken up about that, I recall, but he had jilted her. The gossip columnists played up that angle of the story. Anyway, Mr Hopkins had some sort of digestive ailment. He was the White House's leading Ulcerite. That's what these men who pushed their plates away and turned their noses up at everything called themselves. There were forty-eight items I had to avoid when it came to preparing Mr Hokpins' meals. The president was surrounded by men who couldn't eat this or that and I truly believe that it rubbed off on him over the years. Mrs Roosevelt, on the other hand, wasn't fussy at all.

Much of her summer that year was taken up by the World Youth Congress. She believed the future of the world depended on its youth and she put her money where her mouth was. Despite protests from the Catholic Church, because the delegates were thought to be communist, she went up to Vassar College where it was held. I remember seeing a picture of her on the front page of the *Post*. She was sitting in a great auditorium, wearing the earphones like everyone else, listening to the delegates speak – and you know what she was doing? Knitting. That picture summed up Mrs Roosevelt for me all over.

45

WASHINGTON DC
November 1938

'You made quite an impact at the press conference this morning,' Iris said impishly as she slid into the booth opposite Sam.

He looked up from the menu.

'Hammering the president over immigration quotas and refugees. You'll fall from grace if you're not careful,' she teased as she opened the menu. 'What are you having?'

Sam didn't respond.

'Well?' she said, looking up to meet his reproving gaze.

'It isn't anything to joke about, Iris,' he told her harshly.

'I'm not joking about *that*,' she grumbled. By *that* she meant the recent events in Germany – a series of attacks against Jews that had already become infamous around the world as Kristallnacht. 'I'm talking about your questions. Apparently they had the president on the hop. Steve told me all about it.'

'You could have fooled me,' Sam retorted. 'He didn't offer one straight answer.'

Iris sighed, her good humour waning. She returned her attention to the menu, scolding herself for not knowing better. Pretending to peruse the options, she contemplated instead the solemn man sitting across from her. She thought it odd that Sam could take his faith so lightly in some ways, yet consider himself so wholly committed in others. However, it was impossible to query this inconsistency without sparking a disagreement. Sam argued that his fervour in regards to the Jewish situation had nothing to do with his religion. It was a simple matter of taking a stand against fascism, just as he had done in Spain. To debate the subject with Sam was futile. Her rebuttals only made her appear shallow and uncaring.

Iris took his hand. 'I'm sorry,' she said.

'Jews have been stripped of all their human rights. In just one week twenty thousand have been arrested and taken to labour camps.

They're prohibited from attending school and university. My god, Iris, they can't even drive cars any more. Even fraternising with a gentile is unlawful. You and I would be arrested!'

Irritated that her gesture had not been appreciated, Iris removed her hand. 'It's not so different here,' she remarked casually. 'It would be deemed inappropriate if I were to *fraternise* with a Negro.'

'You cannot be serious,' he shot back. 'That is not against the law in the United States.'

She eyed him coolly. 'But in some states it would be perceived as unlawful or amoral and punishment would be meted out. There's really no difference.'

'You sound just like Chapel,' he snapped.

Iris knew provoking him with a reaction would lead to no good.

'The president said there would be no alteration to the quota system,' Sam continued. 'There are tens of thousand of Jewish people seeking asylum and he won't budge an inch.'

'It's not as if he can. He's referring to the National Origins Act of 1924. He can't change policy on a whim.'

'I don't need a history lesson, Iris.'

'I'm just being pragmatic. He's the president, not God. The economy is touch and go. Unemployment is still an issue. Congress isn't going to vote in favour of bringing in two hundred thousand penniless refugees, are they?'

Iris turned her face back to the menu and pretended to read. Her foot tapped under the table.

'Now you sound like a lawyer,' he said, after a pause. His tone had softened.

She looked at his face. His sternness was fading.

Sam leaned across the table and took her hand. 'Why do you always defend him?' he asked. 'You just admitted yourself, he's a man. That being the case, the president is capable of making mistakes.'

'I know that. I've been there when those mistakes were made,' she responded. 'But I also know that he likes to play his cards close to his chest. Right now he's got a Congress that's against him and a State Department that's anti-Semitic and anti-New Deal. What's more, the Judicial Reorganization Bill and the primaries are still fresh in people's minds. And let's not forget the recession. There's just not a whole lot of good will out there for him at the moment. He'll make his move when the time is right,' she said, and returned her eyes to the menu.

'Do you know something, Iris?' Sam enquired eagerly, leaning across the table.

'No, but I have absolute faith in the president.'

Iris did, in fact, know something. Four days after Kristallnacht, the president had bypassed the State Department and convened a meeting in the Oval Office where he stretched his executive powers to the limit by amending immigration regulations to allow fifty thousand Jewish refugees into the country. Only Harry Hopkins, Steve Early and Secretary of State Cordell Hull were present. Steve had relayed the details to Iris afterwards.

'Now for the cherry on top,' Steve had informed her. 'The boss believes that Hitler would not have acted as he did if we had five thousand warplanes and the capacity to produce ten thousand more within the next few months.'

'Really?' Iris interrupted. 'He wants the United States war-ready?'

Steve shook his head impatiently. 'No, the planes would be supplied to the Allies. Hopkins then stated the obvious: that Congress would not appropriate that sort of money.'

Iris nodded. Harry's was an astute observation.

'Then Roosevelt, you know how he gets that cheeky grin then takes a long drag on his smoke before letting fly with a real zinger?'

Iris nodded.

'Well, he told Harry that he could build the planes at no cost to Treasury and call it work relief.'

Iris shook her head in wonder. 'What a scheme!'

'Have you ever heard anything like it, Iris?' Steve said in amazement. 'It's sly, but entirely constitutional.' He sat down on the corner of her desk, marvelling at the president's artfulness. Then Iris noticed his features darken. 'It is constitutional, isn't it?' he asked.

Iris thought for a moment. 'I believe it is. Britain and France aren't at war yet, so the restrictions of the Neutrality Act need not apply,' she answered. 'Why wasn't Tom in the meeting?'

'With his opinions?' Steve exclaimed. 'His Irish Catholic upbringing means he sees any helping hand extended to the Brits as a betrayal.'

Iris replayed the exchange in her mind as she sat across from Sam in the diner, endeavouring to maintain a guileless expression. It was difficult. Iris was torn. Informing Sam of the president's actions would placate him but she couldn't betray the president. Sam would just have to have faith as well, she decided.

Sam was nodding thoughtfully. 'I guess journalists are trained to be suspicious of politicians,' he said.

And of their girlfriends, Iris thought.

'He's a good man,' she said. 'You've spent hours with him drinking and socialising, sailing and fishing. He's invited you, as a friend, into his home. You know he's a good man.'

'But that's the man, not the politician,' he pointed out.

'They're one and the same,' Iris stated firmly.

46

HYDE PARK, NEW YORK
May 1962

By 1939 Spain had surrendered to Franco, Italy was firmly Fascist and the Third Reich was rock-solid. There was a feeling of dread around the White House, you could smell it in the air. There were meetings and conferences going on at every hour of the day and night. Men in suits coming and going – and Miss McIntosh, of course. She was always in the meetings, working hard. It's no wonder she rose to the position she did. Everything was hush-hush. I wasn't supposed to notice a thing, but I was expected to feed them all! With Dad's passing the year before, it was easier for me to sleep at the White House. That way I was on hand to organise sandwiches at midnight and thermoses of coffee at four in the morning.

I didn't have to listen to the radio or read the newspapers to know how bad things were in Europe. I could tell by the president's appetite. He was difficult when the year started and he just got worse and worse. Also, the fact that he had no time to swim every day just added to his crabbiness.

To be honest, all my thoughts in that year were taken up with the royal visit. As soon as Mrs Roosevelt told me King George and Queen Elizabeth would be at the White House for two days in June I saw the opportunity to embark on a rug-buying campaign. Needless to say, I spent most of the next three months wrangling rugs.

The British government left nothing to chance, you know. I was swamped with official orders. Directives about the quality of the water needed to make the royal couple's tea and how many hangers the King preferred in his closet. It was mind-boggling! Months in advance people from all over the country were giving me advice about how I should manage the King and Queen. I'd just laugh and say in my best British accent, 'We'll muddle through somehow.'

As far as planning the menu went, I received letters from chefs, top chefs, telling me what I should cook. But Mrs Roosevelt just said in that calming voice of hers, 'Don't worry, Mrs Nesbitt. We have our plans made and we'll stick to them.' Those words were really a comfort.

The president's mood improved as the visit drew nearer. It was the first time a ruling head of England was to visit the United States and I think the president recognised that he was making history. When I was planning the menu I asked him whether he thought terrapin would be a good idea for their first dinner in the country. You know what he said? He said merrily, 'Terrapin? My good lady, I'll try anything once.'

The Queen ate like a bird, I recall. But she was on a diet. The King, on the other hand, ate and drank heartily. He finished everything on his plate. They were a nice, young couple, with two adorable little girls waiting for them in London. My heart went out to them when the bombing started only a few months later. I took my mind off the horror by baking. The day Britain declared war on Germany, I began my annual ritual of fruitcake making, even though it was only September.

47
WASHINGTON DC
September 1939

Iris and Sam sat next to one another on her sofa. They held hands as they listened to the president's address on the radio. It had become customary for Iris to be at the White House during Roosevelt's Fireside Chats. Usually Missy, Hick, Steve and Harry Hopkins were there too. Sometimes Roosevelt's speechwriters Sam Rosenman and Robert Sherwood were present when they were in town. Mrs Roosevelt always attended, knitting busily as she absorbed her husband's words. When the president finished, a debriefing of sorts would follow over cocktails that Roosevelt mixed himself. Iris enjoyed these evenings. She found the analyses of the speech and its delivery enlightening and entertaining. Exchanging thoughts and opinions with the likes of Rosenman, Mrs Roosevelt and Hopkins was a privilege, the enormity of which never failed to impact on the twenty-nine-year-old.

However, tonight Iris had no desire to dissect this speech as she listened. Neither did she want to deliberate afterwards over its meaning and objective with DC's most erudite and informed. All she wanted on this particular Sunday evening was to listen to the program as other Americans would be listening.

Sitting in her living room with Sam by her side, Iris discovered it wasn't so easy to shake years of experience and she found herself dissecting each sentence and phrase the president uttered. She wasn't sure whether it was terror or confidence she was feeling as Roosevelt's voice came forth from the radio. Iris had come to know his voice and its many nuances intimately, but it was impossible to grasp his exact aim in this particular Fireside Chat. Was he reassuring Americans that the United States would not be drawn into the war or was he preparing Americans for the likelihood of exactly that? The address was double-edged. That was his intent. The president's speeches were renowned for their clarity of purpose as well as their flawless delivery. Why should this speech be any different?

Iris gripped Sam's hand more firmly, knowing the speech was drawing to a close. The President's tone reached a fervent pitch.

'This nation will remain a neutral nation, but I cannot ask that every American remain neutral in thought as well. Even a neutral has a right to take account of facts. Even a neutral cannot be asked to close his mind or his conscience.

'I have said not once, but many times, that I have seen war and that I hate war. I say that again and again.

'I hope the United States will keep out of this war. I believe that it will. And I give you assurance and reassurance that every effort of your Government will be directed toward that end.

'As long as it remains within my power to prevent, there will be no blackout of peace in the United States.'

When the address concluded, Sam stood and turned off the radio. 'What do you think?'

Iris shrugged. 'It sounds to me like the United States joining the war is inevitable, although President Roosevelt is going to try to prevent it.'

'What about a third term? Any more news on that front?'

'Mrs Roosevelt's packing,' Iris said. 'She's got Mrs Nesbitt taking all their belongings out of storage and sending them to Val-Kill and Springwood. As far as she's concerned the Roosevelts are closing up shop.'

Iris stood and moved into the kitchen. Taking the lid off a pot of vegetable soup Daisy Bonner had shown her how to put together when she was at Warm Springs, she stirred the contents before continuing.

'As for the president, he's negotiating a contract with *Collier's* to become a contributing editor. He wants to pen a few articles for them each year, write a bit of history and turn Hyde Park into a working farm again. He's fifty-eight, Sam. He's tired.'

'Do you think he would leave the country high and dry on the brink of war?'

'Not a chance,' Iris returned seriously.

■

It was after dinner that Sam announced his intentions. Iris did not say a word; she merely opened the window and sat on the ledge. Lighting a cigarette, she realised that she should have seen this coming. Of course Sam would want to go to Europe. It was where history was being forged. However, she hoped they had been forging something far more significant together, something a job offer from Edward R. Murrow couldn't undermine.

'Would you go if we were married?' Iris asked flatly without turning to him.

'Do you want to get married?'

She shook her head. 'Not now.'

'Don't be contrary, Iris,' Sam said without emotion. 'This is hard enough.'

Sam cleared the plates from the table and she could hear him doing the dishes. We're as good as married, Iris thought. Sam had given up his one-room apartment six months ago and moved in with Iris. Since then they had fallen into a domestic routine so comfortable that it caused Iris to fret if she was forced to work late or stay overnight at the White House. Waking to the sounds of Sam in the kitchen preparing breakfast was more agreeable to her than wedding bells.

More quickly than she'd thought possible, small exasperations had become endearing; Sam's intensity transformed into passion, his single-mindedness into devotion. The couple had even hit their stride in the bedroom. Within a few weeks of being together, Sam had blossomed into an assured and observant lover. Although it wasn't wonderful every time, it came extremely close.

Iris heard the water draining in the sink. A few seconds later she heard cupboards opening and closing as Sam dried and put away the plates, glasses and silverware. A few minutes after that he re-entered the living room and stood behind her, placing his arms around her waist.

'You didn't even ask me to come with you,' she stated quietly.

'It's dangerous, Iris,' he explained. 'In all likelihood Britain will be bombed.'

'It was just as dangerous in Spain and you asked me to follow you there.'

'But your place is so firm at the White House and you love it. Also, you're graduating next year. I'm not going to ask you to give up everything you've worked for.'

Feeling mildly reassured by Sam's response, she decided on a different tack. 'But radio?' She turned to face him. 'You've never shown any interest in radio. You love newspapers and DC will be a great place to be in terms of war reporting, and with your contacts . . .'

'I'll be writing the news reports for World News Roundup,'

Sam went on. 'Murrow is based in London now. That's where he broadcasts from.'

'Is that where you'll be based?'

'I don't know. Probably not. A war correspondent has to go where the war is.'

'So you could be sent onto a battlefield somewhere?' Iris said.

'Ed Murrow has offered me a job. I wouldn't care if I was sharpening his pencils in an office or dodging grenades in a foxhole,' Sam responded, looking at her squarely. 'He's read my book. He admires my work. He hand-picked *me*, Iris.'

'So this is about your need for praise?'

'Absolutely not,' Sam said, turning from her in frustration and striding to the sofa. 'Murrow was in Warsaw when the Anschluss happened. He was on a plane and arrived in Vienna the next day. He described events as they were unfolding. Newspapers don't have that sort of immediacy.' He sat down, his elbows resting on his knees.

The fact that Murrow's offer was the opportunity of a lifetime made it no easier for Iris to accept Sam's departure. She walked to him and sat and rested her head on his shoulder. Automatically, his arm went around her.

'Listen,' he began. 'This past six months has been a dream, Iris, an absolute dream. But I can't let that smother any other dreams I might have.'

'How long?' she asked.

'I can't give you a definite timeframe. Perhaps a few months or, if everything goes well, then maybe for the duration of the war. Then again, they say it all might fizzle out by Christmas.'

Iris found no comfort in Sam's words. The Great War endured for four years, she realised. She could be thirty-three when he returned. Could their relationship survive for that long?

'Of course it will go well,' she said begrudgingly. 'You're brilliant.'

48
WASHINGTON DC
June 1940

The Roosevelts invited Iris to join them on a cruise on the *Potomac*, the presidential yacht. At least once a month, the president liked to escape from the rigours of his office and sail to nowhere in particular. But that year his monthly cruise had become a casualty of his ever-increasing workload. The escalation of the war in Europe, the surrender of France, the evacuation of Dunkirk and the pressure to throw his hat into the electoral ring for a third time meant the president had very little time for pleasure. Iris had come along on these jolly outings before. The usual crew was the president, Harry and Missy, Tom and Steve Early. Monty had often been on board as well. Mrs Roosevelt rarely attended, her schedule taking her away from Washington often. On this particular occasion, though, the only people present were herself and the First Couple. Iris was pleased to be enjoying Mrs Roosevelt's company again. Since she had begun working in the West Wing with Tom Corcoran her time with the First Lady, Tommy and Hick had become fleeting.

The trio sailed south along the Potomac River to where the water course opened up into Occoquan Bay. The president decided to anchor in Belmont Bay, a little further north. The sheltered spot, nestled beneath Mason Neck State Park, was far more picturesque than the larger, gusty Occoquan. Three coastguard cutters anchored about fifty yards away. Mrs Roosevelt packed her knitting into her tapestry bag and unfastened the picnic basket.

'You're probably wondering why we invited you out here today, McIntosh,' the president began. He bit into his sandwich. 'Why on earth will she not put butter on sandwiches, Eleanor?'

'Butter is expensive and fattening, and we can do without it,' his wife responded. 'Weren't you about to tell Iris why we invited her sailing today?'

The president would not be diverted. 'But nothing makes a ham sandwich like butter. Fresh white bread, thinly sliced leg ham and butter, spread thick.'

'Your doctor would argue against that particular recipe,' Eleanor said. 'Iris, the president has a proposal for you. Would you like me to continue, Franklin?'

The president examined his sandwich regretfully before continuing.

'McIntosh, I'm establishing a committee to see if we can't work around Congress in regards to these destroyers Churchill wants. I want you on board to advise on the Constitutional implications.'

'Me?' she asked incredulously, her hand going to her chest. *Advise* was a word she had never heard used in conjunction with herself before.

'You see, Iris,' Mrs Roosevelt continued, 'the president receives a wire or a telephone call weekly from Churchill begging for supplies, munitions. All of that is fine . . .'

'We can call it surplus and get around the Neutrality Act that way,' the president broke in. 'Dunkirk was a week ago. We'll have the Brits completely rearmed in five weeks. But the destroyers – they're a completely different kettle of fish.'

'The fifty destroyers Churchill is asking for have been mothballed. What's Congress's issue?' Iris asked.

'It's the message the gesture will send to Germany,' Roosevelt explained. 'Congress worries the Nazis will view it as an act of war. Also, if Britain surrenders, our destroyers will wind up in the hands of the enemy.'

'And then there's the election,' Mrs Roosevelt added, her gaze shifting furtively to her husband. 'If we run again, that is.'

'The GOP will use it as an election platform – FDR weakening the nation's defences,' Iris realised.

The president and his wife nodded gravely.

Iris looked into the crystal-clear sky as an eagle soared overhead. She followed its journey as she contemplated her response. It was a juicy project to sink her teeth into; it would take her mind off Sam and fill the hole that his departure had left. The eagle swooped low and hovered momentarily above the water. The reason for her hesitancy, she admitted to herself, was that she wasn't certain she was good enough. She had never been tested.

'But what about Tom?' she stalled. 'I haven't even graduated yet. Tom knows the Constitution inside out.'

'Tom can't be a part of this; he's isolationist and anti-Brit,' the president responded pragmatically.

'It's a wonderful opportunity, Iris,' Mrs Roosevelt entreated. 'Don't let your loyalty to Tom hold you back. You'll be at the centre of policy-making.'

Iris scanned the sky for the bird. It was gone. She turned back to the president. 'Thank you, sir. It would be an honour.'

'I'm pleased,' the president said. 'I need people on this I can trust.' He went on, 'I'm overturning the cabinet as well. Henry Stimson and Frank Knox are replacing Woodring and Edison as Secretary of War and Secretary of the Navy. Harry's moving up to Secretary of the War Cabinet.'

Iris understood Harry's appointment – he was an ardent anti-Nazi – but the choice of Stimson and Knox was puzzling. 'But they're Republicans,' Iris said.

'It's essential the war cabinet be bipartisan,' Mrs Roosevelt said. 'Knox and Stimson are interventionists. They also support a repeal of the Neutrality Act.'

'And I'd be working with them?' Iris asked.

The president nodded. 'Among others. Harry, of course. Stimson and Knox want a few of their people on it. Judge Robert Patterson from the Court of Appeals is going to be Stimson's undersecretary. John J. McCloy will be Assistant Secretary. Knox wants James Forrestal, the investment banker, as his undersecretary. Not everyone I've asked has confirmed yet.' Roosevelt and his wife glanced at each other briefly. 'Altogether the team should number about twelve.'

'When do we begin?' Iris asked.

'Monday week. I'll be preparing for the convention, but you, Harry, Stimson and Knox can get started. It's a matter of urgency. We've got to get those tubs to England.' The president added happily, 'And by the way, we're calling the project the Destroyer Deal.'

The president handed Iris a Coke as Mrs Roosevelt resumed her knitting. He then picked up a length of rope and began tying knots. His hands worked quickly as each was tied and then undone. He hummed softly to himself. After a minute or so, Mrs Roosevelt picked up the melody and began to hum as well. Iris sipped her Coke and watched the couple at work.

'Come over here, McIntosh,' the president said, noticing her interest. 'I'll teach you.'

Iris sat next to the president. 'This is a bowline, it's one of the easiest,' he said as he began on the lesson.

The threesome spent the next two hours on the *Potomac* doing nothing more than knitting, tying knots and drinking Coke.

■

The next morning Iris arrived at work early. She poured herself a cup of coffee then sat behind her desk and lit a cigarette. She hastily opened a folder then closed it just as quickly and began to rearrange the objects sitting in front of her, tapping her left foot frantically against the leg of the chair as she did so. She stubbed out her cigarette half smoked. When the door opened she started.

'Tom,' she said suddenly, standing quickly.

'Hi, Iris. How was your weekend?' he enquired casually, moving to his desk.

'Fine, just fine,' she responded vacantly. 'How was yours?'

'Not bad. Judy and I finally saw *Rebecca*. That was some film. Mrs Danvers made Mrs Nesbitt look like a pussy cat!' Tom looked at her in anticipation of a laugh, but the sight of her strained expression prompted him to ask instead, 'What's the matter?'

Iris walked to his desk and sat in the chair facing him. Although she had been over her explanation a hundred times in her mind the words still caught in her throat. She spoke hurriedly. 'The president has asked me to work on – *advise* on,' she corrected, wincing, 'a policy that involves sending fifty destroyers to Britain.'

Tom stared at her.

'He wants *me* to advise on the constitutional ramifications.' She hoped her emphasis was enough.

Tom sat heavily in his chair. 'What have you told him?'

'I've told him it would be an honour,' she replied truthfully.

Tom was quiet for quite a long time. Iris wasn't sure whether she should return to her desk or leave the office.

'Good for you, kid,' he said eventually. He stood and held out his hand. 'I'm happy for you. I really am.'

Iris took his hand. 'I'm sorry, Tom. I just feel terrible about it.'

'Don't,' he said. 'If it wasn't you it would have been someone else. These are your salad days, kid. Make the most of every opportunity.'

Iris wasn't certain what this shift in West Wing dynamics would mean for Tom. If Harry was the president's right hand then Tom had been, up until this point, his left.

'Let's have a drink,' he suggested. 'In celebration.'

'It's not even nine,' Iris protested. Tom shrugged and took a bottle of scotch and two glasses from his filing cabinet.

They drank without speaking. Iris knew it was no celebration. When they had finished he packed away the glasses and bottle and returned to his desk. After an hour or so he looked up from the document he was working on.

'Hey, Iris,' he called.

Iris looked up, expecting him to ask for a pencil sharpener or relay an amusing anecdote that had occurred to him. 'Just remember, no matter how he makes you feel, you're always on your own.'

Tom resumed his focus on the document on his desk. Iris was unable to accomplish much at all for the rest of the day.

49

WASHINGTON DC
One week later

Iris stood alone in the Fish Room of the White House at eight o'clock on Monday morning. She placed her bag on the table then checked her hair, running her hands blindly over her head. She had dressed carefully that morning, with the intention of looking as mature as possible. She'd discovered Knox was sixty-six and Stimson seventy-three; she suspected it would be a challenge to get them to take someone of her youth and inexperience – not to mention gender – seriously. She had been too nervous to eat breakfast. She had carried out as much research on Stimson, Knox, Patterson, McCloy and Forrestal as she could over the weekend but it was the others, the names the president had failed to mention, that had her worried. She checked her watch at two minutes past the hour and then examined the pictures on the walls. Roosevelt had chosen the prints – all fish-themed – himself and had christened the space opposite the Oval Office accordingly.

A coffee urn had been placed on a table in the corner alongside a tray of donuts and coffee cake. After examining the food she turned her back on the array.

Although her jacket only had three-quarter-length sleeves, Iris was growing hot in the windowless room. Staring up at the skylight in the ceiling, she wondered how hot she'd be at midday. Reluctant to take off her jacket before anyone arrived, she instead removed a document folder from her bag and began to fan herself. A moment later the door opened.

Stimson, Knox and a cluster of other sombre-looking men entered; one she recognised as Judge Patterson. Iris smiled at the group and was about to introduce herself when Stimson brushed past her and said abruptly, 'It's stuffy in here. Will you organise a fan or two for the room, dear?'

He proceeded to take a seat and organise his belongings without even glancing at Iris. It would have been an easy enough request for Iris to carry out; the phone was right there near the door and she knew Mrs Nesbitt's extension number.

Instead, she approached the table. 'I'm Iris McIntosh, sir.'

The group looked at her quizzically.

'I'm here to advise on constitutional matters. But I do know the housekeeper's extension if *you* would like to organise the fans.'

She sat down at the table and began to remove her things from her bag. She could feel the eyes of every other person in the room on her. When she looked up Stimson was still staring at her. She met his gaze.

'It's nice to meet you, Miss McIntosh. I apologise for my mistake.' He stood, held out his hand, and then proceeded to introduce the other men at the table, starting with Knox and then Patterson, McCloy and Forrestal. The latter three appeared to Iris to be in their forties, with McCloy the youngest. The others were law clerks and assistants. Stimson then asked the most youthful-looking clerk to make that call to Mrs Nesbitt.

While introductions were still taking place, Harry entered. It looked to Iris as if he hadn't slept a wink. His eyes were red-rimmed, and a cigarette hung from the corner of his mouth. Removing an unwieldy pile of documents and files from under one arm and placing them on the table, he immediately made his way to the coffee. He picked up two donuts and balanced them atop his pile of papers.

'Right,' he said seriously, without any pleasantries. 'We should get to it.'

Iris assumed no one else was expected, which meant she was the sole woman at the table. It wouldn't be so bad, she thought. They all seemed pleasant-enough types and Stimson's reaction to her ploy had been extremely gracious. Then the door opened once again. Before Iris had time to turn to see the identity of the latecomer, Harry said, 'Nice to have you back, Chapel. Grab a coffee then take a seat.'

■

The group called it quits at six o'clock. Little had been achieved. They had partially deconstructed the Neutrality Act and examined it piece-meal, but it seemed to Iris the Neutrality Act was not the issue. The problem they had been tasked to solve was much more simple. The group assembled in that room had to devise a way for the president to bypass Congress. Thomas Jefferson had managed to spend fifteen million dollars and double the size of the United States without consulting them. Why wasn't this president able to send fifty destroyers to England? However, while Iris recognised the obstacle, the unexpected presence of Monty made it impossible for her to concentrate on finding a solution.

When she turned and saw him in the doorway it was as if she were seeing a mirage. He was wearing an officer's uniform. She saw by the shoulder strap on his jacket that he held the rank of major. He took off his hat and introduced himself to the room. He nodded at Iris as he took a seat at the far end of the table. He looked exactly the same, a little greyer perhaps, but just as attractive. Slightly vexed that neither Mrs Roosevelt nor the president had thought to inform her of Monty's inclusion, she also understood why they had not. Monty's presence would have swayed her decision.

Work stopped for lunch at twelve. Sandwiches and lemonade arrived. Monty spent the entire half-hour with Knox, a former Rough Rider and World War I veteran who saw Monty as a kindred spirit. Glancing at him intermittently, Iris waited until the older man excused himself. She didn't want their first meeting in nearly two years to be in the company of Knox. But he didn't excuse himself. When Harry suggested the group get back to work, the two men were still speaking. Throughout the afternoon she could feel Monty's eyes on her. Once when she looked up from the document being discussed, he smiled and winked. She wasn't sure what she was feeling. Excitement, fear and apprehension were all in the muddle of her emotions that afternoon, but a pure sense of delight overwhelmed them all. The memory of Francis Slattery and the other men had faded in the intervening years and she had come to reconcile herself to Monty's tastes, realising that they were no reflection on herself.

'Okay, lady and gentlemen,' Harry said at six, 'let's call it a day. We'll resume here tomorrow morning.'

As everyone packed up their papers and slid them into their briefcases Iris and Monty remained seated, staring at each other across the wide glossy table. Once the room had been vacated, Monty began.

'What's been going on?'

'Not much,' she replied. 'Back from the wilderness?'

'So it seems. This is quite an appointment for you. I was thrilled when I saw your name on the list. An adviser. Not bad.'

'Thanks. Why the uniform?'

'I've been recommissioned. The Brits need help and the boss seems to think I've done time enough in Tokyo. I'll deliver the destroyers to

England and stay on as a special attaché. Keep the lines of communication and supplies flowing.' Then he smiled and added as an afterthought. 'And I know you love a man in uniform.'

Iris laughed at this and stood.

'Will you have dinner with me?' he asked. 'I've reserved a table at Montmartre for seven.'

She nodded. 'I just need to do something first.'

'Okay,' he said with a shrug.

Iris dropped her bag and rushed to where Monty was standing. She threw her arms around his neck and hugged him tightly. Tears welled in her eyes.

'I've missed you so much,' she whispered into his neck.

'I've missed you too, kiddo,' he replied and wrapped his arms tightly around her waist.

■

Iris and Monty immediately fell into their old rhythm. Over a dinner of artichoke hearts and chateaubriand with sauce béarnaise, the pair conversed easily about the last two years. By the time the waiter cleared their table and wiped the cloth clean of crumbs, most of the gaps in their knowledge about one another had been filled.

'You look beautiful.' The compliment surprised her. 'You've put on a little weight and you're rounder than when I left. Grable-esque. It suits you. Mrs Nesbitt always said you needed fattening up.'

Iris was aware of her weight gain. Domestic bliss was the culprit. Although the extra pounds were nothing dramatic, since living with Sam she had gone up a dress size.

'And your hair,' Monty went on. 'How long have you been wearing it like that?'

'A few months,' Iris answered, smoothing the rolls that lay on each side of her head. 'What do you think?'

'I think it's lovely. They call them "victory rolls" in Britain.'

'I like to do my part for the war effort,' Iris responded dryly.

Monty grinned.

'Have you met anyone?' Iris asked after a moment, stroking the stem of her wineglass. 'A woman?' She had hoped to add *or man* as well, to prove to Monty her open-mindedness, but she found she wasn't able.

'Not really,' he answered vaguely. 'I spent a good deal of my exile thinking about you and how poorly you were treated. I wish I could do it over.'

'But are you happy?'

Monty seemed to take this question extremely seriously and thought on it for a few seconds. 'I believe so,' he said finally. 'Japan is such a disciplined and well-ordered society. The government is like that as well. They don't have time for game-playing. They don't have time for politics. It was refreshing. Being there gave me a new perspective.'

He looked at her. 'Tell me about Jacobson,' he said. 'What's going on there?'

Monty listened solemnly as Iris described her relationship with Sam.

'I love him very much, but he left for Europe nearly nine months ago,' she finished. 'He writes, but I'm not sure where that leaves me.' She shrugged wearily; she was tired of thinking about it. 'I'm lonely, I guess, and no amount of work seems to be compensation enough.'

Monty offered no advice or comment.

'Would you like dessert?' he asked after a moment.

'No, I need to get home; I have an idea that I'd like to hammer out before tomorrow,' she responded. 'Are you staying at the Mayflower?'

Monty nodded as he paid the cheque. 'Are you still in 30th Street?'

'Uh-huh,' she replied, stifling a yawn.

'I'll get the taxi to drop you off on the way.'

■

Each day the following week Monty took a seat next to Iris when he arrived in the Fish Room. On this particular Monday morning, exactly one week since they had begun, Stimson sat addressing a point about leasing vessels to a belligerent nation. Monty circled a sentence on the front page of the newspaper and pushed it across to Iris. He had made a note in the margin.

The line from the *Washington Post* read: *Wendell Willkie, the only Republican with sex appeal.* In the margin was a question mark.

Iris hastily scribbled in her notepad and slid it sideways to Monty. *Judging by the Republicans assembled in this room, an astute statement. WW a lifelong Democrat until recently. Explains his sex appeal.* Neither Stimson, Knox, McCloy, Forrestal or Patterson had one ounce of sex appeal between them. Monty smiled and nudged her foot with his own under the table. She nudged back playfully.

Willkie was the likely Republican candidate for the presidency. Iris had to admit he was more attractive than your average politician and the knowledge that the long-married Hoosier was involved in a long-standing affair with editor Irita Van Doren made Willkie slightly more attractive, yet he lacked character in Iris's mind. She just didn't believe he could be president.

'Does anyone have any comments?' Stimson asked.

'Yes,' Iris said after a moment. She took a sip of water. All friskiness had vanished from her demeanour. 'I don't believe the answer is to be found in the Neutrality Act or the Espionage Act of 1917. We've exhausted every avenue.' She produced a folder from her bag. Iris looked around the room; all eyes were fixed on her. She had been working on a concept for the past week. She had researched and double-checked and quizzed her professors about the consequences of embarking on such a path. Although she had confidence in her proposal, in the heat of the room it seemed unlikely that it would be accepted. She feared she might even be laughed at. But there was no turning back.

'Yes?' Stimson urged.

Iris drew a breath. 'The president *can* release the destroyers to Britain on his own authority as commander-in-chief.'

'Leasing the vessels to Britain runs foul of international law,' Monty reminded her. 'And the Espionage Act prohibits even delivering the boats as a gift.'

'We can trade them,' Iris suggested. 'We just have to find something that we want and that Churchill is happy to give away. It's entirely constitutional. I've been over it a hundred times.'

Iris looked around the table at the men considering her proposition. Knox and Stimson were locked in discussion. Iris could not hear their muted comments. Patterson and Forrestal shuffled through documents frantically, either peeved that Iris had solved the problem or simply double-checking the constitutionality of her scheme. The younger clerks followed suit. Harry nodded his head slowly in consideration. She turned to Monty. On his face was an expression she had never seen before, a kind of satisfied half-smile. He winked at her approvingly.

'It's daring,' Stimson muttered slowly, his conviction growing. 'But it just might work.'

'I like it,' Harry began. 'We'll take it to the president. Let's start working on it straight away. Write it up into a paper, Iris, using all the legalese you want.'

'Okay,' she said hesitantly, astonished her idea had been accepted so readily. 'It'll take me a few days, maybe even a week. And it'll need to go to the attorney-general. Of course, I'll need to know what the trade is before I can finish.'

The men nodded. 'We'll come up with something – even if it's fifty pints of warm beer,' Harry joked as they got to work.

50
KISMET, NEW YORK
July 1940

Hick lay on the sofa in her cramped living room, *Fortune* magazine in one hand and a glass of bourbon in the other. Following each sip she'd reach behind and rest the glass on the sofa's arm above her head. Eleanor anxiously viewed this movement from her position at a small card table located behind the sofa, certain the glass would topple.

Once the glass was safe Eleanor returned to her work typing her column. She scanned keys impatiently for the desired letter and, once found, tapped it ruthlessly with her index finger. Why had she agreed to Hick's suggestion to leave Tommy behind in Washington? she fumed silently. She had four columns to write during her ten days in Kismet and without Tommy to take dictation, type the article and then proof it, she had little chance of meeting her deadline. Her thoughts became blocked every time she stared at the keys. She just couldn't work like this.

'Listen to this, Eleanor,' Hick said. 'The poll here shows that if Frank is nominated again he'll win the presidency, but if he doesn't another Democratic candidate will lose in a landslide to the GOP. Interesting, huh?'

Eleanor didn't think it interesting at all and she hoped her husband had not seen the results of that particular poll. She feared it wouldn't take too much encouragement for him to run again.

'Yes, I suppose so,' she said noncommittally, wiping her face and neck with a handkerchief she'd found in her skirt pocket.

'Do you think he'll put himself up for nomination?' Hick asked, peering over the back of the sofa.

Searching for the 'f', Eleanor answered abruptly, 'I have no idea. You know Franklin doesn't tell me everything.'

'I just thought as this concerns you he might have raised the prospect,' Hick ventured cautiously. 'To run for a third term – it's a big thing, privately and historically.'

'I know.' Eleanor found the 'f' and banged it down violently. 'But he hasn't discussed it with anyone. Not even Harry.' She grimaced. 'This typewriter is ancient, Hick,' she declared, placing her hands flat on the table. 'I'm going to buy you a new one tomorrow.'

'I don't know where in Kismet you'll find a typewriter shop,' her friend laughed. 'I doubt there's anywhere on Fire Island. Anyway, that's Old Faithful. I bought her with my first pay cheque. She's never failed me.'

'Why did you have to buy a home in a such an uncivilised little hamlet?' Eleanor grumbled. 'No shops, no telephone, no cars . . .'

'No crowds of people seeking your opinion, no distractions, no committees, no Tommy . . .' Hick continued acerbically before returning to the magazine.

It was true. In the four days she had spent in Kismet, Eleanor had discovered something profound about herself. She had grown to despise putting her own life, work and interests on the backburner for somebody else, no matter how much she loved them. This was a profound discovery because she had always perceived herself as being entirely selfless. The First Lady was unsure when the change had taken place. Hick once again reached backwards for her bourbon.

'For goodness' sake, Hick,' Eleanor snapped. 'Sit up and drink that. You'll spill it everywhere.' She rose. 'And take your shoes off if you're going to lie all over the sofa.' Eleanor walked out the front door and onto the cottage's rickety porch.

Leaning against the railing, she looked out over Great South Bay. The lights of Long Island were growing brighter as the sun went down. Apart from the ferry, there was no way off this island, Eleanor thought. But she had promised Hick she would spend these ten days with her at the home she was so proud of, the dilapidated beach shack she had bought three months earlier. Within minutes Hick was standing next to her at the rail. Eleanor heard a mosquito skim past her ear. It came to rest on Hick's hand. Waiting until the insect had pressed its proboscis into the flesh, she slapped Hick's hand sharply, more sharply than she needed to, to flatten the insect.

'Hey, what was that for?' Hick exclaimed.

'There was a mosquito on your hand,' Eleanor explained calmly. 'You know how they love you.'

'No, I mean what was *that* for?' Hick persisted.

The women watched wordlessly as the last ferry for Bayport departed the dock.

'I'm sorry,' Eleanor said. 'Your constant questions about whether Franklin is running again make me edgy. And it's just so hot here all the time, so sticky.'

'I'm just interested,' Hick said quietly. 'His decision concerns me too. I just want to know the facts. What I might be doing this time next year, for instance. Slaving away for the Women's Democratic Committee or living the life with you at Val-Kill?'

Eleanor nodded. Suspecting the worst, the First Lady could not share her fears with Hick. In January she would have laughed at anyone who suggested Franklin would seek a third term. She had organised work for herself, signed another five-year contract with United Feature Syndicate, agreed to deliver forty-five lectures across the country. She was excited by the prospect, energised at the thought of not being burdened by her husband's office. But now, only six months later, she suspected he would run. She knew he could not walk away from the presidency as the world was falling to pieces. These were the facts she could not divulge to Hick. The truth would break her heart.

'Franklin's keeping his counsel,' Eleanor replied. 'I can't tell you anything more, darling.'

51
WASHINGTON DC
August 1940

'Sit down, McIntosh,' Roosevelt said as Iris entered the Oval Office. He emerged from behind his desk and stopped beside the sofa. He held out his hand and she shook it bemusedly. 'It's done and dusted. Churchill has agreed to the trade. We're getting ninety-nine-year leases on eight British naval bases. The deal has been given the green light by the Justice Department.'

'When's it happening?'

'On the sixth of September we deliver the fifty destroyers to Nova Scotia, where we will hand them over to the Brits,' the president said. 'I wanted you to be the first to know.'

Iris was stunned into silence.

'And Bob Jackson wants to meet you. He was extremely impressed with the paper you wrote,' the president said. 'I told him on one condition: that he doesn't try to poach you for the Justice Department.' Roosevelt grinned.

The attorney-general liked my paper, she marvelled. She sat up a little straighter.

'You've done great work,' he went on. 'And the fact that the transaction wound up being to America's advantage . . . well, even the most steadfast isolationist will find that balm for their bruised principles.'

'It was a team effort,' Iris explained hastily. 'Monty came up with the idea for the bases and Judge Patterson and his staff gave me a lot of help with the paper . . .'

'I know, McIntosh,' Roosevelt said, taking her hand. 'But I'm proud of you. I just wanted you to know. The entire team worked hard, but I'm most proud of you.'

Iris smiled and nodded. 'Thank you, Mr President.'

'Now,' he continued, 'I need your help with something else.' Turning towards the door he called, 'Missy! Bring in our new resident.'

Iris raised her eyes curiously. So buoyed was she by the president's praise she almost believed she could achieve anything. Halt Hitler's advance through Europe? Just give me until six, boss, she thought spiritedly.

Wasn't it odd how circumstances conspire towards one outcome? Wasn't it peculiar, it occurred to her, how individuals are unknowingly moulded by their environment and the people with whom they spend every day? Iris had never imagined she would transform into the woman she had become.

A minute later Missy entered holding a puppy up to her face. She placed the dog on Roosevelt's lap.

'Look, she's spoiling him already,' Roosevelt complained. 'He only arrived this morning.'

'He's gorgeous, though,' Missy cooed. 'How could you not spoil him?'

'This little Scottish Terrier was a gift from my cousin Daisy. She thought I might like a four-legged companion during my next term,' the president explained.

Iris stood. 'He is gorgeous.' She lifted the puppy out of Roosevelt's hands and looked into his face. The pair rubbed noses.

'I need your help with a name. Daisy christened him Big Boy, but Missy despises the name and, to be honest, I don't care for it much either.'

Iris was being tested further. Never having owned a pet, she wasn't certain if she had any talent for naming animals.

'I thought that with your Scottish background you might be able to help us out,' Missy told her.

The puppy licked Iris's face relentlessly. 'He is quite feisty,' she said thoughtfully. 'He reminds me of a character from a poem my father used to recite to me when I was a child. It was called "The Song of the Outlaw Murray".'

She paused as she recalled the ballad whose words altered somewhat each time her father stood at the foot of her bed and performed it. Torrie McIntosh claimed he had penned the poem himself. It wasn't until she became a teacher and discovered the poem in a volume of Sir Walter Scott's works that Iris realised the truth.

'In a nutshell,' she said, 'it's about the leader of an ancient Scottish clan, John Murray. He poached in the King's forest. King James couldn't stop his activities, so he made Murray the gamekeeper of the forest. He became renowned as Murray the outlaw of Falahill.'

She looked from the dog to the president. 'You could call him John Murray?' she suggested.

'How about Outlaw?' Missy offered.

The president held out his arms for the puppy. He scrutinised the animal keenly for a few moments. 'Fala,' he declared.

Missy and Iris nodded in agreement. 'Fala it is,' Missy confirmed, kneeling next to the president and stroking the puppy cheerfully.

'How are you going to celebrate your triumph?' the president asked Iris now a title had been bestowed on his pet.

Iris had not considered celebrating. She hadn't even known until a few minutes ago that there was anything to celebrate.

'I have a campaign meeting tonight, unfortunately,' he explained. The president's hand had been forced a week earlier and he had announced his intention to run. 'Now this destroyer deal is over I can concentrate on Willkie. What do you think of him, McIntosh?'

'Voters seems to like his sincerity and openness, his ordinariness, I guess,' she said. 'But I think that lack of polish will see him falter. That comment about women . . .' Iris whistled and raised her eyes.

The previous week Willkie had announced he would appoint a Secretary of Labor from the ranks of organised labor. He added, 'And it will not be a woman either.' This was a direct dig at Frances Perkins, Roosevelt's Secretary of Labor.

'Why did he have to go and insult half the population of the United States?' the president wondered. 'I feel a little sorry for the kid.'

Iris grinned. 'Don't be too soft on him.'

'Anyway, perhaps after the election the missus and I will host something in your honour, as a way of saying thank you.'

'Then it can be a double celebration,' Iris said as she gave Fala a parting pat and left the president and Missy in the Oval Office.

■

Iris walked across the corridor to the Fish Room to collect her things. The space had become her home over the last two months. She had even fallen asleep there one night over a pile of notes and law books. Waking at five in the morning, she had realised it was either too late or too early to go home. After that she began keeping a change of clothes at the White House.

Monty was waiting for her when she entered.

'Did you hear the news?' she asked.

Monty nodded.

'The president said he wanted me to be the first to know,' she groaned.

'You know what he's like: he wants everyone to feel special,' he said, walking over to her. 'But you were the only one he called into his office. Harry told us.' He took her hands. 'That was quite a rabbit to pull out of your hat. And the paper . . .' He shook his head. 'That was something.'

'Thanks,' she responded before beginning to pile the debris of the previous weeks into her bag. Then a small piece of paper that she had folded and slid into her bag caused her brow to crease. She bit her lip as she stared at the table.

'What's up?'

'I got a message today,' she said. 'From Felix Frankfurter's office.'

'And?'

'He wants me to come in for a meeting,' Iris replied without enthusiasm. 'He didn't say what about.'

'That's big, kiddo,' Monty said, eyes opening wide. 'He wants you working for him.'

'You think that's what it means?' Iris asked sceptically.

'Absolutely. I know Frankfurter well. While we didn't see eye to eye on everything when he worked here, he's a good guy. To get a job offer from a Supreme Court justice is nothing to sneeze at.'

'So you think I should meet with him?'

'Absolutely!' Monty responded. 'You don't have to accept. Just listen to what he has to offer.'

She nodded. 'I guess so.'

Monty touched her arm. 'Don't let your loyalty for this administration hold you back.'

She considered Monty's advice for a few moments then said, 'So I guess you'll be leaving in September with the destroyers?'

'Yep.'

'It doesn't give us much time,' she said.

'Nope.'

'Well, we'd better get started.' Iris knew exactly how she wanted to celebrate.

■

Iris lay in the crook of Monty's arm staring at the closet, another Val-Kill acquisition. Monty always despised Val-Kill furniture. He said it was cumbersome and dreary. But he had grown solemn when Iris informed him that the Val-Kill partnership had been disbanded, how Mrs Roosevelt had so bitterly fallen out with Nan and Marion, how lawyers were now dividing the property and the possessions of the three women and how Mrs Roosevelt had taken to her bed in devastation for a week following the demise of their relationship.

'It's a divorce, I suppose,' Monty said despondently. 'Those three women were so close. It's just so strange how love works.'

And now, behind those heavy walnut doors of the Val-Kill closet, were Sam's clothes. His suits, shirts, shoes and trousers were lined up on their hangers, obediently waiting for their wearer to return. His ties – four of them – were hanging on the back of the left-hand door. Moving her head slightly, she was able to see the medicine cabinet through the bathroom door. In it, along with her make-up and perfume and toothbrush, were a razor and shaving cream. His books, records, cufflinks, comb were scattered around the apartment. All of it confirmation of the life they had shared together, a life that was still present, even if distant.

She snuggled more firmly into Monty's side. The sun was only now setting. Was it guilt she was feeling? Guilt and regret, she decided. Regret at what might have been. She had given in to loneliness, she realised. When she and Monty had arrived at her apartment that afternoon and undressed it was as if they were seeing each other for the very first time. Iris had opened the window but pulled the curtains on the still afternoon. However, the sun still managed to penetrate, creating a tranquil haze in the room. They got into bed and pulled the sheet over them then lay on their sides staring at each other for quite some time. Iris was aware of the noises from the street below – voices, cars, a siren. She liked that she and Monty were creating their own haven.

Besides the uniform and a few more grey hairs, he was exactly the man she had first made love to seven years ago. But it seemed so different. They kissed each other softly, tentatively, perhaps fearful of what they might discover. Similarly, when Monty ran his hands lightly over her skin, the assuredness she remembered in his touch was absent at first. Iris followed the puckered trail of his scar with her fingertips.

He readily accepted her touch. She moved closer to him until their bodies were aligned. Caressing one another gently, whispers passed between them, reassurances of the path on which they were about to set foot. They lingered over each other's bodies until they could bear it no longer. When they finally made love it was without pretence. At no time had she thought of Sam.

Monty breathed in deeply and then opened his eyes. 'It's nice to have you back,' he said sleepily. 'It wasn't as I remembered. It was better.' He kissed her forehead. 'What time is it?' he asked.

'About eight, I think,' Iris answered.

'Do you have anything to eat?'

'I should have. Will you fix something?'

'What do you want?' he asked, throwing the sheet off and sitting up.

When she didn't answer immediately, he looked over his shoulder at her. 'Well?' he prompted.

'I want you to give up your suite at the Mayflower and move in here until you have to leave,' Iris said emphatically.

Monty slid back under the sheet. Leaning on one elbow, he looked at her curiously. 'Where does that leave Jacobson?'

'The same place he's been for the past eleven months,' she responded without hesitation.

Monty eyed her sceptically.

'This isn't revenge. I love Sam, I told you that, but it's been almost a year.'

'Then what . . .' he began.

'We've got too much history to be coy with each other, Monty. My feelings for you run so deep it scares me. You're like nourishment . . . I'm not making sense.' She groaned at her inability to articulate or even understand the nature of her love for this man. 'I want to live life with you, even if it is just for a month. I've got some vacation time owing. We could go away for a week or two.'

Monty rolled onto his back and placed his hands behind his head. He stared at the ceiling.

She put her head on his chest. 'Sometimes I wish I had gone to Japan with you,' she said mournfully.

He looked at her and laughed then ran his hand over her head. 'Be glad you didn't,' he said cheerfully. 'Japan is a man's world. You would have been miserable.'

He got out of bed and began pulling on his trousers. 'Of course I'll move in here. I'll ring the Mayflower now and tell them to send over my things.' Monty leaned down and kissed her. 'It'll be nice living like husband and wife for a while.'

Pleased by his response, she lay in the bed watching as he dressed.

When he had reached the doorway he turned. 'Clear some space in that God-awful closet of yours before my things arrive,' he ordered brazenly before grinning and picking up the telephone.

Iris glanced at the closet and considered the consequences of this seemingly trivial request.

52
HYDE PARK, NEW YORK
November 1940

Iris sat on the bench overlooking the bluff. A crowd was inside the house, friends and staff, taking the returns. Although the first-floor lights were on, there was not a sound coming from the house. She wondered whether that was a good or bad sign. Iris held her watch up to the moonlight and tilted her wrist slightly. Midnight. Her mind drifted to the Thanksgiving when she and Sam had sat on the same bench and had ever so fleetingly come together, only for him to leave moments later. Then she thought of Monty. Thirty-six glorious days and then he had left as well.

A cheer went up in the house. Startled, Iris turned towards the building. Good news. Iris contemplated whether she should return. While she was doing so, the door opened. She recognised the silhouette walking her way. It was Harry.

'It's over, Iris,' he called happily. 'We've won!'

'Do you have the figures yet?' she asked.

Harry sat. 'Not yet, but Frank's carried every large city except Cincinnati. We've carried thirty-eight states to Willkie's ten and we've picked up six seats in the House.'

'That's great, Harry,' Iris said. 'I knew there was nothing to worry about. Those speeches he delivered . . . That one in Cleveland last week.' She shook her head in disbelief. 'He had the voters eating out of his hand. He was all the Barrymores rolled into one.'

'I wasn't so sure, Iris,' Harry admitted. 'It was touch and go there for a while.'

'"I see an America devoted to our freedom – unified by tolerance and by religious faith – a people consecrated to peace, a people confident in strength because their body and their spirit are secure and unafraid,"' Iris quoted from the president's final campaign speech. 'It's hard to beat, Harry. Willkie calling the president a warmonger, he deserved the beating he took.'

'Nobody has faith in the boss like you do, Iris.'

She shrugged, unsure whether Harry's observation was a compliment or a slight. 'The Roosevelts can't leave the White House. The country wouldn't be the same without them.'

'What are you doing out here all by yourself anyway?' he asked. 'Feeling a little lonely?'

'A little bit,' she confessed.

'Me too,' he said quietly. 'Who do you miss most – Chapel or Jacobson?'

The frankness of his question startled her.

'I don't know,' she admitted. 'I miss them both in different ways. But I worry about them both in the same way.'

'Because of the bombing in London?'

Iris nodded. 'It's wrong – the bombing of civilians to break a country's will.'

'It's a tactic the British themselves pioneered in Iraq in the twenties,' Harry reminded her.

'That makes it even more sickening somehow,' Iris responded.

'Is Jacobson still in London too?'

'Yes. But he's covering Paris. I'm not sure what that means.'

The pair sat in silence for a while. It seemed to Iris that outsiders like Harry viewed both men as being central to her life. Why did it have to be either/or? she wondered.

'But you've got Diana,' Iris said eventually, referring to Harry's daughter.

'I'm not a great dad, Iris,' he remarked. 'I spend too much time away from her, working. We hardly know each other.'

'What happened with Dorothy Hale?' Although she had only met the actress briefly, her odd coupling with Harry and her subsequent suicide had always troubled Iris.

'I met her at a party and she threw herself at me,' Harry said in amazement. 'It was so soon after Barbara's death and I was still pretty shaken . . .'

'I understand,' Iris assured him.

'But we had nothing in common. You knew Barbara – she was the antithesis of Dorothy.' He paused briefly. 'I don't believe Dorothy killed herself over me. We certainly weren't in love. She was lonely. She was just a very lonely woman.'

Iris and Harry sat side by side for a minute or two as the Hudson flowed below them. Iris contemplated Harry and his life. Widowed, ill and distanced from his child, he spent every moment working. Even when the cancer is at its worst and he's bedridden, she thought, his only relief comes from the telephone and newspapers at his side and the constant stream of communication between his bedroom and the Oval Office. The prospect of such a future terrified her.

'Look at us!' Iris exclaimed finally. 'Aren't we two sad sacks? Let's get inside and start celebrating.' She jumped to her feet and took Harry's hand, pulling him off the bench. The pair walked arm in arm back to the house and the festivities.

THE THIRD TERM
1941–1944

Commander-in-Chief

53
ANTIGUA, CARIBBEAN SEA
December 1940

'How long's he been like that?' Harry whispered, eyeing the president as he lay on a deck chair, the pages of a letter clutched in his hand.

Iris was standing behind President Roosevelt and slightly to one side. It was impossible to see his face. 'Since he received it yesterday,' she answered. 'He hasn't eaten, he doesn't want to fish. He's just been sitting there or in his cabin.'

It was an odd sight to see the president in his open-necked shirt and well-worn straw fishing hat reclining on a deckchair in the shade of one of the USS *Tuscaloosa*'s heavy guns.

'What are you two up to?' Missy asked playfully as she approached. 'Spying on the president?'

Iris and Harry laughed quietly.

'You must know what's in that letter?' Harry enquired.

Missy shook her head. 'It came on that navy seaplane that set down alongside of us yesterday. He won't tell me anything. Just shoos me away whenever I get near him.'

'Well, he seems reflective, not panicked or anxious,' Iris suggested hopefully. 'I'm sure he'll tell us when he's had time to mull over whatever it is.'

The three of them parted. Iris decided to go back to her cabin and write to Sam. Although they corresponded frequently, it had been fifteen months since she'd seen him. He had telephoned from London when she graduated in September but it had been a bad line and she could barely hear him. Initially their letters to one another had been romantic; they spoke of longing and desire. Iris had allowed her feelings to flow freely onto the page. Now the language she used was stilted and strained. Iris knew this change of tone had to do with Monty. She felt like a phoney filling pages with her yearnings and regrets when she had spent thirty-six days with Monty in the apartment that she and Sam had once shared. She also wondered, on occasion, usually in the darkest hour of the night, whether Sam might have met someone else. Even though she knew she was being unreasonable, the idea depressed her. Fifteen months was such a long time for lovers to be separated. Iris sat, pen poised. She began. Twenty-five minutes later she was finished and read over her words.

The election was covered in the first paragraph. She knew he would be up-to-date with news from DC, so she attempted to include some information that was not in the newspapers. She briefly outlined Mrs Roosevelt coming to her husband's rescue at the convention by convincing the delegates to accept Henry Wallace as his running mate even though everyone despised him, including herself. Iris wrote, 'It was a forceful speech that successfully managed to inspire the delegates' sense of loyalty. The situation irritated Mrs R. immensely, but she told me she saw it as one of the small compromises for power.'

Iris skipped over her work on the destroyer deal in one sentence. Nevertheless, those few words allowed her to segue smoothly to her current situation on board the USS *Tuscaloosa*. The president had decided to use the newly acquired British naval bases as an excuse to embark on a tour of the Caribbean. 'After picking up cigars in Cuba,' Iris wrote, 'we are now anchored off Antigua in the West Indies. In between fishing excursions and swimming the president has managed to inspect a few of the bases. But really, it's an excellent opportunity for a little R and R before official business begins again in January.'

Her final words were, 'Take care. All my love, Iris.' She wasn't satisfied with her closing, but anything more passionate seemed misplaced.

As she was addressing the envelope there was a knock on her cabin door. It was Missy, letting Iris know that the president wanted to see her.

After placing her letter in the post bundle to be sent out, she made her way to the Officers' Room.

■

Already assembled when Iris arrived were Missy, Henry Stimson and Frank Knox. They were only waiting on Harry. The president seemed grave, but not troubled. Copies of a document sat on the table in front of two spare seats. Iris sat and began to read what the others had already begun.

It was a letter. Iris skipped to the final page – page eight, she noted. It was signed 'Yours Sincerely, Winston S. Churchill.' Iris raised her eyebrows briefly then returned to the first page. Harry entered, took a seat and began reading also.

Essentially, it was a four-thousand-word plea for financial assistance. Britain's coffers would be drained within the month. Without cash to pay for war supplies from the United States, Churchill concluded, Great Britain would 'stand stripped to the bone'.

When they had finished reading all eyes turned to the president. 'So cash-and-carry no longer applies as Britain has no cash. What's the solution?'

Iris re-read the contents of the letter. The cash-and-carry aspect of the Neutrality Act allowed the United States to sell war supplies to Britain. As long as the Brits could pay for and pick up the goods themselves, they could buy what they liked. But without funds, Iris thought, there was just no way of getting around it.

'We're not talking about fifty mothballed destroyers, boss,' Harry said. 'Churchill here is asking for supplies for the duration of the war. We can't come to the party.'

'But we have to, Harry,' Iris insisted emotionally. 'Without aid Britain will be devastated.' She hastily returned her eyes to the document, hoping the edge of desperation in her voice had gone unnoticed.

'I agree,' Knox added. 'Let's say Britain manages to win despite the odds and without our help. What then? The American people are able to go on enjoying a free world, but at what cost?'

'And that's the best-case scenario. Consider the worst,' Stimson said seriously.

The group sat speechless for a few minutes.

'Okay,' Harry said. 'Where do we go from here? Ladies first.' He turned to Iris.

She thought out loud. 'Congress can't be bypassed on this one. The president can't just give goods away and Britain doesn't have enough naval bases to trade.'

'I can't see how we can keep letting them place more orders,' Knox said, shaking his head. 'But we've got to.'

The room became quiet, but there was an expectancy in the air. The same kind of expectancy that occurs a minute or so before dawn.

'Fortunately, ladies and gentlemen, I believe I've come up with a solution,' Roosevelt stated.

The group turned to him.

The president spoke carefully. 'We are going to *lend* Britain whatever they want at no cost. They will repay us, when they are able, by giving back what they've borrowed or they can pay us back *in kind*. I'm taking the dollar sign out of the equation and substituting a gentleman's agreement, if you like.' He paused briefly. 'Lend-Lease, that's what I'm calling it. We'll thrash out the details back in Washington, but I believe this is a sound solution.'

'Do you think Congress will buy it?' Harry asked the president.

'Congress will buy it if the country buys it. I'll sell it to the public first. Inspire them. Americans need to know what they've got to lose.'

As those gathered rose from their seats, the president asked, 'What do you think of the name?'

'Well, it's better than the Fish Room,' Harry said.

54

WASHINGTON DC
December 1940

One week later Iris climbed the steps to her apartment. She was happy to be back in DC. The salt water had revived her while the sun had sizzled away mournful thoughts of Monty and Sam. The realisation that both men were in her life had arisen gradually. It was neither startling nor revelatory. Iris now had to consider which roles they were to play. There couldn't be two leading men in her life.

When she reached her door she placed her suitcase on the ground and searched her purse for her key, which had sulkily worked its way to the bottom since she'd been absent. Before she found it the door opened. Sam was there.

'I heard you from inside,' he said. 'You're tanned.'

Iris stood, mouth slightly agape, with the key in her hand. 'I've been on a cruise,' she said when she could speak. 'In the Caribbean. I sent you a letter but you wouldn't have received it.'

'Gee, it's good to see you, Iris.'

'When did you get in?'

'Just about an hour ago,' he replied. 'Come in.'

He picked up her suitcase and she walked into her apartment. 'Why didn't you wire me that you were coming?'

'I didn't know until a day or so ago. Roosevelt contacted Murrow from the Caribbean. He wants to give an interview about Lend-Lease. Murrow knows my history with the president, so . . . And I wanted to be home for the holidays. Hanukkah begins on the twenty-fourth this year. But that's all by the by . . .' He broke off and took her in his arms.

When they kissed Iris realised she had come to no conclusions regarding the men in her life. Her longing for Sam was torment. 'I've missed you, Sam,' she whispered. 'I've missed you so badly, but fifteen months is such a long time.'

He stared at her for a second, his gaze shifting from tender to accusatory.

'What does that mean? *But* fifteen months is a long time?' He released her and took a step back, putting his hands in his pockets.

Immediately regretting her careless use of words, Iris backpedalled rapidly.

'I was worried that you might have found someone else,' she said as evenly as possible.

Iris could see immediately by the colour of his expression that there had been no other women. He was hurt that the notion had ever entered her mind. To Sam, the idea was entirely unfathomable.

'I can tell you honestly, Iris, that I have not even looked at anyone else. Have you?' he asked, clearly unsettled.

Iris sat, weighing up the implications of telling Sam the truth. It was far too dangerous, she decided. While her conscience would be eased, she hated the thought of what the truth would do to Sam. Before she could speak, he interrupted her to say, 'I know Chapel was here.'

Uncertain whether he meant *here* in the apartment or *here* in DC, Iris mentally scanned her apartment, scrutinising every corner, every surface, every cupboard for evidence Monty had lived with her for more than a month last summer. Had she overlooked something? Was there a toothbrush forgotten? A pair of socks left in a drawer? Aware of how small Capitol society was, she and Monty had been cautious, extremely so. She sat and looked down at her knees in order to conceal her frantic deliberations, ashamed of herself for doing so.

'He was in Washington,' she hedged. 'He worked on the destroyer deal. Surely it was all over the news in Britain?'

'Did you start up with him again?'

'We worked together. We had dinner a few times. That's it.' Then she raised her head slightly and looked at him squarely, the way she'd seen the president do a thousand times. 'Nothing happened. I love you.'

The truth of her last statement did nothing to allay her guilt.

Sam took a seat next to her. He placed his hand on her knee and squeezed it firmly. 'I'm sorry,' he said. 'I'm tired and a little keyed up. This isn't how I wanted it to go. I actually planned something much more special.'

She raised a quizzical eyebrow.

'You see,' he went on, 'I was going to open the door and get down on bended knee and give you this.' He reached into his coat pocket and withdrew a small velvet box. 'But you just looked so surprised to see me that it kinda threw me.'

Iris took the box from him and opened it. Inside was a princess-cut diamond on a fine silver band.

'Wow, it's beautiful,' she remarked quietly. 'Were you going to say anything?'

'Uh-huh.'

'Well?'

'I was going to ask you to marry me.'

Iris didn't respond.

'I figured now that you've graduated we could get married,' he explained.

'Are you planning to stay in the States?'

He shook his head. 'No, I'm going back to London in the new year with Murrow. I want you to come with me.'

'What about the Blitz?'

'I've thought that through,' he told her. 'We could get a house in the countryside, in Hampshire or Surrey. I could keep my flat in London and join you on the weekends. It's how Ed and Janet Murrow live.'

'Is there much call for constitutional lawyers in Hampshire or Surrey?'

He was quiet. Iris closed the ring box and placed it on the table.

'I'm hungry,' she said after a minute, 'and I don't have any food in the place. Let's get some dinner.'

■

When they returned to the apartment the ring box was still there on the table. They both ignored it. It struck Iris that it was probably the smallest elephant in the room she had ever encountered. After taking off their coats, Iris took Sam's hand and led him into the bedroom.

'I'll just be a minute,' she said as she walked into the bathroom.

Iris undressed and washed her face. Staring at herself in the mirror, she examined her features intently. She remembered the morning in the diner, the morning she had met Mrs Roosevelt, how despondent she had been. Leaning in closer to her reflection, she ran her fingers softly down her face from brow to chin. Was she the same girl? she wondered. Would that girl have looked Sam in the eye and lied?

Throughout dinner she had considered Sam's proposal carefully, weighing up the situation and how they could make it work. She had concluded, just as her peach cobbler was placed in front of her, that it couldn't succeed. To marry Sam now was utterly impractical.

Sam watched her as she walked to the bed and slid between the covers. She pressed herself against him and placed her arm across his chest.

'I'm not going to marry you,' she said. 'Thank you for the proposal and I think the ring is lovely, honestly. But I can't leave Washington now and live the quiet life in England. It would ruin us.'

He breathed in and exhaled heavily. She watched her arm raise and lower as he did so.

'But,' she continued, 'I don't think my refusal should be the ruin of us either.'

'What do you suggest?' he asked.

'Let's enjoy the holiday. All we can do, I guess, is enjoy the moments we have together. But I don't want the moments that we're apart to be wasted waiting for each other.'

He nodded and squeezed her shoulder. 'You're very practical, aren't you?'

'Not always,' she sighed. 'But the possibility of war is likely, Sam. We can't afford to be sentimental.'

She nestled her body into his more firmly. 'Who can say what might happen next year or the next? I would never have thought seven years ago, not even in my wildest dreams, that I'd be where I am now.'

He held her more tightly and their bodies intuitively sought the other's hollows and curves.

'One moment at a time then?' he whispered.

'One beautiful moment at a time,' she agreed.

'Perhaps the war might end,' he suggested after a minute.

'Perhaps.'

'You'll be out of a job anyway in four years,' he teased.

'Maybe,' she said, and felt a shiver of fear at what life outside the White House might hold.

5 5
HYDE PARK, NEW YORK
May 1962

Christmas 1940 was uneventful. Fortunately, I finished all the fruitcakes and baskets by the week before, so there wasn't all that last-minute kerfuffle like there usually was. Anna and the children came across from Seattle. James was there, of course. He and Betsey divorced that year so she had the children with her in Baltimore. But that was all well and good as he was recovering from surgery for his ulcer. Mr Hopkins and Diana were at the table, as were Mr Henry Wallace, the new vice-president, and his wife Ilo.

But the big event of 1940 for me fell on the twenty-ninth of December. That was the evening that Mr Clark Gable came to dinner. He was a great supporter of the president and he and his wife, Miss Carole Lombard, were invited by Mrs Roosevelt to listen to a very important radio broadcast by Mr Roosevelt. The president delivered more radio broadcasts than I can count during his time in the White House, but this one was different. During the week before, the special address by the President of the United States was advertised constantly on CBS and NBC. Everyone knew there was something in the air. Washington was a ghost town that night. I was listening in my office with Elizabeth the cook.

The line from that speech that stays in my memory most strongly is: 'No man can tame a tiger into a kitten by stroking it.' I turned to Elizabeth and said, 'He's talking about Adolf Hitler and Mr Chamberlain, you know.' The president always had a clever turn of phrase. To my mind he was preparing the nation for war.

Afterwards, knowing how fond I was of Clark Gable, Mrs Roosevelt asked me to join the group for coffee. Mr Gable and Miss Lombard were congratulating the president when I walked into the dining room. Mr Gable was complimenting the president on the line: 'We must be the great arsenal of democracy.' I remember he joked that he wished Hollywood scriptwriters could have such a way with words. He was right. With that one speech the president was able to sell the idea of Lend-Lease to the people and to Congress.

Mrs Roosevelt introduced me to Mr Gable. He told me straight away that he loved the dinner. It was only chipped beef, our regular Sunday supper, and I told him so. But he insisted it was magnificent. *Magnificent* was the word he used. After a while I got up enough courage to tell him that *Gone With the Wind* was my favourite movie. Why, I saw it at least five times. It had been a good way to distract myself when Dad passed in '39. Despite all the accolades that Mr Gable and that movie received, he seemed extremely pleased that I liked it so much even though, I informed him, I didn't care for the ending.

When the president did eventually declare war, Mr Gable joined the air force. And it wasn't for show, either. He flew combat missions over Germany and wound up a captain. He even earned the Distinguished Flying Cross for his efforts. Miss Lombard did her part as well. She travelled all over the country selling war bonds for the president. It was tragic when the plane she was flying in crashed in '42. Poor Mr Gable took her death very hard, I read in *Photoplay* magazine.

The president's appetite was extremely good during that time, I recall. I can't remember him being churlish about anything. But why would he be? Public support was on his side and Congress passed Lend-Lease. But it didn't last long. By the summer of '41, he was picky personified.

56

WASHINGTON DC
July 1941

Iris and the president rode together in the back of the presidential car, a Lincoln that the president had nicknamed the Sunshine Special on account of its retractable roof. Even though the sun was bright as they pulled away from the house, Roosevelt requested that the roof remain closed. The presidential pennants had been removed from the bonnet. Mrs Roosevelt followed in her own car. A large bunch of purple lisianthus lay across Iris's knees.

'She'll like those, McIntosh,' the president commented quietly, indicating the bouquet. 'What are they?'

'Texas bluebell is their common name, sir,' she answered. 'The man in the shop told me they're a sturdy flower with the appearance of delicacy.'

The president smiled. 'They're very pretty.'

They were the only words spoken during their fifteen-minute journey.

When they parked at the back entrance of Doctors Hospital in Georgetown, three members of the Secret Service were waiting. A hospital wheelchair appeared at Roosevelt's door and his bodyguard proceeded to lift the president from the vehicle. Mrs Roosevelt was waiting by the entrance. She carried a large basket of fruit.

The First Lady led the group along the hospital corridor to the elevator. The hall was empty, apart from another four agents. She pushed the button and waited for the others to reach her. When the elevator door opened, the party entered. Three agents escorted the president and his wife. The other men remained on the first floor. When they reached the room, Roosevelt asked his bodyguard to stay outside. Iris, the president and the First Lady entered.

Missy was lying in the bed, her head and shoulders propped up slightly. Her eyes were open and her gaze passed along her three visitors when they entered. Her left hand rose an inch from the bed in a gesture of welcome. Following dinner with the president two weeks before, the forty-three-year-old had suffered a stroke. The violence of the attack had rendered her face unrecognisable, its right side distorted in a strange and unnatural way. It disturbed Iris to see Missy LeHand in this state, her fine features altered so dramatically.

Mrs Roosevelt gave her basket to the nurse in the room and spoke to her briefly. On her way out of the room the same nurse relieved Iris of the lisianthus. The president sat by the bedside of his closest companion for the last two decades and held her hand. He looked into her ink-blue eyes and smiled warmly. It was the saddest thing Iris had ever seen. She noticed the stress in Missy's face as she attempted a similar gesture of affection. Mrs Roosevelt busied herself around the room – removing dead flowers from the array of vases, refreshing Missy's water jug and straightening her bedclothes and robe.

Iris moved forward to the bed and spoke to Missy, offering her best wishes and prayers. Missy's mouth opened faintly, her focus fixed hard on Iris. Disappointment clouded her eyes when she realised no sound had been emitted.

'That's okay, Missy,' Iris said. 'You don't need to say anything.' She walked to the window.

Missy's room was spacious and private, with a view overlooking the hospital gardens. It was a glorious summer day. Iris watched the staff on their breaks and patients walking slowly around the garden's perimeter, escorted by their visitors. She turned back to the scene in the room. Mrs Roosevelt now sat knitting at the foot of the bed. Iris counted twelve vases of flowers in the room as she waited for either the president or his wife to speak. The silence was excruciating. After a few minutes, she sat down by Missy's side.

'The place isn't the same without you,' Iris remarked.

Missy turned her head in Iris's direction and Iris recognised the attentiveness in her eyes as Missy placed her left hand over Iris's.

'Harry just got back last week from Russia,' Iris said brightly. 'Can you imagine Harry Hopkins and Josef Stalin thrashing out the whys and wherefores of the German invasion?' Iris paused for a moment. 'But he seemed to like Stalin and said his determination to whip the Germans was impressive.'

Missy squeezed her hand.

'I mean, I guess you would be determined if your so-called ally sends four million invading soldiers your way.'

Iris sighed.

'The president has declared the Soviets eligible for aid under the Lend-Lease Act.' Missy's eyes flickered. 'The State Department was up in arms about it, as you'd expect. They argued that communism was more of a threat than fascism.' Iris shook her head in bewilderment.

Mrs Roosevelt approached the bed. 'I must leave now, Missy, dear. I have a train at eleven.' She leaned over and kissed the patient on the cheek. After farewelling Iris and her husband, she left the room.

'Mrs Roosevelt is beginning another lecture tour in a few days. She's heading to Florida. Can you imagine how hot it will be down there?' Iris glanced at the president. The glitter of tears was visible in his eyes.

'We should go now too, Mr President,' Iris suggested before turning back to Missy. 'It was good seeing you. Now don't worry about work. Everything is taken care of.'

Iris walked quickly to the door and opened it. 'We're leaving now,' she said to an agent.

Returning to the bed, she went on, 'I'll see you in couple of days, Missy.' She kissed the older woman's cheek. 'Let me know if there's anything you'd like me to bring in for you.'

As the bodyguard stepped forward to take the handles of the president's wheelchair, Roosevelt raised a hand.

'Wait,' he ordered and then turned back to Missy.

'Goodbye, Missy, darling,' he said tenderly. 'I won't be able to get in for a few weeks. I'm going away, on a fishing trip of sorts.' From her position on the other side of the bed, Iris saw the president wink, quickly yet deliberately, and she wondered whether it had been a conscious action. As she watched the president's face for a further sign she identified something else far more eloquent. The hint of a kiss was apparent on his narrow lips, but from his wheelchair it was impossible for him to reach Missy. The longing that passed between them at that moment was devastating to witness.

The bodyguard pushed Roosevelt from the room. In the corridor outside Iris said, 'I'll meet you at the car. I'll just find the rest room.'

In the ladies' room at the far end of the corridor, Iris entered a cubicle and locked the door. There she allowed the tears to stream down her cheeks unchecked, the acceptance of a burden that the president could not bear.

5 7
WASHINGTON DC
August 1941

Iris looked up from her work when she heard a knock. Harry stood in the doorway.

'Some fishing trip you and the president went on,' she smirked, placing her pencil behind her ear and leaning back in her chair.

'I'm sorry, Iris,' Harry said. 'It was top secret. I couldn't tell a soul. Even Mrs Roosevelt was in the dark.'

Reading the *Washington Post* that morning Iris had discovered the meaning of the president's wink. He and Harry had embarked on a covert mission to meet with the British prime minister off the coast of Newfoundland. Ostensibly heading off on a ten-day fishing trip off the coast of New England aboard the *Potomac*, the select group of men instead rendezvoused with the Atlantic fleet and the president boarded the *Augusta* and set sail for Newfoundland; all the while the *Potomac* sailed back to Massachusetts flying the presidential colours and sending frequent bulletins ashore for the sake of the press. The outcome of their three-day conference was the Atlantic Charter, a joint statement regarding allied war goals. Iris had stared flabbergasted at the front page until her coffee turned cold.

'What a ruse!' she exclaimed now as she stood. 'I cannot believe it. Not even Mrs Roosevelt was in on it?'

Harry shook his head. 'Just me and the boss and the Secret Service.'

'Nice work, Harry,' she said, sitting on the corner of her desk and folding her arms. 'Nice result, too. What was Churchill like?'

Harry sat in a chair near the door and crossed his long legs. As he was lighting a cigarette he said, 'Different to the boss.' He closed his eyes for a second as if struggling to describe the British prime minister. 'A keen drinker. Serious, but jolly at the same time. He pressed for a declaration of war. That was obviously his agenda. Nevertheless, they got on like a house on fire. The boss was more honest with him than I've ever seen him with anyone.'

Following a long drag on his cigarette he added, 'And he was funny, really funny.'

'Funny amusing or funny peculiar?' Iris quizzed.

'Amusing.'

'More amusing than Stalin?' Iris grinned.

Harry laughed and nodded. 'Hard to believe, I know. Collectivisation and those purges were a great prank.'

As the president's chief adviser went on detailing the secret mission, a wave of something – pride or honour or privilege – washed over Iris. Perhaps it was all three. How strange it was, she thought, that she was taking part in history. It hadn't been so long ago that she had been thumbing down cars and riding the rails. Iris could not recall the last time when money had been a concern. Nor could she remember the last time she was hungry, really hungry. Working in the White House was a dream come true, even though it had never been her dream. Her brow furrowed as she watched Harry's lips move in speech. She pondered what her father would have made of all this – working with the president, conversing with his closest adviser about Winston Churchill. Would Torrie McIntosh have ever dreamed this for his daughter? Then again, Iris thought, she probably wouldn't be at the centre of policy making in the Roosevelt administration if not for the tragedy of her parents' deaths. It all made sense and yet it made no sense at all.

58
WASHINGTON DC
October 1941

At ten minutes to five Iris stood up from her desk and shut her door. Hanging behind it was the dress she'd purchased to wear to dinner that evening. Iris had been immediately attracted to the colour more than the garment itself. The shop assistant called it 'tango pink'. But as she examined herself in the mirror, with the shop girl waiting expectantly to the rear, she had to admit the dress fit very well and the effect of it slowly grew on her. The ruched bodice from the low, linear neckline to the hips made her figure appear more hourglass-like than it was in reality. And she liked the natural fall of the skirt to mid-calf. The only thing that Iris hadn't warmed to were the square shoulders. They reminded her of epaulettes without the fringing. Iris didn't care for the military look that had been creeping into women's fashion since the start of the year. It was an ominous trend, she thought. Taking the pins out of the tight roll at the back of her head, she redid her hair in a more elegant fashion. As she was doing so there was a light knock at the door.

'I volunteered to find you, kid,' Hick said, poking her head through a small opening. 'What's taking you so long?'

'I'm sorry,' Iris responded, flustered. 'I had a stack of work to finish.'

On entering the office and seeing Iris's dress Hick whistled. 'Is that for Monty?'

'I guess,' Iris confessed reluctantly.

'Is Sam still on the scene?' Hick enquired.

'Occasionally,' Iris said equivocally. 'It's just not realistic to carry on from opposite sides of the Atlantic.'

Hick nodded shrewdly.

'You get back,' Iris told her. 'I'll be there in a minute.'

After fixing her make-up and brushing her hands down the front of the skirt, Iris left her office and made her way hastily along the corridor to the office of the president.

When she entered the room she was breathless. Scanning the assembled faces, she realised she was the last to arrive. Even Harry was present, taking a shift as the president's drinks waiter.

Iris saw the person she sought; he was seated on the sofa, martini in hand, chatting with two men. One she assumed was the Japanese ambassador. The other was Joseph Grew, the US ambassador to Japan. Iris hoped Monty would notice her before anyone managed to ruin her entrance. Then he laughed at something one of the ambassadors said. His head turned slightly to the left and she came into his line of vision. Placing his glass on the table and nodding politely to both men, he stood and approached her in the doorway.

'That is some dress,' Monty said, raising his eyebrows. He kissed her on the cheek and took her hand, twirling her around in order to see the dress in its entirety. 'What do you call the colour?'

Pleased he had asked, she replied, 'Tango pink.'

'Perfect – named for the dance of love,' he said seductively. 'Let's get you a drink.' He led her to the bar.

It had been more than a year since she'd seen Monty and it wasn't until that moment that it occurred to her just how deeply she'd missed him.

'I'll introduce you to Nomura later,' Monty promised, indicating the ambassador. 'Tell me, what's been going on around here?'

For the duration of Children's Hour she and Monty chatted about DC and London. They had agreed not to write when Monty departed for England the year before, lest frequent correspondence proved an encumbrance.

'Harry told me about Missy's stroke,' Monty said. 'I couldn't believe it. The boss must have been broken up?'

'It was agonising,' Iris replied. 'There's not been much progress with her recovery. The president has had her moved to a care facility in Virginia. It's nice. I try to get over there every couple of weeks. He sees her regularly, as does Mrs Roosevelt. But it must be lonely for her.'

Monty nodded solemnly and took her hand, gently stroking her fingers.

'And how's Grace doing filling her shoes?' Grace Tully had been Missy's assistant.

'Well, she's no Missy, but she's organised and efficient. Everything you want in a secretary, I guess,' Iris responded. 'She doesn't have Missy's sixth sense though.'

'Perhaps that's a quality only a true partner can possess,' Monty said thoughtfully.

Iris thought on Monty's observation for a few seconds as she gazed towards the president. She finally asked, 'How long are you back for?'

'A week or two. Hopefully two.'

'Are you intending to stay with me?'

Monty grinned. 'Where else?'

■

Iris glanced around the table as the president spoke. Stimson, Knox and Harry were nodding in eager agreement, looking from Roosevelt to the Japanese ambassador. Monty, Grew and Mrs Roosevelt were leaning back in their seats as they listened, grim with concentration. Hick had not stayed for dinner. She had cited an early-morning meeting in New York, but Hick never hung around for evenings such as this.

'There's plenty of room in the Pacific for everybody,' the president remarked. 'It would do neither of us any good if we got into a war, Admiral. Now the best course of action is continued discussion between yourself and Cordell Hull.'

'I'm pleased you feel this way, Mr President,' Nomura said politely. 'I'll pass on your feelings to Tokyo immediately. But I'm afraid my negotiations with your Secretary of State have not progressed in the direction my government had hoped.'

'Now, for the last time, Admiral,' Roosevelt deflected casually, 'will you call me Frank? You once did, I recall.'

Nomura nodded fleetingly.

'You see,' the president said, addressing the table, 'the admiral and I know each other from my days as Assistant Secretary to the Navy when he was a naval attaché in Washington. I know it's protocol, but it doesn't sit well for an old friend to call me Mr President.'

The ambassador nodded once more.

'It would be good, Frank, if you could meet with the prime minister,' Grew advised. 'He's keen for a meeting if you two could agree on a spot. Konoye has suggested Hawaii. Alaska might be another possibility.'

'Well, let's see how the meetings with Hull go and then we'll discuss further steps,' Roosevelt replied.

Iris saw Grew's eyes flash at Nomura. She looked at Monty as he listened to the discussion, his mouth fixed tight with concern. He pushed his plate of Oriental chicken away untouched.

'Do you really think Cordell Hull is the right man for this?' Mrs Roosevelt asked, referring to the Tennessee-born and bred Secretary of State. 'He's extremely inflexible and a little . . . outdated in his ideas.'

'He's the perfect man for the job,' Harry replied. 'The State Department has to be involved in this matter.'

Stimson and Knox muttered their agreement.

'Perhaps it's wise to do as Joseph suggests and meet with Prime Minister Konoye,' Mrs Roosevelt pressed.

'I agree,' Monty urged tactfully. 'The Japanese are a unique people. Negotiations need a deft hand.' He nodded in respect to Nomura.

Iris stayed quiet as she weighed up the arguments being presented and the make-up of the two distinct camps. Obviously, her sympathies drew her to Monty, but her intellect was persuaded by Hopkins and the hardliners. Iris liked Nomura. He was courteous and shrewd. However, as she evaluated the situation in the Pacific, she believed it all might be too late.

'We'll see,' Roosevelt said again as his plate was removed. 'We'll see.'

The president's evasiveness prompted Nomura to show his hand.

'Mr President,' the ambassador began, 'I have a deadline. The prime minister requires a resolution by November.'

'Or what?' Roosevelt asked.

'War, Mr President,' Nomura replied unemotionally.

■

Nomura departed immediately following dinner. Monty tapped his coffee spoon joylessly on the tablecloth, an improvised death march. Knox, Stimson and Hopkins vigorously argued the advantages of playing for time. Grew stroked his moustache soberly. The president listened gravely. Mrs Roosevelt rose and requested another round of coffee. Finally there was silence. Monty placed the spoon on the saucer and spoke.

'You got me back here from England to advise on this situation,' Monty said flatly to Roosevelt. 'Meet with Konoye. That's my advice. If war with Japan is to be prevented then this is the only way.'

'The fact is, Monty,' Harry said, 'we are not prepared for a war in the Pacific.'

'There doesn't need to be a war in the Pacific,' Monty told him. 'If we go to war with Japan then under their Tripartite Pact with Germany and Italy we are immediately at war in Europe as well.'

'That's exactly why we need to delay,' Stimson cut in.

'The Japs are determined to conquer South-East Asia. Nothing is going to stop that. They've already moved into southern Indochina,' Knox added. 'Burma, Malaya, the Dutch East Indies and the Philippines are next.'

Monty turned to the president. 'If you meet with Konoye and lift the embargo on oil they might pull back. They are expanding to ensure resources. They are a trade-dependent nation.'

'*Might*,' Harry emphasised. 'If they don't then it'll be seen as appeasement. We'll have another Munich on our hands.'

'I've been doing some figuring, Harry, over the last few days,' Monty said, changing direction. 'This freeze on exports to Japan will result in a significant downturn of the Japanese standard of living.'

Iris could see that the group had not been swayed.

'Let me put it this way,' Monty continued. 'The living conditions for the average Japanese would become comparable to the most poverty-stricken American families in the worst depths of the depression.'

He waited for the table to digest the facts he had laid out before them.

'The United States is bankrupting Japan. That's why they're expanding into new territory: we have given them no choice,' Monty concluded.

Hardliners angered him, Iris knew. There was always room to be flexible in any situation, he believed. Iris looked at him sympathetically.

'What about China?' Stimson asked, unmoved.

Monty stared at him curiously.

'I'd advocate a temporary lift of the embargo if the Japs pull out of China,' Stimson asserted.

'When the Japanese invaded China four years ago this country didn't lift a finger to help the Chinese. In fact, we increased our exports to Japan,' Monty reminded him. 'Now you want to begin negotiations with a demand? That's not the way to do business with the Japanese. I lived in Japan for two years. I know how they prefer to operate.'

Monty took a calming breath before going on. 'Our relationship with Japan has steadily soured since the turn of the century. The State Department's attitude has always been one of condescension and bigotry.

Hull is exactly the wrong person to handle this. He is arrogant and Southern.'

The strenuousness of Monty's argument stunned the table.

'The dinner that Mrs Nesbitt prepared so thoughtfully for Nomura this evening represents exactly what is wrong with this nation's dealings with Japan,' he continued.

Iris recalled the congealed plate of sautéed chicken, pineapple and almonds that she had not touched.

'The United States of America knows nothing about the Japanese. Americans see the cartoons of Japanese servicemen portrayed as buck-toothed morons in horn-rimmed spectacles and believe them. We underestimate their military capacity.'

'Japan can't be measured with the same yardstick as other nations,' Grew interrupted. 'It would be hazardous to believe economic pressure will not lead to war. Have I ever steered you wrong, Frank?'

Harry grimaced. 'The reality remains that everything we have is tied up in Europe and the Atlantic. We cannot afford a war in the Pacific. The Japanese navy in the region is greater that the combined fleets of Britain, the Netherlands and the United States. The only option is to stall until we can get our forces primed.'

'When will that be?' Mrs Roosevelt asked.

'Early next year.'

There was silence, a stalemate. Iris could see the president was torn.

'Is war inevitable?' Iris posed the question to the gathering after a minute or so.

No one responded to her enquiry.

'What are you thinking, McIntosh?' Roosevelt asked.

'I agree with Monty. Hull is old and obstinate and should be removed from the equation.' Her focus shifted momentarily to the president. 'A meeting between you and Konoye would be most beneficial. You're an expert at negotiations and I'm certain you'd be able to smooth the waters.'

She looked at Monty evenly across the table before going on.

'However, if we can agree that Japan is determined to expand into South-East Asia and you give them the oil to do it . . . it would be disastrous. Like Harry said, it would be another Munich Agreement.'

'And that settlement led to the downfall of Chamberlain,' Harry added.

Monty cleared his throat. Iris looked at him.

'Forty years of sour grapes can't be remedied with one meeting – it's too late.' She spoke only to Monty now. 'Like Hitler in Europe, Japan wants its share of the pie in Asia. They don't want to be dependent on our exports any more.'

'Nothing is inevitable, Iris,' Monty responded calmly.

'I fear this might be,' the president said.

'What are you suggesting, Franklin?' Mrs Roosevelt asked impatiently. 'That the country sits back, prepares the fleet and waits for Japan to fire the first shot?'

'That's exactly what I'm suggesting,' the president said gravely. Iris had never seen the president's jaw so noble.

■

It was three in the morning when Iris and Monty arrived at her apartment. Following the president's decision, Mrs Roosevelt had rung for more coffee and the group had thrashed out the situation for a further two hours. Monty acquiesced eventually, reluctantly, to Roosevelt's course of action – or inaction, as he wryly pointed out. With the group confident that the Japanese would attack some time after November, all that remained was to attempt to intercept Japanese dispatches in order to determine where and when. The Japanese were unpredictable in this regard, Grew informed them. Harry was to notify the commanders in the Pacific that hostilities with Japan were likely and due precautions should be taken.

The couple had walked the entire way to 30th Street, mostly in silence. They held hands the whole way. Now, in the aftermath of the debate and the subsequent strategising, Iris was pensive and fearful. Knowing what was coming made it no easier to rationalise. She could not remember the first war but Monty could.

He removed his hat and coat and sat down on the sofa. As he loosened his tie, he held out his hand to her.

'Are you angry with me?' she asked before sitting.

He shook his head. 'Sad.'

She tilted her head.

'You were brilliant tonight,' he clarified. 'You cut through the bullshit and paved an incredibly clear path through the mess. You didn't need any help, you didn't falter.'

'Then I don't understand.'

'You don't need me anymore,' he explained. 'I used to instruct you in policy, in foreign affairs, in sex, confident that my knowledge impressed you.'

Iris moved closer. His arm wrapped around her body.

'I bet you could even best me in the kitchen now,' he quipped.

She raised her chin and smiled weakly, tears forming in her eyes. He hugged her more tightly and they sank contentedly into each other. Iris kicked off her shoes.

'Perhaps Howe was right all those years ago,' Monty said wistfully.

'How so?'

'He used to call me a Bolshie,' Monty told her. 'Perhaps I am more red than I care to admit.'

'It's not red to care whether the country goes to war,' she commented.

Monty groaned in exhaustion and leaned his head back. Iris closed her eyes.

'Hey,' he went on energetically, patting her thigh. 'Did you ever meet with Frankfurter?'

'Yes, I did,' she answered with a slight laugh. 'That seems like ages ago.'

'Well?'

'He offered me a job – clerking for him,' she stated. 'It was a nice offer, but . . .' Iris shook her head.

'I understand,' Monty said compassionately. 'You love it, don't you?'

She nodded.

'I'm tired,' he said and groaned again. She moved a fraction, but he kept her close. 'No, not at this moment. In general.'

'In general?'

'Watching you tonight, your energy and excitement . . . I've lost that. Government is a game that I used to relish. Now it bores and frustrates me.'

'That's understandable,' she said. 'You've been working in Washington a long time. Perhaps that's why you enjoyed Japan and England so much – they're not Washington.'

'Perhaps,' he replied.

'The prospect . . .' He stopped, then corrected himself. 'The *inevitability* of another world war frightens me silly. I never thought I'd see another.'

Iris was reminded of the boy's photograph she had discovered at Warm Springs. His insistence that the president meet with Konoye sprang from a purely compassionate source.

'Tell me,' Iris said after a few moments. 'Is that why you took Howe's death so hard?' Monty's reaction to Howe's passing had not faded from Iris's mind.

Monty was silent for a long time. Iris thought he'd fallen asleep. Finally, when she was near sleep herself he spoke.

'I guess,' he answered. 'He was the last of the old guard. A brave soldier.' He paused. 'I'm getting sentimental and morose in my old age.'

'You're not old.'

'I'm fifty in a couple of months. Does that worry you?'

'Not in the least,' she replied sleepily, stifling a yawn. 'Does it worry you?'

'A little,' he said, looking down at the woman in his arms. Her eyes were heavy. 'Where do you stand now with Jacobson?'

'We take it one moment at a time. We can't plan any further than that. I suppose he'll come home if we go to war.'

'I see,' he responded, kissing her forehead. 'I see.'

'I'll always need you, Monty,' she said before her eyes closed. Despite her weariness, her tone was unequivocal.

Monty stood, lifted her from the sofa and carried her into the bedroom.

59

WASHINGTON DC
December 1941

Iris heard Mrs Roosevelt's familiar tread as she approached the Oval Office. When the First Lady saw her she stopped and held out her arms. The women embraced for a time. Mrs Roosevelt smelled of soap. Lux. It was odd, Iris thought, how something as inconsequential as the scent of a soap could comfort in a time of dire urgency and alarm.

'I have to get back to my visitors, Iris,' she said. 'They know nothing about the attack. I have to act as though all is well.'

'How is he?' Iris asked.

Mrs Roosevelt thought carefully before responding. 'Serene,' she said before walking on.

Iris approached the Oval Office. She hesitated before knocking. Would it be the same man behind the door? she wondered. When she entered the president was on the telephone. Harry stood and hugged her. His face was ashen. As he exited Grace entered and held a handwritten note in front of the president's face. He nodded and took the paper then gestured for Iris to sit. When he finished on the phone, he called out, 'Hold my calls for thirty minutes or so, Grace. I need a break.'

The president sat back in his chair and folded his hands across his stomach. He took a deep breath and closed his eyes briefly. When he opened them he spoke.

'Have you had lunch?' he asked.

She shook her head.

'Will you fix us a ham sandwich?'

She nodded, slightly surprised by the request. He wanted something comforting, she guessed. Something everyday and normal like a ham sandwich when nothing was ever going to be normal again.

'Nesbitt is in the kitchen sorting out this luncheon for Eleanor. Don't let her have any hand in it. Slice the ham thinly, Iris,' he instructed.

'I know, and plenty of butter on the bread,' she added.

■

'Mrs Roosevelt described you as serene,' Iris said as they ate.

'Was it an accusation?'

'Not at all. Just an observation.'

'The die has finally been cast. I'm meeting cabinet tonight and going before Congress tomorrow.'

'To declare war?' she asked.

He nodded.

When Iris had finished and wiped her mouth on the napkin, she said, 'I'm sorry that it came to this.'

'It was no surprise. You know that. But the location . . .' He shook his head in consternation. 'All our intelligence pointed to the Philippines. I thought they'd take a pot shot at a sentry. I never dreamed of anything like this. The fleet has been devastated. And there's the casualties. Reports are estimating more than two thousand enlisted men and civilians.' He sighed as he folded his napkin carefully, smoothed it on his knee and then placed it across his plate.

'It's not the fact that by tomorrow we will be at war that troubles me.' Roosevelt rubbed his forehead. 'It's the loss.'

Mrs Roosevelt had embraced her. So had Harry. Iris imagined that when the news broke there would be millions of Americans seeking solace and comfort in each other's arms. She wondered if anyone had shown the president a similar gesture of love and support. Standing, she walked around the table. Crouching beside the president's chair, she put her arms around his torso and pressed her cheek to his. It was an awkward position, her knees rubbing against the wheel, but within seconds she sensed his back rise slightly in order to accommodate her arms. His own encircled her body and she felt his large hands on her back. The odd posture immediately felt more natural. Iris kissed him on the cheek before she straightened.

'Everything's harder when you're in a wheelchair,' he said. He wiped his eyes with the back of his hand. 'Thank you, McIntosh.'

'My pleasure, Mr President.'

'Now,' he cleared his throat, 'I'm sorry to get you in here on a Sunday, but there's something I'd like your help with.'

'Of course.'

He placed a cigarette in his ivory holder. 'Grab a notebook and sit down. I'm going before Congress tomorrow. I'd like to dictate my message. It'll be short.'

'But shouldn't Grace . . .?' Iris suggested.

'I'd like you to do it.' He looked at her solemnly. 'I want Hopkins in here as well.'

'I understand.'

Iris retrieved a notebook and pencil from Grace's office. When she re-entered the room Harry was waiting. The three regarded each other for a minute, aware of the import of the moment. Then the president nodded, as if the time had come. The deed could not be delayed any longer. He moved behind his desk.

Harry and Iris sat and waited for him to speak.

'Right,' he said confidently. 'Let's begin.'

60
WASHINGTON DC
December 1941

'That was a lovely dinner, Iris,' Janet Murrow said. 'Let me help you clear the plates. Thank you so much, by the way, for letting us stay.'

'A room can't be had for either love or money in DC at the moment,' Iris said ruefully. 'I'm just sorry you have to sleep on the sofa and the floor.'

She allowed Janet to begin clearing and instructed Sam to turn on the radio.

'We've still got ten minutes,' he said as he looked at his watch.

'I just don't want to miss anything,' Iris insisted as she stacked plates and glasses into a manageable pile.

'Iris is devoted to the president, Ed – a true believer,' Sam explained with a smile.

Edward R. Murrow stood, lit another cigarette and made his way over to the sofa. Iris hadn't formed a firm opinion yet about Murrow. She described his appearance later to Sam as dapper in a doubtful way. He was slightly older than herself, she guessed, and wore a well-cut, English-made suit that didn't sit comfortably on him. Despite being the voice of CBS News, he was reticent at dinner, allowing his more genial wife to take the lead. The only topic he had spoken enthusiastically on was his childhood. He described movingly his meagre but happy upbringing as the son of farmers in North Carolina and then the years after the family moved west to Washington state.

'How long have you worked with Roosevelt?' Murrow asked Iris.

'I've worked at the White House since 1933,' she replied. 'First for Mrs Roosevelt as a secretarial assistant, but now I work mainly for the president.'

'Iris played a major role in the destroyer deal,' Sam elaborated.

'How did you wind up working for the administration at the height of the depression?' Murrow enquired.

'The usual way,' Iris looked at Sam briefly before continuing. 'I responded to an advertisement in the paper.'

'Weren't you a teacher?' Murrow probed.

'I must have been the best applicant, despite my lack of secretarial skills,' she responded flippantly.

Iris was unsure of how much the Murrows knew of her past. It would be uncharacteristic of Sam to expose too many details. Iris was still ashamed of the morning she had met Mrs Roosevelt at the gas station and feared her rise up the White House ladder would be construed by a journalist such as Murrow as favouritism.

'What do you do in London?' Iris asked his wife.

'At the moment I'm coordinating the Bundles for Britain scheme. I'm a writer too,' she added with a nod to her husband. 'But I've given that up. To tell you the truth, I don't think Ed wants the competition.' She laughed. 'Anyway, Ed needs me at home to act as hostess and to support his work. There can't be two stars in a family.'

'Bundles for Britain has been a great success.' Iris observed. 'You should be extremely proud of what you've achieved.'

'It's starting,' Sam interrupted.

The four hushed and listened to the president's address. As Iris listened she watched Murrow. He lit another cigarette using the butt of the previous one. The only change in his expression came when he squinted against the rising smoke. He sat in the corner of the sofa, legs crossed, occasionally leaning forward to ash his cigarette. Iris noticed that he still wore his coat. Sam had taken his off when they arrived, and loosened his tie.

When the broadcast finished twenty minutes later Iris inhaled deeply.

'Would you like coffee?' she asked. 'It's going to be rationed in the next few months.'

'Is that off the record?' Sam asked with a grin.

'You'd better believe it. There'll be hoarding otherwise.'

From the kitchen she heard Sam and Murrow analysing the minutiae of the speech. Unless especially invited by the Roosevelts, Iris now listened to all the Fireside Chats in her own apartment. She preferred to have the voice of the president wash over her without feeling the need to study the words too closely. She had discovered it was a mood the president hoped to convey. The details were merely padding.

When she re-entered the living room, Sam asked, 'What did you think?' He turned to his guests with a smile. 'Iris will be able to quote it back verbatim.'

'It was good. Very good.'

'But what made it good?' Murrow quizzed.

With an ironic lifting of her eyebrow, Iris quoted. '"We are now in this war. We are all in it – all the way. Every single man, woman and child is a partner in the most tremendous undertaking of our American history. We must share together the bad news and the good news, the defeats and the victories – the changing fortunes of war."'

Iris placed the coffee pot casually on the table and returned to the kitchen to retrieve the cups.

'Was that verbatim?' Janet asked, looking at the men. 'I thought you were joking, Sam.'

'She probably read the speech beforehand,' Murrow suggested.

'President Roosevelt never lets anyone besides Hopkins, Rosenman and Sherwood see his speeches,' Sam assured them.

'Can you recite the entire broadcast?' Janet enquired.

'No,' Iris said with a laugh. 'Just those three sentences, the most important ones. That's all he really wanted you to hear.'

■

The couples retired late.

'The bombing in London has stopped,' Sam whispered hopefully when Iris emerged from the bathroom. 'The Blitz is over.'

The blackouts on her windows, a preemptive measure, made it impossible to see. Sam pulled the bedclothes down and Iris slipped into bed beside him.

'It would be safe for you to move to London with me.'

'To act as hostess or support your career?' Iris asked sardonically.

'Janet does more than that,' Sam explained. 'It's not only Bundles for Britain that she's involved in. She was crucial in the move to transfer children from cities to rural locations during the Blitz. Janet Murrow does more to help on the home front than most British women.'

'I know, but I'm not that type of woman.'

Sam didn't respond.

'You're hardly in London,' Iris said. 'Last week you were in Moscow and you'll be in Hawaii in a few days. I'd be alone.'

'We wouldn't need to get married,' he said.

'It's not the marriage part that frightens me,' Iris told him.

'We don't have to end up like Murrow and Janet.'

'I know. With any luck we never will.' Iris hoped that would put an end to the conversation. To ensure that it was put to rest, she added, 'Churchill is coming.'

Sam propped himself up in the bed on one elbow and peered at her through the dark. 'Why didn't you say anything at dinner? That's momentous!'

'Shush,' she ordered impatiently. 'I know I can trust you not to leak anything. Murrow I'm not so sure about.'

He didn't attempt to defend his friend's ethics. Sam had worked in Washington long enough to know the score.

'When does he arrive?' Sam asked.

'The end of next week, supposedly. It depends on the crossing.'

'What?' Sam exclaimed. 'He's coming by ship?'

'Shush!' Iris repeated. 'Battleship. The president tried to delay the visit – the Atlantic is bombarded with U-boats at the moment – but he wouldn't be put off.'

'Who's coming with him?'

'A bevy of military chiefs. Lord Beaverbrook, of course.' She paused. 'Monty's coming too,' she added, fully aware of the peril. 'He's working with the Combined Chiefs now and liaises between here and London.'

Iris heard the rustle of sheets then nothing else for a minute or so.

'So the Jerries could sink virtually the entire British war command with one well-aimed torpedo,' Sam said. 'If the British people are even half as audacious and brave as their leaders . . .'

Sam lay on his back. Iris placed her head on his chest and traced its outline with her finger.

'It's a shame you won't be here for the press conference. Churchill is extremely entertaining, Harry told me. He and the president should make a great double act,' she murmured.

Sam wriggled down more comfortably in the bed and inhaled the scent of her hair. They said nothing more for quite some time but Iris sensed from his breathing that he was still awake.

'Every night I close my eyes and I picture you,' he said drowsily. 'Every night the image changes slightly. Sometimes you're wearing that red skirt that I like so much. Sometimes you look as you did when I first saw you on the balcony at the White House. The picture of you changes constantly. But the smell of your hair never changes. No matter where I am in the world I can smell it. You don't know how lovely that is.'

Iris kissed his chest.

'When I picture you it's always on the jetty at Campobello Island. Remember?' she asked. She felt his head nodding against hers. 'I just wanted to kiss you and make all your frustration disappear.'

'I didn't know that; I wish you had kissed me,' he responded. 'I remember we talked about baseball and books and childhood dreams and it was very windy. You had on sneakers and I was cold.' He pulled her closer and murmured, 'How long will I have to share you for, Iris?'

Fearing his response, she whispered, 'Share me? With who?'

It took Sam a moment to answer. Iris's chest heaved in anticipation as she stared into the black.

'It's sounds stupid, childish, but with the president. With your work.'

Iris licked her lips. Her body relaxed.

'You have all of me,' she said as her breathing returned to normal. 'I'm here with you now, aren't I?'

'I love you,' he said.

'I love you, too.'

They rolled together and kissed for a few moments until Iris forced herself to pull away. 'Murrow and Janet are just on the other side of the door,' she whispered, edging to the opposite side of the bed.

'We can be quiet,' he insisted, and pulled her firmly across the sheets.

61
HYDE PARK, NEW YORK
May 1962

It was as if a tornado hit the White House when Winston Churchill arrived. I've never seen a man with such energy. Mrs Roosevelt ordered the redesign of the Monroe Room as the Map Room. We moved furniture from here to there and back again trying to imitate his London command post. There was even an armed guard on the door! The president was funny, though. When he rang down for lunch he always asked me to send the most stupid usher with the trays. Then there would be no chance of him stealing away with any war secrets.

Mrs Roosevelt put the prime minister in the Lincoln Bedroom, Mr Howe's old room. That didn't sit well with the prime minister at all. He tried out the bed and said, 'Won't do. Bed's not right.' He then conducted his own tour of the second floor testing all the beds and checking the rooms for storage space. He finally settled on the Rose Bedroom.

I remember he came out of one of the bedrooms and bumped into Fields, the butler. He right away gave him a string of orders. There was to be no talking outside his quarters and definitely no whistling in the corridor. He couldn't abide whistling, he said. Furthermore, he had to have a tumbler of sherry in his room before breakfast, a couple of glasses of scotch and soda before lunch and French champagne and well-aged brandy before bedtime. He was quite a character.

The president instructed the household to indulge his every wish. The Brits had been rationed for quite some time by that stage, you see, and he wasn't going to have them eating economy-style. Well, that was just fine, I thought, because they were only staying a week. I shouldn't have any trouble stretching the budget a little further for a just a week. Well, he ended up staying for three and a half weeks!

It reminded me of that play, you know, *The Man Who Came to Dinner*. Mrs Roosevelt sent me to New York to see it as a special birthday surprise only the year before. It was a big hit. She chose that play, she told me, because she thought the subject matter would interest me.

But I have to admit that even Mr Churchill looked hungry and much trimmer than I had imagined him. I fixed a lot of roast beef during his stay because I knew that was the hardest commodity for the English to lay their hands on and I knew how much they all loved it. Those Brits ate and drank us out of house and home while they were staying. When they were leaving, the president gave them each a case of lemons and oranges.

The president and Mr Churchill got on like a house on fire. They mostly were locked in the Map Room with the other army and navy chiefs and they kept very different hours, but I remember them scooting in and out of one another's rooms like schoolboys, Mr Churchill wearing one of those zipper suits he was so fond of, like a cross between a baby's romper suit and a pair of overalls. He had them in all sorts of fabrics and colours. I'd never seen a man wear such a thing before, but I suppose he had to be comfortable. And bare feet. He was always in bare feet or socks.

6 2

WASHINGTON DC

December 1941

'Mr Prime Minister.' John Lambert from *Newsweek* rose to his feet. 'Isn't Singapore the key to the whole situation in the Pacific?'

Churchill paused deliberately for a moment or two as he puffed on his almighty cigar. 'The key to the whole situation is the resolute manner in which the British and American democracies are going to throw themselves into the conflict.'

Steve Early identified another reporter from among the faces and pointed. 'Rex Wells, *New York Herald Tribune*,' Early said.

'Mr Prime Minister, can you tell us when you think we'll lick these boys?'

'If we manage it well,' the prime minister opined, 'it will take only half as long as if we manage it badly.'

The reporters and staff assembled in the Oval Office for the press conference erupted into laughter.

Iris leaned over to Monty and said, 'He's better at dodging questions than the president.'

Monty nodded. 'He's an entertainer, there's no doubt about it. Look at Roosevelt.'

Iris saw that the president was smiling broadly.

'He's showing off his new best friend.'

'That seems like a good note to end on, boys,' Steve Early shouted over the laughter. 'Thanks for the questions. The president and the prime minister will see you back here next week.'

'What are you doing after work?' Monty asked as the reporters filed out of the office. 'I'm off tonight if you'd like to have dinner. A special dinner, I mean.'

'The president has asked me to take a swim with him, but then I'm free.'

'I didn't think you two did that any more.'

'We don't. Well, we haven't in ages. But he memoed me this morning.' She shrugged.

'Be careful; Churchill's proclivity for skinny-dipping is renowned in London.'

Iris's eyes opened wide as she looked at the pudding of a man seated next to Roosevelt. 'No! Really?'

Monty nodded and grinned. He squeezed her knee before he stood and departed.

■

It was snowing and dark as Iris made her way across the Rose Garden. She wore snow shoes, a bathing cap and a swimming costume. A thick terry-cloth robe was wrapped tightly around her body. The force of the heat coming from the pool room was enchanting. It drew her swiftly across the lawn to the door. The windows were completely fogged but she could see light. She was met with a magical sight upon entering. Steam wafted from the water and hovered just above the surface. The cut of the president's stroke lasted only a second before its edges became blurred and vapour filled the void. Iris smiled when she noticed the underwater lights were aglow. The president rarely used them, as Mrs Roosevelt said that they wasted too much power. But they created an ethereal, otherworldly effect that Iris loved. Apart from those underwater, the only other illumination came from the strings of Christmas lights strewn around the perimeter of the room. This was a new addition. Iris was pleased. Despite the attack and the declaration of war, the president was in good spirits. Fala jumped from his seat on the president's chair and greeted her joyously. She bent to pat him and then placed the dog back on the chair.

Removing her shoes and disrobing quickly by the edge of the pool, Iris put on her goggles and made a hasty entrance into the water. She swam three or four lengths before she noticed Roosevelt had stopped. She swam over to him.

'You're a top-notch swimmer now, McIntosh,' the president said as he trod water. His powerful arms made only the slightest ripple on the surface. 'I don't think there's anything else I could teach you. My work is done.' He laughed and Iris joined in.

'Thanks, sir,' she said. 'You've created a charming atmosphere. It makes swimming all the more enjoyable.'

Roosevelt smiled before beginning on another series of laps. Iris did likewise. It was after six by the time she stopped. She rested her elbows on the side of the pool and kicked her legs slowly in the water. Within a minute the president was by her side.

'There's something I'd like you to handle for me,' he said. The seriousness of the proposal was evident in his tone.

Iris turned her head a little.

'There's a push from California calling for the removal, relocation – whatever you want to call it – of Japanese-Americans from the Pacific coast,' he explained.

She nodded and her legs halted their graceful movement through the water.

'The Native Sons and Daughters of the Golden West are leading the charge. The farming community has jumped on the bandwagon. They see an opportunity to regain any profits Japanese cultivators have made over the years,' Roosevelt said.

'What would you like me to do?' Iris enquired.

'I want to know whether it is constitutional.'

Iris turned to face him, stunned that he was even considering giving in to bigotry and greed.

'I can tell you right now that it would not be constitutional. The Fourteenth Amendment guarantees American citizenship to all those born in the country, regardless of their ethnic background or the status of their parents,' Iris fired back. 'What's more, they're considered citizens of the state in which they reside. You might be able to remove the first-generation immigrants who were denied citizenship under the Immigration Act of 1924, but not their children who were born in America and live in California.'

To mention the Fifth Amendment's guarantee of life, liberty and property would have been too brazen, too obvious.

'See if there's a way around the constitution,' the president instructed quietly. 'The Native Sons and Daughters are concerned about sabotage. They're gathering public support.'

He's worried about losing California if he decides to run again, Iris realised.

'How many Japanese-Americans are there on the Pacific coast?' Iris asked, more in an effort to delay her response than from curiosity. The numbers wouldn't make any difference; to remove citizens from their homes and livelihoods was criminal.

'There's forty thousand first-generation immigrants who were debarred from citizenship and then there's roughly eighty thousand who are citizens by birth.'

'Where would they be relocated to? Back to Japan?'

'This is all just speculation at the moment,' the president replied indifferently. 'We'd relocate them to some other state.'

'Buy them homes?' Iris pressed.

'No, they'd probably be housed in internment camps for the duration of the war,' he said. The president's tone was what upset Iris the most; he spoke as if it was the most normal thing in the world to remove people from their homes and place them in prison.

Iris lifted herself out of the pool and sat on the edge, looking into the water. She pulled the bathing cap aggressively from her head.

'Just look into it,' Roosevelt ordered. 'That's all I'm asking. Talk to Eleanor, she's just back from California. Get her read on the situation.'

'I have to go, Mr President,' she said, standing. Disenchantment threatened to overwhelm her. 'Thanks for the swim, but I have to be somewhere.'

Without drying herself, she quickly donned her robe and her shoes and made her way back across the Rose Garden.

■

Iris walked, almost ran to Mrs Roosevelt's suite. She knocked rapidly. Hick opened the door.

'Look what the cat dragged in, Eleanor!' Hick called. 'Come in. Sit by the fire. I'll get a towel for your hair.'

Hick disappeared from the room. Mrs Roosevelt was sitting on the sofa in front of the fire. She turned and looked at her bedraggled visitor. Mrs Roosevelt and Hick were both dressed for dinner. Placing her knitting on the seat next to her, she stood and led Iris to the fire. Iris was comforted that the room had never changed. Perhaps a rug or a wall hanging but nothing significant. It was the same crimson sofa, photographs still littered the mantel and William Henry Harrison still stood watch over the space.

'Sit down, dear. Have you been swimming?'

Iris indicated that she had with a twitchy nod. It was impossible to form words through her chattering teeth.

Hick re-entered the room holding a glass of scotch and a towel.

'Sit on the floor,' Hick instructed, holding up the towel.

As Iris sipped the drink, Hick rubbed her hair dry from a seat behind her on the sofa. Mrs Roosevelt resumed her knitting.

'Will you be at dinner tonight, Iris?' Hick asked.

She shook her head. 'I've got a date,' Iris responded through the shivers. 'With Monty.'

'Is that still going on?' Hick asked wryly.

'It's on and off,' Iris answered, unoffended.

'I know how that feels.' Hick grinned. 'There you go. All dry.'

'Now, what can I do for you, dear?' Mrs Roosevelt said, looking towards Iris.

'How was your trip west?' Iris began, repositioning herself on her knees.

'Productive,' the First Lady said. 'There's a great fear among the population that they'll be attacked. If the Japanese got to Hawaii . . . you know the way people think. I hope I was able to reassure them of their safety.'

Mrs Roosevelt's fingers controlled the needles deftly.

'Is there any fear domestically?' Iris probed. Mrs Roosevelt looked at her enquiringly. 'That Japanese-Americans will turn on their white neighbours or commit acts of sabotage?'

'I believe there is, but I cautioned against vigilantism,' the First Lady replied. 'Many Americans can only come to grips with Pearl Harbor by viewing it as the result of sabotage.'

'The Pacific coast is racist, Iris,' Hick interrupted abruptly. 'It always has been. Negroes, Jews and especially the Japs. They're worse than the Nazis over there.'

'Hick, really!' Mrs Roosevelt admonished.

'It's a fact.'

'What about the press, Hick? Do the papers editorialise racism?' Iris asked.

Hick shook her head. 'The *LA Times* is incredibly balanced. It's a good rag.'

'Why all these questions?' the First Lady asked.

Iris rubbed her eyes. 'The president has asked me to look into something . . . something that doesn't sit well with me. I was just curious about the atmosphere in California following the attack.'

Mrs Roosevelt squinted in concern before returning her gaze to the needles in her hands. It was pointless elaborating further. Iris was certain of the First Lady's stance. She would offer the one hundred and twenty thousand displaced Japanese board and lodging in the White House if she had the room. She would be devastated to learn of possible internments.

'Follow what's in your heart, dear,' Mrs Roosevelt advised. 'You're the one who will have to live with your actions.'

As the scotch began to take effect, Hick gestured to Iris with a hairbrush. Iris edged herself back between Hick's knees and the older woman began to brush Iris's hair.

'What are you knitting, Mrs Roosevelt?' Iris asked.

'A sweater; I'm knitting sweaters for everyone,' Mrs Roosevelt stated. 'The White House is going to be an extremely cold place when we have to start conserving electricity. How's your knitting coming along?'

'Sporadically,' Iris answered. 'I don't have your patience, Mrs Roosevelt.'

'Nonsense,' the First Lady admonished.

Iris hoped this evening was a dream. The warmth from the liquor in her stomach and the heat from the fire were making her sleepy. She yawned. Hick smoothed her hair down gently with her hand and then took a seat next to her on the floor.

Iris closed her eyes, weighing up the morality and legality of the president's request. The clock on the mantel chimed once. Her eyes shot open.

'I have to go,' Iris said, rising to her feet. 'I'm meeting Monty in forty-five minutes and I have to shower.'

'I hope I was of help,' Mrs Roosevelt said.

Iris smiled. 'Enjoy your dinner,' she said, opening the door. 'You'll love the PM, Hick. He's a riot.'

■

'What do you think?' Iris asked when their appetisers arrived.

'You know what I think,' Monty responded as he loosened an oyster from its shell and brought it to his mouth. 'It's exactly the kind of attitude that got the country into this predicament in the first place.'

'Is it just me?' Iris asked, concerned. 'Am I particularly sensitive when it comes to issues such as these? Situations that see people forced out of their homes and work.'

'It's not just you, although your history probably plays a part,' Monty replied. 'You can either refuse the president or honour his command.

Justify it to yourself as an act of presidential privilege in wartime. An extremely vulgar display of presidential privilege, I might add.'

'But it's the Constitution, Monty,' Iris pleaded. 'If I collude to evict and relocate all those people, where will it end?'

Moreover, the president's decision to relocate Japanese-Americans threw into doubt her entire career, she realised. Without a Constitution to uphold, what was there to believe in?

'The Constitution never interfered with the wartime policies of any American president,' Monty replied. 'Take Lincoln for example. During the Civil War he abused the Constitution every which way. Yet, we have him to thank for the Thirteenth Amendment.'

'I hate this war already,' Iris said sulkily. Monty grinned. 'Everything's changing. Workmen are destroying the White House gardens and lawns to put in bomb shelters, streets are barricaded and the city is just bristling with soldiers and police. Suddenly it has all become so real.'

Iris raised the spoon to her mouth and tasted her chestnut soup. It was delicious. Then she pushed her bowl away in disgust.

'What you're confronting is your first real moral dilemma,' Monty pointed out. 'Neither course is going to be particularly compelling. What do you fear most? Losing your job?'

She hadn't even considered that as a possibility.

'Be realistic, kiddo,' Monty said. 'Your job is to do the president's bidding. Look what happened to Tom Corcoran.'

It was true. Tom had been subtly pushed out. He was cut out of meetings and the scope of his workload had quickly diminished once it became obvious he would not do the president's bidding in regards to the British. Eventually Tom resigned, on good terms, of his own accord. His resignation had boosted Iris's own rise. But it was obvious to her now that Tom's hand had been forced.

'If you're not afraid of losing your job, just what are you concerned about?' Monty asked.

Iris looked down at her hands on the tablecloth. 'Nothing, I guess,' she replied.

Monty regarded her thoughtfully for a few seconds.

'Then do what you think is right,' he concluded as their plates were cleared from the table.

6 3
WASHINGTON DC
February 1942

Iris read about President Roosevelt's approval of Executive Order 9066 via a memo she received at eleven o'clock on a Thursday morning. The order authorised the forcible evacuation of persons of Japanese ancestry from the Pacific coast. It was signed Franklin D. Roosevelt.

When Iris had approached the president in his office on Christmas Eve and refused his request she told him she believed that if she carried through with his request that her integrity would suffer. She had rehearsed her speech many times, choosing the word *integrity* over *ethics* and *morals* as the least incendiary. Roosevelt merely nodded and went back to his work as though she had declined a cigarette or a Coke. Iris wished him a happy Christmas before departing.

The president had not mentioned it again, but she had heard from Harry that he'd asked Stimson to handle it. Stimson could see no way around the Constitution either, and passed the problem on to John McCloy who, since working on the destroyer deal, had found a home at the War Department in domestic security. He was a good guy, Iris believed, but he was ambitious just like everyone else.

It was clear to Iris in the opening paragraph of the order how McCloy overcame the obstacle of the Constitution: *the successful prosecution of the war requires every possible protection against espionage and against sabotage to national-defence material, national-defence premises, and national-defence utilities . . .*

The relevant paragraphs from the relevant acts were cited. It was tenuous at best, Iris thought.

She stood, put on her coat, grabbed the memo from her desk and left her office.

■

Fifteen minutes later Iris was sitting opposite John McCloy at Blair House, still clutching the memo in her hand.

'Would you like a coffee, Iris?' McCloy asked as he sat down. 'Have you heard from Monty?'

'No thanks, and not for a while,' she said. 'I'll be quick. I know your time is valuable.'

He nodded.

'This order . . .' she said. She placed the memo in front of McCloy on the desk. 'The opening paragraph. There's something that's been troubling me.' She paused.

'Go on,' he said pleasantly.

'Well, I was just wondering if there's been any evidence to substantiate the suggestion that acts of sabotage and espionage have taken place or ever will?'

'This is what this order guards against,' McCloy replied.

'I know. But is it a military necessity that Japanese-Americans are relocated?'

'There was the report from the Roberts Commission,' McCloy stated.

Iris had read the report thoroughly when it was released in January. It found that the strike force that attacked Pearl Harbor had been aided by Hawaii-based Japanese spies. No evidence was provided to verify the statement, yet it had provoked a surge of anti-Japanese sentiment among the public and the press, which in turn prompted the president to push ahead with the relocation.

'Yes, of course,' she replied. 'Did you interview Admiral Stark about any potential threat?'

'Yes. Stark and General Clark both gave testimony.'

Iris waited for McCloy to continue. He didn't.

'And?' she urged. 'I can get a copy of their testimony, John.'

She could see him wrestling with the facts in his mind.

'Come on, John. I know the score. Just tell me the truth. Friend to friend.'

He leaned back in his chair. 'They both agreed that there was no threat of attack by the Japanese on the Pacific coast,' he admitted tersely. There was more he wanted to say, though; Iris could see it in his pursed lips and rigid frame.

'Is there anything else?'

'Clark was strenuously against the notion of allocating troops to assist in the forced evacuation,' he admitted. He looked at his hands, clenched on the desk, for a moment. 'In fact, he seemed to think that the evacuation in itself could endanger our war effort. Look, Iris, may I be entirely frank?'

'Of course.'

'If it is a question of the safety of the country or the Constitution of the United States – well, the Constitution is just a scrap of paper to me.'

Iris remembered what Monty had told her: the Constitution meant nothing to a wartime president.

'I see,' Iris said. 'And President Roosevelt agreed to it?'

'He told me to go ahead on the line that I thought best.'

Iris rose. 'Thanks, John.' She held out her hand. 'Thank you for your candour.'

Iris left Blair House and wandered into Lafayette Square. The White House appeared so distant. She couldn't go back and carry on as if all was well. She sat on a bench in front of the equestrian statue of Andrew Jackson for almost an hour. The grass was still wet with morning mist. Although it was after one, the sun was yet to make an appearance. She pulled the collar of her overcoat tight around her throat. As she gazed at the stone president sitting on his horse high upon a pedestal, she was overcome by loneliness. It crept in through the soles of her shoes and through her woollen overcoat. It seeped through the pores of her skin. By the time the cold had numbed her face, feet and hands, Iris knew exactly what she needed to do.

64
WASHINGTON DC
April 1942

Iris had been ordered to take nothing with her when she departed the White House for the final time. All her files, documents and memoranda were to be packed in boxes and handed over to the State Department. It was five o'clock on Friday afternoon and no one from the State Department had appeared to collect the boxes. She stacked them on her empty desk and wrote on their lids, *Property of the State Department. Documents from the office of Iris McIntosh.*

Apart from a lipstick, compact and comb in her desk drawer, Iris had very few personal items to collect. There were no photographs on her desk or mementoes accrued during her nine years of service. As she was wondering whether that was normal, there was a tap at her door. When she turned Hick was standing in the doorway. She had lost some weight, Iris noticed. Working at the Democratic National Committee must agree with her. Had she finally found a home away from the offices of Associated Press? Iris wondered. Perhaps it *was* possible to change direction successfully.

'Anyone home?'

'Come in,' Iris said. 'When did you get in?'

'Only about an hour ago and I come bearing gifts.' Hick beamed. 'First, here's the sweater that Eleanor knitted for you. She only finished it this morning; it's for next winter.' Hick handed Iris a heavy-knit, multicoloured pullover. Iris looked at it dubiously.

'She's trying to conserve wool now,' Hick explained, shaking her head. 'And this' – she pulled from behind her back a bottle of eighteen-year-old Chivas Regal – 'is for now. Where are the glasses?'

Iris opened her filing cabinet. Two tumblers lay at the bottom of the middle drawer.

Hick poured generously. 'Here's looking at you, kid,' she said. They clinked glasses and Hick swallowed the entire contents. Iris followed suit. Hick immediately refilled both glasses.

'How are you feeling?' she asked.

'Sad, excited, regretful, inspired . . .' Iris said. 'I realise I can't stay any longer. It's my decision to leave, but this place is . . .' She looked into her glass without finishing the sentence.

'Home?' Hick offered.

Iris nodded and sipped her scotch. 'Mrs Roosevelt said goodbye yesterday before she left for New York,' she said. Iris had cried when Mrs Roosevelt wrapped her arms around her. She had wanted to remain in that embrace forever.

'All of us must experience new challenges, Iris,' Mrs Roosevelt had said in consolation. 'It's good for us to be tested.'

'I'm so scared,' Iris confided. 'This is all I know.'

'You've outdone every expectation I had of you,' the First Lady said gently. 'You're an absolute star. Believe in yourself.'

'I haven't seen the president in days,' Iris said to Hick now.

'He's at Hyde Park,' Hick explained.

'I know,' Iris replied. 'It's just that he hasn't said two words to me since I resigned. I thought he would have said goodbye.'

When she had approached the Oval Office with her letter of resignation he wouldn't even see her. She had to leave her letter with Grace. The next day she received a memo that read only, *Resignation accepted. FDR.* She hastily threw it in the trash.

'He's disappointed, Iris. I suppose he feels betrayed.'

He betrayed me first! Iris wanted to shout, but didn't, knowing it would sound childish. It was a harsh word to use and it cut Iris to the quick.

'Do you think I betrayed him?' she asked dolefully.

Hick shrugged and considered her response carefully.

'He put you in an impossible situation, Iris,' she said. 'If you can't stomach this administration any more then there's no point hanging around. You did what you had to do.'

Hick's words made the situation no easier for Iris to bear.

'Anyhow, working with Felix Frankfurter at the Supreme Court, that's a nice gig and I bet it pays better,' Hick said with a laugh.

Iris sat down behind her desk. Hick moved the boxes aside and took a seat opposite. Iris sipped her scotch as she contemplated Hick's wisdom. It was true. Executive Order 9066 had made her sick, but she still believed Roosevelt was the only leader with vision enough to see the country through the war. She regretted that she no longer figured in the picture. Iris had at one time believed she would be a part of the administration until its final hour.

'You know,' Hick continued as she poured further from the bottle, 'no matter how important you believe you are or how much you're loved, the office will always come first with them. Every year is an election year to them.'

Iris turned her gaze in Hick's direction. To be the First Lady's intimate friend had come at a great cost to Hick, Iris was aware. Sacrificing her career and her independence, Hick had finally surrendered in her battle to come first in her lover's life. She had resigned herself to the position of a bit player.

The women drank in silence for a short while until Hick began to whistle. Iris thought hard through the liquor haze, striving to recognise the tune. Her mind was a fog, the name was lost.

Iris swivelled in her chair. Tom had said as much as well, she remembered. Regardless of how important you thought you were, the administration always took priority.

Then nausea rose in her stomach. Iris scanned her office for a suitable receptacle. She grabbed the litter basket by the side of her desk and vomited until nothing remained.

■

Iris arrived at the home of Felix Frankfurter in Bethesda. She carried a bottle of wine in one hand and a bouquet of flowers in the other. Iris had hesitated over bringing wine. She could recall seeing Frankfurter only once at Children's Hour. Moreover, Iris knew Frankfurter was Jewish, albeit of the non-practising persuasion. His family had emigrated from Vienna when he was twelve, and he'd spent the rest of his childhood on the Lower East Side of New York. He had married the daughter of a Congregational minister against the wishes of his mother. They were childless and his wife had been described to Iris many years ago as 'frail'. Iris had finally decided that it would be wise to offer a token for each of the Frankfurters: wine for him and flowers for her.

Although he had been one of the president's advisers during the New Deal, Frankfurter was rarely seen around the White House. He wasn't a member of either the president's or the First Lady's inner circle. Iris had always been under the impression that he was tolerated more for his brain than his personality.

Frankfurter had graduated from Harvard Law School with an exceptional academic record and subsequently had helped found the American Civil Liberties Union. He was appointed to the Supreme Court in 1939 by Roosevelt. There was no doubt that Frankfurter was brilliant. He had mentored Tom Corcoran, who had praised his mind and his talent endlessly. There was no one better at interpreting the law than Tom, in Iris's opinion. He had been mentored well.

Iris knocked at the door, which was promptly opened by a po-faced Negro in a sombre black suit and tie – the Frankfurters' butler, she assumed – who showed her into the house and, much to Iris's chagrin, relieved her of her gifts. Left with only a clutch purse and her light spring dress, Iris felt exposed.

Following the butler to the living room, Iris noticed that the furniture, the wall hangings and the rugs were ostentatious, every object crying out for attention. It was deafening. The pictures on the walls primarily depicted naval battles from the Napoleonic wars. The grand foyer was a near replica of the president's foyer in Springwood.

In the living room, the Frankfurters were waiting. The lights had been dimmed.

'Good evening, Iris,' Frankfurter said. 'I'd like you to meet my wife Marion.' The women shook hands briefly. 'Marion, this is the young lady I told you so much about: Iris McIntosh – my new clerk.'

Iris smiled and, as she looked at the couple, realised she had underdressed. Frankfurter wore a dinner suit, his dainty wife a floor-length musk-coloured gown. Iris's simple cotton frock (she now hesitated even to call it a dress) was barely adequate in the face of the pair's regal attire.

'It's lovely to meet you, Mrs Frankfurter,' Iris said.

The butler glided into the room with a tray of iced tea.

As the three sat sipping their drinks, Frankfurter and Iris made small talk while Mrs Frankfurter remained silent, smiling vaguely, her green eyes darting back and forth between her husband and Iris. She was in her fifties, Iris reckoned, petite and pale. Her hair was collected on top of her head in a bun. A small, silver tiara studded with rubies sat on her crown. Her hair was greying but Iris guessed Marion Denman Frankfurter would have once been an extremely striking strawberry blonde. Now she appeared slightly shrivelled and frayed, a little like Iris imagined her own mother might have looked if she had lived.

The judge continued to sing Iris's praises, filling his wife in on the destroyer deal and how he had heard of her work from Tom Corcoran initially and later from Henry Stimson.

'She's even had the good fortune, Marion, to meet Winston Churchill.' Frankfurter grinned and looked at Iris expectantly.

'That's right,' Iris responded uncertainly. 'He was everything you'd expect a British PM to be.' She knew it was a lame response, but she wasn't in the habit of discussing White House guests.

Iris could see Frankfurter wasn't pleased by her reply. He wanted details, gossip perhaps, regarding Churchill's visit.

'When you telephoned me last month, Miss McIntosh, it was quite a surprise,' Frankfurter said after a moment. 'I didn't think I'd hear from you again. Your enthusiasm for the president and your work made me think, Now here's a girl who'll be working with Roosevelt until he's gone.'

'I used to think that too,' Iris remarked. 'But things change. Nine years is a long time.'

'I telephoned the president when you got back in touch,' Frankfurter informed her. 'He said you were a solid worker who had served the administration faithfully.'

'Is that all?' Iris hadn't realised she'd uttered the words until they hung uneasily between herself and the judge like dirty laundry.

'They were his exact words. Tom Corcoran and Harry Hopkins were far more effusive.'

Iris hoped her disappointment was not too evident. She looked at her virgin drink and longed for something harder.

As the threesome moved into the dining room, Iris marvelled at just how unremarkable the president's testimonial had been. Could he have chosen a more mundane description than 'solid worker'? Iris thought not.

The butler served the appetiser and as the three began to eat, Iris wondered how her relationship with the president had soured so quickly. She believed she had worked tirelessly and passionately and devotedly at the White House for nine years. Yet one rejection had wound up with her sitting at the table of Felix Frankfurter sipping watercress soup. Iris looked up from her bowl and caught Mrs Frankfurter staring at her.

'You're a very fortunate young woman, Miss McIntosh,' she said. 'To be so successful at such a young age. To have worked with the president and his wife. You would be the envy of women and men all over America.'

Iris took in Mrs Frankfurter's praise as a stark realisation slowly dawned on her. Her own foolishness was as vivid and as daunting as the green liquid in her bowl. It was her decision to refuse the president's request. It was her choice to resign. She had found a new place at the Supreme Court. Why couldn't she be happy with the turn her life had taken?

Iris smiled at her hostess, determined to embrace the opportunity and her good fortune. 'I recently read the book you edited about Sacco and Vanzetti. It was a remarkable case,' she said. Hoping to make a good impression at dinner, she had researched the Italian anarchists who the couple had fought to free in the twenties.

Marion Frankfurter nodded. 'I don't work any more,' she replied. 'I've taken to running the house since we moved to Washington.'

'You're from Boston, I understand?'

'My wife is from Boston, yes,' the judge broke in. 'Now Miss McIntosh, tell me more about your meeting with Winston Churchill.'

The butler entered the dining room and began to clear the table.

Iris looked at the judge who sat at the head of the table. Above his head on the wall hung a painting. Iris recognised it immediately. It was Homer's *Prisoners from the Front*. It was the most hushed of all the works Iris had seen in the house. There were no sinking ships, crashing waves or exploding cannons, just four men standing in a field at Petersburg, Virginia. She turned to the woman sitting opposite her. Mrs Frankfurter's smile was warm and genuine.

Her gaze returned to Frankfurter's. 'Well, Judge,' Iris began enthusiastically, 'he's one of a kind. He likes to wear these all-in-one suits when he's working . . .'

Frankfurter leaned forward and nodded avidly as Iris divulged the domestic habits of a great world leader.

65
WASHINGTON DC
May 1943

'It's strange – ironic, you'd probably call it – that I've just finished with two actions both arguing the case for Executive Order 9066 and there's another one pending.'

'How will the court find?'

'In favour of the United States,' Iris replied.

'Congratulations.' Monty grinned. 'If it's any comfort at all, your work must have been up to scratch.'

'That, and the fact that eight of the nine justices were nominated by President Roosevelt,' Iris added, cynically. She laughed before continuing, 'Anyway, I've got another case coming up. This one is different, though.'

Monty raised his eyebrows in interest.

'Fred Korematsu – a twenty-four-year-old Japanese-American welder who didn't report to an assembly centre in May last year and was subsequently arrested.' She shook her head. 'He was born and raised in Oakland, California. He swam on the school swim team, for Christ's sake, and now they want to intern him. Is there any wonder he's objecting?'

Monty smiled and touched her hand sympathetically. 'Would you like another cup of coffee?'

She nodded.

Monty gestured towards the waitress then proceeded to tap his spoon on the table. 'Where's Jacobson at these days?'

Iris bit her lip for an instant. It was difficult to keep track of Sam. His career had taken off with the same velocity as her own.

'He was in North Africa until a couple of weeks ago. Now he's gone back to London. He's not sure where the next assignment will be. You tend to fly by the seat of your pants when you're one of Murrow's boys.'

'You're obviously still together,' Monty stated, adjusting his place setting.

'Yes, but he hasn't been home since just after Pearl Harbor. Christmas 1941.'

'Do you miss him?'

'Yes, I do,' she affirmed. 'Very much. Just as I miss you.'

'I wasn't asking for my own sake,' Monty explained. His expression was grave. 'I want to know that you're happy. When this war's over and Sam comes home do you think you'll be happy together?'

'I guess,' she answered uncertainly. 'I haven't thought that far. Why all the questions?'

'I'm looking out for you, that's all,' he said with the briefest of smiles.

His expression, his mood, his choice of subject matter all troubled Iris. Monty was rarely this sombre.

She changed gear. 'Tell me about this conference the PM's here for.'

'Now the Germans have surrendered in North Africa, Churchill and Roosevelt want to decide on the next line of attack. Do they "crack on" in the Mediterranean and attack Germany in its "soft underbelly"?' Monty did a remarkably good impression of Churchill. 'Or do the Allies plan a cross-Channel attack? Hit the Nazis directly.'

That's better, Iris thought. 'Is that what the president is pressing for?'

Monty nodded. 'Do you think he'll run again?'

Iris shrugged. 'I wish I knew,' she responded.

'That reminds me,' he said, chuckling. 'He said that if he does run it will only be so that he can fire Mrs Nesbitt.'

Iris offered a listless grin.

'You wish you were still inside, don't you?' Monty said.

She rolled her eyes self-deprecatingly. 'It's a yearning I'm still struggling with,' she admitted. 'But I'm enjoying working under Frankfurter, although the atmosphere isn't quite as convivial.'

She wanted to ask Monty whether the president had mentioned her but there wasn't a way she could frame the question without appearing needy.

'How long are you in Washington?' Iris asked instead.

'However long the conference takes. You know how Churchill can spin these things out,' he replied. Iris sensed his uncertainty from across the booth as he tapped the table gently with a teaspoon.

'What?'

'There's something else,' he said hesitantly. 'I won't be able to stay with you.'

'Why?' she enquired immediately. On his previous two visits they had lived together and had a wonderful time. 'Is it Churchill or Beaverbrook? They want you close at hand, right?'

Monty shook his head. 'I've met someone, you see. In England. It could be serious.'

'I see.' It was all she could manage to utter, yet she wanted to say so much more. Monty's admission threw her own deviousness and infidelity into stark relief. Why was he suddenly taking the higher ground? She was stunned. Dumbstruck. The words wouldn't form in her mouth.

They sat for a number of minutes without speaking.

Finally she said, 'The last ten years – that wasn't serious?'

'Yes, it was serious. Of course it was serious. It just never felt permanent.'

'Because of Sam?'

'Not really. To be honest, that never bothered me.' Monty looked at her for a minute, shaping his response. 'That evening all those years ago when I walked you back to your room after the duck fiasco . . . do you remember?' She nodded. 'We said goodnight and you were in such awe. You looked at me like I was everything. Since then there's been a nagging voice in the back of my mind telling me that one day you'd grow up and you wouldn't need me any more.' Monty stopped momentarily. 'You haven't looked at me in the same way since Warm Springs. That expression, I think, was the lifeblood of our relationship.'

Iris turned her head and focused on the other patrons. There were a few tables occupied by men in uniform and their girls and her mind returned to that evening in 1933. Monty was right. He had been everything and now he wasn't. But that didn't mean he couldn't be something, she reasoned.

'I think that day has come,' Monty continued. 'I think it came a while ago but neither of us wanted to acknowledge it.'

'You also told me that night I wasn't alone,' she responded. 'Do you remember that?'

'I remember,' Monty replied. 'But our situation isn't feasible any longer.'

His turn of phrase annoyed her. 'I'm not Roosevelt or Churchill or the Combined Chiefs,' she said sharply.

Monty didn't react.

'I'll always need you.' Her words were barely audible. 'Can't we go on as we have been? Perhaps we could pull back a little on the throttle . . .'

Monty shook his head. 'We're standing in one another's way.'

He placed a few dollars on the table, put on his hat and slid out from the booth. He looked down at her and took a deep breath. 'I don't think we should see each other for a while,' he said quietly. 'This one has to stick.'

She didn't move.

He touched her hand. 'I love you, kiddo.'

The urge to respond was overwhelming, but she just couldn't.

Monty left the restaurant.

66

WASHINGTON DC
December 1943

Sam helped Iris down from the stepladder after she had placed the star on top of the tree. They had carried it back to the apartment together. It was the first Christmas tree Iris had ever had in her home. She had never seen much point. Spending so many hours at the White House, she just adopted the grand spruce that stood in the foyer each festive season as her own. Last year she had been invited to the Frankfurters' for Christmas. Iris had no decorations or baubles or sentimental reminders from childhood so she went to Macy's in her lunch break and fought the crowds to buy adornments.

'Not bad,' Sam mused, eyeing the length of the tree. 'From a Jew's point of view, that is.'

Iris laughed and walked to him. They wrapped their arms around each other as they admired the tree. 'The image of us here, now, would make a great greeting card,' he joked.

'I don't know what John Sands would make of the menorah in the foreground of the image,' she observed.

'A greeting card for unorthodox families,' he said, smiling.

Sam's words made her break away. 'Is that what you and I are?' she questioned seriously.

'I guess we are a family,' he said, pulling her closer. As he leaned in and kissed her Iris realised that it wasn't the word *family* that had startled her. It was the word *unorthodox*.

Monty's departure in May had affected Iris profoundly on two levels. Not only was she hurt, devastated that he had broken with her, but the separation also unleashed a rush of feelings in regards to Sam – guilt being foremost among them. It was clear to her that the only means of ridding herself of this burden was to confess her wrongdoing. But she was a coward. She assumed Sam, who was scrupulously honest and decent, would never forgive her for her actions. However, it struck her at this very moment that his use of the term *unorthodox* might indicate a more yielding mind.

'You know,' she began doubtfully. He looked at her expectantly. His brown eyes brimmed with love. She stared into them for a moment and contemplated her next utterance but all she could see reflected was her own selfishness. Nothing would be achieved by telling him the truth, she decided. It was over with Monty. Iris resolved to live with her remorse as punishment for her misconduct.

'Do I know what?' he said.

'This is the first time it's ever really felt like Christmas to me,' she said.

He hugged her closely.

'I should get started on dinner,' she said after a moment.

'Wait,' he said. 'Sit with me for a while. I just want to soak you up some more.' He led her out to the fire escape.

'It's cold,' she complained. 'Why are we going outside?'

'I want to soak it *all* up,' he explained. 'You, the city, the lights . . . I've missed it all.'

Apart from a brief visit in July, Iris and Sam had not spent any time together for two years. Sam had been all over the world, from the jungles of Malaya to the deserts of North Africa. Iris had been lonely, painfully so at times. There had been letters but there were cavernous gaps in their knowledge of each other. Iris could barely express how her resignation had affected her; she certainly couldn't put in on paper. That would make it permanent, she told herself. He wrapped his arm around her shoulders.

'I wish you weren't leaving,' she said. 'It feels like this is our time and we're missing the window.'

'My offer still stands,' he said.

Iris thought of the ring. Sam had refused to return it to the store or even keep it himself. The black velvet box was sitting in a kitchen drawer next to wooden spoons, spatulas and Monty's whisk.

'Thank you. You're a very patient man, Sam Jacobson,' she replied.

'Are you happy with Frankfurter?' he asked.

'Yes, I am,' she stated. 'But it's not the West Wing or even the East Wing. It doesn't feel like home.'

'Why did you resign? We've never had a chance to talk about it. Your letters were sketchy.'

Iris realised she hadn't discussed the entire situation with anybody. Monty knew part of the tale, as did Hick. But as Iris related the whole episode to Sam, unabridged, it all came into perspective.

'You know what the hardest thing about the whole sorry affair was?' she asked. 'I knew I had disappointed him. I hadn't lived up to his expectations.'

Sam gazed at her sympathetically.

'Pathetic, aren't I?' she said.

Sam placed both arms around her. He hugged her protectively and she allowed her tears to surface for the first time.

'Poor sweet darling,' he whispered. 'Let me take care of you.'

Iris had never heard Sam express such sentiments before.

'There's nothing you can do,' she stated flatly, drawing in air and bracing herself. 'It's all over with and working at the Supreme Court with Justice Felix Frankfurter isn't such a bad position to be in.' Iris found a handkerchief in the pocket of her coat and dried her eyes.

'It's all a compromise, isn't it?' Sam said after a moment.

'What do you mean?'

'Washington. Politics. When you refuse to bend you wind up out on your ass in the cold.'

Iris kissed him, grateful he was there.

67
TOPAZ, UTAH
March 1944

'Good morning, Mr Korematsu,' Iris said as she sat opposite the young man. 'My name is Iris McIntosh and I work for Justice Frankfurter at the Supreme Court. I'd like to ask you a few questions in regards to the review of your case.'

Fred Korematsu nodded politely and smiled. Iris asked the guard to leave them.

She contemplated removing her coat for an instant, but then decided against it. 'It's cool here at the moment,' she said as she slid a folder from her bag. 'I thought it would be warmer.'

She quickly considered the makeshift iron shed in which they sat. Her home at the Hooverville in Chicago had been better built and warmer, she thought.

'I have a file here from the American Civil Liberties Union. They have been extremely thorough and very helpful,' she added. 'But I wanted to meet you myself so I'll be able to give the justices a clear profile of you and the case.' She paused for an instant before asking, 'Are you happy with that?'

He nodded again.

Fred Korematsu was a well-built, good-looking young man dressed in denims and a red flannel shirt. He looked neat, Iris observed. He was clean-shaven and his thick black hair was combed. The shirt he was wearing was done up to the top button.

'Would you like anything? A glass of water or a soda?'

He shook his head and placed his hands in front of him on the desk that stood between them. Although he had not said a word, Iris sensed no hostility from the round-faced twenty-five-year-old.

'Mr Korematsu,' Iris began, 'can you tell me something of your upbringing? You were born and raised in Oakland, is that correct?'

'Yes, that's right,' he confirmed in a perfect American accent. If Iris closed her eyes she could have been speaking to any American man.

'I went to Castlemont High School and worked part-time in my parents' business.'

'What business are they in, Mr Korematsu?'

'Call me Fred,' he requested. 'The flower business. They owned a nursery in San Leandro.'

'I see.' Iris made a note. 'Good grades?'

'I guess. I never had any problems.'

'Are you an only child, Fred?'

He nodded.

'So am I,' Iris responded and looked up from her notes. 'What did you do after high school?'

'I worked at the nursery for a few years and then I tried to join the navy.'

'And that didn't work out?'

'The recruiting officer said that he had orders not to accept my kind.'

'What do you think he meant by that?' Iris asked, gauging his grievance.

'Japanese,' he replied plainly.

'Do you have a girl, Fred?'

'I did,' he said. 'Ida Boitano. We called it quits the day she told the police where they could find me.'

Iris looked up from her pad and saw the gleam of humour in his eyes. She struggled not to grin.

'What prompted your refusal to report to the assembly centre on the ninth of May last year in preparation for your eventual evacuation to an internment camp?' Iris pushed on.

'I didn't believe it was just for someone like me to be interned,' he responded.

'Someone like you?'

'I'm an American. Just because I look a little different doesn't make me a threat to national security.'

'You managed to hide for twenty-one days, Fred,' Iris stated as she perused her notes. 'Did you get any help from anyone?'

He shook his head. 'My parents, aunts, uncles, cousins – none of them agreed with what I planned to do. They told me to be a good citizen, report to the assembly area and maybe the authorities would realise their mistake and let us all go.'

'But you didn't think that was likely?'

'Nope,' he said. 'Most of my family kept away from Americans. But I knew what they could be like.'

'You're talking about bigotry?'

He nodded.

'Can you give me an example?'

Fred thought briefly and then sighed. 'When I was turned away from the navy I trained at night school to become a welder. I thought I'd be able to contribute to the war effort in that way. Anyway, I got a job at Moore Dry Dock in Oakland.

'For one week I worked my shifts, and there were no complaints about my work. Then I was fired. When the supervisor returned from his vacation and saw the new hire was a Jap, well, that was that.

'After Pearl Harbor I couldn't get work anywhere. I went back to working for my folks.

'It's just not fair, Miss McIntosh.'

Their eyes met. She wanted to agree with him.

'Is your family supportive of your efforts now?'

'No. I'm seen as a troublemaker by my family and treated like an outcast by the other inmates. They all still believe I should show loyalty to the American government.'

'Do you have any family in Japan or any friends you're in contact with?'

He shook his head. 'No. I'm not a spy. I haven't been trading secrets. I'm just a normal guy trying to get on with life. I can't do that in prison.'

'This isn't prison,' Iris reminded him.

'I get paid twelve dollars a month to dig up rocks in the desert. I have a bedroll in an old horse stall. There's a light bulb and nothing else. We're treated like animals, Miss McIntosh.'

'Things will improve,' Iris said. 'The centre is still under construction.'

Iris knew the standard of the facilities was not the point, but she needed to offer him something. The authority of Executive Order 9066 seemed irrefutable. She couldn't have done a better job herself.

Iris had completed her questions. Korematsu's responses had been succinct and eloquent and the interview had taken less time than she'd anticipated. Nevertheless, she remained at the Central Utah War Relocation Centre for another ninety minutes talking to Korematsu about the conditions at the camp, his childhood in Oakland and his plans for the future.

After she shook Korematsu's hand and said goodbye a guard escorted Iris through the dust to the gate in the twelve-foot barbed-wire fence that surrounded the camp. A car was waiting to take her to her hotel in Delta. She gazed at the barren landscape one last time before getting into the vehicle.

'This must be one hell of a place in the summer,' the driver remarked before closing the door.

Iris lay her head against the seat and closed her eyes. His observation settled into the dust as they drove away from the camp.

■

For the following week Iris was troubled by thoughts of Fred Korematsu. He was a kindred spirit of sorts. Life had been snatched from his control and now he was wrestling to get it back. It was plain to Iris that the young man had grit and was up for the fight.

Iris perused the documents in front of her – witness statements, character references, intelligence reports stating the likelihood of sabotage and espionage by Japanese-Americans. It occurred to Iris that while Fred Korematsu was an upright citizen who had done well at school and his jobs, he was of Japanese ancestry and America was at war with the Japanese empire. Iris couldn't see how he could win with his defence. It wasn't a case about racism, as Korematsu's defence claimed, it was a case about military security. They had to prove that Japanese-Americans were not a threat to the nation.

She reordered and shuffled the documents and tallied each one against the log, ensuring nothing was missing. Iris flicked through them once again. According to the log nothing was amiss, but Iris knew the pile of documents was lacking a report from Naval Intelligence she had commissioned herself on behalf of the solicitor-general. Iris had met with an officer, Lieutenant Farrow, in November last year. The report from the Roberts Commission was flawed and dealt only with possible saboteurs and spies in Hawaii. The court needed proof there were Japanese-born subversives living on the West Coast. Iris rang the Department of Naval Intelligence.

■

'Ah, Miss McIntosh,' Charles Fahy said when Iris tapped on his door. 'What a pleasure it is to receive a visit from you.' Even though they had worked together for two years, the solicitor-general refused to call Iris by her Christian name. It was the Southern way, Iris supposed. She was holding the Korematsu file and the log. She entered and sat opposite Fahy and placed them both on his desk then crossed her legs. The pair exchanged pleasantries for quite some time. Fahy liked to talk. Iris considered him extremely amiable and fair-minded, though his appearance – narrow eyes, pointed nose and sharp chin – suggested otherwise. He leaned back in his chair, undid his coat buttons and lit a cigarette.

'Would you like one?' he asked.

Iris declined.

'So what can I do for you, Miss McIntosh?'

'I was just running through the Korematsu documents and I believe one is missing,' Iris explained.

Fahy stood, pulled down his waistcoat firmly and went to close his office door. Iris waited until he returned to his desk before continuing.

'It's a report from Naval Intelligence,' she went on. 'It was written by a Lieutenant Farrow. I rang his office forty minutes ago. He told me the report was sent to this office on the twenty-fourth of last month. I've not seen it and it wasn't entered into the log.'

'Hmm,' Fahy said dourly. He rubbed the sides of his nose between his thumb and forefinger for a moment before opening his desk drawer. He withdrew a dark green file and handed it to Iris across the desk. 'That's the report you're missing, Miss McIntosh. Have a quick read and tell me what you think.'

Iris looked at him, confused, then hurriedly scanned Farrow's report.

Fahy lit another cigarette and glanced over some papers on his desk while he waited for Iris to close the file.

'The findings are of concern, yes?' he asked casually when she had finished. He stubbed out his cigarette.

'Yes, they are. They are of great concern.' Iris straightened the papers and then handed the file back to Fahy.

'Thank you, Miss McIntosh.' He slid the file back into his drawer.

'That's Korematsu's case,' she said, bewildered. 'The report torpedoes the validity of 9066. There has been no evidence of espionage activities on the West Coast in the last two years.'

'Exactly,' Fahy responded coolly. 'That's why the report is being buried. Naval Intelligence and the FBI have disavowed any knowledge of it. It's just a shame nobody thought to tell Farrow.' The solicitor-general shook his head in amusement. 'Naval Intelligence. Such a misnomer.'

'Who's decision was it . . . to scuttle the report?' she asked flatly, unimpressed by Fahy's light-heartedness.

'Mostly mine but the justices were privy to my actions.' Fahy placed his elbows on the desk and looked at her squarely. 'If this report became public knowledge, Miss McIntosh, it would not only sink Executive Order 9066, it would shake the presidency to its foundations. There's an election on the horizon and the country is at war.'

'But there's an innocent man, innocent people, sitting in internment camps,' Iris protested. 'Their entire lives have been stolen away . . . It's not right. That's not justice!' Her voice had grown louder. She stood. Her face was red-hot.

'Calm down, Miss McIntosh,' Fahy said soothingly, as if to a skittish horse. He moved out from behind his desk and led her by the elbow to the sofa near the window. 'Sit down. Take in the view for a moment.'

Fahy waited for Iris to settle before he explained reasonably, 'We're a team, Miss McIntosh. The justices, the clerks, the solicitor-general, the deputies and the assistants – everyone who works in this building.' Iris looked into his dime-sized brown eyes and wondered where he was taking his allusion. 'Do you know who the captain of our team is, Miss McIntosh?'

'The United States Government,' Iris answered.

'That's correct, Miss McIntosh,' he responded. 'And we're not only fighting for justice, Miss McIntosh, we are fighting a war! And if there is one dissenting voice in the team, one *weak* player, then the entire lineup falls apart and the other side wins.' He paused for a brief instant and smiled. 'And it is the captain who is the first to tumble.'

Iris nodded.

'Do you know who'd be the second?' he asked. It wasn't a threat.

'The player who fumbled the ball,' Iris replied quietly, staring ahead of her.

'Quite right, Miss McIntosh. I can see exactly what Frankfurter saw in you.' He stood and looked down at her. 'You seem quite bewildered, Miss McIntosh. I hope I've made myself clear on this matter. Have I made myself clear on the matter?' His tone was pleasant.

Iris stood and looked him in the eye. 'Crystal,' she replied.

6 8

HYDE PARK, NEW YORK
May 1962

The White House was rationed just like every other household in the country. It was brought into effect by the Office of Price Administration in January 1942. By the following year we needed coupons to buy most everything, but what affected me the most was the rationing of sugar, coffee, meat and butter. In just one month I had to stretch our points to feed four presidents, one prime minister and his war-starved staff, a Norwegian princess in exile and her two young children, and Madame Chiang Kai-shek! Although the latter ate like a bird, I can tell you those ration stamps caused me plenty of anguish and a host of sleepless nights.

I talked over the situation with Mrs Roosevelt and we worked out a plan to make those stamps stretch a little further. First, large-scale entertaining was cut down by half and three of the seven days of the week became meatless days. The president didn't like that at all, but I could work wonders with a dozen eggs and a pound of cornmeal. Next, butter was allowed at breakfast only. Dinner rolls were served dry at lunch and dinner. One cup of coffee per individual was permitted, but no cream was allowed.

The president became fussier and fussier about his food, especially as D-Day – 6 June 1944 – approached. That day had been in the planning for months and it took its toll physically and emotionally on our dear president. No matter what I served he'd pick up the telephone and yell something insulting down the line. I recall once he telephoned me in my office after lunch and shouted, 'I don't want any more damn chipped beef!' I replied, 'Well, what would you like?' And he fired down the line, 'Steak!' It was the first time I'd ever heard the president curse. That 'damn' sure sounded mighty loud to me on the receiving end. He never did get that steak.

His anger was understandable. He just didn't get a break. No sooner had he pulled the country out of the depression than it was plunged head first into a world war. That would be enough to make anyone a little temperamental. He took it out on the food and on me, without a doubt, but that was a small burden to bear in the face of everything he was up against.

The president wasn't only thinking about the soldiers and sailors and airmen who were fighting overseas at that time, he also had to make plans for them when they came home. It was a marvellous day when he signed into law the G.I. Bill of Rights in June 1944. That took the edge off the Allied invasion for me. It meant that all returning servicemen received federal support for college and vocational training. The president also planned for low-cost mortgages, medical care, job counselling and unemployment insurance for our boys who were coming home. The bill was passed unanimously in both houses. That was a great day as both my sons would, God willing, be returning home soon.

It wasn't until July 1944 that the president announced he would be running for a fourth term. He was tired and he looked it, and so was Mrs Roosevelt. They hadn't wanted a third term, so I had no idea how they'd cope with a fourth! Mrs Roosevelt began travelling more than ever in the last year of the war. She started calling the world her home. She went to England, the war-torn Pacific – why there was even a picture of her in the newspaper rubbing noses with a Maori woman in New Zealand! When Miss McIntosh was still working at the White House I had been complaining to her one day about all the First Lady's travel. How it was wearing her down and that she should take it easy for a while. Miss McIntosh said something really insightful, I thought. She explained that Mrs Roosevelt was the president's legs. She had to do all she did for the sake of the administration.

69
CAMBRIDGE, MASSACHUSETTS
August 1944

'Do you think the president will attend?' Judge Frankfurter asked.

'He and Missy were very close,' Iris responded tactfully. 'But I'm not sure if he's in town at the moment. If he doesn't attend, then Mrs Roosevelt will be there.'

Dejected, Frankfurter slumped a little in his seat. Iris returned to her notes.

'Who else?' he asked.

'I couldn't tell you, sir.' Iris's eyes didn't leave the pages in front of her.

'Could you take a stab?' he encouraged.

Iris smiled and closed the folder she had only seconds before opened. She had anticipated a silent journey from DC to Cambridge. She and her employer had little in common, apart from the law, and even less rapport with each other. They had stopped the previous night in New York. This was a necessity, according to the judge, as long car trips made him queasy. He stayed with his brother on the Upper West Side and Iris told him she would stay with friends. Instead, she got a room for herself at a Midtown hotel at her own expense.

'Grace Tully, Harry Hopkins, maybe Henry Wallace . . . Really, sir, I have no idea,' she said.

He nodded brusquely and looked out the window. Iris reopened the folder. She too hoped the president would be at the funeral. She believed enough time had passed for them to speak, for their bond, if there ever had been one, to have been repaired. Nervous about the possible meeting, she resented the judge's pestering. Iris discovered very early in her relationship with Frankfurter just why he hadn't been accepted into the Roosevelt hearth. He ingratiated to excess. It was cloying. It didn't surprise Iris that the president had nominated him for the Supreme Court; he was just the sort of man Roosevelt would want to remove from the White House and position on the bench.

'I know Joseph Kennedy is attending,' the judge noted.

Iris looked up briefly. She wanted to advise Frankfurter that Kennedy was no man to hitch his wagon to. Kennedy had less influence in Washington these days than Frankfurter. Instead she nodded without bothering to feign interest in the remark.

Grace Tully had told Iris about Missy's death and then she had seen the obituary in the newspaper two days later. It was a small notice, only about an inch long. The president's statement, which appeared under it, ran to about an inch and a half. Iris had visited Missy regularly since her infirmity, first at the hospital, then at a clinic in Virginia. Missy had spent her final days with her sister in Potsdam, New York. Iris wasn't sure why she was being buried at Mount Auburn Cemetery in Cambridge, but she had heard it was one of the most beautiful graveyards in the country. She was certain the president would have had a hand in it. He wouldn't have wanted his beloved Missy spending her afterlife in an overcrowded burial ground in New York.

■

The president didn't attend the funeral. Mrs Roosevelt stood in his place. However, he had chosen a beautiful spot for Missy. The air was syrupy with the scent of honeysuckle and azaleas. Missy's plot was adjacent to a light-leafed plant which was small enough to be considered a shrub, but large enough to provide shade. Iris wondered what it was called. Apart from the priest's low murmur, all Iris could hear was the distant psalm of crickets. The priest referred to Missy throughout the service as Marguerite. What an exotic name, Iris thought. As the coffin was lowered into the ground, Iris examined the face of each person in attendance. The sun through the nameless tree gave each mourner a mottled appearance. Most of them Iris knew from the White House. There was a woman who looked similar to Missy who must have been her sister, along with several other women in their forties who stood together. Iris guessed they must be old school or college friends. Harry wasn't present. The judge would be disappointed by the turnout. The Catholic priest overseeing the service was Bishop Richard Cushing. Apart from the First Lady, the bishop was probably the most influential person at the gathering.

When the rites had been completed, the mourners began filing slowly back towards the road that led to the exit. Iris worked her way over to Mrs Roosevelt, who was walking with Tommy and Grace Tully. It was Tommy who noticed her first.

'Hi there, stranger,' she said quietly as she looped her arm through Iris's. 'It's good to see you. I wish it could have been under different circumstances.'

Iris smiled and pressed Tommy's hand. She fell into step with the women as they made their way along Beech Avenue in silence.

When they reached Bigelow Chapel they halted and Mrs Roosevelt took Iris by her shoulders and hugged her closely.

'I'm so happy you came,' she said. 'It would have meant so much to Missy. She appreciated your visits.'

'The president couldn't make it?' Iris asked.

Mrs Roosevelt shook her head. 'He's in Alaska visiting troops at the base in Adak.'

'How is he?' Iris asked.

'Up and down,' Mrs Roosevelt answered. Iris wasn't certain of her meaning but she did notice Grace and Tommy swap a doubtful glance. 'Hopefully, this campaign will buoy his spirits. You know how he loves a good fight.'

'He does relish a challenging campaign, but I don't think Dewey will be much of an opponent,' Iris said.

'Humourless and stuck-up,' Tommy agreed. 'He's the groom on his own wedding cake.'

The accuracy of the observation made the women laugh quietly, even conspiratorially, in the shade of the Gothic chapel.

'Anna and the children are back in Washington,' Mrs Roosevelt continued. 'That makes her father very happy.'

'I thought she and John were established in Seattle,' Iris said.

'They were, but then John went off to cover the war in Africa so her father asked her to come to DC and act as his aide. With all our sons serving it's nice to have Anna close by. She travels with him, gossips, organises. She's become his right hand.'

Iris could only nod. A sense of her own failure surged in her chest. It quickly compounded into an irrational and blazing jealousy. She leaned against the cool stone of the chapel.

'How's work?' Mrs Roosevelt enquired.

'I'm faced with a new challenge every day,' Iris answered, brightening. 'You were right about that.'

'What about your knitting?' the First Lady asked. 'How's that coming along?'

'To be honest, I really don't have much time,' Iris answered. 'My hours are extremely long.'

Mrs Roosevelt smiled sympathetically and looked to her right. 'I see Felix over there with Kennedy,' she said, somewhat reluctantly. 'I should go and say hello.' She and Tommy moved off.

As Mrs Roosevelt walked in the direction of the judge and Joseph Kennedy, Grace moved forward and took a place next to Iris against the wall.

'He's mostly down,' Grace admitted.

Iris straightened. 'What do you mean?'

'The boss is sick, Iris.' Her voice was soft.

'How sick?'

'His doctor has diagnosed congestive heart failure. He's got circles under his eyes, his hands shake so much he can't even light a cigarette and he's so thin. You wouldn't recognise him.'

Iris touched her arm. She wasn't certain why Grace was confiding in her with such candour.

'Then why is he running again?'

'He doesn't know the worst of it. He thinks he's got high blood pressure and a little angina,' Grace explained. 'That's why they've dumped Wallace from the ticket.'

'You mean it's unlikely that the president will live out the fourth term.'

Grace's nod of confirmation was nearly indiscernible.

'But – but when I left he was fine,' Iris stammered. 'Fighting fit. He's only sixty-two.'

'It's the war, Iris. It's this goddamn war,' Grace said ruefully. 'In the last eighteen months he's been to Casablanca, Quebec City and Tehran and you know how hard it is for him to travel. Churchill's been back twice to Washington and the Combined Chiefs are virtually living at the White House. He's on call day and night. I can't remember the last time he's had more than three or four hours' sleep.'

Iris was upset. 'I'm not sure what to say. Is there something you'd like me to do?'

'I just needed to tell somebody. Everyone else is carrying on like it's business as usual.'

'What about Harry?'

'He's got his own problems,' Grace said. 'He had surgery again in May. The doctors removed most of his stomach. He's still recovering.'

Iris had never considered the prospect of a political landscape with a leader who wasn't Roosevelt. The vista was alarming. Moreover, the idea of travelling the eight hours to DC with Frankfurter was crushing.

'He misses you, Iris,' Grace disclosed. 'He mentions you often. Something will remind him of you or he'll say, "I'd like to ask McIntosh how she'd handle this situation." He still tells everyone that you named Fala.'

The women smiled feebly.

'Have you heard from Monty?' Grace asked after a minute.

'We broke it off,' Iris answered, and then corrected herself. 'He broke it off in May last year.'

'Really? That's odd.' She looked confused. 'But you know he got a posting with a battalion and that he's in France at the moment. Well, that was the last we heard.'

'Fighting?' Iris cried. 'He's fifty-three years old!' Her mouth turned dry and she sat heavily on the steps leading into the chapel. The thought of losing Monty as well was overwhelming.

'Hey,' Grace said, producing a handkerchief from her purse, 'you're sweating.' As she dabbed Iris's brow and cheeks, careful not to leave streaks in her make-up, she continued, 'I thought you would have known. He's an executive officer. He requested the command.'

'I didn't know,' Iris responded.

'That's really weird, then,' Grace said quietly. 'Monty put you down as his next of kin. I completed the paperwork for him in May.'

Iris couldn't dwell any more on the topic. Nor could she go back to Washington with Frankfurter. 'How are you getting home?' she asked.

'Driving. Mrs Roosevelt and Tommy are going to New York, but I'm driving straight through to DC.'

'Can I bum a ride?' Iris wasn't sure what she'd tell the judge, but she'd come up with something.

'Of course,' Grace replied.

■

A week later, on a Saturday afternoon, Iris took a Coke from the fridge and turned on the radio. It was the first time she had listened to one of the president's broadcasts since she had left the White House. This wasn't out of spite or malice; she just didn't want to be reminded. She sat cross-legged on the sofa as she waited. She wiped the condensation from the bottle onto her skirt and looked at her watch. Any minute. Her fingers tapped the bottle in time to the Harry James Orchestra playing 'Two O'Clock Jump'.

At two o'clock the announcer began with the usual introduction. The president was speaking live from the fantail of a destroyer at the Puget Sound Navy Yard in Bremerton.

Roosevelt's voice was muffled by the sound of the wind. At first Iris told herself it was the quality of the broadcast that stilted his tone and bungled his delivery, but within just a few minutes it was obvious the weather condition and sound equipment had nothing to do with the rambling, clumsy nature of the address. She struggled to find the one message that he hoped to convey in the speech that went on for over an hour. At times he faltered and she could hear his notes rustling in what sounded like a gale.

As he continued, Iris uncrossed her legs and lit a cigarette. She walked to the window and sat on the ledge. She lifted her skirt slightly and felt the warmth of the sun on her thighs. Willing him to stop, she attempted to focus on the street outside – the boy from downstairs chaining his bike to a lamppost, a mother across the road tending to a small child who had just fallen over – but it was impossible not to hear every word, every stammer, every overwritten analogy. Unpolished and verbose, the address Iris assumed was meant to be a report about the progress on the war in the Pacific degenerated into a long list of dates and locations, which was neither gripping nor particularly informative. Even though their radios are on, Iris thought, no one will be listening. The speech was a shambles.

When the broadcast eventually concluded Iris stubbed out her cigarette and put her Coke to her lips. It had gone warm and flat in the sun.

70
WASHINGTON DC
November 1944

Iris left work earlier than usual, stopped at the market on her way home and used up all of her red stamps to buy the makings of Sam's favourite dinner. Two sirloin steaks, potatoes, cream, butter, green beans and cheese. Sam would have stamps too, she reasoned; he could feed them both for the week he was in town. If he stays the week, she thought, and was instantly rattled.

As she sliced the potatoes carefully, ensuring the slivers were paper-thin, fear gripped her chest. She stopped for a moment and took a deep breath. She was going to go through with it, no matter what, Iris told herself. Earlier in the week Sam had sent a wire from London. He was coming home to cover the election. He would be in Hyde Park but he would join her in Washington on the eighth. Iris decided immediately to tell him about Monty. The war, Missy's death and the president's ill-health had made her extremely sensitive to life's margins. She didn't want to waste any more time. She wanted to get on with her life, with Sam, with a clean slate. Iris hoped Sam would see her confession in the same light. Moreover, the Korematsu case had been argued in October. Aware of the outcome, Iris was already working on Frankfurter's concurrence. Korematsu's loss weighed heavily on her. She needed to be relieved of at least some of her guilt. She planned to inform Sam of her infidelity after dinner.

When she heard Sam's key in the latch the pommes dauphinoise were ready for the oven and the table was set. The beans were topped and tailed and resting in a pot and the steaks sat on a tray anticipating the broiler. She hastily removed her apron and threw it back into the kitchen as she emerged.

She walked to him as he stood in the doorway and took his duffel bag. They hadn't seen each other since the previous Christmas. Sam had been in France and Moscow mostly, filing regularly for Murrow. By special invitation of the president he had been in Hyde Park on election night. Now he was in Washington for one week before returning to London and then Normandy, where he would be covering the Allied invasion. He appeared a little thinner and she noticed some grey hairs beginning to sprout just above his ears. They stared at each other for a moment, hastily recalling one another, before they kissed.

'Welcome home,' she whispered. Sam pulled her closer and kissed her again. When they parted he examined her face for a moment. She looked into his eyes and was instantly discomfited.

'You're even prettier,' he murmured. 'How is that possible?'

Realising she couldn't wait until after dinner, Iris simply shrugged. 'Come in,' she said. 'Do you want a drink?'

'Thanks.'

Sam took off his coat and hat then sat down on the sofa, loosening his tie. Iris went to the kitchen and leaned her forehead against the refrigerator for a few seconds before taking out two bottles of beer. She returned to the living room.

'Cheers,' Sam said, clinking his bottle against hers.

Iris took a small sip then scrutinised the label carefully.

'Is something wrong?' Sam asked.

She shook her head. 'How did everything go at Springwood?'

'Good,' he said brightly, taking another sip. 'Mrs Roosevelt asked after you. So did Grace. They haven't seen you for a while?'

'I've been busy at work. I guess I keep more to myself these days.'

He glanced at her and, noticing his concern, Iris changed tack. 'An historic fourth term. It's big,' she said, without much enthusiasm for the subject. 'What was the mood?'

'Sober. The president is tired. Everyone's tired. But he didn't have a choice. With the war going so well for us, I don't think he could have lost if he tried.'

Iris murmured her agreement.

'What's up?' Sam asked seriously.

Iris placed her bottle on the coffee table and forced herself to meet Sam's anxious gaze.

'I've got something to tell you but I'm not sure how I can,' she said.

'Just open your mouth and let the words come out,' he suggested.

She nodded and wet her lips.

'I've been seeing Monty Chapel. I was seeing him up until May last year,' she admitted.

Iris could tell immediately her revelation was entirely unanticipated. Even if Sam had suspected her, he certainly wasn't expecting Iris to divulge it. The colour drained from his face. Silently he put down his beer, stood, and walked over to the window.

'But it's over,' she went on more confidently. 'It is definitely over. I promise you.'

'Then why did you tell me?' he asked faintly, staring out the window that overlooked 30th Street.

Surprised by the question, Iris stood and went to stand next to him. 'I thought you deserved to know. I thought we couldn't have a life together after the war with *that* hanging over our heads.'

'It would have only been hanging over yours,' he commented unemotionally, and turned to her. She couldn't bear to have him look at her like that. All the love in his expression had been replaced with a foreboding mix of dismay, contempt and shame.

'What do you want, forgiveness? Do you want to be chastised? Is it understanding you're after?' he asked, slightly dumbfounded.

'I just wanted you to know,' she said ineffectually, stretching out her fingers towards his arm. He pulled away and turned to examine the living room.

'In this apartment?' he asked. 'Were you together in this apartment?'

She exhaled slowly, as though it were her last breath, and nodded once.

'For Christ's sake, Iris,' he snapped, his anger rising. 'You know what this town's like. Everyone from AP would know what you've been doing behind my back . . . You've made me look like a fool.'

Iris stared at him, mute. She had never fully considered the wider impact of her betrayal. Although she and Monty had been discreet, she guessed the love affair had never been secret. Her behaviour had been cruel and flagrant. 'I'm sorry . . .' she began wanly.

'I don't recognise you any more, Iris,' he cut her off. There was a sorrow in his voice she'd never heard before and it was terrifying. 'You bear no resemblance to that girl on the balcony. That girl who sat at the Roosevelts' table and told her story. That girl who sacrificed her own welfare for the sake of a young man who didn't know better. Where has that girl gone?'

Iris couldn't respond because she didn't know the answer. When exactly had she lost herself? she wondered. Her eyes filled with tears. She tried to take a deep breath but her throat was too tight.

'Why?' he asked after a minute. 'When I've asked you to marry me so many times? You couldn't have doubted my feelings.'

Here was the opportunity to tell him everything. She longed to explain to him the enormity of the losses in her life and her craving for Monty. How could she explain to Sam the need and the loneliness when he would only see it as weakness? She shook her head. 'I can't explain it,' she said pitifully. 'But it's over. I promise you. I . . .'

Aware of the banality of her words she halted. There was nothing more she could say, no more assurances she could offer. Sam would just need to have faith in her and their relationship.

'Is Chapel the reason you've refused to marry me?' he asked quietly.

'I don't believe so,' she answered honestly. 'I don't want to give up my career.'

'Maybe that's what you have to do for us to work,' he said. 'Commit to me only.'

Iris looked at him hopefully. A semblance of optimism returned to her blue eyes. She touched his hand.

'And sacrifice everything else?' she asked gently.

Iris could see him striving to reconcile her independence with his own.

She drew him to the sofa. They sat together.

'Do you really think we can work?' she asked. 'Even after this?'

'We have to,' he replied. 'I've loved you for too long.'

Iris's face darkened. It was a defeatist response. She turned to him, wanting something more certain, more promising.

'I need some time,' he went on. 'I need to think things through by myself.'

'I understand,' she said reluctantly.

'What did you expect, Iris? Did you really think you could tell me you've been sleeping with Chapel and that I'd then open a bottle of wine and have dinner with you?'

It was exactly what she had hoped. How selfish and short-sighted she had been.

As they sat without speaking Iris wondered what was next. The silence was agonising. After a while she glanced at her watch. It was already eight.

'Let's go to bed,' he said, lifting her to her feet.

'But . . . I thought you needed time.' She searched his face. There was love present in his dark brown eyes but also weariness. Iris regretted that she had made him feel this way.

'Commit to me.' He drew her to him.

'Risk everything for you,' she refined.

'Prove to me that you're willing to risk it for me.'

She shook her head. 'You're asking too much.'

Sam took Iris firmly in his arms and kissed her tenderly on the mouth. Her head fell back in pleasure and he showered her neck with a trail of soft kisses. He ran his hand gently down the length of her torso and found her legs and swept her off the floor and into his arms. Such an audacious romantic gesture was out of the ordinary for Sam. Iris yielded to the drama of the scene and allowed him to carry her into the bedroom.

THE FOURTH TERM

January–April 1945

The President's Lunch

71

WASHINGTON DC
January 1945

Iris had set the alarm for six o'clock. It was difficult to get out of bed. She walked sleepily into the kitchen and turned on the light. These days she wore only her underwear, wool socks she had knitted herself and Mrs Roosevelt's handmade sweater to bed. The latter was large enough to serve as a decent winter nightdress. The heating wasn't turned on until seven. She shook the kettle and placed it on the gas then stood in the kitchen stamping her feet on the cold linoleum. While she waited for it to boil she opened the jar of peanut butter sitting next to the stove and scooped some up with her finger.

By seven Iris was out the door. A heavy blanket of fresh snow covered the street. She didn't attempt to hail a taxi. Even though the sun's first hint could only just be glimpsed on the horizon and white flakes fell on her nose, she wanted to walk. There was a great sense of contentment that came from walking on fresh snow. Georgetown was deserted. That wasn't unusual for a Saturday morning in the belly of winter, but it was unusual for this particular morning. Many sidewalks hadn't been cleared and she had to detour onto the road in order to find passage. It was a laborious journey downtown although she enjoyed the sound of the snow crunching under her feet. By the time she reached St Matthew's Cathedral she had seen only two other people – a man shovelling snow from the M Street sidewalk and a boy of about twelve delivering newspapers.

When she turned right onto Connecticut Avenue there were more signs of life. Here a path had been channelled along the sidewalk and the steady flow of footsteps south had begun to turn the frosty causeway slippery and muddy. Cutting through Lafayette Square, Iris made her way across to the South Portico of the White House.

A reasonable-sized crowd of well-wishers had already assembled by eight thirty, although Iris had thought there would be more. She edged her way as close to the front as possible. Perhaps Roosevelt's decision to repeat his fourth oath of office at the White House and not the Capitol steps seemed to some an anticlimax. People loved pageantry but this year there was none. Iris had read the president was also doing away with the traditional military parade. That made sense, she thought. Who was there left to march?

An hour remained before the inauguration was due to begin and Iris felt the cold creeping through her boots. Still, even though her nose and lips were numb, she didn't regret refusing the ticket Frankfurter had offered. All the justices and their staff were attending the inauguration and the subsequent lunch. Frankfurter and his cronies would be inside right now, she guessed. No doubt the judge would be thrilled to be more than a mere onlooker to the festivities. When he had offered her the ticket, Iris decided she couldn't go back to the White House as a member of his staff. It just wouldn't seem right.

Iris tugged at the sleeve of her overcoat and pulled down her glove in order to see her watch. The cold bit her wrist. It was nearing ten. Family prayers would be taking place about now. At ten o'clock precisely the band began to play 'Hail to the Chief' and Iris heard her name called from somewhere behind. She turned and saw Mrs Nesbitt pushing through the crowd.

'Coming through,' she cried. 'White House staff. Coming through.'

'Everything's white this morning, isn't it?' she said when she'd reached Iris, speaking loudly to make herself heard over the band. 'White House, white lawn . . .' She laughed. 'I recognised you from back there.' She pointed. 'Still as pretty as a picture.' The housekeeper put her arms around Iris and gave her a firm hug.

'It's good to see you, Mrs Nesbitt,' Iris replied. 'Taking a break from the kitchen?'

'I wasn't going to miss this one, Iris,' she explained. 'There might not be the hoopla of the previous inaugurations because of the pressure of the war, but this one is the most historic of all of them in my book.'

'It certainly is,' Iris agreed happily.

'Anyway, everything in the kitchen is ready to go,' she added.

'What's for lunch today?' Iris asked as the band continued.

'Well, the president asked for Chicken à la King,' she began. Iris knew this was Roosevelt's favourite dish. 'But I said, "Chicken à la King for two thousand people? Not on your life." It would be impossible to keep warm. So instead we're having chicken salad, rolls, cake and coffee.'

Iris tilted her head as she considered the austere menu. Chicken à la King, even Mrs Nesbitt's Chicken à la King, would surely be more palatable on such a bitter day than cold chicken salad.

Seemingly mistaking Iris's surprise for disapproval of her extravagance, the housekeeper went on, 'No butter for the rolls or frosting for the cake, of course, and only one cup of coffee per person.'

'Of course,' Iris said seriously.

The band stopped and the president emerged onto the balcony on the arm of a young man in uniform.

'Is that John or James he's with?' Iris whispered during the prayer.

'James,' Mrs Nesbitt confirmed.

Roosevelt walked slowly to the lectern, leaning against his son.

'Does he wear the braces very much any more?' Iris asked.

The housekeeper pursed her lips. 'Well, he hasn't delivered a public address sitting down yet.'

'He looks ill,' Iris said. The skin on the president's face was like parchment and he was thin – too thin. 'And small,' she added. The president had always seemed such a big man, his head, hands and shoulders larger than those of any other man she knew. Not any more.

'He's been very ill,' Mrs Nesbitt said as Roosevelt took the oath. She shook her head as if the president was to blame.

As Mrs Nesbitt spoke Iris scanned the faces on the balcony. Justice Harlan Stone delivered the oath. James stood behind the president, to his right. Mrs Roosevelt and Anna stood further back. There were many men in uniform standing in the background. Iris couldn't identify Harry, although the columns supporting the portico blocked much of her view.

'I've had to rewrite my entire menu catalogue to accommodate him,' Mrs Nesbitt complained. 'What's more, he just won't stop. He's off again the day after tomorrow, to Malta!'

As the oath was completed Iris wondered what there was in Malta the president had to attend to.

Roosevelt, with the aid of his son, moved closer to the lectern and began to speak. His bold, confident voice belied his appearance and Iris was glad. Mrs Nesbitt began to speak, but Iris held up her hand.

'I'd just like to hear this, Mrs Nesbitt,' she said politely.

It was a brief address, the shortest Iris had ever heard Roosevelt deliver. It wouldn't have been any longer than five hundred words, she estimated. But she listened closely. Then she smiled. There they were: the lines he wanted her to hear.

'We have learned that we cannot live alone at peace, that our own well-being is dependent on the well-being of other nations far away. We have learned to be a citizen of the world. We have learned, as Emerson said, "The only way to have a friend is to be one."'

The speech ended shortly after this and there was applause. The vice-president stepped forward to take his oath. As he began to speak, Mrs Nesbitt leaned towards Iris and asked, 'Who's that mealymouth?'

'The vice-president, Harry Truman.'

'I haven't got time for him,' Mrs Nesbitt said, a look of disgust on her face. 'I've got to get back to the kitchen. There'll be two thousand folks stampeding into the East Room soon, demanding lunch.' She hugged Iris again. 'It was swell to see you. Don't be a stranger.'

Iris smiled and, as she watched the woman disappear into the crowd, marvelled at her staying power.

■

The ceremony took just twenty minutes. There was to be no inaugural dinner or ball, just the lunch that Mrs Nesbitt was providing. As the spectators meandered off, Iris wondered if this had more to do with the president's health than the pressure of the war, as Mrs Nesbitt had indicated. Iris stopped to let some people pass. As she did so a fleeting swell of nausea rose in her stomach. Within a second it had receded and she continued on her way.

She was glad she had come, she decided. While the president's physical appearance was alarming, his voice and mannerisms, the inflection of his voice, were just the same as they had always been.

When she reached Lafayette Square she realised she was starving. Apart from the finger scoop of peanut butter at six am, she hadn't eaten anything all day. Her lower back ached from standing in the cold for hours. As she began to cut through the park to the coffee shop on the other side, the same queasiness that she had experienced earlier returned. Halting by a trash can, she placed her hands on the metal rim and leaned her body weight against it. Despite the cold, she was perspiring. She could feel moisture running down her back and chest.

As the biliousness intensified, she stared into the depths of the trash can and breathed deeply, attempting to forestall the inevitable. But the stench was overpowering and before her stomach was able to protest, she fainted.

∎

'Is there someone we can call for you to see you home?' the nurse asked, notepad and pencil at the ready. She was much younger than her patient. Iris guessed she was in her early twenties. The name on her badge read *Miss Preen*.

Iris shook her head. 'There's no one, but I'm feeling fine,' she insisted through a piece of gauze she held to her mouth. Her lip was still numb from the lidocaine and she had the sensation she was drooling.

'It's hospital policy, miss,' Preen explained. 'Someone has to escort you home in case you faint again and the doctor said that is a possibility. Your blood pressure is extremely low.'

She moved Iris's hand from her face and examined the stitches. 'The swelling should go down in a day or two.'

'I'm sure if I just get a cab, the driver could walk me to my door. I'll be absolutely fine.' Iris feared her slurred speech wasn't helping her cause, but she just needed to go home.

'What about your husband?' Preen asked deliberately, looking down at Iris's unadorned hand.

'He's in the war. Fighting in Europe,' Iris responded flatly.

The nurse then found a use for her newly sharpened pencil and stood by the bed writing on Iris's chart. Iris felt certain she was scrawling the word 'harlot' across the page.

'Well, there must be someone,' Preen declared.

Iris didn't know her neighbours that well and her colleagues were eating cold chicken salad and dry rolls at the moment. Once she would have called Monty or Mrs Roosevelt in such a situation, but Monty was in a battalion HQ in Europe somewhere and Mrs Roosevelt would be busy with her duties as First Lady. Sam was probably sitting in a foxhole in France or Holland and Grace Tully would be unavailable today as well. As she inventoried her friends and acquaintances she became increasingly despondent. There really was no one.

'Hick!' she finally exclaimed to herself. Her heart lifted momentarily.

'Excuse me, ma'am?' the nurse said.

'I've just thought of someone,' Iris explained. 'But I'll need to make the call myself.'

Miss Preen eyed her dubiously.

Iris had no intention of attempting to explain why this was the case.

It would be hard enough to get through to Hick during the inaugural lunch without the request coming from a sneering nurse.

'I will have to make the call,' Iris repeated sternly.

The nurse complied and led Iris to the telephone in the nurse's station, staying within earshot for the duration of the conversation.

■

Hick arrived promptly at the hospital. Miss Preen hovered invasively in the cubicle while Iris dressed. She looked at Iris unkindly, with misgiving. Was this the way everyone would perceive her now, as a woman not to be trusted? Iris and Hick mutually avoided all conversation until they were back at Iris's apartment.

Iris filled Hick in on some of the tale in the cab. Once ensconced in Iris's living room, she asked, 'How did you get to the hospital?'

'Someone picked me up and shoved me in a cab,' Iris said. 'I woke up in the back of the car. The driver told me where we were heading.'

'Friendly Washingtonians,' Hick remarked with a laugh.

Iris raised her hand and ran her fingers gingerly from her nostril to the top of her lip. The stitches were stiff and crusted with blood. She wanted to pick at it, but it hurt too much.

'The lidocaine is wearing off,' she told Hick.

'Where do you keep the aspirin?'

'In the bathroom cabinet.'

Hick disappeared into the bathroom and returned holding two aspirin and a glass of water.

'I'm sorry I'm keeping you from the White House,' Iris said as she swallowed the pills and the water.

'Don't worry,' Hick said offhandedly. 'There were too many people, lunch was a bust and it was dry.'

Iris knew she wasn't referring to the absence of butter.

'I can barely endure the thought of another term,' Hick added dolefully after a moment.

She had stalled her life for twelve years, sacrificed her career and her reputation. Now Iris was facing a similar dilemma.

'I was glad you called.' Hick took Iris's hand. 'Now, what have you got to drink?'

'In the kitchen. Top right cupboard. Take your pick.'

'How do you think bourbon will mix with lidocaine and aspirin?' Hick called from the kitchen.

'Pretty well, I think,' Iris said wearily. She took off her shoes and put her feet up on the sofa.

'You're still very pale,' Hick noted when she entered the living room holding a bottle. 'Why did the doc say you fainted?'

'Low blood pressure.'

Hick nodded. 'Have you been eating? Are Meatless Mondays to blame?' she joked in an effort to get Iris to laugh.

Iris shook her head. 'The doctor believes I might be pregnant.'

Hick was speechless. She moved across to the sofa and sat on the edge. She rubbed Iris's shoulder gently.

'He did a test, but I won't know for a few days. Wednesday, he said.'

'Gee. Christ,' Hick murmured. 'I'm sorry, kid. What do you think the likelihood is?'

'I'm late and I've been feeling queasy on and off, and then the fainting . . . The doctor said all the symptoms pointed to the same thing. But they had to do a blood test to make sure.'

'So that's why the nurse was being such a bitch?' Hick asked.

Iris nodded and handed Hick her glass. 'I can't drink any more,' she said. 'I'm beginning to feel sick again.'

Hick took the glass and poured the contents into her own. 'Lie back,' she instructed and took the rug from the end of the sofa and placed it across her friend's legs.

'Who's the father if it turns out you are pregnant?' Only Hick could ask this question without making a woman feel like a tramp.

'Sam,' Iris responded bleakly. 'I haven't seen Monty since forever.'

'Have you considered what you'll do?'

'I'm still coming to grips with the possibility of being pregnant,' Iris replied. 'I can't see beyond that at the moment.'

Then she clutched Hick's hand. 'Please, Hick, don't tell Sam.'

'Of course I won't.'

Hick finished her drink and sat in the armchair. 'I have the number of a doctor,' she said quietly. 'Eleanor has contacts too. Let me know if you'd like to speak with them. You have options, Iris.'

Iris looked at her, shaken by the suggestion.

'When you know where you stand, that is – after Wednesday,' Hick added.

'Don't tell anybody about this, Hick. Promise me you won't. Not even Mrs Roosevelt – especially not Mrs Roosevelt,' Iris pleaded suddenly, overcome with emotion.

'She's the best friend to have in a situation like this.'

'Please,' Iris repeated. 'I'll tell her when I'm ready.'

'Okay, you have my word,' Hick responded reluctantly and then added, 'I nearly said, "Mum's the word."'

Iris smiled and the women began to laugh.

'Hopefully, it won't be the word,' Hick joked.

Iris began to laugh harder and somehow that release sparked another and she began to cry as well.

'Shut up, Hick,' she moaned.

'Are you laughing or crying?' Hick asked.

'Both,' Iris exclaimed. 'My lip hurts.'

Iris put her hand to her face. She forced herself to stop laughing. Her lip was stinging. She took a series of deep breaths until the tears and giggles subsided.

The women sat for a time without speaking. It wasn't so bad, Iris thought, to be pregnant, if she was. It hadn't been planned but she could manage, surely. She had been in much more serious fixes.

'It's after four, Hick,' she said. 'You should be getting back.'

'Not a chance,' the other woman said. 'I'm staying here while I'm in DC, at least until you hear from the doctor. The next four days are going to string out into an eternity. You shouldn't be alone. Anyway, you can't go to work looking like you've gone ten rounds with Joe Louis.'

'What about Mrs Roosevelt?' Iris asked as she settled her head down into the cushion.

'Eleanor's leaving for the West Coast tomorrow morning and Frank's heading to Yalta in day or two,' Hick explained.

Iris smiled as her eyes became heavy. 'Yalta,' she whispered.

'It's in the Crimea, on the Black Sea,' Hick told her. 'He's meeting with Churchill and Stalin to divvy up the spoils of war.'

'That should be some meeting,' Iris muttered as her eyes closed and she fell asleep.

■

Over the next four days Iris confided in Hick more than she'd thought possible. She described her last night with Sam and how, when she had woken up in the morning, he had already departed. She cried when she told Hick that she hadn't heard from him since.

'He just wanted to have all of you for once,' Hick explained. 'I can understand that.'

'He *had* all of me,' Iris protested.

'Not really.'

'But why did he go? Why didn't he stay for the week, like he'd planned?'

'He was angry. You've got to allow him that. He's got some thinking to do.'

They also discussed Monty and Iris told Hick about their parting, how it had pained her, broken her heart. She struggled to describe her attraction to him, her longing.

'Your old man checked out early, didn't he?' Hick asked.

Iris nodded.

'You and Monty, your devotion to Frank – you know that this all stems from your father, don't you?' Hick spoke as though this was a fact, obvious to all, yet Iris was horrified. The idea had never crossed her mind.

'It doesn't mean you're perverted and it doesn't mean you were in love with your father or the president,' Hick went on. 'It just means that your experience of him has shaped who you are now.'

Hesitantly, Iris accepted Hick's assessment. It was true that Monty shared many traits with her father, as did the president. It wasn't completely incomprehensible that she was seeking out her father in both men.

'My pop was an asshole,' Hick stated. 'He was a drunk who beat me black and blue every chance he got. Perhaps that's why I'm attracted to women. Who knows how the heart and the mind conspire to create the people we become?'

During the four-day duration of Hick's impromptu visit, Iris was nursed back to a semblance of normal with the aid of Henry James and Hick's blueberry pancakes, chicken soup and grilled cheese sandwiches. One night Hick even cooked a goose that she boasted had been filched from Mrs Nesbitt's store.

'My father raised geese for a while when I was a kid in Wisconsin,' she explained when she entered the apartment holding the bird, loosely wrapped in brown paper, under her arm like a football. 'So I know a thing or two about cooking them.'

Hick's meals were improvised, spontaneous and she liked to cook and serve them at odd times. The women shared chicken soup for breakfast and then blueberry pancakes for a late supper. Grilled cheese sandwiches were good at any time of the day or night, Hick advised. And cupcakes. Hick loved to bake cupcakes that she would subsequently adorn with fluffy, pastel-coloured frosting that looked as though an angel had had a hand in its creation. It amused Iris that Hick got butter and sugar from the black market while other women bartered for silk stockings. Like the grilled cheese, cupcakes were permissible at any hour.

It was in the kitchen late one night as Hick iced cupcakes that Iris divulged her greatest regret. As Hick leaned over the bench piping baby-blue frosting onto a batch of cupcakes, Iris hoisted herself up onto the bench and related the story of Fred Korematsu and how she had conspired to keep the young man interned, digging up rocks behind a twelve-foot-high barbed-wire fence.

'I'm so ashamed of myself, Hick,' Iris moaned. 'I've fallen so far and it's all been my own doing. I've made some horrifying choices.'

Hick stood up straight and handed Iris a cupcake. 'You're more screwed up than I am, kid, and that's saying something.' Hick grinned and bit into one of the recently frosted gems.

Iris joined her in the tasting.

'You know, it probably wouldn't have a made a difference,' Hick said. 'The war will be over soon anyway. What do you think Yalta is all about? Japan will be the next to tumble. Fred Korematsu will be released before the year is out.' Hick's words were of no comfort. Korematsu's detention and perceived guilt would haunt him for the rest of his life.

■

The following afternoon at ten minutes past four o'clock, the telephone rang. Hick loitered on the sofa while Iris spoke to the doctor. She placed the receiver back into its cradle, turned to her friend and nodded.

'Congratulations!' Hick rejoiced. She stood and embraced Iris warmly. 'Everything will be fine. Tell Sam. He's a good guy and he'd want to know.'

Iris looked at her doubtfully.

'This is good news, kid,' Hick explained. 'Joyous news, in fact. Be happy about it.'

Having been remade over the years into the woman she was, Iris now wondered what sort of mother she would be.

72

WASHINGTON DC
April 1945

Iris raised her head from her work and saw him standing in the doorway.

'Aren't you a sight for sore eyes,' she said.

Monty entered her office. Iris rose from behind her desk and went to hug him. She hesitated to kiss him, but she allowed her face to rest between his shoulder and neck for longer than she should have.

When at last they drew apart he took her hands and examined her in her fullness.

'My little girl's all grown up,' he declared.

'And then some,' she agreed. 'I can't hide it any more. There're already rumours.'

Monty nodded. He didn't ask about the father but he did glance fleetingly at her left hand.

She touched the silver oak leaf that adorned his breast. 'You've been promoted,' she said. 'Congratulations. Lieutenant colonel?'

'That's right.' Monty released her hands and walked to the window.

'I'm glad you're safe,' she said after a moment. 'When Grace told me you were in France leading a battalion . . .'

'I couldn't tell you myself,' he replied without turning. 'I couldn't say goodbye knowing that it might be forever.'

Iris joined him at the window that overlooked the Capitol.

'Why did you request a field command?' she asked, clasping his hand. 'It seemed that all you took away from the last war was heartache and that gruesome scar across your belly.'

'It's difficult to explain.'

'To someone who has never served,' she finished for him.

He nodded.

'How long are you in town?' she asked after a pause.

'I'm not sure,' he replied. 'The European campaign is coming to an end. I've been given a couple of weeks' furlough. There're a few things they need me for at the White House. I'm not sure what will happen after the Germans surrender.'

'Do you think you'll be assigned to the Pacific?'

He shrugged. 'It's hard to know.'

Iris gripped his hand more firmly.

'Can we have dinner tonight?' he asked. 'I'll reserve us a table at Montmartre.'

'I'd love to,' she said glumly, 'but I get tired so early these days. After a full day at work I just need to put my feet up. I'm sorry.'

'Don't be silly,' he said, turning from the window. 'I'll get something and cook for you at your place. I've still got my keys.'

'Okay,' she responded, and then remembered her change of address. 'But I don't live on 30th anymore. I've moved to Q Street. Apartment six, number sixteen. It's closer to Logan Circle than Dupont.'

Iris walked to her desk drawer and withdrew her house keys from her purse. She threw them into Monty's hand.

'Moving up in the world,' he noted as her telephone began to ring.

'Hardly,' she said, looking down at her expanded girth. Iris answered the incoming call as Monty departed her office with a formal salute.

■

As Iris wearily ascended the four flights to her apartment, the smell of onions, garlic and bacon frying drifted down the stairwell. The odours were a tow rope, hauling her heavy body up the stairs. Iris was certain from the scents that Monty was preparing coq au vin. He had cooked it for her countless times before and she was familiar with each step of the recipe, although Monty never needed to refer to one.

When she reached her door she knocked and waited for it to open. Monty was there in an instant. He wore her apron over his uniform.

'Come in, I'm just adding the wine. I'll be with you in a minute.'

Monty bustled from the entrance and through to the kitchen.

'What grade of mess have you made in my kitchen?' she called.

'I clean up after myself these days,' he shouted back.

Iris hung her jacket in the closet, kicked off her shoes and proceeded to the living room. Monty had bought her flowers, many bunches she guessed, which he had placed around the room. Candles had been lit and a glass of wine waited for her on the coffee table. Even though she had no stomach for it now, Iris picked up the glass and took a sip.

Soon Monty joined her in the living room.

'This is a nice apartment, kiddo,' he said approvingly. 'Good neighbourhood. Spacious and a nice view of the park across the road.'

'I had someone in mind when I took it.' She indicated her bump.

Monty smiled. 'Can we talk about that?' he asked.

Iris nodded and sat down. Monty joined her and tapped his thighs. She placed her legs across his lap and he began to rub her feet. Iris wasn't certain whether he expected her to begin relating the whole hopeless episode, but she did so regardless.

'It's just all such a mess,' she admitted. 'I haven't heard from Sam since November. He's in France, I think. Perhaps Belgium. I'm only guessing. The baby is due in three months and other than this apartment, I have nothing. I don't even have a crib yet!'

'Does Sam know about the baby?'

She shook her head.

'You need to tell him,' Monty ordered. 'The rumours have started and they'll spread like wildfire. He needs to hear it from you.'

'But you don't know the whole of it.' She paused. 'I'm worried . . . the way he left. He was mad. Sometimes I feel as though this baby was his revenge.'

Monty stopped rubbing her feet and looked at her quizzically.

'I told Sam about you and me. He was angry and hurt and humiliated. Then . . .' Iris stopped. She wasn't able to confide in Monty about that night with Sam. She still hadn't deciphered its meaning herself.

'Jacobson's not like that,' Monty said. 'He's not the vindictive type. What are you worried about?'

'I'm worried that if I do tell him . . .' She halted once more.

Monty resumed rubbing her feet. 'You're worried that if you do tell him he won't come back? That he won't want you?'

Iris nodded.

'Just like your grandparents,' he concluded.

She wondered how he knew. The only person she'd ever told about her grandparents was the president.

'You undervalue yourself. You always have. Of course he'll want you.'

'Maybe he doesn't even want to know about the baby,' she said in a low voice.

'He'd want to know,' Monty insisted. '*I'd* want to know.'

Iris let his admission come to rest. She wondered whether Monty wished it was his child she was carrying. Had he returned to save her?

He hadn't seemed shocked when he'd seen her. The candles and flowers, the wine. Was this a renewal or were her erratic hormones deceiving her, leading her to make false assumptions?

'Are you still seeing the person in England, the person you were getting serious about?' she enquired after a few minutes.

'That didn't work out,' he said reticently.

Iris wondered whether there had ever been another relationship. Perhaps Monty had been setting her free. If so, she had squandered her freedom. There was a time when she had not squandered anything. Not a front door nor a floury apple nor the chance of a ride along a desolate highway.

'Thank you for not judging me,' she said.

'Who am I to judge?' he replied, then went back into the kitchen to check on dinner.

■

During the meal the pair chatted easily about the war and the Supreme Court. Iris expressed her disappointment with the internment cases she had worked on with Frankfurter but failed to mention Fred Korematsu.

'You seem disillusioned,' Monty suggested.

'I saw Mrs Nesbitt at the inauguration,' she began. Monty's eyes brightened. 'She's never compromised. Her principles have never been shaken. Her kitchen has been responsible for the creation of the worst meals I have ever eaten. But despite constant complaints from the president of the United States she has never conceded. Yet she remains the one constant in the Roosevelt administration.'

Monty grinned.

'In the last twelve years some have died, some have been forced out quietly and some have been reassigned, but Mrs Henrietta Nesbitt remains a fixture.'

'What are you saying, Iris? Are you saying that you have compromised and it's got you nowhere?'

'I think I'm saying that I'm sick of Washington, the politics, the bargains, the struggles that lead to nothing.' She paused and looked across the table earnestly. 'I've been contemplating moving, possibly to New York or Boston. A lawyer can work anywhere.'

Monty began to laugh uproariously. He threw his head back and banged his hands on the table, making the plates and silverware clatter.

'What?' Iris asked, astounded by his reaction.

'You'll never leave Washington. You love it too much. It's in your blood now.'

Iris watched him, thinking.

'You're astonishing, Iris McIntosh. Even if Jacobson doesn't come back, you've handled much tougher than this. You have a roof over your head, a job, money in the bank. This baby couldn't find a more resourceful, capable or beautiful mother.'

Iris stared into his face from across the table, drinking in his presence. As her mouth widened into a generous smile she realised there was no one who could lift her spirits quite like Monty Chapel.

■

Iris asked Monty to stay with her while he was in Washington. He slept on the sofa. On only one occasion had she asked him to crawl into bed next to her and hold her in the dark. When he was free from White House duties he painted the second bedroom in a creamy shade of yellow the man in the paint store called vanilla. She had been doubtful of the colour, telling the paint store manager that she thought the colour too adult for a nursery. He had reassured her by declaring, 'Everyone loves vanilla.' Iris couldn't argue with that. When Monty had applied two coats he began assembling the crib Iris purchased on the same day as the paint.

It was at the beginning of Monty's second week in Washington, on 12 April, that he showed up unexpectedly at her office in the Supreme Court building at around four in the afternoon. Iris saw him from the corner of her eye.

'I can't finish yet,' she said without looking at him. 'I'll probably be here until six.' Then she raised her head. 'Weren't you supposed to be working today?' Monty entered her office and took off his hat. His face was ashen and his jaw clenched tight. His ready smile was absent.

'Will you come for a walk with me, Iris?' he suggested. His pleasant tone failed to mask the urgency in his words.

'Why?' she asked, standing. Her eyes narrowed. 'What's wrong? You never call me Iris.'

'Just come for a walk,' he insisted.

Their journey from the third floor to the outside seemed like the longest walk she had ever taken. Monty's expression was as cold and severe as the Alabama marble that lined the walls of the building. Iris wondered what had happened to upset him. He was usually so even-tempered.

By the time they reached the outside of the building, Iris's mouth was dry and her heart was pounding. 'What is it?' she asked. Then, seeing the despair on his face, she knew. 'It's the president, isn't it?' she said softly.

Monty replied with a brief nod.

'Gone?' she asked.

'About thirty minutes ago,' Monty confirmed. 'I came over here as fast as I could. I didn't want you hearing the news from someone else. You were special.'

She sighed. 'Where?'

'Warm Springs.'

'Mrs Roosevelt?'

'She's on her way down to Georgia this evening.'

'How's she holding up?' Iris asked.

'Stoic,' Monty answered. 'Stoic, as usual.'

'I should call.'

'Wait,' he advised. 'You won't be able to speak to her properly until she reaches Warm Springs.'

Iris took a deep breath and leaned back against one of the building's ivory-coloured columns. She glanced at the passers-by as they made their way up and down the steps and considered the impact of his death – on her, on Mrs Roosevelt, on the passers-by, on the world. She placed her hands on her belly. Already there was a huge chasm forming, hollowing out her insides.

'Are you okay?' Monty enquired.

'Not really,' she responded. She hadn't spoken to the president in two years. She hadn't even said goodbye to him when she left the White House. Misery washed over her. She should have contacted him. 'What about you?'

Monty shook his head. 'Presidents have died before,' he said, 'but not one like Roosevelt. I can't see a world without him. I just can't envisage it.'

Iris held out her arms and Monty walked into them and they embraced. When they parted, Monty's eyes were moist. She touched her hand lightly to his cheek.

He turned away for a moment and looked beyond the steps over 1st Street. He turned back, his composure restored.

'Steve Early was notifying the press associations when I left but there's going to be an official announcement on NBC just before six. He's called a press conference.'

Iris nodded.

'They want me back,' he went on. 'Everything's kinda frantic. Do you want to come with me, sit in on the press conference? Nobody would mind. You're family over there.'

Iris shook her head. 'No. Thank you, but no. I'll listen to the broadcast on the radio tonight like everyone else.'

He took her face in his hands and kissed her tenderly on the lips.

'You'd better get over there,' she urged. 'I'll get my things and go home and wait for six o'clock. I'll see you later on.'

Monty kissed her briefly again, then ran down the steps two at a time and hailed a taxi. It disappeared up 1st within seconds.

■

When Iris got home she ran herself a hot bath. Her doctor had told her that hot baths were no good for the baby but she turned on the faucet nonetheless. What was good for her was good for the baby, she reasoned.

She remained in the bath until the water was tepid, staring at her protruding belly. Inhaling, she slid her head under and stayed like that for some seconds. She was a product of the Roosevelt administration, it occurred to her, fashioned by the skilled hands of master craftsmen: the president and the First Lady. Everyone of her generation, the depression generation – millions of people, she guessed – had been shaped by the Roosevelts. She wondered what lay ahead. Who and what would shape her baby? Bubbles rose to the surface of the water and fear rose in her throat as Iris contemplated the enormity of these questions.

■

By five thirty Iris was settled in her pyjamas on the sofa waiting for the broadcast. When she switched the radio on to NBC, the station was transmitting a doleful piece of harp music. She listened for a few minutes to the dreadful dirge before becoming angry. They should be playing 'Happy Days' or 'Anchors Aweigh', jubilant tunes of triumph associated with the president. She frowned and snapped the radio off.

As she did so the telephone rang.

'Hello, Iris speaking,' she said into the receiver. She thought it would be Monty on the other end checking on her. There was a long pause on the line and a lot of static. 'Hello,' she said again more loudly.

'Iris.' It was Sam. Even through the crackling and hissing she recognised his voice. He sounded so far away. His voice was tiny, as though he was shouting across the Atlantic. 'Iris, it's me. I'm sorry. I'm so sorry about the president. How are you?'

Iris held the receiver to her ear but didn't speak. Her knuckles turned white around the handpiece.

'Iris, are you there?'

'Yes, I'm here,' she said, attempting to calm herself. 'How are you?'

'I'm fine,' he responded. 'I thought we could listen to the broadcast together.'

Having difficulty settling her breathing, Iris couldn't respond.

'Like old times,' he added. 'Iris? Did you hear me?'

'I heard you,' she responded. 'Thank you. Thank you for calling.'

'What was that?'

'I love you,' she called.

'I love you too,' Sam yelled down the line.

■

When Monty came home it was just past midnight. Iris walked out into the living room to greet him.

'I thought you'd be asleep,' he said.

'I was waiting for you,' she replied. 'How're things at the White House?'

Monty related the events of the evening as he took off his coat and tie. Mrs Roosevelt had departed for Warm Springs and would travel back with the president in two days' time. Steve Early had the media under control. Flags were flying at half-mast all over the country.

When he had finished, Iris said, 'Sit down. I need to talk to you.'

'What's up?' he asked.

'Sam telephoned this evening. I told him about the baby. He was happy, really happy.' She gave a bemused smile. 'He's coming home. Straight away, I think.'

Monty smiled in return. 'That's good, kiddo. I'm glad.'

'I'm not sure where that leaves you and me,' she went on.

'It leaves you and Sam and the baby,' he responded kindly, taking her hand. 'No me.'

'That's what I figured. I just wasn't brave enough to say it.' Her voice trembled.

He leaned back and placed his arm around her shoulders. Iris nestled against his body.

'The end of an era,' Monty remarked quietly.

'The end of an era,' Iris affirmed.

They sat together for a long time, each lost in thought, each contemplating the last twelve years together – privately and professionally. Iris ran through the various settings in her mind. The Mayflower, Montmartre, her 6th Street snug, her apartment on 30th and, of course, the White House. It seemed like a century ago that she had approached Mrs Roosevelt in that Virginia gas station. She could barely remember the day.

'I drafted my resignation tonight,' she said eventually.

'What?' Monty said, sitting up, alarmed. 'Shouldn't you wait until a less emotional time to make a decision like that?'

'This is the perfect time,' she explained calmly. 'I have to take a leave of absence anyway and . . . I don't really like who I've turned into, Monty. It has become way too easy to compromise my values.'

He nodded thoughtfully for a moment and then commented with a grin, 'I can picture you as a housewife.'

Monty settled back into the sofa and pulled Iris close to him once more. 'You've made a lot of momentous changes tonight, haven't you? But that's your style, I suppose. You've always been hungry. Hungry for more. Hungry for something more satisfying.'

'I guess,' she responded, considering his observation. 'There's one more thing.'

He looked at her.

'I rang Grace Tully in Warm Springs,' she told him. 'I'm going down there on Sunday. I need to move past the president and the White House. I should have done it years ago. I don't want to regret anything else.'

'I understand,' Monty whispered into her hair. 'But you know he didn't hold a grudge. He only ever viewed you in the most brilliant light.'

Iris nodded as she fought back tears. 'It's just a trip I have to make.'

73
WARM SPRINGS, GEORGIA
April 1945

Iris reached the gates of the Little White House just before noon. As she watched the taxi drive off along the road into town an odd sense of freedom overcame the thirty-five-year-old. All her concerns of the previous few months seemed to be carried away by the gentle, azalea-scented breeze. Monty had escorted her to Union Station. They knew it was their final goodbye. It had to be. He wouldn't be at her apartment when she returned.

As Iris approached the sentry box at the gate a marine emerged carrying a clipboard. His rifle hung casually over one shoulder and he wore a black band around his upper arm.

'Is there something I can help you with, ma'am?' the young man asked politely. Iris guessed he was from the South but couldn't pinpoint his accent exactly.

'Good morning,' she said. 'My name is Iris McIntosh. I believe Mrs Bonner is expecting me.'

The marine scanned his clipboard.

'Grace Tully organised my visit,' she went on. 'The president's secretary . . . the late president's secretary,' she corrected. Iris had spoken with Grace on Thursday evening then telephoned Mrs Roosevelt at Warm Springs on Friday to convey her condolences. Monty had described the First Lady as stoic. Grace Tully informed Iris that Mrs Roosevelt had been 'completely composed' when she arrived at Warm Springs. Iris was wishing for something more, a greater reaction, and was pleased when she gleaned a hint of sorrow in the First Lady's warbling cadences. It wasn't that she had articulated her grief. Nor had her voice trembled. But there was a remoteness in her tone that Iris had not heard before.

'I see your name right here.' The marine smiled. 'Would you like me to drive you down to the house?' He glanced at her belly.

'No, thank you. I've been on the overnight train from Washington for fourteen hours. It'll be good to stretch my legs.'

Iris smiled as she picked up her small overnight bag and began to walk. She passed under the oak canopy that bordered the drive and recalled her previous visit to Roosevelt's Georgia retreat in March 1938. What a crisis in her life that week had ignited. Now here she was again, seven years later, at a similar turning point. When her train had pulled away from Union Station Iris had imagined she would be devastated. She had dreaded the moment of departure. When the train began its roll along the tracks Monty had waved at her through the window and offered a smile. It was not his most charming, but it was one weighted with denouement. She placed her palm on the glass in response and waited for the vicious tug. It never came. The knowledge that Sam would be returning to Washington by the end of the week was thrilling. Desperate to be with him again, Iris was eager to begin the next phase of her life. She hadn't experienced such a sense of urgency in a very long time. Not since she had left the White House. There was something to fight for again.

When the fountain was in sight she stopped for a moment and put her bag on the ground. As Iris tidied her hair she could clearly envision Dorothy Hale in her splendid evening gown with her glorious burnished shoulders smelling of jasmine. Even though it was almost seven years since Hale had killed herself, Iris frequently thought of the actress and considered the all-consuming power of loneliness.

By the time Iris reached the house Daisy Bonner had already rounded the corner from the side entrance.

'My goodness!' she exclaimed. 'Look at what we have here!' Daisy held out her arms and the women hugged. When they parted Daisy scrutinised Iris's mid-section closely.

'How many months?'

'Just six,' Iris answered.

'You're tiny, aren't you?' Daisy marvelled. 'Women are always the most neat with their first. Miss Tully didn't tell me you were having a baby.'

'Grace doesn't know,' Iris explained. 'Neither does Mrs Roosevelt. I'll tell them the news when . . . when everything is over.'

Daisy nodded and Iris recognised a trace of doubt in her angled smile.

'What?' Iris asked.

'It seems to me they might have found the news a comfort at a time like this, that's all,' she commented casually. Daisy picked up her guest's overnight bag and led the way into the house.

'You're staying in here again,' she informed Iris when she opened the door to the room Iris had once shared with Monty.

'I've got a booking in town, Daisy,' Iris said. 'I don't expect to stay here.'

'Don't talk nonsense,' Daisy replied offhandedly. 'I'm staying here for a few days while I pack the president's personal items for Mrs Roosevelt. I'd be glad of the company for the night.'

Iris agreed. Absently fingering the engagement ring she had begun wearing since her conversation with Sam, she took an easy stroll around the room. The quilted bedspread, the jug and bowl on the chest of drawers, the crocheted drapes, the side tables and the glass ashtrays — nothing had altered. Then she caught sight of herself in the mirror. Iris smiled at the image.

Daisy was watching her. 'Why did you come?' she asked curiously. 'Why didn't you stay in Washington and wait for the funeral train to arrive?'

Iris sat on the bed and ran her hand over the comforter. She wasn't certain why the urge to make the trip to Warm Springs had been so fierce. Monty told her that when the funeral train arrived in Washington a huge procession was planned. From Union Station, soldiers and horses, carriages and mourners, brass bands and officials would escort Roosevelt on his final journey to the White House. Thousands were expected to pay tribute to the president. Iris supposed she simply wanted to honour the man in the place where she had seen him happiest and most at ease.

'I'm not too sure, Daisy,' Iris replied.

'You loved him very much, didn't you?' the cook asked.

'Yes, I did,' Iris responded with certainty.

■

Like the bedroom, the living room too was unchanged, apart from one addition. An easel holding an incomplete portrait of the president sat in the middle of the room. Iris examined the work closely for some minutes.

'I don't think it looks a bit like him,' Daisy whispered from behind.

It was an unusual portrait, Iris thought. And while there was no mistaking the face as that of the president, Daisy was right — it didn't look like him. The watercolour likeness did nothing to capture Roosevelt's magnitude. The eyes possessed none of the president's astute spark and his jawline conveyed not a skerrick of his characteristic nobility. The portrait had no heart, Iris determined finally.

'It was a Russian friend of Mrs Rutherford's that painted it,' Daisy went on. Iris turned her head towards the cook in surprise. 'I think she was just doing it as a favour to Mrs Rutherford. You could tell her heart wasn't in it. Neither was the president's. But Mrs Rutherford pestered them both until they just gave up tryin' to argue.'

'Lucy Rutherford was here in Warm Springs?'

'She was. The president wanted her here. She was real gracious and you could tell that they thought the world of each other, old friends that they were.'

How interesting it was, Iris considered, that after all those years it was the face of Lucy Mercer the president wanted to see as he lay dying. It must be close to thirty years since their relationship ended.

'Anyway,' Daisy continued, 'it was while he was posing for that picture that he collapsed. I was out back, in the kitchen, about to serve lunch. Two hours later . . . well, that was that.'

Iris put her hand on Daisy's shoulder and squeezed it affectionately.

'I'll fix you something to eat, Miss Iris,' Daisy said after a moment. 'Are you still Miss?'

Iris nodded. 'But not for much longer,' she said happily. 'You'll join me, won't you?'

Daisy seemed reluctant.

'I don't want to eat alone.'

Eventually Daisy agreed with a gentle nod.

'Who else was here with the president?' Iris asked as she sat down at the table in the kitchen. 'Can I help you with lunch?'

Daisy waved away Iris's offer casually as she opened the refrigerator. 'Miss Tully, of course. Two of the president's doctors, Mrs Rutherford and her painter friend, Miss Shoumatoff. Mrs Roosevelt arrived the next day, the day after he passed.'

She turned to face Iris. 'She was as calm and strong as ever. When she arrived she comforted all of us before we even had a chance to sympathise with her. After about fifteen minutes she told us that she wanted to see her husband. When she came out of the bedroom, just a few minutes later, her mood hadn't changed one bit.' Daisy shrugged, seeming perplexed by Mrs Roosevelt's reaction. She was right to be confused, Iris thought, but Mrs Roosevelt was never going to be anyone's definition of a conventional grieving widow.

Iris attempted to imagine the First Lady in the room alone with her husband. Did she speak to him? Did she offer him a final kiss? What a marriage they had shared and then, one day, not shared, Iris thought. Yet as individuals and a couple they became so much greater together. It was a paradoxical relationship that made perfect sense. Such compromise and acceptance and judicious bargaining it must have taken in order to survive as joint and equal partners in their marriage for forty years.

'She's a remarkable woman, Daisy,' Iris said. 'I know she didn't come down here much and you never got the opportunity to know her well, but she is an extraordinary woman.'

Daisy nodded solemnly.

'How's Lonnie, by the way?' Iris asked after a moment.

'He joined the army in '41 like everybody else,' Daisy replied.

'Where is he? Europe or the Pacific?'

'Europe. They had him driving a truck for a while, carrying supplies from here to there. Then one day, around Christmas last year, Eisenhower decided to hand him a rifle.' Daisy shook her head in disbelief as she sliced a loaf of bread.

'The army needed replacements, I guess, during the Battle of the Bulge,' Iris explained. 'You must worry.'

'All the time. All the time,' Daisy said. 'But tell me about yourself. It's been so long since I've seen you.'

As Daisy moved around the kitchen, from refrigerator to cupboard to table, Iris described her change of career, her position at the Supreme Court, Sam, the baby and finally her resignation from Frankfurter's employ.

'What will you do now?' Daisy asked.

'Get married, have the baby, be content for a little while,' Iris answered.

'And then after a little while?' Daisy asked with humour.

Iris shrugged in complete and happy compliance with her ill-defined professional future.

Daisy placed a plate containing ham and salad on the table. There were pickles and mustard, and a few pieces of cold fried chicken.

'This looks wonderful, Daisy. I'm so hungry,' Iris exclaimed.

'It's just leftovers. Nothing special.'

Iris waited for Daisy to seat herself and then began buttering a slice of bread distractedly as she conversed. 'How was the president while he was here?' she asked.

'It's the strangest thing, honey,' Daisy began, pushing her spectacles along the bridge of her nose. 'When he got here he was sick. Sicker than

I've ever seen anyone – deathly pale and thin as a rake. The president knew he was going to pass. He said to me on the first evening, "You cooked me my first meal here at Warm Springs, Daisy, and it looks like you'll be fixin' my last as well."' Daisy smiled at the recollection.

'Then, as the week went on, his health improved. He put on a little weight and his blood pressure went down. The doctors couldn't believe the change. Everyone was so happy. Although it shouldn't have been, it came as a shock when he collapsed on Thursday.'

Iris placed the bread on her plate and reached for the ham. 'Was he happy?'

'Very,' Daisy replied. 'He credited being here for the upturn in his health.'

Iris thought about the president's final days as she carefully laid the ham on the bread. When she brought the two halves of the sandwich together she stared at it closely for a few seconds and then was struck by what she had inadvertently made.

'What were you cooking for lunch on the day he passed?' she asked.

'Brunswick stew. Chicken and tomatoes, lima beans and okra. It was one of the president's favourites. He didn't get to eat a bite of it.'

Iris shook her head. She would have delighted in telling Daisy about Henrietta Nesbitt and the diabolical meals she had prepared for the president for twelve years. But it wasn't the right time. Not many people would understand the depth of the president's suffering at the hands of his housekeeper. Iris bit into the sandwich and closed her eyes briefly in pleasure.

'It was quite a scene when they took the president away,' Daisy said sombrely. 'Patients, doctors, nurses and attendants gathered at the front of the cottage to bid their final farewell. The children were sobbing. Everyone was sobbing. It was sad.' Daisy placed her silverware on her plate and wiped her fingers on the napkin. 'I don't believe I've ever seen anything sadder.'

The women were silent as they finished lunch. Completely satisfied, Iris leaned back in her chair.

'Will you have seconds, honey?' Daisy asked.

Iris considered her appetite for a moment before replying.

'In a little while,' she said and experienced a flutter of movement in her abdomen. She placed her hands on either side of her belly, anticipating further action, and smiled.

POSTSCRIPT

Henrietta Nesbitt stayed on in her position as housekeeper under the new president, Harry S. Truman. Most thought the homey style of Mrs Nesbitt would suit the Missouri-born, farm-bred president. However, within weeks of assuming office, Mrs Truman asked the housekeeper for a stick of butter. Mrs Nesbitt refused to give her one. The White House observed rationing just like every other house in America, Mrs Nesbitt said. President Truman dismissed her that afternoon.

AUTHOR'S NOTE & ACKNOWLEDGEMENTS

One day in 2010 I was scouring food sites for something special – roasted potatoes with a twist. Once the recipe was sourced from *Gourmet* magazine, I stayed on their site and began scanning the featured articles. Here, I came across a piece, by American culinary historian Laura Shapiro, titled 'FDR's Anti-epicurean White House'.

What followed was the astonishing tale of Henrietta Nesbitt. I found myself amused, disturbed and saddened that Franklin Delano Roosevelt, the man who navigated the United States through the Depression and World War Two, was rarely served a tolerable meal. The relationship between the leader and his housekeeper would have been a wonderful premise for a Frank Capra film, I thought. Then it struck me that I should tell the story instead. In searching for a recipe, I had found my twist!

In *The President's Lunch* Monty suggests to Iris that Mrs Nesbitt is Eleanor's revenge. This theory was formed by Blanche Wiesen Cook in her outstanding, two-volume biography of the First Lady (*Eleanor Roosevelt*, Penguin Books, 1992 & 1999). I believe it is partly true. Eleanor Roosevelt was an extraordinary individual, who used her immense intelligence, compassion and power in positive ways. However, she was also a complex and nuanced woman of varying and volatile moods and tempers.

On the other hand, after reading Henrietta Nesbitt's diary (*White House Diary*, The Country Life Press, 1948), I learned the housekeeper was not a multifaceted woman like her employer. Mrs Nesbitt's steadfast belief that she was a 'vital cog' in the administration was astounding, yet there was something about her that appealed. Perhaps it was her homespun wisdom or, as Iris remarks, her 'staying power'.

The most expensive book I purchased for research purposes was Henrietta Nesbitt's cookbook (*The Presidential Cookbook: Feeding the Roosevelts and Their Guests*, Doubleday & Company, 1951). I unearthed it online from an obscure bookstore and it cost $US99 plus postage. A stamp on the inside cover revealed the book had been previously in the ownership of the Fairfax County Public Library. Fairfax County, Virginia is where Iris and Eleanor first meet in my story – another coincidental twist.

I horrified my family for several nights by trying some of Mrs Nesbitt's recipes in my own kitchen. I am happy to confirm that Iris's revulsion at the veal roast she shares with the Tweedsmuirs and Monty's claim that Mrs Nesbitt's Oriental Chicken is responsible for America's tensions with Japan are entirely reasonable reactions. Other sources I utilised for food guidance include *American Regional Cookery* by Sheila Hibben (Gramercy Publishing Company, 1956), *From Hardtack to Home Fries: An Uncommon History of American Cooks and Meals* (by Barbara Haber, Penguin Books, 2002) and, of course, Elizabeth David's *French Provincial Cooking* (Penguin Books, 1960) to learn 'what French onion soup should taste like' (chapter 19).

It was from Cook's acclaimed biographies and Eleanor Roosevelt's remarkably frank memoirs (*The Autobiography of Eleanor Roosevelt*, HarperCollins, 1961) that I discovered most about the First Lady. Similarly, Jean Edward Smith's award-winning biography of the president (*FDR*, Random House, 2007) helped me to shape the character of Roosevelt in the novel. Other books I found valuable and would recommend to anyone wanting to gain further insight into the couple are *Eleanor and Franklin* by Joseph P Lash (W.W. Norton & Company, 1971) and Jonas Klein's *Beloved Island: Franklin and Eleanor and the Legacy of Campobello* (North Bay Books, 2000). The only invented characters in the story are Iris, Monty and Sam.

I have tried to allow the real-life people to come to fictional life in a manner that is faithful to their real personas. For instance, Eleanor's confession to Hick about 'the old days' in chapter 4, and her admission to Iris in chapter 33 regarding her bigotry, are her own words. Likewise, FDR's first press conference in chapter 10 and the president's joint press conference with Winston Churchill in chapter 62 are, for the most part, as they actually played out. In chapter 23 Sam relates to Iris how the president casually announced his decision to float the dollar. This was how the news actually became public. And John McCloy did, in fact, compare the Constitution to a 'scrap of paper' (chapter 63). Eleanor's short speech to the Bonus Army in chapter 15 and FDR's explanation of Lend Lease in chapter 53 are almost verbatim. Finally, Roosevelt did think it was 'a good time for a beer' following his first Fireside Chat (chapter 8) and Hick did like to kiss 'the soft spot at the corner' of Eleanor's mouth (chapter 4), a lovely detail I discovered in a love letter Hick wrote to her friend.

In chapter 31 Iris reads aloud from an article Sam has written on the court-packing scandal. For weeks I attempted to come up with something bold and dramatic, befitting Iris's praise, but my attempts sounded corny. Then while searching newspaper archives for a piece I could use as inspiration, I found the perfect article, one that encapsulated Sam Jacobson's eloquence and passion. It was written by the reporter Mark Sullivan and appeared in *The Oshkosh Northwestern* in March, 1937.

I would like to express my appreciation to the National Park Service for their precious information regarding the Roosevelt homes – Springwood, the White House and Val-Kill – when I visited Hyde Park and Washington DC in 2013. My immense thanks goes out to Anne M Newman from Roosevelt Campobello International Park, who generously spent a very snowy morning during the Canadian winter guiding me through the Roosevelts' cottage (which was closed for the season) and sharing her great knowledge of the couple with me.

I would also like to thank Hachette Australia and my publisher Bernadette Foley for her understanding and patience, as well as editors Kate Stevens and Ali Lavau for their good humour, enthusiasm and discerning eye. Finally, as always, this book could not have been written without the constant support of my husband, Chris.